THE
ATHELING

Books by Grace Chetwin

★A Tor Book

THE

Volume I

of

The Last Legacy

tetralogy

GRACE
CHETWIN

TOR

THE ATHELING

Copyright © 1987 by Grace Chetwin

First printing: January 1988

A TOR Book

Published by Tom Doherty Associates, Inc.
49 West 24th Street
New York, NY 10010

ISBN: 0-312-93059-3

Library of Congress Catalog Card Number: 87-50877

Printed in the United States of America

0 9 8 7 6 5 4 3 2 1

Pad: this one's for you.

Now the great Bear and Pleiades
        where earth moves
Are drawing up the clouds
        of human grief
Breathing solemnity in the deep night.

FROM "PETER GRIMES,"
BENJAMIN BRITTEN.

CHAPTER ONE

PITAR ELLISEN

10.05 Hours 19 September 2047
Bentnose Peak

CONTROLLER Pitar Ellisen V stared across his desk over the wide polished floorboards toward the tall gray windows where bare aspen and sumac clawed a bleak flat sky.

Ellisen liked what he saw: a somber world; not dead, like the real world way up there above ground, but suspended, waiting, he part of it. Waiting to release locked energy on a whole new cycle of life.

Ellisen's fingers drummed lightly on the desktop.

For four days now he'd waited gazing upon that projected wilderness while in reality the stricken slope above him shimmered in the late summer heat. For four days now Pitar "The Viking" Ellisen, Controller of the PanAmerican Federation had privately sweated it out, awaiting the vote that would decide who sat in the next World Council chair.

He wanted that vote badly.

Like dominoes the commitments had fallen to either side of the meridian dividing the Feds from the Reds, half to him, the other half to General Voltov of the Sino-Soviet bloc. Now everything hung on the United African consensus and M'boda.

Which way? Which way? Ellisen's fingers abruptly stopped. The Emirates surely wouldn't come out for Voltov, not against

Ellisen's package: a bigger share in the arms race and a piece of Hengst.

A blue light winked on the desk sensorband to Ellisen's right hand. Susann's light. He reached out, touched it lightly.

"Yes?"

"Pitar . . ." A small silence. "Let me wait with you."

He let the silence lengthen.

"All right. Shall Sven and I see you for lunch then?"

"I don't know. Get back to you later, okay?"

Another pause, and he could picture the firm full lips compressing into a tight straight line. "I guess."

"Susann—say good morning to Sven for me."

"Say it yourself, Pitar. He's right here."

Ellisen bit the bullet. "Hi, Sven. What's up today?"

No reply. It was hardly a bright question, Ellisen had to admit. Apart from the small gym, a tub-sized swimming pool and the slingball court, there was precious little else for that one to do except sleep and read and watch antique movies. Still, if their son chose to sulk it out, that was his affair.

When the blue light winked off, Ellisen, his mind already back on Hengst, barely noticed.

Hengst, not the war, had killed Grandfather.

Manfred Hengst, squatting like a spider in his space web high above a festering Earth. Space Tektonics, Inc: five miles of conglomerate, pickings from the war. Research stations, observatories, shipyards, factories, foundries, mines. Manfred Hengst, grown fat on an ailing Earth.

But not for long. From the World Council chair Ellisen would pick Hengst's legs off slowly, one by one.

A yellow light pulsed with a faint buzz like a polite cough behind the hand. *M'boda?*

"Yes, Katz?"

"Sir." The voice sounded thin in the low-ceilinged room. "Palo Alto. On red."

For a moment, Ellisen was blank. *"Palo Alto?"* A two-bit relay outfit below swirling red grit that would flay the hide off a buffalo in ten minutes flat. Who in firehell was calling the

Northeastern White House direct from there—and for what?
"Palo Alto?"

"On red, sir."

Red. Top security encoded. *For the Controller's eyes only.*
"Come."

Another touch on the sensorband and instantly the comfort-ing winter scene was gone to a world chart on which tiny lights blinked, clocks flashed, and schools of quick bright arrows tracked earth-encircling clouds of swirling radiation borne on prevailing winds. Great crimson blotches, like some mutant leprosy, or malevolent lichen splashed across the chart: lethal zones devoid of human life: London, Moscow, Tel Aviv, New York, Canberra, Nairobi, Calcutta, Peking. Other patches, pale pink to gray marked more "fortunate" areas that had not been leveled but hit by antipersonnel bombs and virus carriers. In these gray zones now thousands lived out short, useless lives in appalling conditions because there weren't enough protective domes even after all this time, and the underground shelters were crammed to danger point. And up there Hengst played Nero, tinkered with star drives and star fleets while the world below rotted to death.

Damn, where was Katz?

Ellisen's eye moved across the chart to a tiny beacon eighty miles west of Ticonderoga: his present position, the Northeast-ern White House, under the bossy mass of the Adirondacks.

The heavy oak door rumbled aside to let Katz through, looking, as usual, more like a scholar than the veteran civil servant that he was. The glow from the chart reflected off the neat gray hair, the gold-rimmed antiques that he affected to wear, off the polished genuine leather shoes. The gray jumpsuit—wool, Ellisen would swear—was knife-edge sharp and the rim of white collar above it was starched and plain. At his waist hung a swatch of plastic "keys," a swatch containing the command key to Ellisen's personal communications unit. With that card, Ellisen knew, Katz had just routed the red line from the outer office console directly through into the study.

Katz stood inside the closing door, the original paneled door of the old mountain house with its added core of solid ergomentium that once closed rendered the room airtight and soundproof.

"Big screen, sir?"

"Uhuh."

Katz went to the wall beside the world chart, slid aside a wooden panel to reveal the master sensorband. Two touches and the chart was gone, and a giant face blinked patiently in on them, a lean angular face, sunlamp brown under a shaven head. The eyes were blue as Ellisen's own, but heavy-lidded, giving them a sleepy look. The tag on the collar said, MacAllister, A.E. Rating #794/8.

"Go ahead, now," Katz commanded. "Re-ident yourself."

"R.S.W. 32 calling Bentnose on red, on red." The voice was even, unhurried, showing no sign of nervousness. A lowly radio rating, a "rat," calling Bentnose Peak from some godforsaken dusthole direct without clearance? Ellisen glanced to his desk chronister. Oh-seven hours Pacific time. The red-eyed end of the night watch. What had happened that the man couldn't wait an hour until the day brass showed? And how in firehell had he managed to enter code red direct without the second key? Ellisen eyed the face with growing interest. Some radio rat. Resourceful, but quite possibly a fool. He'd hit the alarm, called out the brigade. There'd better be a fire . . .

"Continue, R.S.W. 32. The Controller is waiting."

The man blinked once. "I'll see him first."

Katz was thrown, Ellisen knew it, but it didn't show. He merely pressed the sensorband again and Ellisen knew that MacAllister, A.E. rating #794/8, could see his Controller now. God, this had better be good. Ellisen nodded the man to speak.

"Man just walked in, Controller. Pylar Fazhakian. Hesikastor. He has data you should see. Transmitting . . . now." The face cut.

Pylar Fazhakian. Ellisen swore. There he was waiting to hear from M'boda and the line was taken up by this. As he reached out to cut, columned figures began scrolling slowly up the screen. Codes. For what? Ellisen lowered his hand. PanAmerican missiles, currently deployed in silos about the territory. Highly classified, sensitive material.

"Katz, what in firehell—"

Katz pointed to the bottom of the screen. Less familiar codes now, but still recognizable. Ident tags for equally classified warheads similarly deployed over in the Sino-Soviet bloc. And those, coming now—derelicts of ten years or more, foisted onto the North African Emirates. Some, Ellisen didn't know at all, but now the gist was clear: this was a list of active warheads from around the world, all stationed and pointing somewhere, all set to trigger. A list for which certain heads of states would trade theirs sons. Ellisen would.

The scrolling stopped. "That it?"

MacAllister's face was back again. "Yes, Controller."

"Fazhakian still there with you?"

"Yes, sir. He wants to speak with you."

"Put him on—no. Secure yourselves until further orders. Over and out."

Katz cut. "You want me to call in Security, sir?"

"No. Wrap them up and bring them in."

Alone, Ellisen sat down again and tapped for a printout. With a whisper, a shiny white scroll slid from a slit in his desktop to rest at his right hand. He ran his finger slowly down the columns, trying to think. Where could a man like Fazhakian have gotten such material?

Katz came back in. "They're on their way, sir."

Ellisen pushed the printout across the desk. "What do you make of it?"

Katz crossed over, read the scroll up and down. "He's either running the slickest grubbing operation I've ever seen, or—"

"Or?"

"He's sniffing entrails again."

"Hmmm." All thought of M'boda gone, Ellisen stared at the columned figures. Spy? Prophet? He couldn't buy either. "What do we have on him, Katz?"

A quick smile, a baring of the teeth. "There is a file."
There would be.

Ellisen crossed to the fire, stirred it, then leaned back in his blue chintz armchair beside it. "Pull it," he said.

"Yes, sir. Screen or holoverter?"

" 'Verter."

Katz cut the lights and the screen and all at once the firelit space between wall and desk filled with tiny hologram figures in a brilliant landscape of sea and sky. Of whitewashed cottages on sunbaked cliffs. Of urchins loping along a flat wide beach with an improbably floppy brown dog.

"The tallest boy is Pylar Fazhakian, now Hesikastor. Dog was called Lupy. Place, Kkannakale on the Black Sea. Wiped in '25, of course."

"Go on."

More clips of that extraordinary life. Hazy, disjointed, but not short of a miracle, when most records of anything and anybody had gone up in the war along with half the civilized world. Newscasts of the old man's emergence as the Hesikastor and the spread of his message of brotherhood and the simple life. The poor man's guru, the media had called him, tongue in cheek. His growing popularity. Peace rallies. Mass following. The tabloids full of the old man and his gloomy prophecies of global holocaust. And all around him the Alliances being forged and broken. Betrayals, petty wars, more treaties.

Ellisen sat up. July 2025. Archived glimpses of Chambertin, then United Nations President, his turtle's wattles upstretched toward a dark and intense Hesikastor, whose own lean length was stooped to speak in the presidential ear; Chambertin, the bumbling old appeaser, shuffling back and forth between hot spots. There, off to Israel from his last meeting with the Provisional Palestinian Government, eye on the newscasters, nodding gravely and looking wise. But for all the warnings, the wise nods, the fedayeen broke out and the first bomb fell August fourth on Tel Aviv, the key log in the jam. Almost on reflex the rest followed, escalating to cover half the globe. On that day millions perished and during the days and months and years following millions more in a sick, maybe dying, world.

Wasn't he judging Chambertin harshly? Since Ellisen's own rise to power the Hesikastor had tried to reach him several times in vain.

Could the old man really have the gift of future sight? Was history just about to repeat itself, with him, Ellisen, a second Chambertin? Hadn't his rise to prominence in the World Council been through his shuttle diplomacy over rearmament? Ellisen returned to the parade before him, the Hesikastor now emerging after the war, long-haired and black-bearded now, a latterday saint on barefoot pilgrimage across the smoking cinders of Europe to give comfort where he could. Ragged survivors weeping, kissing his feet, clinging to the hem of his robe.

When Katz spoke suddenly, Ellisen started. "He pulled some of them together under the Balkans. Couple of thousand, they say." Katz cut and looked across the room to Ellisen, obviously awaiting his reaction. "Built quite a complex I understand."

It would be, that size. "With what?"

"Bootstraps. His people pooled their resources, dug a hole with their bare hands, and fitted it with scrap. And by barter."

"*Barter*?"

"The old man swapped goods and services for—" Katz coughed. "Healing."

"*Healing*?"

Katz restored the light. "That's official, sir. The old guy has no credit, no known assets."

No credit? It didn't compute. Outside the system a man was nothing but a bundle of rags with the life expectancy of a dog. He'd have to call in Security after all. "I want him scanned, Katz. Get Pearson."

"Er—"

"Something wrong?"

"Controller, if the man's genuine, Security can't handle it."

"Alternative?"

"Psionics."

"For God's sake, Katz! Anyway, who'd be left in that field?"

"Nobody much. Schiller's gone. Wong's almost: leukemia. I found a Tannis Ord over in Denver."

"Any good?"

"There're no credits, no publications, but he'd only just gotten going by '25. Bought the old Estralita silo in 2023. Set up his own center. The Psionics Institute of New Mexico."

"In an old bomb silo?"

"Apparently."

"You're not saying he's still there? Surely we requisitioned the place."

"We did, sir." Katz steepled his hands. "But it appears to have fallen between the cracks."

"And so we never got around to using it. You're not telling me he's still down there?"

Katz shook his head. "He was posted to the Denver Hospice in '25. Shall I put in a call?"

"Let me think about it."

Alone, Ellisen pulled himself out of the armchair and went back to his desk. A moment later cold snowlight shone once again into the room, this time with sound: faint outdoor twitterings and the strident calls of canada geese—recorded, the geese being long gone along with everything else out there larger than a cockroach. He remembered the far times his grandfather took him hunting, how he'd listened to those wild compelling cries and willed the birds away. Despite his secret, silent urgings, one by one the bodies exploded from the sky and his grandfather had sent him to gather the ragged bags of blood and feathers from out of the mud and bring them back to the blind.

August four, 2025: the first global atomic war.

Next stop: Armageddon.

How long before the prediction came true? Last time, it had

been a little over six months. Prediction? Or lucky guess? Or plain coincidence? Believe the old man and the World Chair wasn't going to be much of a sinecure. He glanced to the chronister. Eleven-thirty. Within the hour he'd be here. Pylar Fazhakian. *Hesikastor.* Spy? Or prophet? What would Ellisen say to him? How would their meeting go?

Eleven-thirty! Fires of hell! He reached out to call Susann, set up a late lunch, but Katz buzzed again. "Chief M'boda, sir. On red." An authorized call this time, vectored through an eastern station, second-keyed, scrambled, and properly relayed.

After all the waiting, suddenly this was it. "Come."

Ellisen activated the miniature tri-co-beamer in his desk and at once the small lens slid up, already crammed with the vast bulk of an African of indeterminate age with shining blue-black face and gray grizzled hair.

M'boda leaned forward, eyes shining, obviously enjoying the moment. Ellisen fought to keep his face still, his eyes from betraying to the man the importance of that moment to him. Far away beneath the mountains of Tanganyika the African took a wheezy breath.

Ellisen beat him to it. "President M'boda. Good to see you."

The man nodded, the flesh of his chin folding about his high white collar on the rebound. "Controller. It is my duty to inform you that the Emirates met two days ago." A chair creaked as M'boda clasped his hands on the desk before him. "There were hold-outs."

Silence. The squeak of Katz's shoes across the floor.

"Right up until fifteen minutes ago six fiefdoms leaned to General Voltov."

So?

"But now we're all agreed. Controller, I'm happy to inform you that the Emirates are with you to a man. May I be the first to offer my congratulations."

Ellisen, aware of the adrenaline swamping his gut, allowed

himself a slight nod. "I thank you. You'll of course keep it quiet until the twenty-fifth?"

M'boda's slab teeth gleamed white against full lips. "Count on it, Controller—or should I say, Mr. Chairman?"

"Not yet, President M'boda. Not yet." The smile irritated him, with its claim to familiarity. It was almost as though the man had actually reached out and laid hand on him. A word or two more—after all, M'boda had just delivered the deciding vote and knew it—and Ellisen cut. For a moment he remained staring into the blank 'beamer, then leaned back and closed his eyes.

"Congratulations, sir."

"Yes." Ellisen stirred, looked up. All those months of dealing, making promises. Hoping, scheming. The adrenaline was gone, leaving him flat. He thought of Susann. He was suddenly sorry he'd cut her off. Why had he done it? She'd gone with him so far, so long. The last few months must have been hard. The last few days, harder. As soon as Katz was gone, he'd call her in. No—the old man was due within the hour. Maybe he'd buzz her, set up a late lunch.

Katz rounded the desk on his way out, but before he reached the door the red light winked again on the sensorband. Another signal code red. Ellisen looked to Katz, puzzled. After a second's hesitation, he opened the channel.

"Controller here."

"Ellisen?" A gravel voice loud in the quiet, with the stridence of one used to shouting into lesser ears.

Stunned, Ellisen pressed visual and at once the lens filled with a square, solid face in a bare skull as squat as the shoulders it sat on, a gray stone ball on its gatepost. Hengst.

"Controller, I offer my congratulations. I'll be discreet, of course, until after the fact. Then I shall look forward to celebrating your success. You'll come up I hope the week after the twenty-fifth, perhaps the twenty-eighth? Bring your wife. Stay a day or two, look around. Make a break for you before you take up the slack, eh? Until then, over and out."

Ellisen cut, his eyes dark with shock and outrage. "Damn!"

He jumped up. "The bastard!" The man had actually penetrated impossible atmospheric layers, bypassed the relay stations, and directly accessed their cable line. How? *How?* And for how long?

Even Katz looked shaken.

Furling hell! Not only accessed, but broken the scrambler code. Hengst must know about Palo Alto as well. But not about Ord, though. Thank God they'd not called the man.

Katz made for the door. "I'll alert Ciphers and Communications, sir," he said, without much conviction.

"Right away," Ellisen said. "And chill the red line." They couldn't call Ord now. If Ellisen wanted him, they'd have to pull him from Denver direct and unofficially. But how?

Ellisen subsided, stared out at the snow-locked mountainside. A couple of hours before everything had seemed so secure, and now twice in as many hours there'd been a major breach in security. Bloody Hengst, playing God again and getting away with it. A fresh flood of adrenaline washed though him, rage-triggered this time. He remembered Eheim, took a deep breath, spread his hands out on the desk until the anger had subsided. MacAllister had also breached security, and he without Hengst's advantages. And MacAllister was on the side of the angels. Interesting.

His humor partly restored, he called Susann. No reply. Damn the woman. Never there when he wanted her. That wasn't fair. He'd hardly spoken to her the last four days, had even taken breakfast there in his study. He paged her. A minute later her voice came breathlessly over the intercom. "Darling? Sven and I were on the slingball court. Do you know, he's suddenly as tall as you are? I swear he's sprung an inch overnight."

"Susann? Susann, look: let's make lunch around two, okay?" Maybe, he thought, he'd tell her about M'boda's vote. "In here, all right?"

"There?" When she spoke again, her voice was guarded. "Did— Has—" Unexpectedly, she laughed. "Oh, all right," she said and, somehow, it was.

"Love you," he said, suddenly glad that he'd called her. Maybe after lunch they'd take time off together. Upstairs.

Katz buzzed. "Sir: The Hesikastor's approaching now."

"Good. Go meet them."

Faintly excited, Ellisen deleted the winter scene, called out the entrance scanner, and the big screen caught the silver tail of a hopper descending under an already closing airlock port to the decontamination chamber. He counted out five minutes then switched to inside, watched the elevator doors open on the gleaming craft, watched it roll across into the shadows of the tiny service hangar opposite. The area was deserted, secured from local personnel.

Beside the open hangar doors Katz waited in a small yellow cart for the hopper's two passengers.

For a moment, nothing, then shadowy figures emerged from the gloom of the hangar out into the bright, white, floodlit passage and moved toward the waiting cart.

CHAPTER TWO

12.27 Hours 19 September 2047
Bentnose Peak

THERE were not two passengers, but three. MacAllister, Fazhakian, and a girl in a thin white jumpsuit, loose blond hair down to her middle, medium height, slight, even frail between the two men. Who was she? Where had she come from, and who'd given her permission to go along?

Another strike for MacAllister, probably.

The man was big, big as Ellisen himself, topping the Hesikastor by a good two inches. He moved well, Ellisen noted, and— Ellisen watched him turn, hand first the girl into the cart to sit beside Katz, then the old man, to sit next to her, then climb himself into the empty backseat.

A *gentleman* radio rat. What do you make of that, Katz?

He watched the cart move off, the backs of the heads dwindle into the distance. The old man hadn't changed much as far as Ellisen could tell. He still had his beard, the long hair swept back behind his ears like vigorous wings, but now the black was gone to silver. His step was firm enough, though, and his back straight. How old was he? Ellisen wondered. It was impossible to judge.

He got up, paced about. He looked toward the windows,

21

then on a sudden thought crossed back to his desk. A touch of the sensorband and a live projection of the real early afternoon sun from up there flooded the room. How many times since he could remember had he gazed out through infinite light and space from the comfortable confines of that dark and solid window bay?

He turned away. Sometimes it worked, and he could almost believe that he was once again up on the mountain looking out through real glass panes, could almost feel the high winds shaking them as though to loose them from their anchorage to shatter them against the rocks below. But not now. The screens and the outside scanner projections were only what they were: surveillance tools subverted to comfort him with subtle sophistry.

He went to the fire, threw on a log. Not that it was cold. In fact the fire placed an unnecessary burden on the recycling system, but he liked it. The study had always felt cool, even in summer, and the hearth had seemed so gloomy unlit.

His back to the screen, he stood staring into the new, bright flames, rocking back and forth on his heels. He could have followed the cart's progress on the 'beamer, but now he was too restless. Strange, he'd not felt like this in a long while. As though he were waiting to greet distinguished guests at a dinner party instead of gearing himself up to conduct an interrogation. *Two* interrogations.

At last the door signal and Katz was ushering his party through.

Ellisen found himself walking over to greet them.

"Hesikastor." He shook the proffered hand, nodded to MacAllister.

"Glad to meet you at last, Controller." The old man's voice was unexpectedly mild with a rolling Russian accent. "Permit me to present Shira, my granddaughter."

Ellisen looked to Katz in surprise. She'd not been in the files.

The girl looked up at him from under thick dark lashes— striking contrast with the hair as pale as Ellisen's own. The face was small, oval, with uptilted eyes and Slavic cheek-bones. There was not a sign of a blemish on her, Ellisen noted. Or, come to think, on the old man either, apart from age's normal mottling.

To his amazement the girl made an abrupt curtsy. "How do you do."

Ellisen took a hold on himself. Waved them to the couch beside the hearth, sat himself down in his armchair opposite. Katz, without a word, took an upright chair to Ellisen's right hand.

The Hesikastor smiled. "Such an astounding feat, the complex, Mr. Controller. A credit to the Ellisen foresight and sense of responsibility."

Was the old man being sarcastic? Anti-Ellisen snipers had long made issue over the family's almost feudal relationship with nearby Ellistown. Was the old man referring to that, or to the refugees harbored behind the tunnel walls?

"And the house. To come through miles of permaplast to . . . this." The Hesikastor waved his hand about. "Mr. Katz told me how you brought the house down piece by piece. The sudden sight of a three-story mansion after the tunnels was . . . shocking."

Shocking? Again Ellisen felt the discomfort. Was the man complimenting him, or calling him extravagant? Moving the house hadn't been extravagant, not at the time, for the bombs hadn't gone off then, nor were they ever expected to for the most part. And they hadn't for full fifteen years after the shelter's completion. For fifteen years the house had nestled in its protective plastic bubble under the mountain like a giant artform in timber and stone. For fifteen years the complex of cells and tunnels had stood empty save for Ellisen's visits. For fifteen years the locals had called the gutted foundations up on the mountain "Ellisen's Folly."

"If I had only known in '24 that the Ellisens were of like mind about the coming war," the Hesikastor went on, "I'd have sought their help then."

"You wouldn't have had much joy," Ellisen said. "Grandfather was too wrapped up in his lunar mining operation, and I was just a Capitol Hill cadet. The shelter was purely a family affair.''

"Pity, for had the war not happened your grandfather might not have lost his precious lunar mining rights to Mr. Hengst, is that not so?''

Ellisen didn't like the sudden turn of conversation.

"All this empty space feels strange," the girl said suddenly. "How many people live in here?''

"You mean the shelter? Or the house?''

"Both." Her eyes were intent on him, unusual eyes, light brown, almost gold, like a cat's.

"The complex outside houses a couple of hundred." Ellisen paused. "The house remains for my family's sole use. I assure you, there's plenty of room for everyone out there. In fact, I only wish we could accommodate a greater number," he went on quickly. "But the life-support system won't sustain any more. In fact already the population's increased past the limit by five percent over the past fifteen years.''

Now why had he said all that? Since when did he have to justify himself? All over the place the wealthy survived comfortably in their small private shelters, whereas at least the Ellisens had taken the additional trouble to provide for their less fortunate neighbors during an era of high optimism when building shelters had been considered at best an eccentric indulgence, an unfashionable and expensive waste of time.

"The increase is good," the old man said. "It speaks well for your system. Elsewhere the populations are failing. How do you do it?''

"I do nothing," Ellisen said. "The place is run independently of the house by qualified professionals. All credit must go to them.''

The girl again. "Didn't anybody transfer topside?''

"Where to?" Ellisen shrugged. "The domes fill faster than they come.''

"Do you have break-outs?''

"We did in the beginning, Miss Shira, along with everyone

else. But not now." After twenty-two years of living like a mole, people lost the urge to feel the sun and die. The in thing now was leukemia.

"Do your folk ever get out?" The girl was persistent.

"They do. There's a shuttle roster to the Boston domes every month."

The girl nodded, apparently satisfied.

"I guess we're underneath the old garnet mine, Controller?" This from MacAllister.

"By a good half mile."

"I hear your great-great-grandfather won Bentnose Peak in a poker game, 1888, right?"

Ellisen eyed MacAllister sourly. It was right, all right. The legends were rife about his raunchy ancestor and that drunken poker game. But if the man knew that much, he certainly knew the rest.

Whose inquisition was this anyway? Ellisen turned to Katz. "I'll speak with the Hesikastor now. Alone. Our other guests will take lunch out in the anteroom meanwhile."

The girl snapped around to look at her grandfather. As though she'd actually spoken, the old man shook his head slightly. She took his arm and looked stubbornly across to Ellisen.

"Controller, I'll stay."

Ellisen forced a smile. "I'm sorry, Miss Shira. He won't be long."

The girl's eyes went dark, angry, then just as suddenly her face cleared. She flipped back her long fair hair and stood up.

"Very well," she said.

MacAllister got to his feet after her and the pair of them followed Katz through the door.

Alone, Ellisen gestured toward the robocaddy standing beside the hearth. "A drink, Hesikastor?" Or was it too early?

"Thank you. A glass of water would be most welcome."

Ellisen splashed ice water into a crystal goblet, handed it over, then sat. "You certainly got to me this time."

"Desperate days call for desperate measures, Controller."

"The data. How did you get it?"

The old man took a sip of water. "It came to me."

"How?"

The Hesikastor tapped the glass to the side of his head. "In here."

Ellisen leaned forward. "You mean you had a sort of vision?"

"Oh, yes. Just like before. Just like before. Do you know in '24, '25 I saw everything just as clearly as I'm seeing—things now. It's going to be much worse this time, you know. There'll be nothing left."

Ellisen jumped up, crossed to the desk, took up the printout, and dropped it into the Hesikastor's lap. Then he stood over him, his back to the fire.

"Those numbers—you saw them written just like that?"

The irony was plain. But the Hesikastor only looked up mildly.

"Oh, no. No, I sorted them out afterward."

"Then where did you see them?"

The old man's voice came in a whisper. "Like last time. On the sides of the bombs."

"You expect me to swallow that? Hesikastor, what do you want?"

"An end to the insanity, before it is too late."

"If you've already seen the end, how can you change it?"

"I don't know, but I believe it could be changed, somehow, by some act of grace. Anyway, I can only try. I take my visions as warnings, you know. I have to believe that with effort and grace things can be changed. I didn't succeed last time, I know, and yet I cannot just stand by to watch the human race commit suicide. Even now . . ." He stopped, shaking his head.

"Even now, what?"

The old man sighed. "It may be too late. The life chain is broken, perhaps irrevocably. The ecology's gone wild. But this next letting will surely set the seal. Controller, if you have any wish at all to save this Earth you must heed me."

Ellisen looked down on the old man speculatively. Suppose, just suppose he were for real. My God! He sat down. *Armageddon.*

"When, Hesikastor?"

"Soon."

"Can you give me a date?"

"I'm afraid not."

"This year, maybe?"

The old man shot him a guarded look. "Maybe."

Maybe. But where? The Big Powers were still thinking mere survival. If trouble lay anywhere it was down the central strip. The buffer zone. The so-called neutral chain of States separating East and West that had in fact triggered the horror of '25.

Very soon.

What to do?

The immediate answer would be to work to adjust the arms balance all the way down the buffer strip. Shore up the Emirates against the Zionists. Zultan against Old Iraq. How much, and where? The old man would have to feed him more data. *If* he proved genuine.

"This claim of yours, Hesikastor: you'll consent to verification?"

The Hesikastor nodded. "Yes, yes. But after verification, then what?"

"Excuse me?"

"Surely you have wondered why I have come to you?"

"I assume that you, too, have the matter of world survival at heart."

"Indeed. Controller, you are a powerful man. You could do so much. I have come to ask that you work with me toward world disarmament."

Ellisen stood up. "Disarmament?" After his last election platform? "Be practical, Hesikastor. The world hasn't taken to it over the last two thousand years, it's certainly not going to now."

"Not after '25?"

"Especially not after '25. Everyone is scrambling for a better weapons system to prevent a repeat, and a better defense net to offset it."

"I beg you, Controller. Please at least consider the option."

The old man must think him crazy. "And commit political suicide? No, Hesikastor. No deal."

"Then how can I do work with you? Where you will call the nations to arms, I will urge them to lay their weapons down. I must."

The old man got up. Ellisen thought of all of the data he might be taking away with him.

"I'm not for armament, exactly. Only redistribution. Perhaps we can still work together, Hesikastor."

"You think so, Controller?"

The old man looked toward the door, which annoyed Ellisen immensely.

"Since we differ so radically I wonder you came to me at all."

"You were the one," the old man said simply. "It was you, or no one."

Startled, Ellisen looked into the old eyes, saw his grandfather twenty-two years before, his ruined face starting from his pillows. *Pitar, remember you're an Ellisen, and the Ellisens came over here to make their mark. Mine was Lunar Mining and now I've lost it. Get it back, my boy, and take that Hengst apart. It's you, or no one.*

The log, shifting in the hearth, flared into flame then subsided into smoking charcoal. Ellisen took up the tongs and resettled the log briskly on its cradle.

Armageddon.

He mustn't let the old man go.

"You'd permit verification then, Hesikastor?"

The old man set down his glass and stood up. "I am in your hands."

Ellisen rang for Katz.

Fires of hell, it was thirteen thirty hundred hours already

and there was still the MacAllister fellow. He'd have to buzz
Susann and make it dinner instead.

"Sit down." Ellisen nodded MacAllister onto the high-
backed chair across the desk. MacAllister sat, loose yet wary,
a mountain cat up in a noonday tree.

"Perhaps you'll now tell me exactly what happened this
morning."

MacAllister's eyes went to the sensorband.

"Off the record. You have my word."

MacAllister nodded, apparently satisfied. "It was oh-five-
forty-two. My second was on his break, when the old guy
arrived."

"How? How did he arrive?"

MacAllister's lids came up briefly. "I have no idea. the
airlock trig blew and there he was, just standing there. Dead
center of the primary scanner."

MacAllister stopped, as though expecting comment.

"Go on."

"Which was strange, because none of the perimeter trigs
had blown. And the hopper pad was empty. Anyway, there he
was, looking straight into the 'eye as though he knew exactly
where it was."

"His granddaughter with him?"

"Not that I could see then."

"Where was your second all this time?"

"Still out. There was the old man in his topsuit, looking like
one of us. When I asked for the password he gave it, just like
that." MacAllister snapped his fingers. "Do you know it's
changed every watch, double blind?

"I opened up. That was when the girl zipped in quick as a
quark."

Ellisen nodded. "When they were down, what?"

"The old man showed me the data, asked me to get it to you
urgently. When I saw what it was I did."

"You recognized the material?"

A pause. "Call it a lucky guess, Controller."

"MacAllister, you'll please not play games with me."

"I have some knowledge of Ciphers."

"I see." Ellisen let it go. "How did you know I was here?"

"The Hesikastor said so."

"He's a persuasive man."

"Indeed he is."

"How did you access my red line without a second key?" The lids came up again. "You a radio rat, Controller?"

"No."

"Then you wouldn't know if I told you. But I'd be glad to talk to a Communications man, if you like."

Ellisen refused to be rattled. "State your credentials, MacAllister."

Another pause. "I had a Chair in Communications in '25. Edinburgh University, U.K. My place of origin. I was before that a free-chartered Mercantile Space Pilot, First Class." A brief sad smile. "Grounded by marriage. There was a doctorate in Quantum Electronics, an associate chair in Ciphers at Berkeley, and a research fellowship in Space Engineering with P.S.R.C."

"You can verify all this?"

"Can you?"

Ellisen reached for Katz, remembered Eheim, took a deep breath, and spread his fingers on the desk. "And so now you're a class 8 radio rating in Palo Alto. How come?"

"I'd rather not say."

"You'd better."

"Controller, it's personal. As to what I did today—I had to act fast. Make the right decision for you, for the old man, for—" He sighed. "For everybody."

Ellisen stood up. "Drink, MacAllister?"

"What is there?"

"Name it."

"Scotch. Double. Neat."

Ellisen felt the man's eyes on him as he went to the robocaddy, poured a generous tumblerful, held it out. "Here."

MacAllister padded across the wide room, took the glass, and dropped onto his former place on the couch.

Ellisen mixed himself a Brown Lady—heavy on the rum, light on the kuva—and went to stand on the hearthrug. "Skol."

"San Fairy Ann." MacAllister raised his glass, but instead of drinking straight away, he swilled the Scotch around and around slowly, eyeing its amber currents against the warmth of the flames. "I'd almost forgotten," he murmured. He took a deep, appreciative sniff, then a sip.

"MacAllister—" Ellisen checked himself. He was acting on impulse, something he'd not done for years. MacAllister was looking at him across the hearth, waiting. "You still fly a hopper?"

"You still ride a bike?"

Ellisen laughed. Touché. "I'm sending you to Denver. Fetch a party. The thing is, he won't know you're coming."

"When?"

"Now."

"My pleasure."

Ellisen stood up, set down his glass, rang for Katz. "Sir?"

"Have a hopper ready. And a flight log for Denver. Mr. MacAllister's fetching Ord now."

Katz looked from one to the other. "He need Security detail, sir?"

"Absolutely not. After this morning the right hand knoweth not what the left hand doth. Set up Security gear, Katz. And a hazer. You handle firearms, too, MacAllister, no doubt."

MacAllister ducked his head slightly.

Katz went to the door, stood waiting for MacAllister to follow.

MacAllister stood, peered into his glass, then reluctantly tossed back the remaining contents.

"Don't worry, MacAllister, if all goes well, there'll be more, and the time to enjoy it," he said, and saw from MacAllister's quick look that he'd said quite the wrong thing.

To Ellisen's surprise, the man put out his hand. "I hope things turn out, Controller."

Ellisen seized the waiting hand, pumped it hard, once. "So do I, MacAllister," he said. "So do I."

As the men crossed the room, Ellisen glanced to the chronometer. If Susann hadn't yet eaten they'd maybe still make it. And even if she had, they might still make it. Upstairs.

Ellisen walked over to the intercom.

16.00 Hours 19 September 2047
Bentnose Peak

He lay on his back staring up at the beam-and-plaster ceiling. His neck ached, and his arm had gone to sleep but Susann lay curled in the crook of his elbow and he hadn't the heart to shift her. He wiggled his feet to the end of the bed seeking a patch of cool sheet. Catching his movement, Susann stirred, murmured. He reached down, stroked her tousled head. "You say something?"

She opened her eyes, looked up at him with dark brown eyes that turned down at the corners, giving her a vulnerable look bordering on hurt. Irresistible.

"I said, this sure beats slingball."

He sat up, reached for the last of the burgundy.

She came up now and took her glass, the sheets slipping from her breasts. He reached out, cupped one of them lightly, and raised his glass. "To the future First Lady of Earth," he said and drank.

"You don't sound so thrilled."

"I am really. I guess I'm tired. Susann—thanks for putting up with me. I've been a bastard at times."

She put a finger to his lips. "Don't. It's been rough. But we came through. As always." She pulled away slightly, her eyes quizzing him. "Pitar, what now?"

He leaned back, closed his eyes, resting his glass on his chest. What indeed? How long before the world exploded once more into a mess of blood and feathers? This time there'd be nobody left to pick them up, if the old man was right.

Hengst was the key, ultimately. He was the one who dealt the cards. He was the one to decide really who got what and when and how. The game was still between him and Hengst even though the rules must now change. If the old man was right, there'd be no time to take Hengst apart. They'd have to get to him some other way. And fast. But how? And with what?

"Pitar? The Hengst business. Are you still going for him?"

He looked down at her, his eyebrow raised. "Why?"

She turned to face him. "Darling, if you do, don't look back. Don't get bogged down in a private vendetta. Your grandfather's dead, and we're alive and there's a world at stake out there."

Ellisen set his wine down, spilling red onto the white linen cloth of the robocaddy. *Private vendetta.* If she only knew. He almost told her then, that old Pylar Fazhakian was over in the guest wing. But God knows what that would bring about his ears. She'd want to meet him, the girl even. Because she, General Cleary's daughter, was as much against his armament platform as was the Hesikastor.

That's why the rift, why things had gotten so hard, only they didn't say as much, not in so many words. There weren't any left.

His mouth went tight.

As if she were the only one who cared about the ecology. *The life chain's broken. The ecology's gone wild.*

Ecology! How did you poison a dead man?

He shifted, angry at his thought, at Susann. The desire for her was suddenly gone. He swung his legs to the floor.

"I have to go."

"Pitar!" The eyes were hurt now. "You said we had until six."

"I know. But there's something I thought could wait that won't. I'll see you at dinner," he added, and reached for his liners.

"Pitar—something bad is happening to us."

He pulled on his navy jumpsuit, clipped the belt shut. "Don't be so melodramatic, Susann."

He turned to go.

"Why," she called after him, "are you going off like this?"

"Later, Susann," he said, and went downstairs.

CHAPTER THREE

TANNIS ORD

16.55 Hours 19 September 2047
Denver Hospice

ORD was taking a pee when his wristic went off, the sound skimming the urinal walls with the whine of a mutant mosquito.

Ord let it. With deliberate speed he finished what he had to do, resealed the front of his whites, and smoothed them down. The wristic still making urgent demand, he washed his neat pink hands with precise economy, waved them gracefully under the vacuheat, then with his palms he fanned the meager strands of red-brown hair across his freckled skull.

Aieee. Aieeeeeee. The tyranny of the moribund.

Somebody had to make a stand for the living.

Outside in the passage, he leaned into the curve of white permaplast and spoke into his wrist. Smitty, no doubt, yanking him back to the assembly line. Goddamn evangelical bleeding heart.

"Dr. Ord, please report to Dr. Saunders immediately."

Ord's heart skipped. Not Smitty. The voice, husky, seductive, and coming from no human throat, pulled him off the wall. *The Bitch.* What had he done?

There were a couple of things he could think of straight off.

He set out at a trot toward the central dome. Every year this

35

place spread like a mushroom patch, blowing him with the spores farther and farther from the parent head.

Non-specialist Personnel Relocation, they called it. During the early years, he and others like him had been displaced by an army of shrinks brought in to deal with the mass breakouts by poor buggers taken with post-atomic claustrophobia syndrome—P.A.C.S. After the pacs wave of breakouts, he'd been moved out even farther by hematologists working with the first wave of leukemics, or lukes. And there they waxed fat, those goddamn shrinks and bloodsuckers, living off the best of everything, with money to burn while Basic M.D.'s like him labored in the goddamn outback for slave gelt.

Halfway down the passageway stood a skid cart, idle, empty. Thank God. His throat was burning already. He hopped on and jerked it into gear. Still puffing, he slid along the glassy floor, tracking the reflected lightstrip line down its center. Fast as the cart ate it up, more unrolled ahead. He stopped at an airlock, while the doors clicked severally and whirred aside to grudge him through.

Twenty-two years, each year worse. On he went, curving now into a bypass. Goddamn war, screwing up his life. He'd had enough. That's why he'd quietly put in for transfer.

Had Boston turned him down? Obviously, and now Saunders knew, and he'd have it in for him forevermore. The rest of his life he'd have to sweat in that goddamn death factory, shunting lukes through and out. Shoveling mud up a landslide.

He'd rather break out. He'd considered it often, but he'd never do it, he knew. He'd actually seen a breakout once. In the early days, the peak time. An orderly; just a kid. He was out only twenty minutes before they hauled him back. Classic case: laughing, waving, and looking into the sun. Ran and shouted and rolled in the blue-gray dirt until all you could see were the whites of his eyes. Put him through detox but it was no good, of course. Funny, they shipped him over to Ord's sector to die. Ugh. There were better ways out.

An image, a flash, no more, of the silo, dark and silent. And his baby deep inside awaiting rebirth.

If only he dared.

He veered from the thought superstitiously. Even the blip of a wish could draw trouble.

There was the high main dome, a round white well arching forty feet over the round white floor. The whole place was white, sick, sick white. Blind and sterile going nowhere, like endless pointless days.

Ord jumped off the cart, crossed the busy floor.

Beside the door was a sign. *Dr. H. P. Saunders. Chief Administrator.*

And under the sign, the Bitch lying in wait. Not much of a face: access slot and small round grille underneath.

The sweat was starting already. A fine, misty sheen. He wiped his palms down his sides. Every time his I.D. hit that slot he waited for her to pick up on Estralita. Why she hadn't in all this time, why they hadn't back in Washington was a mystery to him. But they hadn't, and he sure as hell was not about to tell them.

He pulled his I.D. card, and with the usual misgivings, put it to the slot. With his spare hand he smoothed his hair across his scalp, hitched his shoulders back. Why did he always have to take the gloomy side? Cowards died many times before their deaths. Julius Caesar. Saunders was likely only pulling him in to confirm his transfer.

More likely not. Boston was only another mushroom patch with the same problems as this one and just as overloaded.

He pushed the card through. A click, pause. That was new. The skin pricked on the back of his hands. *Bitch! Bitch! Bitch!* She'd done it!

Another click, and his card shot out, through his shaking fingers to the floor. The airless voice came, smooth, beguiling. "Go right in, Dr. Ord. Dr. Saunders is waiting." The door swished aside.

In front of Saunders's desk—Ord's gut shrank to a tight hard mass—a stranger sat on one of two upright chairs. A big man in a dark jumpsuit with a visitor's I.D. clipped to his collar. And a hazer at his belt.

Security. The guy was absolutely from Security.

Terror. Then, oddly, relief that it was all over. That it wouldn't be hanging over him anymore. But in the next moment the fear was back. Lord oh Lord, he prayed, I'm sorry. Sorry. Please. I'll not complain anymore. Only let me keep the silo.

"Ord." Saunders half rose—the most his rank ever allowed him—and waved him to a second chair. Still poised, the Chief Administrator leaned toward the stranger. "Alistair MacAllister, Dr. Tannis Ord. Dr. Ord, Mr. MacAllister," he said, and plunked down again.

Ord stood, uncertain. That didn't sound much like an arrest.

The big man stood, stuck out a large hand. After a moment, Ord took it, tugged it limply a couple of times, then let it go. A strong hand.

"Sit down, Ord," Saunders said.

Ord lowered himself, his eyes still on the big man. The best thing was to keep quiet. They wanted his hide, let them get it.

"You're sure there's nothing more I can do for you, Mr. MacAllister?"

"Thank you, no, Administrator."

To Ord's amazement, Saunders came up again. All the way up this time. "I'll say good-bye, then."

Good-bye?

Nodding briefly to Ord, Saunders passed him and went out.

"Dr. Ord." The man reached into his pocket, held up a bright blue Security I.D.

The sweat popped out in large wet beads. "I can explain," Ord said.

"The Controller would like to see you right away."

The *Controller?* Ord's knees dissolved. "You mean, Mr. *Ellisen?*" The man nodded. "But what can he possibly—"

"I'm only the driver. Shall we go?"

"What, right now? Like this?" Ord looked down at his whites.

The man stood, towering over him. "Like this."

Ord let him take his elbow, help him out of his chair. He looked up into cool blue eyes, his lower lip beginning to tremble.

For a silo? A lousy, goddamn, rundown silo? He'd never even gotten around to painting the place.

20.34 Hours 19 September 2047
Bentnose Peak

"Dr. Ord, sir."

The gray man practically shoved him into the room, then backed off, leaving Ord standing alone while the heavy wooden door rumbled shut behind him, blocking his retreat. Thock. Whumph.

The room was vast. Low-beamed, *dark*, in spite of all the light. The walls. It was the walls. Paneling. Overpowering smell. Fruitwood of some kind. Cherry. His temples throbbed, and his inner gyroscopes were spinning wild. What was he doing here? Any minute now he'd throw up on the polished wooden floor.

"Dr. Ord." A man rose from behind a far desk. "Come."

Ord walked toward him.

He was bigger than he looked on the public compuscreens. Big as the Security man who'd brought Ord from Denver. But not as fit. Bit too much flesh around the jaw and the color was a touch high. Still good-looking, though, Ord conceded. The famous charisma.

"Sit down."

Ord sat.

"Good journey?"

Ord considered what to say. It had been bloody awful. Too high, too fast, too loud, and bumpy—Christ!

"I haven't flown for a while, sir."

"Hmm."

There was a tri-co-beamer on the desk. Ellisen glanced into it, then back to him.

"Dr. Ord. You're a psionicist."

Careful. "I was."

"Was?"

"I've served in the Denver Hospice since the war."

"Nevertheless. My chief aide tells me that you read minds."

The response was automatic. "Sir, no reputable psionicist would make such a claim."

"I see. You can't read minds after all, then."

A touch of impatience now. "No, sir." Danger, he was on the edge of it, somehow. "That is—" *Fool. Think. Think!*

"Can you or can't you?"

"Maybe, sir."

"Make up your mind, man."

For one agonized moment Ord hugged his precious secret close then offered it up. "In '25 I'd just finished working on a device. A synergizer. I was testing it when everything broke loose. It did work."

"You're saying that with this—synergizer—you *can* read minds?"

"Yes, in a way."

"What way?"

"It reads only visual imagery, sir."

"Pictures in the mind?"

"Yes, sir. Even the ghost of a hint. I even—" Ord stopped short. He was getting carried away, letting on too much. But it had been so long inside. Ellisen, however, only nodded him on. "The way I worked it, you have the vaguest picture and the synergizer extrapolates, fills in the gaps. *Enhancement*, I call it."

"So we get nice clear pictures." Ellisen looked happier. "Any more?"

"Actually, I almost had sound." Would he ever, now?

"You still have this thing?"

"Yes, sir."

"Back in Denver, I suppose."

"Oh—no, sir."

"Estralita? Dr. Ord—answer."

Ord hardly could. "Yes, sir," he whispered, and waited for the worst.

But Ellisen only leaned back. "Good. We shall fetch your synergizer, Ord. I have a subject for you."

Momentary relief gave way to fresh anxiety. "It won't transport, Controller. It's large and complex. And built in."

"Fires of hell!" To Ord's surprise, Ellisen spread his hands out on the desktop and closed his eyes. *Eheim.* Good God. Fascinated in spite of his anxiety, Ord watched him breathe deep, watched the fire subside. "Very well. Muhammet shall go to the mountain. Tell Katz what you need to get things going down there. You'll want assistance, I take it."

"Yes, sir."

"Give Katz their names. If they breathe they're yours." The Controller pressed the desktop.

"Sir?" Ord recognized the voice. The Controller's right hand. The Gray Eminence. Ord had feared him on sight. The legend who knew everything about everybody. Ord knew in that moment that it was Katz, not the Bitch, who'd sniffed him out.

"Katz, bring in the Hesikastor. Alone."

The Hesikastor? *Pylar Fazhakian?*

"By the way, Ord, you'll need this." Ellisen reached down, brought up a familiar small gray metal box which he set on the desk before him. His sickness rising again, Ord watched the man raise the lid and take out an oval green card. Estralita's front door key. "We brought along your things, Ord. All your creature comforts." The Controller dipped into the box and held up a thick swatch of bonds. "You should have been a stockbroker, buying into space when everybody else was still grubbing about in the dirt." He fanned them, picked out a gold card, held it up.

"Ellisen Lunar Mining. Original shares, I see. Worth quite something now." Ellisen laughed shortly. "I thought Hengst had them all."

He set the green card on the desk then replaced the bonds and closed the lid. When he looked up again the smile was gone.

"Keeping the silo constitutes high treason, Ord."

Oh, God.

"You know that all properties of convicted traitors are confiscate?"

"Yes, sir."

"No doubt you hoped that at some future date when things got better you'd cash those things in and head back to your burrow."

Damn him. *What did he want?*

"A deal, Dr. Ord." Ellisen tapped the box. "Get what I want from Pylar Fazhakian and you keep this. Maybe even the silo, too. Maybe. Understood?"

Ord found himself nodding eagerly.

To Ord's great relief, the door slid open and Katz ushered in the Hesikastor. Ord watched the old man cross the floor with interest. He knew him from the newscasts before the war, the shoestring guru, arms always lifted Moses-like over acres of faces. Intense eyes, shockblack hair, silver wings tipped back.

God, he'd aged. The eyes were mild and wet and faded, the beard, the hair long and totally white. And the fire was gone to melancholy. On the other hand, he still stood pretty tall, and when he smiled like that— What had he been doing since '25? And what was he up to now that Ellisen wanted verified?

The Controller was around the desk to meet the man, which was more than he'd done for Ord.

"Hesikastor, may I present Dr. Tannis Ord? Dr. Ord is the man who'll conduct the verification, if you'll agree."

Piqued, Ord looked from one to the other. It hadn't escaped him, either, that Ellisen had presented him to Fazhakian and not the other way around.

"An honor, sir," Ord mumbled, but Ellisen had already turned back to the old man.

"Would you also agree to removing down to Estralita, Hesikastor? Dr. Ord apparently can't conduct his examination here." It sounded like an accusation.

The old man shot Ord a brief and charming smile, and there again came the quick flash of energy, then almost apologetically, he turned back to Ellisen. "Can I refuse, Controller? However, I ask that my granddaughter accompany me. More for her peace of mind than for mine, you know."

Ord watched them talking over his head as though he were part of the paneling, but as he listened, the tiniest feeling began to nibble. There he'd been, half dead from fear and worry, thinking himself ruined for sure, and here he was, bound for heaven with a subject any psionicist would give his eyeteeth for. He relaxed, allowed the worried look to leave his eyes.

"And then we'll have results, eh, Ord?"

"Oh, yes, sir," Ord said, and as he said it, he caught the Gray One's eye on him and the fear snapped back. The synergizer. All these goodies depended on the synergizer. What if, after twenty-two years, *the bloody thing didn't work?*

10.40 Hours 20 September 2047
Estralita

Ord walked slowly down the fifth level passage, listening. He was here. His lovely, beautiful silo was alive again. It was all about him, the fierce energy of the power drive, the recycling plant, the steady thrum of ventilators, the warm waft of wind as the heater kicked in.

He paused for a moment, hands in his jumpsuit pockets—the dark Institute green—ran his hand down the brown concrete wall. Only hours before he'd been tooling along endless white permaplast tunnels to Saunders's office, full of dread and dire misgivings. And here he was now, in paradise. A properly functioning paradise.

Not perfect yet, however. He walked on. MacAllister was due within the hour with the old man and they didn't know whether the synergizer itself would work. It had been a scramble just to get the silo going, so they hadn't yet broken it out. Ellisen sure didn't give a man much time.

Ord stopped before the elevator. Of course the thing would work. He mustn't be so bloody negative.

He stood listening to the whine as the cage gunned up the shaft. Bump. Clank. Old army standard. The doors hissed open and he stepped through, pressed for level six, one down. Lab level. There were six levels in the silo, enough room for an army, but Ord had only ever used the two. Five as living quarters. Six, the bottom level, the working floor.

More than enough space for three people. Six, when MacAllister and the Hesikastor arrived. With a granddaughter, if Ord had heard right.

He had to give the Gray Eminence his due, finding Suk and Prosser. And fast. So fast. If he'd had to choose only two of his former assistants, they'd have been the ones.

Brilliant light spilled from lab A's open door, shadows slid back and forth over the passage floor as Suk and Prosser went about the preliminaries. How familiar that scene was, and the old comfortable feeling of proprietorship it all gave him.

Suk and Prosser looked up as he entered. Suk, little slip of tallow with her brilliant eyes and helmet of hair, still looked like yesterday. But Ord couldn't get used to Prosser. The jowls. The stoop. He was only in his mid- to late forties, like the rest of them. God, they'd all been so young in the old days. Prosser's job had done it, of course. Lugging dead bodies around all day for twenty-odd years took its toll. Suk on the other hand had landed a job over in the Washington State Overspill servicing plant.

"All set?"

"All set." Prosser turned to the instrument wall at the right of the door, eyed the visiplates. "Temperature, check. Humidity, check. Air filter, check. Ion reading, check."

"Right, then. Let's go."

First, the outer casing, airtight, hard as permaplast. Suk handed Ord the laser saw. Ord took it, weighed it in his hand, then, in growing excitement, he put his thumb to the trigger.

A few minutes later the silver couch floated above discarded layers of sheathing and packing, clear and clean as it had been the day Ord had put it up.

Carefully removing the shredded cocoon, Ord reached over, took from Suk the bright leads one after another, Suk calling off their names in her clear Oriental voice and Ord repeating them as he connected them to their appropriate terminals at the head of the couch while Prosser monitored the results. And suddenly, there was the system, live, connected, waiting for someone to slip on the headband and let the thoughts flow through . . .

Ord crossed through into the little observation cubicle just inside the door, fetched out a dark green bottle and three glass beakers.

"Courvoisier. I stashed it when we left," he said, and bet that even Ellisen couldn't boast such a prize. He set it on the table by Prosser's wall ready for when the testing was through, then waved Suk up onto the couch and slipped the headband over her temples. His hands shook slightly, touching her after all those years.

There were creases where the dimples had been, but otherwise the smile hadn't changed much. She must also have been thinking of the passing of time, for she tapped her head as he straightened up. "Don't get your hopes too high, guys," she said. "It's not so much fun in here anymore."

"That's okay, Suk. No time for porn right now. Prosser, the TS."

At once the large transducer screen in the wall behind Suk's head lit to a bright silver.

Suk coughed, sniffed, shifted about a bit, then lay still. Her visual sense was better than Prosser's. And, if Ord remembered, her powers of concentration had been good. Yoga, though she'd always maintained it was the sex. "Give us a circle, Suk. Black on white."

The screen went dim, cloudy, then a dark patch began to form, vague, amorphous, pulsing in and out. Partly Suk's flabby concentration, but that shouldn't matter. "Center, Prosser. Focus, focus."

The screen went whiter, whiter. To Ord's great satisfaction the patch began to sharpen, intensify. Then without warning the light cut and the screen went dead.

Bloody hell! "Prosser!"

Prosser scanned the wall. "I don't get it. Everything's still rolling. It's got to be the transducer."

Suk slipped off the headset, sat up. "Or the lead. Or something. Nothing big."

Five hours later, Ord was gazing morosely at a disemboweled visiplate wall. At least they'd narrowed the problem down to four possible sources. Another month or so might do it.

A bell shrilled through the closed space, starting him unpleasantly.

The front door.

On top of everything else the Hesikastor had arrived.

18.32 Hours 20 September 2047
Estralita

Ord got to his feet, leaned against the couch surveying each visiplate critically. Suk peered brightly out at him from the first crawl space. "Well?"

"Nada. Pull the auxiliary exchange board."

He watched Suk turn about, and crawl ass-up back into the wall.

Ord picked up a cross 'ducer, bounced it in his hand. They'd overhauled every damned thing at first reach. Replaced almost every unit. If the problem went any deeper they were really in trouble.

"Hi. I guess I shouldn't ask how it's going?" The Security man ducked his head under the lintel. MacAllister.

"Where's Fazhakian?"

"Resting." MacAllister looked around the room. "Seems like fun. Can anybody play?"

Suk popped her head out. Her hair was mussed and her eyes were shining dangerously and she looked about twenty-five. Ord felt an old tic of jealousy. "I hardly think—" he said, but Suk was quicker.

"He's it, Ordy. That way I can bone up on the old crash pac, and back up Pross."

Good idea, but the decision must be his. "Yes, well. Nobody's going to do anything if we don't get this show on the road—except maybe take a quick ride back where we came from."

Prosser came alive. "Sir—look!" The TS was silver again.

"Interesting," MacAllister said. "What is it?"

Ord unbent at the sight. "That is a live and functioning transducer screen. TS. We hope. Okay, MacAllister, you play. Onto the couch."

While Suk scrambled out from the crawl space Ord got MacAllister down, fitted him with the headband. "Relax. It won't hurt. All you have to do is picture whatever I tell you to. Okay? First a simple set sequence to establish your norm."

"Sounds easy enough," MacAllister said. "But if it's not going to hurt, why all that first aid stuff?" He looked over to Suk now standing in the middle of the crash pac.

"Don't let it bother you, MacAllister. It's just routine."

MacAllister sat up on one elbow. "Some routine." He pointed now to Suk and the crash pac. "You're sure the old man's not in any danger from all this?"

Ord ignored Suk's quick glance. "Absolutely not. As I said, it's just part of normal procedure."

MacAllister lay down again. "If you say so. But if anything happens to the old guy, the Controller won't be too happy, you know?"

"When you're ready, MacAllister."

MacAllister closed his eyes.

"Right now. Try to picture, if you will, a circle. Black, on a white background. Can you do that?"

The silver of the screen began to shimmer until all at once the light flickered, dimmed. Ord turned to give the order to cut. At that moment the screen came up again, and gray mist began to swirl like a nascent galaxy in its center.

Its core darkened, spread out.

"Prosser, focus."

The core shrank, condensed, and the whole mass slowed, then began to turn the other way. A flash, a snip on the screen of Suk's face grinning up from the crawl space. MacAllister waved a hand in apology. "Ooops. Sorry. It's not so easy, is it?" The grayness came back, swirling, swirling.

"Try harder, MacAllister. Concentrate."

The swirling slowed, stopped finally and the dark shadow in the center resolved into a circle, nebulous, unsteady, but a circle. A quiet cheer from Suk.

Ord let it by. One circle did not a working synergizer make. "Okay, Prosser. Enhance enhance."

The hazy circle grew smaller, sharper. "Good, nearly there. Keep going, keep going." Suddenly, it was gone. "Damn," said Ord. The whole bloody thing, kit and caboodle, had gone and flinked out again.

20.07 Hours 20 September 2047
Estralita

Ord straightened up, rubbed his palm wearily over his scalp. Three more times they'd gotten things going, and three more times something had gone wrong, a different thing each time. At last they were ready to try again. He crossed his fingers. "Okay, MacAllister. Black circle on white."

The screen went silver, gray, swirling, swirling, swirling. Dark center. And—the image was coming through . . . coming through . . . flicker. Before Ord could curse this time the fault righted itself and held. The dark central core on the screen swelled, centered, good old Prosser, and suddenly there it was: a perfect circle. Beautiful. Ord allowed himself a breath. "Thank you, MacAllister. And thank you, Prosser. We're finally getting somewhere. Let's try for two threes. Arabic. Red on blue. Hold it, Prosser. Center it, now steady, steady. Okay."

Two hours more of visualizations. Still and moving, each more complex, each requiring more of the enhancer, before Ord called it a day.

They relaxed, played back the strips through the tri-di-corder. Great images; clear-cut, color true.

"Great little machine." MacAllister stood up and stretched out.

"It's only as good as its operators." Ord smiled at Suk and Prosser. They'd done real well. Tomorrow if the synergizer held up they might get some halfway decent readings. MacAllister hadn't done so badly either.

"Maybe you'll join us in a little libation."

In a rare burst of good feeling Ord fetched a fourth beaker from the little observation cubicle, poured four generous toasts, and handed them around.

"To—" What?

Ellisen wanted one man tested, and quick. After that?

Ord pictured himself back in whites walking down the endless white passageways, bending over bed after bed after bed looking down on fleshless white skulls and dying eyes.

"To every man his dream," he said, and drank.

11.16 Hours 21 September 2047
Estralita

"Okay. Break."

Ord leaned over, brushing past the granddaughter, removed the headset from the old man's head. The girl pushed in behind him, reaching out to help her grandfather up. Her breasts were small, hard, not to Ord's taste at all. Weird, she was. Fey. Come from haunts of coot and hern. Thurber's. And so caught up with the old man. Not healthy, not healthy.

"An hour, Hesikastor." Ord spoke past the girl. "Then we shoot for real."

"That is good." The Hesikastor swung his legs to the floor, stood stretching.

Shira took his arm. "We'll be in our sitting room," she said. "Grandfather will rest now."

Smiling fondly, the old man let her steer him through the door.

Grandfather will rest now. Ord glared after them. Why did she think he'd called the break? Silly cow.

"So far so good," Prosser said.

"Hush. You want trouble? Suk, get a stand for that I.V. pac."

Suk, nodding, went out and down the passage to the supply lockers. Ord couldn't help but notice her brush past MacAllister in the doorway.

The big man leaned against the lintel. "There was something like your synergizer over in the U.K. '24. Guy called Sturnman. Imagector. Armchair. Stuff didn't come through near as clear as this, though."

Ord remembered him all right. And a good half a dozen others racing for name and fame. But Ord was the only one who'd really come through. "The imagector gave you only what the subject saw." Ord bent down, reset the tri-di-corder. "You can see for yourself how much more the synergizer can do. Mind you," Ord went on, switching off the 'corder, "the old man didn't need too much enhancement."

MacAllister ambled off down the passageway toward the elevator. Suk fetched beakers of hot soycaf from the observation cubicle, passed them around. Ord sat himself up on the only stool, Suk perched on the couch. Prosser, after a moment's thought, slid down the wall to squat on the floor.

"A penny for them, Pross," Suk said through the steam. "You're too quiet even for you."

Prosser looked up with his tired sad eyes. "I was thinking. I can't click to all this. It's unreal. Like we'd all died and now we're back as ghosts."

"Pross, don't!" Suk shuddered theatrically. "I felt weird yesterday, but now I'm feeling more okay. How about you, Ordy?"

How about him? He'd been under too much pressure since he'd arrived to indulge in such fancies. "It's great to be back. And I'm amazed how fast you two have clued in after so long. Kudos, kudos, my children."

"Hark at him!" Suk cried. "What's he got? A year, two, on us? What've you been up to, you sly devil? How's Denver?"

"Don't ask. How about you, Prosser?"

Prosser stared down into his beaker. Something had changed in the man. He'd had a wife and kid. Not mentioned them once, neither had Suk asked after them. Suk herself, Ord knew, had lost her folk over in Malay.

"I could be worse." Prosser kept his head down. "All those people. Hundreds, thousands. Shattered. Lost. Because what it was that made them what they were is gone. I can't help thinking, the hotshot guys like Ellisen—they're still doing what they've always done. They still know who they are."

Ord glanced around. They weren't bugged, not unless MacAllister had slipped something under something. Nevertheless, better say a positive word just in case. "That's why it's so great to be here, if just for a while, doing our thing again."

"Yeah." Prosser looked up. "But it doesn't feel the same. It's been too long. I wonder— Oh, forget it." He hung his head again.

"Wonder what, Pross?" Suk leaned down, stroked the nape of his neck.

"Whether we'll ever—get back to normal?"

"I do!" Suk cried. "I can't believe that this is all there's going to be!" She straightened up, smiled across to Ord. "You're sure you don't know what we're supposed to see this afternoon, Ordy?"

"I told you. Ellisen's testing blind."

"Wow. We're back to Saturday matinees. Any bets?"

"Only a fool would place a bet on your table, Suk."

"Still as cautious as ever, I see. Pross?"

Prosser shook his jowls. "No dice. Though given the star lead, I'd say hold the popcorn."

Suk slapped him playfully. "Don't be such a pooper, Pross. Who knows, it might be fun."

12.32 Hours 21 September 2047
Estralita

"Four sevens, Hesikastor. Green on brown. Good. Now clouds. Sunset. All the colors you can imagine. Great. Fine." Ord glanced to Prosser, who gave the thumbs up. At Suk, standing by the crash pac. He crossed his fingers briefly and prayed that everything held. "We're all set. Now, clear your mind, if you will, and breathe deep, in and out three times. As soon as you're ready, run through the data as well as you can recall it, and we'll take care of the rest."

A soft grunt from the old man.

Ord watched the eyes close, the chest rise and fall three times. The girl was right by his head, pressed into the wall. He glanced to the TS. Colors swirled clockwise, pastel, like a light show. They slowed, turned direction. The small room was very still. All eyes, Ord's, the girl's, MacAllister's, Suk's, and even Prosser's—who should have been looking at the instrument wall—were on the TS above the pale beaked face.

The pastels turned to grays and blues. Then, without any help from Prosser, things began to happen fast. The colors resolved into shapes. Mountains, a mass of cloud and stone. High, very high. Suddenly, silently, a huge lumbering shape cut across the foreground in a streak of black and yellow and tilted away, dwindling up and over the mountaintops.

Ord watched, his attention carefully divided between TS and visiplates.

The old man's psi level was climbing fast.

Abruptly, the scene was gone, replaced by a sprawling city, midafternoon. Public aerial cars crowded with commuters going home for the day. A narrow high bridge across a wide blue estuary crammed with pedestrians, tiny craft in the harbor down below. Hong-Kong, Ord was sure. A silver pencil streaked the sky, striped with black and yellow. Everything stopped as the pencil hovered then suddenly exploded and all was silent screaming and shouting and darkness and pain. Ord saw people running everywhere, tearing at their clothes, their hair, streaming down to the water's edge and, would he ever forget it, half a face turned upward, toward the vanished sun. Almost before Ord registered they were off again, amid gray desert, stony, hot. A shaft opened, black hole in the ground and like angry wasps rockets swarmed out, so close that Ord could see quite clearly the Cyrillic stencils on their sides.

Night now, and the sky flashed with laser and antimissile missiles.

Then, oh my God, was that New Washington? A flash, and a huge dirty cloud mushroomed upward, obliterating the clustered permaplast domes.

Things happened faster. In place after place rockets soared, exploded, lasers flashed, and people and parts of people screamed and writhed and died or crawled away into the smoke pall.

The smoke cleared, fanned by fierce winds, revealing flat grassland. The place? Who could tell? Nothing stood against the bare skyline: no tree, no roof, not even the stump of a shelter wall. High in the sky a dirty sun filtered down and lit the shiny floor.

There came a soft sound from somewhere in the room. Startled, Ord looked away. Across the couch, among the clutter of I.V.'s and respirator, Suk was crying.

CHAPTER FOUR

08.01 Hours 22 September 2047
Estralita

"CONTROLLER. This is an honor." Ord stepped forward as Ellisen emerged from the elevator followed by MacAllister. "May I offer you breakfast?"

"Thank you, no. I must move along. The Hesikastor is ready?"

"Waiting in the lab as you requested."

"Good. Let's go."

"So this is the synergizer."

Ord watched him take in the lab: the couch, the monitor wall, the lines and wires, paraphernalia of the crash pac. God, Ellisen and MacAllister in there together practically crowded it out.

Fazhakian was waiting by the far side of the couch, Shira beside him.

"If you'd care to sit down, Controller."

Ord drew out the stool but Ellisen waved it away. He did, however, accept a beaker of soycaf from Suk.

Ord waited for the command to begin, trying not to let his anxiety show. Ellisen had come for a live demonstration of the machine. And after? Would they all be rewrapped and shipped back into hell?

"Hesikastor. As you can guess, we couldn't verify all your data," Ellisen said. "But enough. I'm prepared to accept your prediction as a working hypothesis."

Working hypothesis. Ord listened, stunned. He'd fought away the visions of yesterday, pushed them from his mind. But now this man was standing there with a beaker of soycaf coolly talking of Apocalypse.

"I understood," Ellisen went on, "that what Ord sent me yesterday was a memory of your vision as processed and recorded through this machine. I congratulate Dr. Ord on his achievement, and you, Hesikastor, on your phenomenal power of recall. Now as we discussed, Hesikastor, I'd find more of these visions useful. Tell me, do you have as much control over them as over your conscious thought?"

"No. But through meditation I am lucky sometimes."

Ord sensed reluctance on the old man's part.

Fazhakian was too honest. Ellisen was going to use him. He knew it, but he couldn't stall by lying.

What did this mean to Ord?

God. To have found a man who could shift from mental to psi mode.

Ord had never run a live vision through the works. He remembered the psimeter the day before, its sudden surges. Had the Hesikastor been on the verge of a shift then? Oh, Lord that Ord would be lucky enough to see it.

"I see," Ellisen said. "Hesikastor, I want you to stay here. Work with Dr. Ord. Get into a prophetic frame of mind. Dr. Ord," Ellisen turned to him now, ignoring a stifled protest from the girl. "I stressed yesterday the urgency of the situation."

"Quite, Controller." Anything, Controller, only let us stay.

"On the twenty-fifth of this month I take the World Council Chair—"

"Congratulations, Controller."

"Thank you, Ord. From there I intend to move with all

speed to prevent what you saw from happening. With the Hesikastor's help."

The old man smiled wryly. "You want more visions, Controller."

"Yes."

"And if I refuse to cooperate?"

"I'll have you held for treason."

"You can't! He's not a PanAmerican citizen."

"Miss Shira, my authority is now supranational. Think, young lady. Your grandfather may be about to have the distinction as the first man to be held for treason against Earth. Hesikastor?"

"You think to cow me with threats, Controller." The old man shook his head. "I shall stay, but not to fan the flames of war. Remember that I reserved the right to serve my own ends within the limits of our common cause."

"And I shall see that you don't. Are you ready, Ord?"

Ord moved to the couch. What a pair they made, those two. Two cock birds squaring off across the synergizer. The hawk and the dove.

Aware of Ellisen's eyes on him, Ord laid the Hesikastor down, adjusted the headband, and straightened up. "We'll just run through a simple visualization routine, Controller. The sort of thing we use to establish the personal norm."

As he said that, he saw the psimeter, noted with a stir of excitement that the old man's psi energy was at a new high. He caught Suk's quick glance. Cool, Suk, keep cool. Maybe they'd all see history today.

Ord pointed to a row of visiplates partway down the monitor wall. "Those plates register the Hesikastor's vital signs, Controller."

Everything normal so far.

"And these here on the row beneath," Ord ran his neat little hand over the crystal panels, "monitor his brainwaves: type, intensity, and so on. As you can see, already the Hesikastor is at deep alpha level, that his mental concentration is high and rising."

"And that?" Ellisen pointed to the psimeter, its bright green indicator already rolling along like an Atlantic wave in a force five gale.

"That is the psimeter, sir. It monitors the psi energy, and also indicates if and when the subject slips over into psi mode."

"Psi mode? He'd be having a vision then."

"Exactly, sir." Ord nodded briskly, as though that would be perfectly normal and that it happened all the time. In fact, in no test that Ord had ever conducted had he witnessed anything of the sort.

The old man's eyes were closed. Ord bent down. "A circle, Hesikastor, if you will. Black on white," he said, and kicked himself. He was acquiring an almost superstitious suspicion of that test, the rock on which the day before the synergizer had foundered every time.

He crossed his fingers and prayed.

The TS came up silver. Thank you, Lord.

Gray mist began to form, then twirled slowly, slowly anticlockwise. It slid sideways a little, then Prosser caught it, and focused. The circle came, smaller, sharper. Nice, nice.

Ord glanced to the Controller, saw with satisfaction the beaker of soycaf balanced on his knees, forgotten. He was just turning back to the instrument wall when suddenly the TS went blank. Oh, no! Not now.

"Sir," Prosser said just as Ord himself saw the psimeter.

In that same moment the old man's face contorted, his body jerked, and every blip broke sync. Needles and lines ran wild at crazy speeds, and the luminous green of the psimeter rolled like a bloody great riptide, swamping the visiplate.

The old man went into spasm.

A cry from the girl.

A quick glance from Suk. An "I told you so?" Or a "What to do?"

"Crash pac."

At Ord's command, Prosser broke out an I.V., clapped it to the old man's arm, while Suk opened the sluices.

"What is it? What's happening?" Ellisen was on his feet.

A brilliant flash exploded from the screen, making Ord blink. Then another, and another, a whole string of them, like sheet lightning.

"Ord?" Ellisen said, but Ord barely heard him.

The old man's adrenaline had reached an impossible high. Ord watched Suk pan it down again. This wasn't like '25. That woman had only gone catatonic, for a spell. This was something much worse. The pulse rate was faster than a hummingbird's and the respiration, shallow. The eyes opened, rolled up under the lids.

The lips were going cyanotic.

Oxygen.

Ord himself placed the mask over the old man's face, adjusted the feed.

No change.

The TS was now a blinding, continuous white. Whatever it was was killing him.

Suk looked up, pointed surreptitiously toward the headband.

He shook his head. To remove now it might only make things worse.

The brilliance cut abruptly, leaving the TS dark.

And in that instant Shira looked up. "He's gone," she said. She laid her head on the old man's chest and began to cry.

What did the silly cow mean, he'd gone? That he was dead? How Ord despised that sort of thing. He scanned the visiplates. She was right, though. They looked as though a storm had passed through them, leaving them totally wiped. Oh, God, what was he going to do?

"Ord, what in firehell is going on?"

Ord took his courage in both hands. "Controller, we have an emergency. I must ask you all to leave. MacAllister—and Miss Shira—now."

"No!"

"Shira," Ord chose his words as much for Ellisen as for

her, "wherever your grandfather is, we'll get him back—if you'll give us space. Please—you must wait outside."

She put her arms about the old man's shoulders. "You get out," she said. "Leave us alone. You've done enough! Grandfather should never have come here!"

MacAllister went over, tried to draw her away, but she only clung the tighter to the old man.

Ord looked to Ellisen for support.

"Shira, come. Let them do what they have to. We're only in the way. But the moment you know anything, Ord, I want to hear."

"Of course, sir. The conference room's just that way down the hall."

MacAllister pulled Shira, still resisting, away from the couch and through the door after Ellisen.

Ord closed the door on their heels, then leaned against it and closed his eyes.

"How could you! How could you say we're going to get him back?"

Ord turned on Suk defiantly. "We can at least try. Have faith."

For ten minutes they gave the old man everything they had. But finally even Ord gave up. God, what now?

Suk bent down to remove the respirator.

"Hold it!"

Her eyes flashed. "Why? It's not doing him any good."

"It's not him I'm thinking of." Now he had to go down that passage to tell Aunt Rhody that her old gray goose was dead.

"You don't give a dam, do you?"

Ord was mildly shocked. He'd never seen her so mad.

"You knew something like this could happen, but you didn't say. Maybe the old man had a condition, or something. You never checked. And here we were, only the three of us, with this antiquated junk!" She kicked the side of the resuscitator tank.

"I had no choice, Suk. The point is, he's gone, and we're still here, and we're just about to fry."

"You're just about to fry! And I'm glad. You're a cold, conniving, selfish son of a selfish lousy bastard and I'll be glad to get back to the Overspill!"

"Sir." Prosser turned from the wall, a swatch of tri-di-corder strips in his hand. "You want to look at these?"

"What? Oh, yes." Ord turned from the ghostly face under the shining sheath of the respirator, from the heat of Suk's anger. Thank God for Prosser.

The flashes. There must have been at least four minutes of them, including the continuous light. At that point, the old man's psi reading had been off the wall.

"What do you think, Prosser?" Ord took the strips, fanned them across his palm.

"It looked to me like a flash burnout. As though something tapped into his psi and stripped him of everything in one fast go."

"Something?" God, was Suk still mad. "You mean the goddamn synergizer. We should never have used it again without more testing. I should have said. The man could still be alive."

"Don't blame yourself," Prosser said. "Don't blame anybody. The whole thing happened too sudden and too fast."

That was true. It had been fast all right. Ord thought of the flashes blinding the room. Flashes!

He turned to the wall, patched in the slomojector, tuned it to the lowest setting, and set it to run through the auxiliary viewing screen. Then he slipped in the first strip.

Bingo.

The screen filled with a jerky succession of blurred stills. What had they caught? One frame in five hundred, maybe. But then the images had come through so fast.

Christ! Too fast for any human mind to visualize—and survive.

"Why, that's Earth," Prosser said slowly.

Ord gazed at the screen, at the blue-green globe slowly turning, tilting and wobbling slightly on its axis. It was. Pre-war Earth, all mist and soft blues and salty greens. Shadow overtook the globe, and there, suddenly, tiny flashes broke out all over the surface. Beautiful, deadly spangles. Light slid around Earth's curve.

The beginning of a new day.

The mist, the blue and green were gone. Now all was red and brown and sickly ochers. Earth as she was now, seen from Hengst's lunar observatory, as shown on the public compu-screens.

"I hate Ellisen," Suk said softly behind him. "And I hate you for helping him. He's going to make all this happen again, can't you see that? Haven't you been watching the news?"

Ord stayed quiet. What could he say? What could he do, one way or another?

He removed that first strip, set it aside. Was it a continuation of what they'd seen the day before? It certainly looked like it, and yet—this was no mere memory of a vision, not according to the psimeter.

Ord put in another strip.

Radically different subject matter, this. Nothing to do with the war, as far as Ord could tell. He was looking at a fuzzy landscape of small whitewashed cottages baking in a bright sun. Urchins running along hazy white sand beside a deep blue sea. A dog ran alongside them, underfoot, its ears flopping wildly in the wind.

Ord rubbed his head, fascinated, puzzled.

"Fires of hell!" Ellisen's voice came angrily from the doorway. "I'm waiting for news and I find you looking at a picture show!"

The Controller strode to the couch. "Is he dead?"

Ord looked pointedly past Suk. "He's—in a coma, sir. We're doing all we can." Go on, Suk. Say it, say it.

Suk said nothing.

"By looking at pictures?"

"They may tell us what happened, sir—"

"You mean you don't know? Was it your synergizer, Ord?"

"I don't think so, sir," Ord found himself saying, and looked Suk full in the eye.

To his surprise, she looked down.

"The answer lies there, sir." Ord nodded at the screen. And for once he meant what he said. On the screen the urchins still ran along the sand, halted in mid-stride. Ord ran it on, watched them splash into the tide.

"Kkannakale," Ellisen said softly. "I saw something very like the other day. Let's see another."

Ord retrieved the strip, slipped in the next one, and there was the Hesikastor, a young man, in India. China. Crossing Africa, on foot. Another strip and he was standing, bearded, arms raised against a sea of cheering faces, their mouths opened in dark round O's.

"The man's life," Ellisen said. "It's a review of his life."

Ord watched the pictures jerk disconnectedly across the screen. The old guy's life. Passing before his eyes at high speed. Oh God. Quickly he slipped a fresh strip in.

A wild assortment of images now took the screen, a mishmash of fragments: animals, birds, fishes, sea, mountains, trees, flowers, a rainstorm. A dinosaur. A whale. A trilobite. Nautilus. Amoeba. Figures—equations. Diagrams, charts, maps, passing across the screen now at blinding rate even at that slow speed. God knows how much the 'corder had missed.

It was a living stream of human consciousness.

"It's clear to me," Ellisen said. "It's no more no less than the dying man's life passing before him. Ord, you have much to answer for."

"I don't think so, sir," Prosser said.

"Oh?" Ellisen rounded on him, but Prosser stood his ground.

"What have equations, dinosaurs, nautilus shells and maps and diagrams got to do with his personal life? More likely he was taking inventory."

"Of what, man?" Ellisen demanded.

Prosser turned to Ord. "Sir, I think that for reasons unknown, maybe in response to some unknown stimulus, he suddenly gave out all he knew, not just about himself, but Earth."

"Grandfather!" Shira appeared excitedly in the doorway, followed by MacAllister. She ran to the couch, bent over the old man. "He's coming back!"

"Dr. Ord." Suk's voice came urgently from behind them. As Ord spun on his heel a light winked on the monitor wall. Just one. But it was enough.

The girl was right. Incredibly, the old man was returning to life.

The lines stirred, began to flow across the visiplates. Fazhakian was shifting up yet another notch from wherever he'd been. Against all reason, he was zooming up from the death zone and back into alpha state.

The psimeter surged. No half measures there. That energy was soaring with a vengeance.

Shira ran to the couch, seized the old man's hand. "Grandfather!"

The Hesikastor made no move, gave no sign that he'd heard but when the girl looked up she was smiling. "It's all right," she said. "It's all right now."

How had she known, Ord wondered, but before he could ask her, the TS lit up again, not with quick bright flashes this time, but with slow bands of color.

Like a light show, they shifted and changed, drifting down the screen, mutating all the while, hues for which Ord had no name until gradually, as though by trial and error, they took on a familiar aspect, resembling now nothing more exotic than a standard spectrum testcard for a tri-di-corder.

The bands steadied, pinched in at the center, the ends fanning out to form a rainbow aster. For an instant, it hung motionless, then it began to turn, a color wheel flashing into blinding white.

The screen darkened, and all at once filled with tiny points of light.

"Stars," Ord muttered, then bit his lip in the silence.

The stars wavered momentarily, then began to speed toward them. Incredible.

He glanced to the psimeter. Solid, luminous green. It was happening. The old man must be having a vision!

He turned back to the screen. Now, by some trick of gestalt, he was moving toward the stars, not them toward him.

Suddenly, with a whoosh, the stars smeared and streaked into a tunnel of light through which they were all speeding at a sickening rate. Ord closed his eyes, felt the brilliance flashing upon his lids.

When he reopened them the light had recompressed, foreshortened back into familiar star points again—but in formations never seen from Earth.

The viewpoint slowed, spiraled toward a near sun, grazed its orbit and sped on, executing at last a wide parabolic turn until in the center of the screen now shone a bright disc of light.

The disc grew larger, crowding out the black until it was a globe, all mist, soft blues and salty greens.

The globe became ovoid, flattened at its poles, spinning slowly on an axis inclined at an angle of about twenty degrees.

"Earth," Ellisen murmured, but it couldn't be, Ord knew, not against that alien night.

They arced across the glowing horizon and entered the upper atmosphere to be smothered instantly by thick, white cloud. Seconds later they dropped gently, coming to rest on, what?

Paradise? Another Eden?

Before them, under a cold winter sun, stretched a high lake of deepest, bluest green, ringed in by gray-blue mountains capped with snow. From the lake ran a river: narrow, twisting, falling, tumbling over precipices down into lush green valleys; widening now, slowing, snaking lazily through brackish marshland to a silver sea.

The viewpoint rose some and they were on the move again, toward the lake until mountains shut out hill and plain and sea.

They finally alighted on a small plateau beside the high lake, at the foot of a lesser peak.

Then, incredibly, the room filled with sound: the soft soughing of wind across the rock face, the answering lap of ruffled waters over the cold lake, the creak of branches bending, swaying, in the mountain air.

Suddenly, with a harsh scream that started Ord in his skin, a wild white bird, eagle-beaked and big as an albatross, swooped down from overhead.

This was impossible. The synergizer was not geared for sound. But there it was, and Ord stared entranced, unable to budge.

The air was clear, the sky a deep rich blue. There was life, movement, and he could almost smell the fragrance of the tiny blue flowers at his feet. Somehow he sensed that it was growing warm up there and that it soon would be summer.

He sighed, a deep sigh of release. How good it felt to be in that high clear atmosphere after all those years breathing canned air under a plastic dome.

All at once the picture faded, leaving them all staring at the screen, transfixed, unable to break the spell. The girl stirred first, raising the old man's hand and holding it to her face.

The wall was quiet. Quiet but normal. Vital signs, normal. Mental activity, normal. Psi level, normal—for that one, anyway.

Ord reached over and removed first the air mask, then the headband.

Suk unclipped the sluice-valves and unhooked the I.V.

And the Hesikastor slept on under his own steam.

CHAPTER FIVE

PITAR ELLISEN

13.48 Hours 23 September 2047
New Washington

"**Y**OU'RE sure Hengst can't pick us up?"

MacAllister shrugged. "Who can be sure of anything? Hengst may have moved the state of quantum electronics on since '25. What I'm counting on is the fact we never got QECS working earthside. So he won't be looking for it. And if he's not looking, he shouldn't find it."

"When I call Ord, Hengst will get what?"

MacAllister tapped the little black box patched into the sensorplate. "Plenty. And it might even make sense. But, courtesy of our little random seeder here, the real stuff hitches a ride incognito."

"Unless it hits a quantum detector."

"True."

Ellisen called up the tri-co-beamer, dialed for the red line. It was a risk. But a sensible one worth taking. He trusted this man. "You're sure Ord's got his random seeder set up properly at his end?"

"I went over it several times, Controller."

"Okay. Here goes." With MacAllister standing beside him, Ellisen pressed the red plate on his office sensorband and the call signal leapfrogged cable and short wave relay stations, zigzagging back and forth across the continent all the way down to Estralita.

And there was Ord's pink baby face shining in the lens of the tri-co-beamer. Even before the man spoke, Ellisen knew some gig was up.

"Controller here. How is the Hesikastor?"

"Perfectly well, sir."

That wasn't it.

"Is he there with you?"

"He's sleeping, Controller. Sir—"

Ellisen glanced to the chronister. The old man was all right, which was mainly what he wanted to know.

"Those were pretty brave claims you made yesterday, for a scientist."

Ord's face went red. "I volunteered only the facts, sir."

Ellisen nodded. Indeed, he had. Ellisen had bullied the rest out of him. Such a cautious man. Living in a state of constant anxiety. Ellisen wondered how he'd ever had the gall to keep so quiet about his silo.

"You said, let's see. Quote, that the data from the flashes must have been elicited from the Hesikastor by agent or agents unknown. That in making contact with the Hesikastor they unwittingly destroyed him. That they restored him, and reciprocated by offering data of their own. Unquote. Ord, Ord, Ord. I thought even psionicists were scientists."

"I did say that it was a hunch, sir." Ord looked like a sulky cherub.

"But that hunch raised more questions that it settled. Such as, if the extraction was supposedly too fast for a human being to handle, then who was behind it?"

Ellisen stood up to go, then leaned into the eye of the 'beamer.

"You know what I think, Ord? I think you're covering your ass. You're to stop using your synergizer pending further tests." He reached to cut transmission.

"Wait, sir."

Ellisen waited, his hand to the 'band.

"Sir, this morning at 11.00 hours the Hesikastor had another—vision. It came fast, the moment he put on the headband. We didn't even warm up."

Ellisen drew back his hand. "Subject matter?"

"Similar to yesterday's, sir. A continuation, I'd say. But with a most interesting preamble."

Ellisen glanced again to the chronister. Fifteen minutes late for the next meeting already. He'd told Katz to stall. "How long is it?"

"Five minutes and thirty seconds, sir."

"Be quick," Ellisen said. "MacAllister—secure the door."

MacAllister rounded the desks, took three strides to the door, and set the catch on "hold."

Ord's face gave way to streams of symbols that might have been ancient Urdu: delicate, almost spidery, curlicues and little dashes and dots.

The writing faded to diagrams, one after another in rapid succession, each remaining in view for the blink of an eye. Fine white lines etched on an azure background. Blueprints of some kind?

"Star charts," MacAllister said quietly.

Star charts? Ellisen sat down again. *Star charts?* Was this some elaborate scam? A ruse on Ord's part to stall trouble?

He wouldn't dare.

More figures, this time white on a black background. Columns of words written in bold runes. A crimson circle formed around a set halfway down the central column.

The red circle drew and held Ellisen's attention.

A moment, and the symbols shimmered, dissolved, and reappeared in clear English. Inside the circle now the words read:

3412: 37th year in the 12th reign of the Gnangar Dynasty Being the First Year in the Old Imperial Calendar of Gurnyac

After a moment, both columns and circle vanished and the screen filled with mountains under a high cold sun.

Yesterday's mountains, Ellisen recognized them. And yesterday's plateau overlooking the lake. But now a great gate stood before the peak, separating lake from mountain.

And something more.

The viewpoint panned over the gate for an intriguing glimpse of golden domes flashing in the bright sun. Real gold? No chance to find out for they were whipped away out over the lake, over tiny waves that glistened restlessly, flowing toward a surf collar ringing the far shore.

By the time they reached it, gate, domes, and little mountain peak were lost in haze.

They left the lake, went down through tangled bush and scrub, through swarms of flies and clumsy carapaced insects, following the swirling river from the lake until it slowed, enmeshed in fens crawling with snakes and large slothlike creatures that honked mournfully in the humid heat: down at last into a seaport of tall timbered houses and bright sails.

Ellisen gazed curiously at noisy crowds milling around in dress reminiscent of Europe in the Middle Ages. A Brueghel painting, maybe.

A plumed and ribanded man rode by on a high black horselike creature while before him strode two young boys, threshing from side to side with whips, clearing a way through the press. One of the whips caught a man on the side of the face, opening up a scarlet gash from which blood flowed profusely. The man did not complain but rather melted fast into the crowd.

Brueghel out of Hieronymous Bosch.

The noise was deafening.

Up they went through the air again, along the seashore, turning inland at length toward a dark smoke-pall on the horizon.

Below was undulating plain: dun, dry, monotonous.

As they neared, Ellisen could see that the smoke covered an immense area, close on five kilometers in diameter, maybe. It was erupting from tall blackened brick chimneys atop square squat buildings extending over several hectares apiece. Magically, walls gave way before them and they were under sooty rafters where men and women alike sweated over white hot flame, pouring molten metal into vast vats. The air was thick with black dust; the sweat-slick skins of the workers were streaked with it, and, Ellisen cleared his throat, their lungs must have been full of it.

The heat looked unbearable.

It was a relief to be flying back out again, over what looked like barracks, each flying a pennant with its own distinguishing sign: a mailed fist, a sword, a metal rose.

Ellisen stirred restlessly. What was all this? Did the old man know? Where was this place, first pristine, uninhabited, then teeming with brutish, primitive humanity? Was it a vision, or the dream product of a troubled mind?

They were off once more, toward a ridge of dusky hills on the horizon.

Over their crest reared a great city, a loose collision of tall wooden buildings with a massive fortress in their midst.

Ellisen remembered the words in the red circle.

Was this Gurnyac?

The roads were unpaved. Women, their cumbersome skirts trailing the dirt, went on foot with heavy baskets on their hips, like so many beasts of burden, while men, bright cock-jays in velvet tabards and leggings laced to the knee, rode the not-quite horses.

And everywhere were not-quite dogs, and cats, and goats.

And filth.

Sixteenth century London? Will Shakespeare dodging dog shit underfoot only to catch the amber jet-stream from an up-tipped chamber pot? New York in the late twentieth century? John Doe dodging half-dried human piss trails on his early morning midtown stroll?

And suddenly, Ord was back, the roundness of his pink eager face made rounder by the small bulbous 'beamer lens.

"That it?"

"Yes, sir. Communication broke suddenly. I think the Hesikastor couldn't take any more. But as you can see, it was longer than yesterday's strips. He's adjusting."

"This—hunch—of yours. Any further thought?"

Ord looked wary. "Yes, Controller. But it is only that and subject to verification."

"Go on."

"The nature of the, er, communication suggests to us that the star charts at the beginning give its source. Which is, in our opinion, sir—" Ord broke off."

"Go on."

"A planet located outside the solar system."

"I see." Ellisen watched Ord's face carefully. "How much do you know about star charts?"

"No more than any other informed layman, I'm afraid, sir. I have no idea what they say. I only wish I did."

"What did the Hesikastor say to all this?"

"He won't discuss it, sir. Not without clearance from you."

"Go get him."

"He's still sleeping, sir."

"Wake him."

"It's—not that simple. He's very deep."

"I see. Ord, I'll get back to you. Whatever happens until then don't even think of trying to contact me or anyone else. Whatever happens, you maintain communications silence. Understand?"

"Yes, sir."

Ellisen cut, stood up. He pulled the strips, then cleared the 'beamer. Alien star charts and royal genealogies. If anyone could make sense of them, it was Katz.

He left MacAllister in the office, walked briskly toward the Sessions Chamber. Damn, the way things were happening all at once and so fast. It didn't give a man time.

He walked quickly, absently returning salutes and salutations. Strange, how that place was so like Earth and yet unlike. The horses, for instance. Like Chaucer's chunky beasts, except for the split hooves and whip tails. And the woolly coats, like astrakhan.

Was Ord right? Was this an alien connection?

Or merely an elaborate practical joke on the old man's part?

Ellisen had demanded visions. Maybe the Hesikastor was producing them with a vengeance!

No. The man had died. That had been no joke.

If it were an alien connection—it was certainly an interesting notion. Why, he wondered. Why now, here, and at this time?

He slowed suddenly. Wherever the planet was, *if* it existed outside the old man's mind, it was closely analogous to Earth. And a paradise compared with the fetid sink Earth had become.

He thought of the mountains, and the sea. The city. And the foundries. There must be mines close by. Seams rich in ores. The whole planet abounded with natural resources, as Earth had a century before.

And there was Hengst, up there with his precious voyager ships, all rigged up and nowhere to go. Maybe there was a deal here. Perhaps, instead of going up to see Hengst, he could persuade the man to come down here . . .

Katz. He must get the strips to Katz for analysis.

Ellisen walked on briskly toward the Sessions Chamber.

CHAPTER SIX

TANNIS ORD

20.20 Hours 27 September 2047
Bentnose Peak

ELLISEN stood up.
"If you'll come this way, gentlemen . . ."

Ord left the security of the dinner table for the treacherous expanse of polished floor. The women had already withdrawn: Susann Ellisen and an Abigail Somebody or Other whom Hengst had brought down with him, a Valkyrie of a woman head and shoulders above everybody save Ellisen.

Wishing now that he'd not drunk so much, he followed the rest: Ellisen, Hengst, and Katz, from the dining room, down passages, a flight of treacherous steps, across a hall into another wing—God, this place rambled—and there was the door to Ellisen's study.

Thock. Whumph. Ord felt a fluttering in his ears.

Hengst stopped, square, squat, menacing as a dwarf star just inside the door. "We talk *now*, Ellisen?"

"Momentarily. Drink? Cigar?"

Ord's eyes glazed. More drink?

He took the far corner of the couch beside the fire and watched the others clustered around the robocaddy. Hengst had selected a short, fat cigar from an antique humidor and was busy clipping it. Ellisen handed the man a snifter, then poured

a glass of something for the Gray Eminence. A small glass.
Katz had drunk sparingly throughout the evening. Tiny sherry.
One glass of white wine. A sip or two of port.

Ord wished he'd done the same, but it was too late now.
"Drink, Ord?"

"Oh, er."

Ord felt the blood flushing his face as Ellisen crossed over to
him, bent down, and handed him the snifter.

Carefully holding the brandy level, he watched Hengst,
thick cigar in thick fist, make for the blue chintz armchair
opposite, commandeering it as he no doubt commandeered
everything else. It looked comfortable, well used. Ellisen's
own, probably, and Ord bet Hengst knew it.

To Ord's amusement, Ellisen outmaneuvered him, moving
to stand over him, wide-legged on the hearthrug. Hengst
wouldn't like that. Rumor was that, spaceside, he went about
on stilts.

Katz took a high-backed chair at a discreet distance from the
fire, leaving Ord all alone on the wide couch.

"Well, Controller." Hengst blew out a cloud of fragrant
smoke. "Perhaps now you'll tell me what this mystery is all
about."

Ord looked from one to the other of the men expectantly.

Ellisen raised his brandy glass. "To our future alliance,
Hengst."

Hengst frowned. "Alliance," he muttered. He drained his
brandy and clapped it down on the hearth. "Now. To
business."

"Okay." Ellisen took a sip from his glass, set it up on the
mantelshelf. "I want to talk arms agreement, Hengst. I want to
discuss who gets what and when."

"Go on."

"I'm proposing a trade."

"What? For what?"

"What I want for what you want."

Hengst squinted up through his cigar smoke. "What *I* want?
How can you possibly know what I want?"

"For thirty years you've been probing space. Developing starships, building God-knows-what-sized fleet up there. And there it sits because after all this you haven't yet found it anyplace to go. For all your miles of radio cable, Hengst, and your probes and your observatories you've found not one sign of what you're looking for."

Ellisen paused, then added quietly, "But I have."

Hengst, cigar halfway to his mouth, looked up. "Really."

"I have evidence of a planet, out in deep space, rich in natural resources just begging to be developed. I don't want that planet. I want control of this one. Real, effective control, you know what I mean."

Hengst nodded, barely. "This planet you're talking of, Ellisen. I can't imagine how you found it. What signals get down here go by me."

"They certainly do. And did."

Grunting, Hengst picked up his snifter and went to the robocaddy. He poured himself another brandy and sat down again.

"You say you have evidence of this place. You've obviously got it all prepared."

"You want to see it?"

Hengst nodded.

The Gray One crossed to the far wall beside the curtained window bay. Windows? *Down there?* Ord watched him slide aside a wall panel revealing a sensorband, and, Ord's eyes gleamed avariciously, a Hengst Supronix Mk 6 Tansjector, loaded with extras, including, oh glory, a holoverter.

Katz double-checked the setting, started the run. Ord watched him jealously. They were his signal strips. He should have been working the damn thing.

The lights cut in the room, but for the dim radiance of the sensorband and the glow from the fire.

The center of the room filled with stars. Ord stared, entranced. The sight had been impressive enough on the TS. Through Ellisen's 'verter it was awesome.

The stars began to move. Ord barely refrained from ducking

his head as the outer solar planets whizzed past him, then whoosh, he was rushing out toward the stars. He closed his eyes, feeling dizzy. He couldn't watch the star tunnel on the TS. He certainly wasn't about to go through it via the 'verter.

When next he looked he was nearing the distant sun, and there they were, gliding into the wide parabolic turn. The disc appeared, got larger, and larger, until it was a huge sphere hanging in the center of the room, slowly turning on its axis.

"Earth," Hengst murmured, just as Ellisen had, then, "Hey, no!"

The man leaned forward, his forgotten cigar threatening to burn his fingers.

The strip slid on. What did Katz think about it all, Ord wondered. Did he see the beauty of it, or was it just data to be coded and filed?

Suddenly, there they were, from the viewpoint of the mountain looking out over the lake.

Though he'd been prepared for it, Ord ducked as the huge white bird swooped harshly from the beamed ceiling and faded into the floor.

Hengst looked up at Ellisen. "That is your planet?"

"It is."

Hengst looked thoughtful. "Where did you get the footage?"

"I'll tell you that when you've seen the rest," Ellisen said. "Katz?"

Katz kicked in the second sequence.

Like the Cheshire cat's grin the strange script hung disembodied in the air. A blink of an eye and there were the now familiar words red-encircled:

3412: the 37th year in the 12th reign of the Gnangar Dynasty
Being the First Year of the Old Imperial Calendar . . .

And there, at last, round and gleaming in the gloom, the huge domes high in the mountains, behind the great wooden gate. An exclamation from Hengst, but Ord ignored him, and

Ellisen, the lot of them. Fascinated, he watched as though he'd never seen the stuff before. Such a difference the 'verter made, he didn't want to miss a single second of it.

"Most interesting," Hengst said when it was over. He threw his dead cigar tip into the fire. "I like it. Now will you tell me where you got that stuff?"

Ellisen thrust his hands deep into his jumpsuit pockets.

"Absolutely. A few days ago, I had a call from Pylar Fazhakian—"

"Palo Alto! Good God, Ellisen, that's it?"

Ellisen looked annoyed. "It is."

Hengst waved a fist toward the middle of the room. "He's behind this? I can't believe it." Hengst uncrossed his legs and leaned forward. "Listen, if you're basing your offer on that man, forget it."

"Just a minute, Hengst." Ellisen raised a hand. "I'm not here to waste our time. I can authenticate everything you've just seen."

Hengst smiled up at him coldly. "Mysterious signals that get by my detectors up there. Fancy hologram dreams of a self-styled prophet. I can't buy it, Ellisen."

"The signals that produced those images got by you because you're not equipped to pick them up. They aren't radio in nature, but psionic."

Momentarily, Hengst looked startled. Then he reached for his glass.

"I'd like to see you prove that, I really would."

"You shall. Dr. Ord?"

Ord's middle dissolved and his hands sprang moisture. Here was what he'd been dreading. The reason he'd drunk too much. Now when he needed it, the effect of the liquor had worn off, leaving him alone and scared.

Ellisen and Hengst facing off with him in the middle. Should he stand? He tested his knees and decided not.

Ellisen stirred impatiently. "I introduced Dr. Ord at dinner as an aide, Hengst. Actually, he's a psionicist. Go ahead, Ord."

Ord sat up. "Mr. Hengst, several days ago, Mr. Ellisen sent for me. He said that the Hesikastor claimed to have had certain visions. He was very skeptical of the visions, yet in view of their content, he couldn't afford to overlook them entirely. So he asked me to verify them. This I did, and I'd like to show you the result."

Hengst frowned. "More pictures?"

"They establish the Hesikastor's credibility beyond reasonable doubt."

Hengst's frown deepened. "How?"

"They contain highly classified material, too much for one man to get even were he a master spy. I think you'll agree, sir, that espionage is not Mr. Fazhakian's forte."

Hengst was plainly not amused. Ord ran his hand over his scalp, appealing to Ellisen for support.

Ellisen stayed where he was.

"Very well." Hengst leaned back again and crossed his thighs. "I'll see this material."

A nod to Katz and the center of the room filled with mountains under lowering cloud. Strip one. PanAmerican missile complexes. Sino-Soviet complexes. Then the bombs.

Hengst would recognize them, every one. After all, he'd made the things and shipped them out.

Ord all but cried out as the ancient Z52 swooped like a bloody great Boanerges past his ear to disappear into the hearth in a streak of black and yellow tail band. Chemical code sign, Suk had told him, though God knows how she knew.

Ord fought the urge to turn his head away. The number of times he'd watched this stuff over the past few days, he had it pat. Sick, Suk had called him. But after the initial shock, he'd felt numb. Impressed, but quite unable to connect it with reality. Now here in the hologram it was real all right. So real that he couldn't stand it.

He squeezed his eyes shut.

"I see what you mean," he heard Hengst say at last. "The details are incredibly accurate. How did you do it?"

Ord opened his eyes. It was over. The Doomsday hologram was done.

"Tell him, Ord," Ellisen said.

"I took the images direct from the Hesikastor's mind, sir."

"Be more plain."

"With my synergizer, sir."

Hengst eyed him intently. "Synergizer?"

Ord felt a little surge of excitement. The man, with his hi-tech monopoly, was in for a surprise.

"It's a device that transduces mental and psionic signals into the physical mode, sir."

"Oh. Another Sturnman's imagector. It didn't work."

"Sturnman didn't go far enough, Mr. Hengst."

"You reckon."

"I know, sir."

"I see. Well, I'm open to persuasion." Hengst spread his squat square hands. "I bought out Sturnman in '24. Still have the blueprints."

Sturnman's collateral. Poor sod. The man must have gone bust.

"Ord, I'm interested," Hengst said. "Carry on."

Ord described the preliminary tests, the Hesikastor's rising psi energy, the sudden flashes, the Hesikastor's death and revival.

"When we slowed the impulses on the strips and decoded the recording, sir, we had about eighteen hours worth of material. Snips of his life, his career. Data on Earth."

"The dying man's last moments."

"Not exactly. The data was extracted by an outside agent, and so fast that it killed him."

Hengst's heavy brows came up. "How could you possibly know that?"

"We couldn't, not at first. It was a hunch based on evidence. But a good one. Mr. Hengst; the man died. We were unable to resuscitate him. Whoever killed him *restored him whole.* Within an hour of his death, the Hesikastor's vital signs had returned to normal."

Hengst nodded. "And the star trips?"

"The first one immediately followed his revival. The

second transmission came early the following morning. Each time the Hesikastor exhibited no distress. The speed of the incoming signals, you notice, had now been adjusted to his psi rate.

"And the incoming data? Your opinion on that?"

"We believe that the Hesikastor has been scanned for information. And that whoever scanned him is now reciprocating."

"Ah, yes. The star charts." Hengst turned his attention back to Ellisen. "You said you knew exactly where the planet was."

Ellisen rocked forward on his heels. "Yes."

"I see."

Ellisen stopped rocking, stood quite still on the hearthrug. Ord held his breath.

Hengst swished the last of his brandy around inside the glass, stared down into the bowl.

"Of course, I'd have to see the old man."

"Of course."

Hengst's head came up. "There is one thing. Those ironheads couldn't build a hay cart, let alone mount a caper of this magnitude."

"They didn't," Ellisen said quickly. "There's nobody left on Phrynis now."

Hengst looked from Ord to Ellisen. "Phrynis?"

"The planet."

"Oh. *Phrynis.* What happened to everybody? To the cities, the buildings? The gate?"

And the domes, you greedy bastard, the domes, thought Ord, catching the glint in the man's eyes.

"According to the charts they beamed us, they're long extinct."

"Extinct?" Hengst eyed Ellisen narrowly. "Then who's sending the signals?"

"An automatic beacon triggered by psi energy focused to the right level. Ord, you explain."

Ord cleared his throat. "It seems that the synergizer

somehow boosted the Hesikastor's psi power, sir. I don't know how. It's done it with no one else."

"I see." Hengst stared past Ellisen into the fire. "It's certainly feasible." He looked up. "I wonder why? Why the beacon? Why the exchange?"

Ellisen smiled, relaxing a little, Ord thought. "We don't know, yet. I'll bring Fazhakian in tomorrow morning. Let you talk to him yourself."

"No," Hengst said. "I'll go to him. See him in action. Look at this synergizer."

Ord's breath caught. He felt threatened. The man couldn't take it from him, could he? Ellisen wouldn't sell him out as he was selling the old man?

Panic made him brave.

"Actually, sir, the plant's pretty well outdated now." He glanced across to the window wall. "Just a small screen. Nothing like this."

"Oh?" Hengst's heavy eyebrows came up. He turned to Ellisen. "Then we'd better take a 'verter with us, eh, Ellisen? You got somebody to patch it in, Ord?"

Ord bobbed his head. "No problem, sir." Ord didn't know whether to laugh or cry. In trying to put Hengst off, he'd only gotten himself updated.

"I don't suppose you'll say where he is, Ellisen?"

Ellisen's smile broadened. "Sorry, Hengst. You'll have to go blind. Leave aside your tracer and take us on trust."

Ord winced inwardly. All that smiling didn't fool him. There was bad blood between those two. He remembered Ellisen's laugh as he'd held the Ellisen Lunar Mining Shares. Hengst had taken the Ellisens to the cleaners after the war, as he'd taken everybody else up there. It must hurt for someone to rook you then have to stand aside to watch them get fat on the pickings. God knew he'd feel the same if somebody took his silo. Or his baby.

Hengst gripped the arms of the chair and planted his feet square ready to stand up. "Very well. I'll put a call in spaceside to warn them I'm going to earth for a while, as it were," he said, and hauled himself up. "My God, man, I'm looking forward to this jaunt."

Ellisen led the way to the door.

Ord belatedly stood up to follow them. He hadn't missed Ellisen's glance as he'd left the hearth. Ord had done fine. So far.

He hadn't missed the greed in Hengst's eye, either. There wasn't a thing that that man had wanted and not gotten in the end.

Some deal this was in the offing. Top level shenanigans and his, Ord's future somehow riding on it.

He'd better come through.

09.34 Hours 28 September 2047
Estralita

Ord stood nervously by the couch. God! If anything should blow now! And he didn't just mean the synergizer, either. The air in that small place was loaded.

Ellisen was a smooth one, Ord had to give him that. The way he'd brought those two together. Hengst was thinking of cooperating over the arms situation, he'd told Fazhakian. Such a look the old man had given him. He hadn't been fooled, Ord would swear, but he'd said nothing. Only kept his own council and gotten up onto the couch.

Shira had read pretty well, though. If looks could have killed, the lab would look like Hamlet act five scene two by now.

Then there was Suk.

I hate that man . . . and I hate you for helping him . . .

The sweat was running now. He ran his hands down his jumpsuit.

As if the place weren't crammed enough: The old man on the couch; Shira beside him; Suk, her face a tight little Oriental mask; Prosser by the wall; Hengst with Ellisen just inside the door; MacAllister back of them, with Katz, leaving the floor space clear for the hologram.

Ord couldn't help a small twinge of excitement at the thought. All this time using a tri-di-corder and never being able to see its true results until now. The TS was still operating, of course, but whatever came through today would be there, in its full roundness, filling the lab.

Ellisen waved him on. "Go ahead, Ord."

Ord crossed his fingers and set the headband on Fazhakian's brow.

"We'll warm up," he said. "Go through a check routine we use to establish the subject's norm. Hesikastor, if you will, I'd like you to visualize a black circ—"

That was as far as he got before the TS cut out.

But this time Ord didn't panic. Instead he looked to the psimeter, saw the green flowing, rising with beautiful geometric symmetry.

Gradually, as though one's eyes were adjusting to darkness, the black of the TS changed to the dimness of a dark paneled chamber, the walls of which were . . . Ord blinked and looked again . . . hung with rich tapestries.

The lab filled with shapes and shadows.

A bedchamber.

God.

In the middle of that bedchamber stood a gigantic bed thick with furs and in the middle of that two naked figures, a young man and woman, were doing what came naturally with a fierce energy that made Ord's crotch tighten.

The young man rolled aside, said something into the girl's ear. She, laughing, replied. Her voice was high and clear. Her accents were harsh, yet slightly rounded in the long vowels. But most of the words were familiar enough.

"The Gurnyac krudt is like Adiga's well: the faster it's drawn, the faster it fills!"

Hengst laughed.

"They speak *English* on Phrynis?"

"The signals reach the Hesikastor's mind inchoate, sir. He must be forming them into English for our benefit. I'm sure he could just as well put them through in Armenian or Russian or any other language he speaks."

The bodies rolled, thrashed, and lay back at last side by side, spent.

Oh, God. That would have been the same in any language.

Nobody moved. Nobody spoke.

The man's body shone coppery-green in the dim lamplight. His flesh was firm, tight-stretched over high wide cheekbones, beaked nose and brow, and Ord could see clearly the slate sharp angle of the jaw under the richness of blue-black beard.

He was tall, very tall. Proud. Arrogant. He'd strut high, strong, light on his feet, like a stag. Beside him all of them there in the lab were traveling salesmen, even the Viking. Even MacAllister.

A god, he was. An Apollo. An *alien* Apollo, and alien he undoubtedly was, for all his earthy appetite.

The woman, too, had that same alien *feel* in spite of her Reubens body. Ord stared at her mouth. So ripe and red even in that dim light, swollen from the kissing. Inside, her tongue would be soft and wet and inviting.

Hengst laughed again.

"Earth's greatest moment and what do we get?"

There came a heavy thud from somewhere outside the chamber walls, startling Ord as much as it did the young man on the bed.

The young man raised his head slightly, listening, a young stag sniffing the wind. Then, grunting, he reluctantly rolled over and turned on them a cold blue eye . . .

CHAPTER SEVEN

TORC came up too fast. Puffballs of pain swelled and burst in his head.

Had he heard the sound, or only imagined it?

Naked, he crawled away from the damp warm body curled beside him and fell cursing to the floor. Served him right for drinking too much wine again. He picked himself up and stumbled over polished flagstones to the far wall.

There came a scratching now, then a second thump as something hit the paneling from the other side.

He needed more light.

He made the casement, wrestled back thick harpile drapes but no light came. Cloud had gathered while he slept, smothering bright, full Ao.

He bumped around bulky chests, the stand holding his white pilgrim clothes, to collide at last with the small table on which stood the lamp, on the lowest setting.

He turned it up too fast, squeezed his eyes shut in pain, and turned it back low. He looked, blinking, to the bed. Tanna's flesh glowed in the dimness. She lay on her back, legs splayed, arms outflung: the swell of breast and belly glistening smooth as the dunes of Pruth. One long leg was straight, the other, bent up and out, the dark between the curve of thighs shadowy, inviting.

He seized the lamp, took down a blade from the wall, unsheathed it, and moved back to where he'd heard the noise. There, he raised the arras masking the length of the wall and pressed a knot in the wainscoting. At once a panel swung out, shoulder high, revealing a dark glory-hole beyond.

A youth, enough like Torc to be his brother, fell across the sill, his blood spilling over the flagstones.

"Aravac!"

Torc threw his sword aside and squatted to raise him, cradling the bloody head against his chest.

Aravac's eyes opened, barely, not blue now but dark—black, through the slits. The mouth moved. Blood came out, more blood, warm and thick against Torc's flesh, rich red and shiny as the wine they'd glutted themselves on at the farewell feast but an hour before.

"What is it, Aravac? Answer me!"

Torc looked around the chamber. He must stop the blood. He looked across to the bed. Tanna hadn't moved, curse her for a stupid fallowella. He called out, as loudly as he dared without waking those keeping vigil in the outer chambers. "Tanna! *Tanna*—wake up, I say!"

No response.

Torc's arms tightened. Aravac was dying.

"Aravac! Who did this? Tell me, and he shall pay!"

Still no response.

Torc tried to think. After supper, Aravac had been going back to his chambers. To meet a certain fallowella, he'd said. But here he was, fully dressed. Obviously he'd never gotten there.

Could he have been taken up some sudden private quarrel?

Torc shook his head. No one in all the citadel would dare to raise his hand against a friend of the crown prince, even with just grievance. Neither would Aravac have used Torc's secret back door unless . . .

Torc's eyes narrowed. Had he been right? Was danger come here, into the very citadel, from the Weald? He'd asked Aravac to keep an eye out.

Oh, the blood. He must stop it somehow.

Before he could move, Aravac's eyes opened wide, their whites crazed with blood. He saw Torc, seemed to recognize him. He tried again to speak, but a rush of foam choked the words.

"Aravac—!"

Aravac went limp in Torc's arms.

On a sudden thought, Torc glanced up at the gaping glory-hole. Was he, Torc, in danger now? Could Aravac have led his assassin to Torc's secret back door?

Torc laid Aravac down and peered through the glory-hole into the darkness of the tunnel beyond.

No. Whoever had done this to Aravac must surely be dead, or dying, for Aravac would never risk leading another to him.

What to do now? Get rid of Tanna, then give the alarm, of course—and that was surely going to mean trouble!

He ran to the bed and shook the sleeping girl. "Tanna! Tanna—get dressed, I say!"

For a moment she looked dazed, then she focused on his bloodied chest.

"Highness!"

Torc snatched up her dress from the floor beside the bed and threw it at her. "Out. Hurry!"

She slipped it on, pulled it down, and fumbled the laces, then felt around for her shoes.

"Get to your bed—and keep your mouth shut or it will go ill with you, you hear?" He marched her over to the open panel.

She caught her breath before the glory-hole.

"*Aravac!* 'Tis the lord Aravac! What have you—"

"I said," he snapped savagely, "keep your mouth shut!" He made to push her over the sill.

"But Torc, Highness—" Tanna clung to the edge of the lintel.

Torc's fingers dug into her shoulder. "Go," he said, then

relenting, he released her, and crossing the floor, took up a second lamp in order to light her way along the low crooked passage to the outer panel that opened onto the gallery behind his chambers.

He thrust the lamp at her.

"Here," he said, but Tanna was bending over Aravac.

"Wait. See: his hand."

Torc looked down. The barest tip of what was unmistakably a shuktek protruded from the rigid fist. Now why hadn't he seen that? Frowning, he bent to retrieve it, but his head throbbed with the sudden movement, and for a moment everything went dark. Tanna caught him, steadied him, and by the time his head cleared he found her squatting beside him, examining the stick closely.

Strangely stirred, he snatched it from her and laid it on his palm. He'd been right. Danger was come to the very citadel, and Aravac had found it! He frowned, looking down.

Like all shukteks it was roughly the shape and size of a small knife, but unlike any he'd ever seen it was crude and unpolished.

He ran his finger along the straight edge, picked up a splinter. The other edge was notched in the usual way.

"What is it, Torc?"

Ignoring her, he continued to stare down at it thoughtfully. He knew what it was, all right, but it was not a fallowella's place to know of such things, it being a ritual summons to a meeting less than public. Called to no good purpose, that Aravac should die holding it. Called by whom? Where, and when? He fingered the notches, some deeply indented, some small as the teeth of a wember leaf. There the answer lay. But only for those privy to the call.

One good thing might come of all this: with luck, he might not go to Rm after all. If Gurnyac were threatened, surely the crown prince belonged at home.

He would see his father, now. Take the shuktek to him, make his case. But first he must get rid of Tanna.

He stood to pull her upright, but in that moment Tanna

reached out, took Aravac's other hand, and prising open the fingers, let fall a heavy gold coin.

Torc snatched it up and held it to the light.

It bore his father's head on one side, and on the other the royal Gnangar crest. A thousand gosheng piece, a small fortune—even for Torc.

That clinched it.

He seized Tanna, drew her up, and thrust the lamp into her hand.

"Get back to my mother's chambers, and if you breathe one word of what you've seen this night, your head will hang by the Great Gate and your tongue beside it. Now—go!"

He pushed her through into the darkness and closed the panel door.

"But, Highness—the king sleeps. You know as well as I that one may not disturb him now."

Torc blew fiercely, beat his fist on his palm. It had been easy passing the guards compared to this.

"Gense," he said, glaring down on the old man, "I must speak with Sharroc. It's urgent. Wake him—at once."

Old Gense shook his shaggy locks, pulled on his tousled beard. Torc could well guess what the old gont was thinking.

"I'm not drunk, Gense. I'm deadly serious."

Still Gense eyed him doubtfully.

Torc barely forebore from seizing the old man's beard and swinging him around by it. But that would only bring the guards running. He put his mouth close to Gense's ear. "I swear to you, upon my mother's life and honor, that if you do not wake the king now you'll live to regret it—barely." He fingered the scabbard at his side—a tactical error.

"And since when did even the king's own son think to go before him bearing arms?" the old man cried.

"I wore it through the citadel as self-protection, only." Torc unbuckled his sword, threw it at the old man. "Now—admit me to the king!"

"Protection?"

Gense, staggering a little from the impact, set the weapon aside, went to the king's bedchamber door, and spoke softly into the lock.

There was the sound of bolts sliding back, and a key grinding, then the door opened and he disappeared from view.

A moment later, he emerged, shaking his head, and beckoned to Torc.

"You'd better make good your word, Highness," he muttered, "or prince and steward alike—both our heads will on the morrow mark the Great Gate."

King Sharroc, his grizzled hair caught in a nightcap, filled the boot-chair; his feet, slippered, were propped up on a stool.

How ghastly he looked in the blue agria flare. His face was blotched and yellow, his pale eyes sunken and bloodshot; his jowls hung flaccid as an old adahi's.

Yet, thought Torc, they say I am now as he was when he became of age. Will I therefore one day look like that?

At Sharroc's beckoning, Torc advanced, flanked by the chamber guards.

His father eyed him up and down, taking in his yesterday's clothes, grease-stained and wine-soaked from the feast, that he'd torn off and tossed aside in his haste to mount Tanna. He'd had to shake them out and put them back on. It had been either that or put on his pilgrim's gear—short of rousting out the vigil-keepers guarding his ante-chamber to find him a new suiting, and that would never have done! Oh, whatever the old gont thought, he'd think again, soon enough.

"If this is some wine-begotten joke you'll go to Rm with something to last you your whole stay!"

"No, Father, I swear—"

"State your business."

"Only, Father, when we're alone."

The king's mouth tightened. Torc waited for the usual rush of rage, but, instead, the king nodded the guards—and Gense—outside.

The moment the door closed, Torc knelt by his father's

stool, pulled the shuktek and the gosheng piece from his pouch, and held them out.

His father took them, examined them much as he himself had done, then looked up. "Well?"

Torc told him what had happened, without mentioning Tanna, or his back door.

"Where is Aravac now?"

"In my chamber still, Father."

"And your vigil-keepers—they brought you here?"

Torc shook his head.

"I came alone."

"You came alone?" His father leaned back, his eyes narrowed. "You mean to say that they let that boy pass through to you, then they let you out—*alone?*"

Torc swallowed. "They heard nothing, Father. They—" He stopped.

"You mean he came through the back way? You told him about the glory hole?" Sharroc actually stood up. "When you became crown prince, when you moved into those chambers and I showed you that secret way, what did I tell you? Answer me, boy!"

His father's face went a deep, dark red.

"That—that my life may depend on it some day," Torc mumbled, looking down.

"Say it again, say it aloud!" his father cried.

Torc forced himself to look up. "My life may depend on it," he said, loud enough to placate his father, not so loud that he'd be accused of impudence, or worse.

Sharroc sat down again with a grunt. "Do you know I didn't even tell Brac and Feric," his father said, quietly now. "As close as we were when I became crown prince. But then you haven't half the sense that I had, I've known that all along." He looked up from under his brows. "Who else have you told?"

"No one, no one at all," Torc said quickly, too quickly, maybe, to fool the old gont, but Tanna surely didn't count.

"Humph, so you say." His father pulled his robe about him. "Well now. Your young friend came in on you, woke you, and bled all over your floor. Pity he couldn't have chosen another night, boy. You need your rest. You've a big day ahead of you tomorrow. A nuisance, but a matter for the king? Perhaps you'll explain why you had to bother me with it. With these."

Sharroc held up the coin and the shuktek.

"They were in Aravac's hand."

Sharroc wagged the stick at Torc like an admonishing finger. "You're sure that you weren't gambling in your chamber, boy? You're sure that Aravac lies not dead of a certain hot blade? And that these are not from a gambling tryst? It's not the first time you've killed in wine-anger, boy. And over a lost wager."

"I swear, sire—" Torc's headache was coming back.

"Start again, Torc. Tell the truth this time."

"Aravac came to me—"

"Bleeding all over your glory-hole—"

Torc took courage, repeated his tale—minus Tanna. "And so here I am. Father, I am sure that Aravac was trying to warn me—someone in the citadel is working to no good end," he said, but Sharroc only looked as skeptical as ever.

Torc lost his patience.

"What if it is to do with the riots in the Weald? What if the melks are bringing insurrection through our very own gates? If we ignore these things, then Aravac died in vain!"

Sharroc waved the shuktek between them.

"Many like these were indeed taken in the Weald, and some may even have found their way here as souvenirs." Sharroc peered up at Torc from under his eyebrows. "But their owners are gutted and their heads, poled. The trouble's over, the Brandhouses are purged, and there's an end of it. As for you— whatever hot-headed nonsense that went sour on you—we can't afford a scandal on the eve of your pilgrimage. Have Aravac removed and get some sleep. You've a long journey tomorrow."

Torc stood up.

"I beg leave, sire, not to go."

Anger flared in the king's eyes then.

"Now I see. This has all been but a ruse to keep yourself at home."

Torc started back, truly stung.

"Father! You think for that my friend lies dead?" As near to friend an any Gnangar was like to have. "For a *ruse?* I beg you—at least defer this—farce—until the throne is truly secure!"

Stiff with rage, Sharroc stood up again, and this time Torc stepped back. "Are you suggesting, fratling, that the king can't manage his own affairs? Do you dare come in here, disturbing our sleep, demanding that you *not go!* Since the first Gnangar king, the royal heir has gone to Rm on his coming of age. Not a day before, not a day late. Who are you, eh, that you're exempt? Without his proving in the holy city the king is but a man like all the rest. Already the people line the streets to see their next king ride the route that will make him a demigod. What—shall you stand out there and tell *them* that you'll not go?" He lowered his voice. "Farce or no—and it's not for you to say—of course you'll go tomorrow against a thousand conspiracies, and there's an end to it."

Before Torc could speak another word, Sharroc rang the bell at his side and at once the guard—and Gense—reappeared.

One would think, Torc thought sourly, looking back as Gense helped his father back into bed, that they'd been listening at the door.

"By your leave," he called over his shoulder, but Sharroc didn't even look his way.

CHAPTER EIGHT

TORC stepped out of the darkness of the king's barracks—a misty darkness in which the dew hung, as though reluctant to fall to Gurnyac soil—and into the glare from the porch of the first building.

He met the sentries' challenge, acknowledged their quick salute.

He glanced back at them: fixed blades, fixed stance, eyes and voices flat as the reed beds of Asurdun. Brac trained his sentries well. And yet, Torc's mouth curled slightly, in their fixed stare he'd caught a flash of shock at seeing him in that place at that time and on that night.

He ran up the front steps, squeaked along the polished passageway, breathing in old smells from his earliest childhood. Of scrubbed wood, wax, and metal polish; of tharhide boots, stale hlath, and acrid smoke from strong pipe-moss.

"Stand, in the name of the king!"

Torc stood, heard smart steps behind him, turned.

"Highness! Pardon."

As if the man hadn't recognized him from the back. Quick as a petiwick, the soldier put up his blade, saluted stiffly.

Gibbal: one-time common footclar, long-time campaigner in the field, and now first equerry to the regiment.

"General Feric is awake?"

"Highness." Gibbal clicked his heels again. An unnecessary question, the click said. Feric never slept.

"I would see him."

"Highness."

Double click, then Gibbal led Torc to a door midway down the passage on the right-hand side.

Torc detained him. "I said, *Feric,* Gibbal."

Click. "General Feric is with General Brac, Highness."

The Dryac he was. Oh, well. Better than nothing. Torc had feared he'd be with a woman.

The two generals were bent over a small table on which was spread a map so large it trailed the floor. This time, if there was surprise on having the king's heir announced at that hour of that night Torc got only cool appraisal and a brisk salute.

Brac called for hlath and gestured Torc to a seat by the stove.

"Well, and what brings you, Highness?" Brac outranked Feric; was closer to the king.

Yet Torc looked past him to Feric. Feric, as broad and solid as the other was lean; as square and grizzled as the other was smooth and angular. But Feric was staring down into the flames of the stove, and Torc could see only his profile.

Sighing, Torc addressed himself therefore to Brac, but it was still to Feric that he really spoke.

He told of what had happened, as much as he'd told Sharroc, anyway.

"And so Father holds the shuktek, and the gosheng piece, and I can do no more. He thinks it a ruse to keep from going to Rm. Yet Aravac lies dead of an unknown hand that struck here, somewhere in this very citadel. And the king's gone back to bed!"

Brac raised his hlath.

"Don't sound so bitter, Highness," he said. "To your pilgrimage."

He tipped his cup and drank.

Torc banged his handle down angrily. "You, too, think I'm fooling. I had at least expected you to hear me out!"

"And so we have, Highness," Brac said. "As we heard your father speak to his father on the eve of his going—such a tale as he told on that night, and we but young aides at his side. And when his father wouldn't listen, he kicked up such a racket. One would have thought the world were coming to an end. Do you think that all those before you didn't try one way or another to put off the fateful day? Though I do think, young bruk, that you sailed close to the wind with the king in taking the uprisings as text." He reached out, touched Torc's arm. "Come, half a sunaround isn't so very long, you know. Think of all the wine that will be waiting for you when you get back. And all the other to garnish it!"

Torc stood, looking to Feric, who still stared into the open stove. "I see I waste your time," he said, and strode to the door.

"Stay!"

Feric's voice.

Torc stayed.

"Sit."

Torc went back to his seat and sat.

Feric took up his hlath in his great fist and drank it in one scalding draught as was his custom. Then he set down the cup.

"Why have you come here?"

"Because my father wouldn't listen to me. I thought you would."

"This is the truth that you speak?"

"The truth."

"Not a trick, or a way out of some scrape?"

"That is so."

"What would you have us do?"

"Go to my father. Make him listen."

Feric leaned back, the chair creaking under his weight. His tunic, unlike Brac's, was crumpled at this hour, and open at the neck, and a lock of hair had fallen over his brow.

"You think treason stalks the Citadel." A trace of irony now in Feric's voice.

Torc's temper rose. "Yes I do!" he cried, and knew he sounded peevish. A mistake with Feric.

"Is it not more likely that Aravac, as the king suggested, simply died of a gambler's quarrel?"

Torc calmed down instantly. He looked into the scarred and pitted face.

"Likely, but I don't think so. Since when have even the sons of Gurnyac lords gambled with thousand gosheng pieces? Also—" He hesitated, feeling foolish. "I'd asked him to keep an eye out about the place."

"For?"

Torc looked for a sign of amusement, this time found none.

"Strange faces. It was easier for him than for me."

Feric nodded. "Why?"

"The troubles in the Weald are common talk in the Citadel. Everyone knows you went there last month. And they say that there's trouble still. I've heard—"

Feric took his arm. Torc felt the strength of that hand, that had given him his first small sword; a hand still strong enough to snap his bones in two. "You think your father a gontish pizac, eh? And his two generals doddering incompetents?"

"I didn't say that!"

Feric grinning, tightened his grip. "Don't excuse yourself, boy. There's never lived the Gnangar son worth his salt that hasn't thought his father an old gont best pensioned off. The riots are over, but between you and me I'll own the trouble's not entirely done—"

"Feric!" Brac's voice was sharp.

Feric shrugged. "The lad's of age tomorrow. It can't hurt for him to know." He addressed himself once more to Torc. "But the back of it's broken. It's all a matter of finding the last of the trouble-makers, that's all. And our agents are out there now, doing just that.

"You're still not satisfied, I see."

"No, I'm not, nor would anyone be with half a brain." Torc stopped short. Had he gone too far? Too late. Feric motioned him to continue. "Those riots had to be more than freak outbreaks."

Feric looked interested. "What makes you say that?"

"You wouldn't get random disturbances as far apart as they were—two in the Smeltings, and three in the Foundings—all bearing the same stamp. Furthermore," Torc leaned forward and spread out his hands, "melks are too stupid to be discontent, let alone to organize riots. Somebody is out there, stirring up feeling against the Gnangars."

Even as Torc said the words, and winced at their melodramatic ring, he felt their truth.

But Brac only laughed, and stood up. "Go to bed, Highness," he said. "Whatever plot is hatching out there against the Gnangars is no match for the king and his generals. There's not a man in the world that could unseat Sharroc—" His laugh vanished. "—or you in your due turn. We'll see to that."

He was about to call for Gibbal to see Torc out when there was a tap at the door and Gibbal came in of his own accord.

"The king, sir," Gibbal said, his face stiff as ever. "He requires the generals Brac and Feric in his quarters at once."

Brac and Feric exchanged a quick look. Then Brac nodded, reached for his sword belt to buckle it on.

"You see? Your father's taken you at your word. And thanks to you, we'll probably be at it for the rest of the night. Go to bed, boy, and let those whose task it is do the worrying. You'll have your day. Come, I'll walk you back to the Citadel."

The three of them trod the length of the shiny passageway to the door and down the steps.

"Till the morrow, then," Torc said when Feric halted. Torc had hoped that Feric was going with them.

Feric, massive and dark against the light, bowed his head. "I wish you safe journey and swift return, Highness." He turned back to Brac. "I'll catch you up, General," he said, and strode back into the hutment.

CHAPTER NINE

IT was well into the early hours before Torc lay once more on his back in the darkness. Only a few hours before, the most that had been on his mind was how to get out of going to Rm. And now Aravac was dead, had used the last beats of his heart to reach him, Torc.

Had tried to tell him, what?

Of some sort of trouble, as the shuktek and the thousand gosheng piece clearly testified. But what?

The king and his generals had told him to forget about it.

And yet—Sharroc had summoned Brac and Feric. For all their show of skepticism they'd listened to him.

And so they should.

Take the shuktek. Crude and clumsily carved, it had come from the Weald, Torc was sure, and not merely as a souvenir.

To think that someone here, in the king's very stronghold, was plotting against the Gnangar crown.

Anger stirred in him. He'd sounded the alarm. Seen the danger. And yet there he was still being packed off to nowhere like a child.

Dawn would see him a youth no longer but a man.

How dare they dismiss him, deprive him of the chance to prove himself, keeping him, by their dismissal, a milksop for fully half a round of Demiel?

He tossed restlessly.

While Brac and Feric and his father discussed strategy in the king's tower, Torc had stood in his own bedchamber, watching the bewildered vigil-keepers remove Aravac's body and clean up the mess.

He couldn't help one tiny smile. He'd bet they were sitting out there, still trying to figure how Aravac had gotten in and how Torc had gotten out past them.

His smile faded. Maybe not.

He hadn't been so clever. Everyone must guess now at a secret back door.

He turned over again.

At dawn they'd come for him. And he'd leave behind him so many unanswered questions.

Let those whose task it is do the worrying, Brac had said.

Oh, the endless days stretching ahead.

He thought of Tanna, wanted her to lie with him through that long and sleepless night. He could almost feel the softness of her full, moist mouth, smell the muss of her tawny hair on his face.

But even he couldn't get her out from his mother's stronghold.

Half a sunaround!

He thought of her in her little cell off his mother's bedchamber. Had any of the other waiting-women heard her creep back in? What if they had? Everyone knew to whose bed she was keeping. None would dare taunt her for that.

What a mess this last night had turned out to be.

Mess.

Torc sat up.

The blood! There'd been so much of it. Aravac must have left a trail of it—leading to his back door. Torc hadn't noticed as he'd rushed out earlier. The back galleries, lightly traveled, were badly lit. Spent sconces weren't regularly replaced along them. But tomorrow someone might well spot a dried up blood trail disappearing into the wall.

He rolled out of bed, relit the lamp, and, after bolting his chamber door on the inside, slipped through the glory-hole into the little passageway, sliding the panel shut behind him.

Reaching the far end, he slid aside the outer panel and peered out from threadbare scenes of horn-thar, and dismal fallowellas wading thigh-deep in ice-cold lakes.

All clear. He stepped out and lowered the lamp to the floor.

Strange.

There was not a sign of blood.

A faint sound came from along the gallery.

He stood quite still, wishing for the sword that was back on his bedchamber wall.

"Who goes there?" he called harshly.

There came a faint chink of metal, as of sword sliding from sheath.

He must retreat while he could. Bolt both panels from inside. That should give him time to sound the alarm. The Dryac that he should have to lose his precious back door. Yet better that than his life.

As he darted back behind the arras a voice came out of the dark.

A woman's voice.

"Highness?"

The figure moved toward him, hesitantly, holding a dark lantern.

"Tanna!" Fear gave way to relief; relief to anger. "What are you doing? Why aren't you back in my mother's tower?"

She stopped well short of him.

"I saw the blood, Highness, all the way down the stairs and out. I got a pail and cleaned it up as best I could. I was just done."

The Dryac she did! "Did you follow the trail the other way?"

"Across the inner courtyard, then it suddenly stopped. I walked all around, but couldn't pick it up again."

He went to her, took her hands, and held them out. They were red and wrinkled from the water. He put an arm about her, drew her close.

"For a fallowella, you're smart. Come to bed."

"But Highness, it's not long till dawn."

"Long enough," he said.

A few hours later, scrubbed, shorn, and robed in coarse white latik, he trod the long galleries flanking the Main Hall, around and down a crowded Grand Staircase, across the cold tiled floor of the Hall itself to the Great Door, where Sharroc awaited him looking dourly.

What had finally been decided in the early hours?

He looked to Brac, standing impassive to the king's right hand; to Feric at his left. No joy there.

He'd found himself telling Tanna about it all last night, as much as he thought she should know.

"I wonder, Highness," she said. "Aravac was like enough to you to be taken for your own brother. What if—oh, by the Quaur—what if one had killed thinking him you?"

"Possible," he said. "Yet why me, and not Sharroc? There is only one of him, whereas there are brothers a-plenty willing to step into my shoes."

Tanna came up on one elbow.

"Highness, is that it?"

"Is what what, Tanna?" he snapped, following her thought full well, and feeling unaccountably irritated by it. "The next in line to me is Gar." The name came out as a sneer. "Can you see him—or any of the rest as capable of all this?"

She looked at him doubtfully, which goaded him now to anger.

"Look," he said. "Gar's sly enough, I'll give you that. And he's envious enough, and greedy enough, and ambitious enough. But he has neither charisma nor wit enough. And he's not liked anywhere. Not anywhere!"

"I think, Highness," Tanna began timidly, but Torc was going strong.

"No. We must look elsewhere for Aravac's murderer. As to the reason, you're probably right there. The reason for his death is certainly more important than Father would admit to me, since he did after all send for Brac and Feric. What that reason turns out to be," he went on, his anger rising, "and what comes of it, how will I know, out in the Dryac-crossed wilds?"

She'd stroked his hair, and kissed his eyes. "Don't fret yourself, Highness. I promise you I'll be your eyes, and your ears. Whatever happens, I'll find out and let you know."

He'd laughed then into her upturned face.

"Eyes and ears like yours were made for other uses. And that mouth," he'd said, and in showing her then exactly what he meant his humor had been restored and he'd slept at last for a time.

But as he approached Sharroc now in the cold light he was troubled. The king, though past his prime, was still feared, and his armies were the greatest in the Known World. But intrigue had never been his strength. He who kept the iron Weald with weapons forged from its ore, who'd seized the silver mines of neighboring Duhor in only three days, and who took tithe of the gold even of far Juban might not see menace of a subtle kind.

Torc sighed deeply. He could do nothing now.

Father and son faced each other by the Great Door.

Torc felt Sharroc's scrutiny as he knelt and bowed his shorn head; saw the attendant hand the king the snowy heisha that would cover his naked scalp from the public gaze.

Skod, but he'd suffocate by midmorning.

Sharroc raised the headgear on high for all to see as Torc touched his forehead to his father's feet. Torc felt the blood and pain rush through his skull, and prayed to the Quaur to help him up again without mishap.

He felt the cool weight of the stuff descend about him, breathed in its strong earthy odor, while the king intoned the age-old words:

"May the grace of the great Lothuri cleanse your soul,

prove your mind and spirit, and send you forth from Rm a future king!"

A vast sigh sounded throughout the entire hall.

Torc stood, fighting the blackness rushing in, acknowledging the slow thigh-slapping from the ranks crowding the serried tiers overlooking the Hall, the spiral stairs climbing up and up to the very central dome.

The moment passed.

Torc received the king's stiff embrace.

His mother stepped forward, kissed both his cheeks.

Torc's nostrils dilated in distaste. Even at that hour Meltha's perfume was strong enough to down a walking battalion.

Behind her, his five brothers and sisters saluted him, their faces formal, expressionless. He barely looked at them: sisters Pregia, Arivia, sly, scheming fallowellas that they were; brothers Gar, next to him in age, Grotok, and Ghein. Fools, all of whom he despised, except maybe for Gar, whom he hated.

Alone now in the space before the door, he cast one last glance around the massed faces and wondered. If he were right, if that shuktek had been for someone here against the king or, as Tanna had said, even against him—*could that someone be even here, in the Hall, watching him go?*

The Great Doors opened. Gar stepped forward to precede him outside. As Torc moved to follow, he glimpsed Tanna, caught in the widening shaft of daylight, almost completely hidden under a wollen overmantle against the morning chill. Only her mouth showed, ripe from the night's hard loving.

Oh, but how good she was!

The one quick glimpse, and he was out.

Rage caught inside him.

Half a sunaround! A whole season's loving! The summer's petals will have flourished and fallen by the time he came home again, and the pods would be full upon their stems.

Be good, Tanna, loile blossom . . .

Outside, his retinue shuffled in the cold.

Gar, as second brother, moved to hand him up onto a daur,

whose fresh-burnished hide glinted on its serpentine neck, whose tasseled ambaree stood open to receive him.

Gar held the mounting platform steady.

As Torc turned to mount, their eyes met and hatred flowed between them.

And something else. A look Torc well knew. Many years before, Gar had stolen Torc's first sword, and his tharling from the stables. He'd smashed the sword and lamed the thar. Gar was beaten for it, of course. But after, he'd given Torc that same look.

Torc set his foot on the lower step and prepared to swing up.

"Keep your sword in your own scabbard, or your head will rot by the Gate."

Gar's lips twisted. "Merchandise has a way of changing hands, brother," he muttered. "Half a sunaround is long for fallow . . . ellas."

Torc aimed his free foot at Gar's head, missed as Gar stepped back.

As he took his seat in the ambaree, Gar grinned up at him widely.

"Our wishes for a peaceful sojourn, brother, and your safe return."

As he spoke the time-honored valedictory, Gar looked back to where they both knew Tanna was now standing.

Torc, masked from open view now by the ambaree's canopy, bit back his rage while the procession got under way.

As the daur turned ponderously and lumbered across the courtyard cobbles, Torc had one glimpse of Gar walking toward Tanna. Then he was passing under the inner courtyard arch and down toward the drawbridge gate.

CHAPTER TEN

WITH each massive tread of the daur's feet, Tanna edged back into the crowd. Torc was really going, out through the Great Gate. She'd believed until this last minute that he would somehow turn things his way, as he always had before.

She shuddered, aware now of the damp cold of the morning air clinging to her heavy mantle. She was so tired. Tired, and shaky in the aftermath of the night before.

Those in front of her began to move away, muttering, toward the dark doorway leading back into the citadel but she lingered, to watch the last of the procession out of sight, the last flutters of the high-held pennants of red and green and black shivering in the breeze.

One other, she noticed, was still standing also, looking out after the departed procession: Gar, more like to Torc than the other princes, but lesser, as though squeezed, like baleful Hawcasyr, by some inner force.

Gar turned and looked her way, as if he knew she'd still be there, and something in his stance made her feel afraid. She pulled her hood down and quickly made for the door.

Too late.

As she stumbled up the step, fingers tight as Torc's own gripped her elbow cruelly under the stuff of her cloak, pulling her into the hall.

"And who'll lead thee to board this day, now the pilgrim's gone?"

Tanna pulled back as much as she dared, conscious of people staring.

"Please let me go, Highness," she said, from under her hood. "I must attend the queen's morning toilette."

Gar laughed, and with his other hand flipped the hood back, exposing her telltale face; eyes bruised from lack of sleep, and love-proud lips. "Very well. But tonight you sit by me and we shall console ourselves and drink to absent friends."

She looked into the eyes so like Torc's, trying to hide her revulsion.

"The queen has also bidden me attend her at evening board, Highness."

A flash of anger, then Gar's eyes narrowed. By the Quaur, she'd only whet his appetite! He pushed her from him, knocking her back against the doorframe.

"Half a sunaround, fallowella, is a long time. For my brother's sake we must keep you trimmed. If you can't please me at board, then you'll please me after."

He turned and ran up the great staircase without a backward glance.

Ignoring those about her, she replaced her hood and swiftly crossed the cold floor toward the back stair, a long way around to the queen's tower but the Dryac take her if she but appeared to follow him.

Three flights up the winding stair left her breathless and dizzy. People passed her, scrots, mostly, on this back way, from whom she was safe enough; some men of higher rank, muttering obscenities, but withholding their pinches and fumbles for were they not all aware that she was Torc's bedmate? Even the queen herself knew of it, although she hadn't said. And why should she? Tanna was nobody, and Torc had these past ten sunarounds been promised to the sairah Broda of Cray.

Tanna reached the level connecting the queen's tower with the main pile and leaned against the wall. She was late. The queen would already be on her way to morning board. But it didn't matter. Tanna had lied. She was free that day. She pulled her mantle more tightly about her. What if—no. Gar would never bother to question his mother about her. He wouldn't discover this particular lie. But sooner or later her lies would run out. And he'd be there waiting.

And Torc? Did Gar warn him of what he was going to do? Was Torc thinking ill of her now?

She walked along slowly, through the galleries leading to the aerial passageway over the Central Courtyard below. She had no illusions on that score. He'd forgotten her already.

But even if he had, she'd promised to stay faithful. And when he came back, he'd see that she'd kept her word. That she'd resisted Gar, somehow.

She must, or lose all. Not for her a concubine's bed, as Torc had promised her three nights ago. Somehow, she was determined, she'd prove more worthy than Broda.

That she'd sworn the first day she'd seen Torc.

"We were just wondering if you'd be back."

The two women peered into Tanna's tiny cubicle, at the tidy chest of drawers, the too-tidy bed, which hadn't been slept in for how long?

"Well, the wondering's over, Magla. Here I am."

Tanna slipped off her dress, wrapped herself in a length of towel, and went to the door. The two women made no effort to stand aside.

"Such a splendid leavetaking, wasn't it?" The taller one, Magla, black-haired, blue-eyed like Torc—a distant cousin—looked down on her.

Tanna shrugged. She pushed her way past and, conscious of them treading on her heels, she went down the passage to the communal bath which steamed and stank of cleansers and emollients at all hours of the day and night.

She tossed aside her wrap and walked down the steps, feeling the warmth and sting of the salted water on her tired skin. They were staring, she knew, but she didn't care. She enjoyed it, rather: the envy, the vain search for flaws in her perfect body; the meaningful glances at the love bruises on her breasts, the bite marks on the inside of her thighs. She'd felt sorry for them once, Magla and Leylin, but no more.

Leylin looked down at her. "What will you do now? Who shall you have after the Gurnyac heir? It will be hard to lie beneath a lesser lord."

Tanna floated belly up, let the water slip silky through her thighs.

She wouldn't answer them. Wouldn't give them the tiniest hook to prick her with.

"Of course," Magla said. "It's common knowledge that he'll take his wife within the sunaround of his return."

"But Tanna could become a concubine."

"*Concubine*? Really, Leylin! A scribe's daughter . . . a *concubine*? Over the queen's dead body!"

Tanna strove to keep her face relaxed. Hadn't she weathered all this long enough? Whatever her birth rank, when her father died hadn't the Lady Folian taken her and made her as good a lady as any of them in that place? And hadn't she in three short sunarounds so proved her worth as an attendant that on Folian's death the queen herself had personally sent for her to join the royal retinue?

She sat up, turned her back on Leylin and Magla and soaped herself all over.

"There's always Prince Gar." Leylin never could let well alone.

"To take her for concubine, you mean?" Magla made a rude noise. "The queen wouldn't let even her second born bond

with a commoner. Though, of course, as one saw, he's game
for a roll in his brother's warm place."

Commoner. That didn't hurt. Scribe's daughter she may
have been, but Folian had laid the title of Lady on her in full
writ, with purse enough to match it. She was the Lady Tanna
now and always whatever they said or did.

Tanna sluiced off the soap, walked up out of the bath, and
taking up her wrap, threw it loosely about herself.

She looked at the two women, seniors past the age for
making a good bonding, feeling suddenly very sad.

"Please excuse me," she said. "I must dress." Before they
could move she was down the passage and into her room with
the door closed behind her.

Tanna stood on the tiny stair, halfway up—or down—
undecided. She'd scarce drunk a drop at supper, to keep her
wits clear. Gar had commanded her company for that evening,
and the queen had bade her obey.

And now Gar was waiting and there she was, skulking
around the back passages like a thief.

Oh, what was she to do? Suppose she hid for this night?
What about the next? And the next and the next?

She wouldn't give in though. Whatever Torc did, and she
didn't doubt that even now he was consoling himself along the
way, she'd keep her word, taking to no other man's bed, least
of all Gar's.

Oh, where could she go? She thought wistfully of Torc's
chamber, a haven behind his sealed doors, but the hour was
much too early to risk the back gallery.

She started down.

She'd go to the stables. There were vacant stalls where the
grooms seldom went, and she'd stay there until the third watch
when it was safe enough to creep back up to the queen's tower
and bed.

She walked down shadowed aisles, treading pungent hay
and sawdust, not minding the scuffle of tiny claws, the snuffle

of thars shifting in their sleep. Every three stalls dim yellow lamps lit weathered doors; shone on the names of the beasts within.

She went on, past Torc's own thar, past rows and rows of them until the lights grew dim and farther between. The grooms were gone for the night. The watch dozed by the front door. She was safe.

Pushing through into an empty stall, Tanna lay back on a pile of straw, and looked up toward the dark skylight beyond which stars pierced the chilly sky.

She sighed, feeling bereft; empty, just as she had when Folian died. Then as now she'd sought shelter from prying eyes, and groping hands; a private place, where none would think to seek her out. And had, one dark night after board, found unlikely refuge here, in a back stall like this one, where she'd lain that night, and many after, until she'd found the courage to live the life expected of her.

She closed her eyes, relaxing in the warmth of the hay. The stables. She bit her lip, remembering what had drawn her to them the first time.

"Father, Sudry says you're not my father. She says—she says I'm a garobol born of the hay. Father, what does that mean?"

"Hush, child. Let me dry your face. Good little fallowellas don't use such words, and sensible ones don't listen to them. Can you remember when I was not your father? Come, and we shall see what is born of hay."

They walked down to Folian's great stables, under the long low eaves, picking up the groomsman on the way, until they came to a stall in which a great black woolly thar lay on its side.

She had never seen a thar down before. Even as they arrived, the beast struggled to its feet and nuzzled a smaller patch half hidden under the hay. Black, like its mother: a newborn tharling, long-legged, too weak to stand, its coat still wet and sticky. The mother began to lick it; Tanna could hear the rasping clear across the stall.

"Yon's cleaning 'un," the groom said. "And brisking life into 'un."

Even as he spoke, the little thing struggled up and stood unsteadily on all fours.

Durac looked to her then back to the tharling.

"Hmmm. Long legs you have, and curly hair, but it is not black, and I don't think it's all over you, is it—is it?" And he seized her arm, pushing up the sleeve, pretending to look for thar-pile, and as ever, by the time he had finished, he'd had her laughing again, jigging up and down in delight, her doubts forgotten.

For many years, she'd believed him, and why shouldn't she? Who in the Castle Folian ever doubted the word of Durac, the scribe? But in the later years as her breasts budded and blossomed the whispers prevailed and her suspicions had grown that she was indeed a garobol born of the hay, a foundling that for reason best known to himself the lonely scholar had fostered, giving her the love of a father she'd never known. And her mother? Gone, he always said, and would never say more.

Those were the happy years, when still a stick-child, she'd sat by Durac's hearth tracing letters on a slate. Safe from the hard castle women who scolded her and harried her, set on bending her to a fallowella's ways.

Happy years. Warm years.

And secret.

Don't tell anyone, Durac would say, tapping his hook of a nose. If they knew what we were at they'd box our ears and throw us to the adahi.

But why? she'd asked him, over and over, just to hear the answer.

Because, and here a sly smile would crease the long dry face, they say this is man's work; that a fallowella—especially a delicious fallowella like you—has the brain of a—a *thar*!

And at that, remembering the great she-thar lying on her side and the little tharling beside her, Tanna would giggle and rub her hands together delightedly between her knees, and set to work again. She secretly learned not only letters with him, but numbers, and the motions of the stars. You, he'd told her once, are the cleverest fallowella alive. But never, never, ever let men know it. You'll never make a binding, else.''

And he'd smiled to ease the harshness of that truth.

Tears came suddenly, hot tears of anger and loss.

No one. She had no one, no one, *no one*.

She turned onto her side, rubbing her face hard in disgust. This would get her nowhere. At least she had clothes on her back, and food to eat, and a decent roof over her head, she who'd started life a hay-spawned garobol.

From stable to lady . . . from lady . . . to queen.

And, if queen, then she must begin to act like one.

She pulled her mantle closely about her, curled up, and fell asleep.

The voices woke her. How long had she slept? She looked up at the skylight. Not long, as she would guess.

She knelt up quietly, listening. Men. Down the far end. Grooms, on some errand? Should she slip out through the side door before they turned the corner, or stay? Too late: they came.

She slipped beneath the hay.

They stopped at her stall wicket.

Not grooms.

Not anybody from Gurnyac. In fact, the dialect was so strange that she couldn't understand a word—save one: Aravac.

The creak of a wicket. Hers? By Forthyr and Demiel she daren't look.

The voices continued.

No. Next door.

She lifted her face and squinted under the partition. Huge

feet, rough-booted, flattened the hay. Hands scuffed it aside, uncovering—her breath came sharp. Had they heard? The body of a man.

Another sound. The soft thropping of a thar being led toward them.

The body was lifted off the hay and the wicket creaked again. She could see the thar's hooves quite clearly out in the passage. The boots gathered around them. The men were laying the body across the back of the thar. A rustling, as of rough hide. They were covering the body. The boots, the thar hooves moved off again, down the empty aisle and out through the very side door that she'd had a mind to take.

Strangers.

A dead man.

Hidden in the deserted part of the stables where even the grooms seldom went.

Could not that dead man have been the one Aravac had fought with? But how would strangers know where to hide their comrade's body until it was safe to remove him, unless . . . they had been directed here by someone from inside the citadel?

Tanna began to shake. Oh that she'd never come into this place! Yet—hadn't she promised to be Torc's eyes and ears?

She waited a minute or two then creaked open her stall wicket.

The aisle was deserted.

She crept out, ran to the side door, and peered through.

Nothing. Only darkness and drifting cloud shadow.

Doubly grateful now for her brown mantle, she slipped across the rough ground, a weedy, no-man's-land behind the main tower, wondering where they would take the thar without being seen.

She walked fast across the waste ground between barracks and citadel. This was the only way they could possibly take. But how would they get past the guards? She was going so fast that she almost bumped into them.

Why, they were going by the barracks itself, along a wooded path privy to but a few. Hadn't Torc himself taken it one restless night when he would walk and pin her to every tree?

Suddenly, one of the men detached himself and started back toward her. She shrank behind a wide trunk, flinching as he passed her by inches.

Which way now? She couldn't follow both men at once. Should she go with the body, or see where the other was headed in the citadel?

She stood a moment, irresolute in the buffered dark, then turning, she followed the one man back the way they'd come.

Tanna slowed, her throat blood-raw, her chest heaving. How long since she'd run like this?

Ahead of her, the man's shadow merged with the massive dark of the citadel wall. She must move on, or lose him. Her sodden skirts flapped between her ankles, and the heel of one slipper was loose.

What if he'd sensed her—heard her, even, and was waiting just ahead to catch her as she passed?

Before her was the central courtyard around the king's tower into which all the outer courtyards led.

She caught sight of the man passing under the flame of a drafty lantern. Surely he wouldn't dare step out into the open at this hour when so many people were about?

She was right. He turned aside and made for a path leading around the peripheries. The backs of her hands pricked. Just ahead was the side entrance to Torc's tower, and the yard where Aravac's blood trail had run out. Was that where he and the dead man had met? Had Aravac done as she was now doing? Followed this man, here, to this spot and then—and then—found too late that the hunter himself was hunted—by another to his rear?

A slight sound behind her, and a massive hand whirled her around by her shoulder. A glint of steel and something sharp pressed against her chest.

"The Lady Tanna. What brings you here at this hour?"

Feric! She stared up unable to breathe. The sword point pricked her mantle.

"Well?"

She looked around. The man was gone. "I—" *Was following someone*, she almost said, but she stopped, staring up at the general. She might ask the same of him.

She felt the trembling begin again, somewhere in her knees, felt it spreading up through her whole body, raising the hairs in her flesh. What if Feric were the one behind everything? The king's left member striking at the royal heart? And hers if she made but one false step now.

She looked down at the sword point lost in the folds of her mantle. Feric made no move to lower it.

"Well?"

She forced herself to meet his look, to speak, hoping to mask the shake with laughter.

"Why, I confess, General, that since the pilgrim left, I've been pulled to and fro, pleasing this one and that—and satisfying none. And now I am late even to Prince Gar's chambers."

Feric's eyes gleamed cold as the faint starlight on his blade. Now, right now, he could kill her, impale her on the point of his sword as a butterfly on a branch, if he chose.

Her smile began to wilt.

Feric loosed his hold and lowered his blade.

"Tell me," he began, but in that moment, Tanna's name came clear across the yard, and Leylin, swinging a lantern, ran toward them across the tussocky grass.

"There you are!"

Leylin raised the lantern to Tanna's face. "Where *have* you been!" She sniffed. "In the stables, as I'd guess." She half turned then, affecting to see Feric for the first time. She bobbed coyly, looking from Tanna to the general, and back again. "Madam the queen sent me first to the prince Gar's quarters to fetch you. His adaide said you weren't there and

that Gar had sent everywhere for you. I hear he's quite put
out." Leylin looked slyly to the general. What, did she think
them to have been lying together in the hay!

"What has happened? Why does the queen seek me?"

"She's had a falling attack. The apothecary has ordered her
to Pruth for full twenty-one days. And we prepare to leave at
dawn, *including* you."

Leave? But she couldn't. She mustn't. Not right now. She
pulled herself together.

"You see, General?" She looked up, coquettish, concerned.
"My sins have quite outrun me. If you'll excuse me, I will
attend the queen."

She lay in her cubicle, ears pricked.

Was Feric traitor to the king? And did he think she knew it?
Or had she managed to look the wanton fool?

If not—

She caught a sound beyond her door, raised her head from
the pillow.

She sank back again, her neck stiff with strain.

If Feric sent an assassin, no one could stop him. Would he
seek her breast? Or her throat? Would it hurt? If so, would he
stop her mouth with his hand? She couldn't bear that. Better
she go to sleep so's not to know.

I'll be your eyes and ears . . .

On this very first night she'd seen and heard plenty: those
men in the stables, the body. And Feric, in the courtyard. He'd
stopped her from following that stranger, from seeing where
he went.

Now what? If she stayed alive, what should she do now?
She'd promised to get word to Torc. But of what? How? And
where? How could such as she reach Rm alone? And even if
she got there, what would she say? Not enough. Not yet. No.
She must brave it out. She must survive. Find out more.

But not, she thought with a sinking feeling, for the next
twenty-one days, not down on that empty shore.

What if things happened while she was away? Terrible things? And she too late to do anything? Maybe she could make herself ill and stay behind. Maybe no one would notice if she didn't go.

Maybe.

CHAPTER ELEVEN

TORC'S ill-humor lasted until well after they reached the first inn. He rode alone in the ambaree, disdaining Sharroc's handpicked adaide, Arad. Not one of his own friends had been allowed to go with him, not one. Some two dozen formed the company altogether: Arad, riding behind on a thar, some twelve or so minor nobles: respectable old gonts of Sharroc's choosing, to provide the pomp and pageantry befitting a royal pilgrim. The rest were armed escort from Brac's own first battalion. The general, it seemed, was not taking any chances with Torc's safety even as far west as the Asurdun road.

The air in the ambaree grew hot and close. Torc fidgeted restlessly. The coarse latik scratched his skin, irritated his scalp. Saturated with his sweat, the stuff threw out its strong and earthy stink.

Why, Torc brooded sullenly in his enforced seclusion, couldn't he have been allowed to travel in his own clothes to Asurdun, put this sackcloth fit only for scrots and groles on there at the last minute? He was growing irritable bordering on murderous, and the sounds of quiet chatter and the occasional discreet laugh coming from the riders behind him didn't help.

In the inn, Torc ate alone, and as he ate, his mood grew even uglier. Three times he had the food replaced. And twice, the wine.

The fallowella serving him he also had sent out and another one put in her place. That one he took to bed.

But she was so terrified of him that he threw her out and sent for the inn-keeper, demanding to see every other fallowella in the place.

It was a motley line. All were in various states of dishevelment. Torc grinned maliciously, wondering whose beds he had plucked them from. One was as tall as Feric, and almost as broad; another was as small as a child, but none of them quickened his blood, not even the redhead with skin the color of harsmilk.

"This is all you have?"

"Yes, so please Your Highness."

"It'll not do, not at all. There was another, the one by the door as I came in. With the brown hair down her back. Where's she?"

The innkeeper bobbed nervously. "That is Faisel, my daughter, so please Your Highness. She is abed this past hour."

"Oh? By whose command? Bring her here."

"But Highness—" The man's voice failed him.

"By the Dryac!" Torc shouted, aware of Arad now standing just through the door. "Fetch her, or else my father shall know of it!"

The innkeeper hurried away.

"Highness." Arad came into the chamber. "Everybody in the inn hears you. Do you think it fitting, on the eve of your—"

Torc reached for his sword. "And since when did I ask your counsel, Kurdin's son? Anything the king's heir does is fitting—or have you not learned that in all your years in Gurnyac?"

The man blinked at *Kurdin's son*. There was no greater insult than to give a man his father's name, but Arad did not challenge it, to Torc's disgust.

Yet still the adaide persisted in his way.

"Highness, the girl is a *true* fallowella, and is still a—"

"By the Dryac!" Torc drew his sword, advanced on Arad a step or two. "My father did you a disservice, sending you with me, for when I'm king you'll not set one foot within the citadel. Get out!"

The innkeeper was back, pushing ahead of him the girl he'd seen on his arrival. She was tousled from her sleep, yet she smelled clean enough. And looked to be shapely under her gown—and the fullness of her mouth reminded him of Tanna. His krudt hardened. Better the girl yield her maidenhood to him than to a local scrot. Why, it was a privilege. With luck, she might even get a brat by him.

"She'll do. See that mine host gets an extra purse tomorrow," he called to Arad, standing back along the passageway. "Two thousand shengs, and I'll give her a ring— if she's good."

Two rings if she restored his good humor, he thought, and, shutting the door in their faces, he hopefully took the girl to bed.

But the following day Torc felt little better. The girl had been as amorous as a pillow. Serve him right. Yet he'd still left her with two rings, two thousand shengs, plus the purse for her father. The inn itself, presently called "The Gray Wether," he'd ordered changed to "The Royal Pilgrim," promising to call in again on his way home.

All that morning he brooded.

On Aravac. On Tanna, and on Gar. That scrot had better keep his puny krudt out of her bed. Tanna had sworn undying chastity but as Gar had said, fallowellas had a way of changing hands. If Gar chose to defy him, Tanna would have very little say in the matter. Whatever her avowed intentions, who could trust a fallowella's word?

*   *   *

The winds blew in low over the sea, sweeping salt and sand together in wide sheets over the hollow dunes. Seated alone by the queen's pallet, Tanna shaded her eyes against the noon light, watching the great blue corlins loop and dive. Such hunger they had, and the scope of the wide skies to sate it.

She tucked a flyaway wisp of hair behind her ears and turned back to the sleeping Meltha. She looked gray without her paint. And withered as a stranded sea-kuzn.

Tanna absently fingered her own cheek, tracing its soft curve from ear to chin. Remembered Torc's hands upon her. Her flesh was sweeter than a pecular's, he'd said.

What was he doing now? Wherever he was, he'd find comfort, even in Rm, she didn't doubt it. Wherever he went in the Known World he'd find someone to lie with.

She shivered. The wind was blowing colder. Soon they'd bring the palanquin to take the queen back up to the pavilion.

She hated the place. It was drafty, full of grit and chitflies. And old. The kitchens swarmed with horebugs and the cisterns were dry. Rumor had it that Sharroc was to renovate it, but that had been in the spring before the troubles began.

She stretched out a leg before her on the sand, rubbed the calf. She must stop her grumbling. At least she was alive, and intact. And safe from Feric.

And Gar.

She stood, wrapped her arms across her chest against the chill of the wind, nursing her small warmth against the shore's wide emptiness.

The vastness of it disturbed her. It was as though it were sucking at her, pulling out her very spirit to blow it away. As though if she were to bide there long enough she would simply cease to be.

She shuddered, as though someone had stirred her remains. Morbid. She was getting morbid. Just because Torc was gone and there was nothing to do.

"Come to Pruth," she said softly. "Come to Pruth and die."

The queen grunted, stirred.

"Your hand, girl. Help me up."

Tanna bobbed, bent to take her hand, but as she did so a shadow passed over her and another arm reached out.

"Madam—take mine."

At the voice, Tanna looked up, the blood draining from her head.

But Meltha, looking past her, extended both her arms, her fat fingers winking in the sunlight.

"My darling boy!" she croaked. "My one! Now shall we see some life! What have you brought your mother, eh? Here, let me embrace you, my own, my son; my dear, dear Gar."

He escorted his mother back to the pavilion, walking beside the palanquin. Tanna hung back, to avoid him. Why had Gar come here? Surely not on account of her?

He caught up with her outside Meltha's chambers.

"You and I have unfinished business," he said, catching her by the arm, whirling her around to face him. "Don't think I've forgotten you." He laughed then. "But you can wait, and ripen. So watch for me in Gurnyac, Tanna. In Gurnyac."

He put his mouth to hers, feeling about her body with practiced hands. With a great effort, she submitted, keeping the stiffness out lest she anger him and make things worse.

Just when she thought she would suffocate, he let her go, and passed through the queen's bedchamber door.

Tanna walked with measured steps back to her room where she subsided onto her bed. He had not come for his mother, surely, for everyone knew how he despised her.

If not for her or Meltha, why, then, and for how long?

She leaned over and buried her face in her hands.

As the sun grew hot, Torc's mind turned to thoughts of the next inn: of a bath, a good meal, and bed.

His luck was in. The wayside house was bigger than the last one, being on a trading route. The fallowellas crowded the hallway to see him arrive so this time at the start he selected three to bathe him and serve his food.

By bedtime, Torc, with practiced eye, had made his night's

selection, and soon proved his choice. Rerry, a one-time dairy maid and harvest queen, pressed into service after the festival at which she'd been crowned. A great day for her family, she told Torc. Her father had gotten full five hundred shengs for her inn-maid's position, and she, luxuries unheard of from satisfied "friends."

She was neither the youngest of the three, nor the most beautiful, for all her claims to the harvest crown, but she had the most, and was eager to share it. But, while properly respectful, she was not too overawed to scold.

"For shame, Highness, to be lying here with me and you a pilgrim bound for the holy mountain." She laughed. "What is it—no meat, no strong drink, and no women for full one half a sunaround before you enter their gates. Yet here you are with half a saddle of game meat under your belt and a bladder full of Gort wine—sharpening your blade between the sheets into the bargain!"

He traced a heavy breast with his finger, then squeezed its overhang. "So? With six days to go they won't know any different." He pressed against her, felt the fullness of her thighs open as readily as the loile blossom to the silfly's tongue. "Even as great as Djunu gorges himself before his long fast, so do I prepare for mine."

The evening board was crowded and buzzing with news of Gar's arrival, and its cause.

The king, it seemed, had remembered his pavilion in Pruth. Rebuilding was to commence, under Gar's stewardship. With Gar was come an army of artisans, freemen all: builders, carpenters, tilers, glaziers, blacksmiths, not to mention drafts-men, with their lead-lines and calipers, whose usages she was not supposed to know.

To Tanna's relief, and to the queen's disappointment, Gar did not attend the meal, but dined alone.

Around her gossip was rife.

"Strange," Magla said to Leylin. "We were sure Tanna would be sitting at the queen's left hand. Now they say His

Highness has brought a new fallowella to Pruth, and is so taken with her that he has no eyes for the rest of us."

"Praise the Quaur," Tanna murmured, raising her glass.

What they said left her only relieved, until the truth came out that he was really busy in his chamber with plans for the morrow's work, and that there was no fallowella in sight.

After board, the queen swept from the dining hall and along to Gar's chamber, dragging Tanna and Magla in her wake.

"You come to your darling mother, and then you act as though she weren't there," she complained. "I thought you'd keep me company."

Gar took his mother's hand and drew her to the door.

"The work begins tomorrow, madam, and what is done by day must be planned by night. I must eat as I work."

Tanna watched him with great unease. Gar the dutiful hard-working son? Never. And Gar without a fallowella in the dark hours? She found it hard to believe.

But apparently Gar meant what he'd said.

From the following morning until the end of the queen's stay, in total disregard of her supposed rest-cure, the hammers fell with great noise, and clouds of dust rose to mingle with the drifting sands. There was much traffic over the dunes, riders coming and going at all hours of the day and night; masons from the town, so they said, certainly strangers to the Citadel.

Perhaps, she thought, Gar was taking the opportunity of Torc's absence to curry favor with the king by rebuilding Pruth.

Rebuilding Pruth!

Tanna looked around the cracked walls, the sagging floors, chipped tiles, the peeling gilt and paint. The Weald was crumbling, the slaves in revolt; the Foundings were idle, and the Brandhouses breaking apart. Treason stalked the Citadel but though Gurnyac fall, by Sharroc's will would the royal pavilion prevail!

Torc arrived in Asurdun midway through the third after-noon.

Asurdun: flat, sprawling, brawling seaport, squatting between marsh and estuary. Foul-smelling to one not used to the
stink of fresh fish.

As was the custom, one of the retinue got down from his
thar and walked ahead, threshing from side to side with a hide
whip, clearing a passage through the crowds.

Halfway along the main street, far enough away from the
racket and stench of the market, was a low, rambling inn.

Torc signaled the column to stop.

"But—Highness—you are expected this hour at Riverside!"

Arad had broken rank and was abreast of the daur, looking
up.

"Oh?" Torc's eyes gleamed silver under his heisha.
"They'll wait. I need a bath and clean gear." He plucked at his
pilgrim's robe, crumpled and sweat-stained from the morning's
hot ride.

A short time later he sat in a hot tub, eyes closed, while two
fallowellas scrubbed him down.

His thoughts turned to his coming journey. To the manner of
boat that would bear him to Rm. A paddle boat, so his father
had said. That took seven days to travel upriver to the high
holy lake.

"Highness?"

Torc shifted irritably.

"Well, Arad?"

"There is a man, Highness. A guide from Rm, seeking you
all the way from Riverside."

Torc kept his eyes closed. "Then he's in luck, for here I am.
I'll see him when I've eaten."

"But, Highness—"

"Out!"

He'd no sooner settled back when he heard the door again.

"Arad, I told you to get out!"

There was no reply.

Torc opened his eyes to find not Arad but a stranger clad in a light blue traveling tunic trimmed in gold with leggings to match. A footclar dressed as a general. Torc took in the stocky body, the wide shoulders, the blunt and weathered face.

The Dryac take Arad for sending him in. "You're the Rm fellow? Wait outside."

When the man didn't budge, Torc yelled for Arad, slapping his hand on the bathwater, soaking the fallowellas through.

The man stood his ground. "You are Torc, of Gurnyac?"

"*Prince* Torc, frat. Now—wait outside before I have you flogged!"

A smile touched the face. "No need. I'll not wait, but leave you altogether, *Prince* Torc. My mistake. I had sought another entirely: Torc, *pilgrim*, bound for Rm."

He turned to go.

"Wait!" Torc was up in a surge of suds.

The man shook his head. "Your place at board is cleared and the pilgrims are embarking. They'd have left an hour since had I not persuaded the head guide to let me seek you out, for the path being long and devious, I thought you might be lost. Now you are too late for I must go at once. You may return another time."

He turned, and left.

Torc leapt from the tub, slipped on the wet tiles, skidding to a stop against a serving girl bringing in his food tray, which crashed to the floor.

Naked, Torc ran out into the passageway, but the man was gone.

Return another time!

"Arad! Arad, I say!"

Arad came running.

"Clothes, man! My clothes! And get two thars!"

Torc, with Arad, inched his way through the courtyard crowds that had gathered for a glimpse of the royal pilgrim.

Without his entourage they didn't recognize him, but that blessing was two-edged, for without whip-boys to clear his path he had to dismount and fight his way with Arad out into the street.

As the guide had said, the road was devious. Twice they lost their way, losing ground, and time.

When at last they rode onto the Riverside quay, the long slim vessel with its white-clad passengers was dwindling upstream. A truly uplifting sight, one man said, and doubly so, it costing not one rak.

"Call them, Arad," Torc cried. "Stop them, in the name of the king!"

Arad, red with heat and embarrassment, pushed his way through to the water's edge. "Ho there!" he shouted. "Return, in the name of Gurnyac!"

"Here," said somebody. "Who do you think you are, yelling at the holy barge? Let's have some respect!"

Laughing, the crowd jostled Arad off the edge of the dock and into the river.

Torc angrily forced his way through and stood, his gear flapping in the wind, looking over Arad's head out into the midstream toward the dwindling boat.

"Missed your ride, have you?" somebody said, tutting, and shaking his head. "What a shame. But it happens, sometimes, when a lad drags his heels." He gave Torc a knowing look. "Never mind. There'll be a fresh lot going in half a sunaround's time."

Half a sunaround's time? And what was he supposed to do meanwhile? Go home? He could well imagine the welcome he'd get.

He looked out, eyed the boat pulling slowly upstream. It didn't look so far. If he acted now, he might reach it. And if he reached it, they'd have to take him aboard.

Ignoring Arad, who was just climbing out of the water, Torc dove in, struck out into the flood, and, cheered on by the crowd, headed upriver.

The waters frothed and boiled, rising, filling the space of the lab floor, swirling and swelling to engulf them all.

Ord closed his eyes and cried out but his cry went unheard.

Just as the waters were surely closing over his head, the tumult faded, the raging river was gone, and the light from the passageway shone in on an empty floor.

CHAPTER TWELVE

SHIRA

23.53 Hours 28 September 2047
Estralita

S HIRA caught a small movement out of the corner of her eye. Her grandfather had stirred slightly on the bed. His head was now turned toward her, and his eyes were open a slit under the glow of the lamp.

"Grandfather?"

Shira stood up and bent over him. His color was back, and he looked rested. "Grandfather, are you awake?"

He opened his eyes wide, stared up at her as though he'd never seen her before, then suddenly, he smiled. "Shira. What time is it?"

She glanced up to the gray army chronister on the wall. "Almost midnight. How do you feel?"

"Well, thank you."

He struggled to sit up. Shira stacked his pillows, then leaned him back against them.

"And so I should, sleeping so long. Shira, my dear, you look so pale. Go to bed."

She sat down again, reached for his hand. "Grandfather, you said all this would be for only a day or two."

"I know, Shira." He fixed on her a look of mock severity. "I also told you to stay home where you belong."

"You know I'd never do that." Shira glanced over her shoulder to the door, then leaning forward, she dropped her voice. "Grandfather, I don't trust these people. May we go inside?"

For one moment he looked so stern she was afraid he'd say no. But then his face softened, and he opened his thought to her.

Very well. For a while. What is on your mind?

Those men, Grandfather. Hengst and Ellisen. They hate each other, and they each want to use you. That Ellisen's a warmonger. The things he's set to do! He'll wreck what's left of Earth. And we'll have helped him. That's the very opposite of what we came for.

The old man spread his hands. *Shira my love, he'll do exactly what he's supposed to do. No more. No less. Just like everyone else.*

Shira shook back her hair impatiently. She hated it when he talked that way. He was holding out on her. And worse, he was playing the prophet. Well, he could act the legend with the rest of the world, even the rest of their family—what was left of it—but if he tried it with her, she'd soon shake him out of that!

I read Hengst. He wants Phrynis. Do you know that Ellisen has promised it to him in exchange for arms?

To her disgust, her grandfather only shook his head at her. *Shira, Shira, Shira. How many times have I told you not to do that?*

Now the lugubrious look. Oh, it was really too much.

Why, Grandfather? Why did we have to come here? You said all along that Ellisen would never agree to what you want.

My child, we all of us must do what we have to do. And this is what I must do, even though I don't really know what I'm doing, being only a small part of the whole. Listen: it will all turn out right in the end. Trust an old man.

Shira eyed him resentfully. Even as she watched the legend in action, she could feel herself getting suckered in. And if she didn't know better, she'd almost think he was getting suckered in, too, he'd been so mild and compliant with everybody, quite unlike his normal self, ever since they'd left home.

Blushing, she stopped her thought dead. What if he'd read her just then? But no. He'd never reach into another's mind unasked.

Grandfather, Ellisen has no intention of working with you.

I know.

And Hengst has no intention of working with Ellisen.

I know.

Her thought grew stronger, more insistent. *Do you realize we're in a trap, that we're prisoners here now? Ellisen's sending in more staff for Ord, and Hengst is shipping down new equipment. They're not going to let us go until this whole thing is done. Do you know how long that will be?*

No, I don't.

Grandfather, what's it all about, this beacon thing?

It's not clear, Shira. Not yet. He smiled at her. *But whatever it is, it's good. The moment that band goes on my head, peace is in me. Even with all those terrible things going through my mind, it's there. As though they're holding my hand.*

Who's "they?"

The old man looked away. *I don't know. So much I don't know.*

His thought trailed off.

Shira put her hand on his. *Grandfather, talk to them, whoever they are, and ask them what it's all about. Why they're doing all this.*

The old man really smiled then. *My dear. They'll tell me in their own good time.*

Shira blew out her lips in exasperation.

Do they know what's going on down here? What Ellisen's doing to you? Can they tell what's going on in your mind?

Oh yes. I am to them as a glass fish swimming in an aquarium.

Shira didn't like the sound of that.

Maybe you are, Grandfather. Maybe we all are. Specimens in a glass box. She shook his hand to make him listen. *What do they want of us?*

They haven't said. Only that they wish to show me part of their history. He looked tired again suddenly. *They won't contact me again for a while. They said I must rest.*

His eyes closed.

Grandfather, I don't care if they never contact you again. They're nothing to us. I want us to go home now.

Shira, Shira, Shira. Why must you always vex me so? Why, of all my grandchildren I had to bring you with me, I cannot imagine. I'll have you sent home tomorrow.

He looked at her now with some of his old asperity.

No! I shan't leave you. Please don't say any more. I'll not complain again.

Did he seem a little relieved?

This is no place for a young girl about to be wed, he scolded her. *Kerrin didn't want you to come, you know. Your place is with him.*

She leaned over and threw her arms about him. *Grandfather, we promised Mother we'd stick together, didn't we?*

There was no doubt about it. She saw it clearly in his eyes. Her heart swelled with pleasure. He was relieved. He didn't really want her to go. He needed her. He was depending on her. That's why he'd brought her with him. Her arms tightened about his slight body. She'd never leave him, not ever. Not as long as he needed her, not even for Kirrin.

Aye. Child of my heart, we did.

Sighing, he disengaged himself, and taking her by the shoulders, held her at arm's length.

I shall sleep again, now, Shira. Go to bed.

Shira kissed his forehead, helped him down again, and tucked him in.

Good night, Grandfather.

Good night, Shiralee.

She lay on her own bed fully dressed, her arms folded behind her head, looking up into the dark, listening to the machines thrum all around her.

Her aunt and her two elder sisters had all told her she belonged with Kirrin, too. It wasn't as though Grandfather had asked her to go with him. She'd sensed his need, had insisted, over all his objections.

Kataïs, her eldest sister, had been so angry. But that was only because she'd wanted to come with Grandfather herself. Shira smiled to herself in the dark. Fat lot of help that one would be to Grandfather, or any of them, for that matter. Little yes-people all, and not a bit of use.

She remembered the row she'd had with Kataïs last year.

"Just because you're the prettiest. That's the only reason he loves you more than us."

"No," Aunt Marita had said. "It's because she's the crabbiest. Just like him. They make a fine pair, I'll say. They deserve each other."

But Aunt Marita had been smiling. She loved her brother, and couldn't say no to him any more than anyone else could.

Except Shira.

And Kirrin.

Kirrin had told Grandfather she shouldn't go. But she'd insisted to the point of almost breaking off their engagement. It was her affair, what she felt she ought to do. "And it will always be so. If you can't take it, then don't marry me."

She saw Kirrin's eyes on her, felt his arms about her. "Such a fierce thing you are," he'd said. "You're no fun, you know, at times."

She'd refused to argue with him. Hadn't wanted to make Grandfather an issue between them.

But he was right about her being no fun.

She rolled over onto her side and drew up her knees, hugging them. She couldn't help it. The world was such a rotten place and she didn't want to live in it.

Bad enough in the Bourg. Hardly a day went by without some major breakdown of the plant, and nobody ever had enough to eat.

Yet that place was paradise compared with this. At least there she was with her own. How she hated all these horrible frugs, abusing her grandfather, taking advantage of him, using him for their own selfish ends. She frowned. Why was he letting them do it? It wasn't like him, not at all. He must know something he wasn't sharing with her. She couldn't think of any other reason he'd let himself be so used.

That Hengst. The things she saw about him on the compuscreen. Such disgusting luxury he lived in up there. They'd never requisitioned his floating complex, his lunar bases, for refugees.

So many people dying down on Earth each day. With so little effort that man could do so much to stop it. One missile. One piece of the defense web would buy a dome for five hundred people for a year. Close just one factory plant up in space or on the moon and fill it with overspill. But no.

Of course, nobody could force the man to. How could they?

Such a farce it was. The politicians like Ellisen with their pretty titles. One snap of Hengst's fingers and their heads would roll. He had the world on a plate. It was for him the ultimate market place.

Pay, or die.

How much money or power did the man need? What more could he possibly want that he didn't have now? He had so much her mind boggled.

He didn't have Phrynis.

Ellisen and Hengst would keep her grandfather down in that horrible place forever. All because of that horrible synergizer. If it weren't for that, they'd never have heard of that planet and none of this would have happened.

But if the synergizer were suddenly gone, everything would come to a stop. She wished it would break down again, this time for good.

She came up in the dark.

What if it did? They'd have to let Grandfather go then, wouldn't they, because there wasn't another machine like it in the world.

If it broke down, the signals from Phrynis wouldn't get through.

Phrynis.

That brutal young prince. And the girl. Such victims, both

of them, of their horrible society. So barbaric. But probably no worse than Earth's, when you thought of people like Ellisen and Hengst.

Shiny bodies like living bronze figures writhing among the furs. Like animals. She pushed the image away uneasily. She didn't know much about that sort of thing. Unlike other communities, in the Bourg young people weren't allowed even to sit together unattended. It was the Hesikastor's enclave, after all.

Shira sighed.

For all his brutality the young man had clearly felt something for his friend, and for the girl Tanna.

She'd be sorry now not to see what became of them.

But wrecking the synergizer was more important, to her mind.

With sudden resolution, Shira slipped out of bed, peeped in at her grandfather. Sleeping soundly. It took but a dozen steps to creep through the tiny sitting room, and out.

She stood before the elevator feeling a little guilty, a little nervous, now.

She tuned in to the surrounding area.

All clear.

But even with everyone asleep, she couldn't risk using the noisy elevator. It would surely awaken someone.

Beside the elevator was a fire door. She took the lever in both her hands and pulled. It gave a little. As she'd hoped, there were stairs behind it, lit by the same flat white airstripping as the rest of the place.

She stepped through, let the door swing shut quietly, and started down.

Three flights of stairs and she was pushing open the lower fire door and walking through into the level six passageway.

The brilliant emptiness was unnerving.

She stood attuning herself to the different sounds of the plant.

Then she started along the passageway, labs on every side, empty, brightly lit through the glass-partitioned walls. Machinery, equipment for goodness knows what, cocooned in silver, awaiting the kiss of life.

She reached the door to lab 5.

It looked even smaller, empty.

She took in the tiny observation box to the right of the door. The right wall full of glass windows. Visiplates, Ord called them. The row of cylinders and dripstands pushed tidily against the partition. The bare couch. The tangle of cables and tubes attaching it to the rear wall, the dark screen above it, and the square red box of the holoverter that Ellisen had brought with him to pull the images from the tri-di-corder and out into the middle of the room.

She walked forward, ran her hand over the couch. What should she do? How could she wreck it without anybody suspecting?

Now that she was there it didn't seem feasible.

She moved to the head of the couch. At the base of the TS wall were hatches. Behind those millions of wires and cables ran back and back. She'd seen the woman assistant crawling under there, bringing out stacks of small square plates. Transducer plates, Ord had called them. Should she pull a few and break the circuits? But how? She knew less than nothing about that kind of thing. And how long before they found out and simply replaced them?

Maybe if she pulled as many as she could, they wouldn't have enough replacements. Ord had complained of almost running out, and they were obsolete, she'd heard Hengst say so. He'd promised to search some out, but he'd sounded doubtful.

She was just bending down to open the first hatch when she sensed another's energy at the edge of her mind. Startled, she ducked behind the couch.

Somebody else was down there, on level six.

Close by.

She waited, heard nothing.

She straightened up, moved quietly to the door, and peered

out to her left. Three doors down in the right-hand wall. The conference room. Whoever it was, was in there.

Dare she scan? Grandfather had told her only that night not to. But she'd already done it by the elevator, in a very general way, and again, just now.

In for a penny, in for a pound.

She reached out with her mind, pressed against such an intensity of concentration that she recoiled. Someone was searching. For what? She crept down the passage, reached the conference room as the door suddenly swung wide. She stood there, caught in the middle of the passageway, not breathing.

In the open doorway stood MacAllister, hazer in hand.

"Shira."

He lowered his hand.

"What are you doing here?"

She stood her ground. "I'll ask the same of you."

He slipped the hazer back into his belt.

"I'm looking for something, young lady."

"Looking for what?"

He eyed her speculatively. "Something someone may have left behind. You?"

She turned away. "I couldn't sleep. I took a walk."

"Oh yeah?" He glanced past her to the open lab door. His eyes widened. "You didn't—"

He strode past her into the lab, looked quickly around, came back. He took her hands in his.

"Listen, Shira. I can see that this is rough on you. But take some advice from an old campaigner: go with the flow. If you make trouble, things will be tougher, for you, for your grandfather, for us all."

She pulled her hands away, stuffed them in her jumpsuit pockets.

"I hate this place. I hate Ellisen, and that lecherous old frug Ord. And I hate what they're doing to Grandfather." Her voice rose.

Ellisen put a warning to his lips.

"I know, but that's not the point. There's a war on, Shira," he said quietly, and Shira could see that he really meant it.

"What do you mean?"

"I mean we're down to basic survival. Not just for me or you, or your grandfather, but everyone out there. Your grandfather's set something going that's going to escalate God knows where."

The heater suddenly cut out, and in the quiet MacAllister stopped talking and listened, looking up the passage toward the elevator. He beckoned her into the conference room, and half closed the door behind them. "Remember that," he went on. "The Hesikastor started it. And you can't start a war then just cry 'out.'"

Shira bit her lip. She hadn't thought of that. He was right. Grandfather had brought all this down on his own head. On all of their heads. All her life she'd always trusted him, and believed in him. Not as the Hesikastor, but as her grandfather, and he'd never let her down. But this time? *Did he know what he was doing?*

MacAllister was watching her. There was one who thought he had all the answers. Pulling her fists from her pockets, she rounded on him.

"You're as bad as the rest of them," she hissed. "You don't care."

He backed off in mock defense. "But I do. In fact, I'll even give you a token of my good will." He waved his hand around. "This whole place is bugged, you know that? Every single cubic centimeter is this whole silo is covered, right down to the bathrooms. Come."

He took her elbow and drew her back out into the passage and on, down to the far end from the elevator. There, in the right-hand side of the wall, was a recessed door, locked.

He took a card from his pocket, touched it to the access slot.

The door slid silently aside, and Shira caught her breath.

The place was lined with monitors.

"In those," MacAllister told her, "you can see everything that's going everywhere. And if you're not here to see, you get a replay later through there." He pointed to a control bench running the entire length of one wall. "I'm not saying they'll ever use all this," he murmured, "but it won't hurt to bear it in mind."

She nodded, grateful to him for the warning. She remembered her earlier uneasiness, realized how it hadn't been so far out after all.

"Thank you." She looked up at him, liking him suddenly. "I'm sorry for what I said."

"That's okay. Now, how about going back to bed?"

Her chin came out. "What, to leave you in peace to go on looking for whatever it is you're looking for? I'm going to help."

He shook his head. "That wouldn't do at all," he said. "Some things you'd better not know about. For your own sake."

Without stopping to consider she sent out her thought, touched the edge of his mind. "You're looking for something quite small," she said. "You looked under the conference-room table. Under the chairs. Around the doorframe. It's not there. In fact, it's not in there at all."

His eyelids came up. What a wonderful blue his eyes were. Like the alien prince's. What people called "piercing," although she knew it only signified recessive genes. She felt herself growing warm under MacAllister's gaze.

"You're quite the mind reader, I see." He folded his arms, eyes hooded again, and leaned against the lintel. "All right. Since you can tell me that much, maybe you can tell me the rest. What it is, and where it's hiding."

She pushed past him, leaving him to close the surveillance-room door behind them, and went into the conference room.

On the table was what looked like a small black flashlight. She stepped forward, picked it up. Buttons, a tiny dial, calibrated.

"What's this?" she asked, as he came in behind her.

"A detector."

"But of no use to you, obviously. Why not?"

He looked at her for minute. "You're a persistent character, aren't you? Okay. Friend Hengst may have left behind a tracer. You know what that is?"

She nodded. "A signal device to tell where someone—or someplace—is."

"Right. Ellisen had him leave his official tracer behind. You know, the one he wears to let his sidekicks up there cover him. But I don't trust him. He's got to have a trick or two up his sleeve. He wants Phrynis pretty badly."

"I know that."

"Well, he's going to get it by hook or by crook. My bet's on the crook, and we don't want that, do we, because that will mean Ellisen will lose his bargaining point, and Hengst'll have your grandfather in his pocket. I've a hunch he's left behind a delayed action baby, one that we won't pick up until it goes off. I may be wrong, but I don't think so. If there is one, and it goes off just for one peep, that's it. Hengst will have us, like that." He stretched out an open palm, curled it up into a tight, hard fist.

"If it's so important, why have you left looking for it so long?"

"Because it's taken Ord all this time to go to bed."

"So?"

"I don't do this sort of thing out loud. It's bad for my image."

"Oho." She shot him an old-fashioned look. "You're Ellisen's spy."

He made a show of looking shocked. "What, me? Let's say I'm looking after our interests down here."

"Ellisen's interests, you mean!" She glared at him.

"Listen. When you're at war, you have to do what you have to do. You look out for me, and I look out for you, okay?"

Warm became hot. He'd tried to help her, after all. She was a brat.

"Sorry again," she said. "Your secret's okay with me."

"Better be, for all our sakes."

"This tracer, what's it like?"

MacAllister shrugged. "I wish I knew. It could be no bigger than a pin head, that's the trouble."

"And if you pick it up in your detector, that means it's too late."

He nodded grimly. "Correct. Let's go."

"Where was Hengst today after I left with Grandfather?"

"In here, in the washroom, in lab 5. I've already covered upstairs."

"And down here?"

"Only this room, so far."

"Okay. I'll check the washroom, you check the lab."

He laughed outright. "Aye-aye, ma'am." He saluted smartly, turned on his heel and went to the door. There, he paused, looking out, then he moved quietly through and left toward the lab.

Shira made for the washroom.

Rough concrete walls, gunmetal gray. Three washbasins, five stalls.

What was she looking for? It could be as small as a pin head, MacAllister had said. And he wasn't even sure there was one.

She closed her eyes, put her mind in neutral, opened them again.

She ran her eyes around the walls.

Nothing.

Under the washbasins.

No.

The stalls?

She walked slowly into the third stall from the door, stepped up onto the toilet seat, and felt along the narrow rim of the left-hand partition.

There! A bead of paint? Better not try to move it, in case.

She jumped down, ran to fetch MacAllister.

A moment later, he gingerly lifted down a tiny silver bead.

"Well, I'll be," he said, grinning proudly down on her. "You did it. That was pretty smart. How old are you?"

"Nineteen," she said primly. "Nineteen last month. Leo."

"Ummm. It figures."

MacAllister put the little thing on the floor, and crunched it under his heel.

"You've just saved our skins," he said, and, taking her arm, he propelled her out toward the stairs. He opened the door, ushered her through. "Now," he whispered, "if we make it back up there all in one piece, maybe we can finally get some sleep!"

CHAPTER THIRTEEN

SHIRA

08.38 Hours 12 October 2047
Estralita

SHIRA hovered impatiently by the bathroom door, listening to the rush of the steamshower. Grandfather was so slow this morning she'd almost believe he was dragging his heels on purpose.

She put her head to the door and called.

"Grandfather. MacAllister's waiting."

His laugh came back. "Nine-thirty, he said, Shiralee. It's a little past eight thirty-five. The man's likely still having his breakfast."

She paced to the door where their small packs lay ready. Oh, to be out of this place, if only for two days!

She took a white plastic card from her pocket and examined the signature flowing across the bottom.

Susann Ellisen.

A gracious hand, flowing from an open, friendly nature, though she could be very private, judging by her closed t's. How did she ever marry Ellisen!

"Dear Shira," she read, "I'm appalled at my husband's keeping you cooped up in that little place without a break. I cordially invite you to spend a couple of days with us at

Bentnose Peak. Your grandfather, too, if he would care for company.

"I do hope you choose to make it. I would very much like a chance to meet with you and to talk about the Bourg, and about your life under there, and so much more. Please say yes, truly, Susann Ellisen."

"But why?" she'd asked MacAllister, who'd delivered it.

MacAllister shrugged. "There's no fathoming the big folks," was all he'd say.

But he didn't fool Shira. He knew why, all right. But he wasn't telling. He was such a strange man. Not unfriendly. *Close.* Since that night they'd met down at level six they'd scarcely exchanged a word. He kept to himself, saying no more than he needed to anyone, only banalities, giving nothing away.

A cipher.

Not to everybody else, though. They all thought of him as Ellisen's gopher. Errand boy. The way Ord ordered him around. The man had no idea that MacAllister had a brain.

Suk liked MacAllister. A lot. Which made Ord mad, even though MacAllister was careful to keep the woman at arm's length. Shira didn't like that idea much, either.

Did MacAllister like Suk? It was hard to tell.

Shira had been tempted to read MacAllister more than once, but she couldn't bring herself to. It felt immoral, somehow, for since that night they'd found the tracer, she couldn't help but think of him as a friend.

She picked up her bag, jiggled it in her hand, felt its lightness, and set it down again. Two jumpsuits, a few liners, and combs for her hair: all she'd brought from the Bourg.

And there they were, she and Grandfather. Two weeks of routine scanning exercises and still a dead beacon. They could surely risk two days more, Ellisen had said last night over the 'beamer.

But she was sure he hadn't meant it. He'd not looked too pleased at the idea of their coming. Susann Ellisen had probably nagged the invitation out of him and now he was stuck with their acceptance.

Was that it?

Were things perhaps not right with those two? Is that what MacAllister wasn't talking about? It might be. He'd seen an awful lot of the Ellisens lately.

Strange.

He'd not met any of them before that day in Palo Alto. Grandfather had certainly set a lot of things going. Now there MacAllister was, shuttling back and forth from New Washington to Estralita and Bentnose Peak.

Bentnose Peak.

She never thought she'd be glad to see that mausoleum again.

The Ellisens had a son, apparently. If he was anything like his father, she wouldn't speak to him.

She darted back to the bathroom as her grandfather cut the suctionair. He was stepping through into his bedroom now, picking up his liners, putting them on. Now his jumpsuit, zipping it up.

"One moment, Shiralee," he called, "and we'll be—"

She waited, straining to hear the rest.

"Grandfather? Grandfather, are you all right?"

She pushed aside the door.

"Grandfather!"

He was lying in the middle of the floor.

She ran to him, turned him onto his back.

His eyes were closed. He was breathing normally. She felt his pulse. Normal, too. And his color was okay. She looked down on him with thunderous face. She knew what it was now.

Oh, Grandfather, how could you? You've wrecked every-thing! Just a few minutes more and we'd have been up and out of here!

He didn't answer her, of course.

He was having a vision.

A Phrynis vision? Not necessarily, but she'd bet it was. Without the aid of the synergizer?

Oh, Lord! His psi must be out of sight. Were "they" responsible? Or the synergizer? Or Grandfather himself, by just going through this whole thing? You got real strong legs by climbing stairs.

She stood up.

What was he seeing in there? she wondered a little enviously. Ord would have a fit. By the time they strapped him in, they'll have missed scads. Whatever would Ellisen say?

She stood there, of half a mind not to tell them. But that wouldn't work. They'd come soon to fetch them into the hopper. If they found Grandfather like that, and her just sitting there, they'd be awful mad.

Remembering MacAllister's warning, she crossed the room slowly and reached to buzz for Ord.

Tannis Ord stood by the synergizer in mauve pajamas.

Shira stood aside as Suk and Prosser got things going. Ord, of course, did nothing but stand and fret. The little toad. The way he always managed to let everybody else do the work!

MacAllister appeared in the doorway. Shira looked to him glumly.

He made a face and shrugged.

What can we do? it said. Shira didn't have to scan to get that.

Somehow, that made her feel a little better, made her feel not quite so alone.

Soon the room would fill with color and shape. Of what? Of the young woman Tanna? The young prince? Or something else? Whatever it was, it was going through Grandfather's mind right now.

If she read him, would she see it, too?

She regarded him uneasily. He'd be so angry, and Grandfather angry was the worst trip in the world.

Still watching him, she tentatively reached out. That, at least, was allowed. *Grandfather?*

No response. He wasn't aware.

She reached a little farther, and farther, then caught her breath sharply. Her mind filled with hazy images. And more.

Words, names, a voice spoke inside her head. Grandfather's voice.

The great gate between Asr-Rm, the holy mountain, and Hn, the holy lake, still stood wide as the last rays of Demiel glanced off the golden domes within the walls. Already in deep-shaded places yellow lamps glowed from niches in white-washed stone as the two gatekeepers emerged from their booth to shut up for the night.

The TS flickered, lit up.

"Cut the lights," Ord said.

A moment later the lab filled with the golden radiance of a sunset, the lapping of water, and the thin wail of high winds. And then, and then: everyone jumped, even Shira, as a great deep bell boomed out.

The two ancients had actually cranked the gate to and were slipping the heavy bar into place when the bell tolled to announce an arrival—once, deep and slow, then again and again filling the air with loud, importunate sound. Through it all, however, the gatekeepers methodically completed their ritual, and only after that did they actually toil up the winding postern stair to see who it could be.

Down below a solitary figure groveled in the fast-gathering dusk, trying to peer under the gate. A pilgrim? In those grimy, tattered rags? The old men looked askance.

From across the steep valley an animal screamed, the echo trailing long after the sound cut off. One of the men called down.

"Who are you, who come to Rm unlooked-for and at this hour?"

The figure scrambled to its feet.

"I am prin— Torc, *pilgrim*, come late to the sohurin. Open the gate."

They drew in their heads, letting the spy-hatch fall shut.

Dusk deepened into dark as Torc waited for the old men to reappear, for the gate to grind open, for them to usher him inside, and still he waited, cursing and fuming, until at long last a light wavered above and a chain ladder looped down in short, spastic jerks.

"You expect me to climb *that*?" Him, Torc of Gurnyac, to enter Rm like a nocturnal thief?

The ladder began to rise again. With an oath Torc leapt, missed, and hit the dirt, and as he hit it, the ladder smacked the top of his head.

"Young man, if you have any mind at all to climb, then do it with speed. It is well past the time for securing the postern."

The voice was mild, but firm.

Torc got up, hoisted the remnants of his robe about his knees, and pulled himself up rung by rung until his fingers found the postern sill.

Hands guided him over and down into the tiny turret room. He was too angry by now to feel stone scrape his shins and hit his temple.

"Careful." A second voice, sharp and thin as a rusted hinge. "You'll set yourself a-bleeding."

Before Torc could speak, Voice Two was off down the turret stair, lighting the way as his partner stowed the ladder and bolted the hatch.

Torc took off after him, fetching up at the bottom with such a thump against the old man that he all but knocked the torch from his hand.

The old man steadied himself.

"You will please come."

Torc seized his arm. "Where to?"

The old man gestured to a low door halfway along the cobbled way that led under the Gate.

"You shall make yourself comfortable while I send word of your coming. Follow me."

Torc's hand tightened. "No. You shall take me to my sohurin. Now."

The gatekeeper looked down. "Not whilst you hold me thus, young man. In that arm, the blood has ceased to flow!"

Torc only tightened his fingers.

"On, or more than blood will cease to flow."

"To what good?" The rheumy eyes glistened in the torchlight. "These gates yield not to threats."

Torc let go.

Behind the low door was a bare white cell, furnished with a small table, an upright chair, and a narrow cot.

"You will please mind your head."

For one moment Torc had half a mind to snatch the old man's torch from his hand and run, but as the old gont had said, *to what good?*

He ducked, went inside, and shut the door in the old man's face. There, he threw himself, wincing, onto the hard cot, and closed his eyes. Faintly through a high barred window came snatches of a ghial in the high register, tinkling sounds, spilling out under the sky, sparkling like the stars far above the dark mountaintops.

How tired he was. Hungry. Stinking filthy. His left leg ached. A deep scratch in his right side throbbed with pus. Under the remnants of his heisha his scalp itched with stubble, and his chin sprouted three weeks of beard.

How he longed for a hot bath, and fresh roasted meat and a handle of hlath.

And Tanna.

"There. Make yourself comfortable."

Torc must have dozed, for he hadn't heard the gatekeeper set a frosted pitcher and washbowl on the tabletop.

He started up, wincing as the man set snowy towels over the chair back. "When you have washed, there will be nourishment."

Torc beat him to the door.

"Wait! Hasn't word gone yet that I am here?"

"Patience, young man. All in good time."

Torc pushed past him to the door, threw it wide, and ran left along the cobbled passage.

The end was barred by two spear guards.

At last! A language that he spoke.

He reached for the first man, only to fetch up against a shaft that jarred him sorely. He tried again, and this time met empty space.

How?

Many times in the barracks he'd taken six such at one time.

He turned on the old man angrily. "Is this how Rm's cowards fight?"

The gatekeeper looked puzzled. "Fight? We don't fight in Rm."

"You lie. What are these armed guards for, then?"

"To watch, merely."

"For what?"

"For stray wildbeasts that would breach our night gate."

Torc looked to him sharply, but the old one's face seemed innocent enough.

Sighing, he let himself be led back to his cell.

While he ate, a guide came in, richly dressed as the one who'd come to him in Asurdun.

The Athor and the Hela had been told of Torc's arrival, the man said, and this was their reply:

Prince Torc, having missed full thirteen days of the current sohurin, was advised to return home until another time.

Torc jumped up, spilling his hot charnu over the flagstones.

"The Dryac you say! Who is this *Athor* and this *Hela* to send away the Gurnyac heir! I'll see them!"

"They see no one after sunset save in grave emergencies."

"Grave emergencies!" Torc shouted. "You think this isn't grave? Go now and say that I would speak with them. If not, my father shall know!"

The guide turned on his heel and left, shutting the door behind him.

Torc threw open the door again and called for fresh food. None came.

He ran out, down the passage. The guards barred his way.

"Food," he snapped. "Bring fresh food. Now."

The guards lowered their pikes. The gatekeeper was gone for the night, they informed him, and the inner gate was locked till dawn.

Enraged, Torc would have hurled himself at them, but as the old gatekeeper had said, *to what good?*

He strode back to his cell, slammed the door behind him, and scraping what he could of the charnu off the floor, ate it, then, still hungry, he threw himself onto the cot and fell asleep.

At dawn Torc was roused and taken to a cold bathhouse to shower under icy mountain water, then handed fresh clothes, not pilgrim's clothes, but garments like the guide's, of thick blue harpile, crimson trimmed, finely embroidered in gold thread; well fit for a gentleman if not a prince.

Torc turned them away.

"I will not put these on. I am a pilgrim. I will shave and put on the robe and heisha.

The guide folded his arms. "There are no pilgrim clothes in the outer city. This is the gear they ordered for you. As for your hair—you were wise to grow it back without delay, as befits a man of your standing, or any other traveler who would go through these mountains at this point of Demiel's ring. The snows are not too far away."

"I am not a traveler. I am going nowhere. I tell you, I shall not wear those clothes!"

Nodding, the man bent to take them up, but then Torc, remembering the ladder and the lost charnu, snatched them back, and, cursing, put them on.

They fitted perfectly.

Without another word, the guide led him back to his cell where a bowl of hot charnu and fresh-baked shnihar waited on the table. Sullenly, Torc ate while the man waited by the door.

The instant his plate was cleared the guide produced a traveling cloak and bag.

"This pack will see you through the worst. The Athor and the Hela regret that you must return on foot, but no journeys are planned down the Lake until the end of the latest sohurin. They wish you speed and hope you'll reach Asurdun before the snows set in."

The guide set cloak and bag before Torc on the table and

stepped back. "Please feel free to leave as soon as you are ready."

Torc stayed put.

"I'm not leaving. I demand to see the—what did you call them?"

The guide stepped forward and leaned over the table.

"I've delivered your valedictory. The gatekeepers are waiting to see you out. If you don't go now you'll be sorry. The shelters are few and far between."

"You think I don't know that?"

Torc jumped up.

"On my father's life I'll not go. Tell that to your Athor and your Hela."

Something flickered in the guide's face.

"So be it."

He bowed his head, and left.

Torc paced the room until, fancying he heard footsteps outside, he stood by the door, listening. Then he paced again, then sat, then fell onto the cot.

Time passed.

Once or twice he visited the tiny urinal in the far wall: an alcove behind a fine rush screen, washed by a spring and fragrant with orat and fresh achan root.

No one came, not even to bring him a midday meal.

He remembered the travel pack. In it was waybread, thung cheese hard as wood, and a flask of water. Two bites of bread and his hunger was gone. He left the opened bag on the table, and lay down once more on the cot.

Light rays slanting in through the high window lengthened then dimmed.

He heard the change of watch. And the sound of laughter across the thin mountain air.

Then all at once he heard the boom of the great gatebell. He heard the groan of hinges, the sound of greetings. He leapt up, crossed the room, and opened the door a crack.

". . . may this stay be as fruitful as the last . . ."

A guide was leading a group of blue-shrouded figures past

his door and into the city. The liars! Not another sohurin for another half sunaround? What was this, then! He had half a mind to rush out, demanding to know.

On second thought, he clamped his mouth into a thin, tight line and quietly closed the door.

He could wait.

It was almost sunset when his guide beckoned him. Without a word, the man led him past the guards, across the yard, and through a high inner arch.

Torc had his first glimpse of the Holy City.

Walls. Stone walls, steep and close. Walls that climbed the mountain slope, high white walls whose fabled golden rooftops were out of sight in mist. Mellow lamps wavered in the twilight from niches cut into those walls, while around them, like ribbons on spools, wound flights of steep steps, crossing, joining, leading everywhere.

They walked and climbed the winding ways, back from the gate, until they reached a rough cleft in the bare mountainside.

Torc labored for breath, and his thighs burned, but his stocky guide never slowed, never gave a sign of effort. But then, Torc thought sourly, he was used to it.

They entered the cleft, walked along rough tunnels, across windy caverns, climbing ever upward inside the mountain, until they came at last to a small door. Torc's chest was fairly heaving by now, and his throat was afire.

Beyond the door, to Torc's surprise, was a small square chamber lined entirely with mirrored panels, even the floor and ceiling.

The guide ushered Torc through the door and shut it behind him, sealing him in.

Torc stood for a moment, leaning over, his hands on his knees, until his breath slowed and his blood stopped pounding his ears. Then he straightened up and looked about him curiously. The light shafted down through slits set in the angle between wall and ceiling, the bright blue light of costly agria.

The air was chilly and damp. Lucky he was hot from his climb.

Time passed.

He began to grow uneasy in that tight, closed space.

What was he doing in there? What was that place? It felt like a mirrored cage. Did they test him, the Hela and the Athor, to see how he behaved? Well, let them. He'd show them how a king's son carried himself.

He held himself still for a while, until, growing restless at last, he circled the room feeling for the door, but so tight was its fit in the mirrored panels that he couldn't find it.

He went to the stool in the middle of the floor and perched with his arms about his knees.

Was the air thin in there? He was beginning to feel really strange.

Giddy.

He spread his hands over his knees and studied them, as though he'd never seen them before.

Funny things, hands. Take his father's.

Sharroc had lost the first joint of the middle finger on his right hand while taking the Barren Lands. Massive hands, they were. Warriors' hands. How many lives had they taken in their time? How many battles won? And how many draughts had they raised to froth their owner's beard?

He turned his own over, thinking suddenly of Tanna. Of soft flesh under his fingers, hard back, moist warmth of thigh.

He jumped to his feet, snarling, clenching and unclenching his hands.

Glancing up, he caught sight of himself reflected on all sides, hundreds upon hundreds of faces twisted like a Gradhlzac's, a very demon army in rich, bright dress, stretching back and back to infinity. Slowly, he revolved, staring at himself in fascination on all sides.

They kept the wild things out, did they?

He drew his lips into a snarl. His jaw cut stark through the young beard, and his skull shone hard and round through the stubble. He grinned at himself, a very Dryac, liking what he saw.

He tipped his head back and laughed aloud.

He turned faster, raising his arms upward and outward to meet the ranks of arms outstretched to meet them, until they all seemed linked in an endless chain of power.

He stopped and closed his eyes, his head, the room, the whole inner firmament, spinning about him.

"The Athor will see you."

Torc started, looked up to find the mirrorspaces filled with the guide's fragmented image, so filled that Torc himself was crowded out.

He dove for the dark rectangle of the open door and followed the guide into a high dark cavern lit by one small pool of light.

On a small rush mat, in rough, unbleached latik robes, sat a golden man.

His face, Torc saw as he approached, was oval and unlined, although he was not young. His nose was long, and straight— sharp, almost. His eyes, dark-fringed, were tawny as a langaur's. His golden hair, shoulder length, was caught at the temples by a latik cord, knotted at every thumb's width.

The man motioned Torc to sit opposite him on the mat, while at a signal, another dressed in dark brown stepped from the shadows to place between them a low wooden table, on which stood a pitcher of water and two small brass bowls.

"I am Athor, of the Inner Ring. You asked to see me."

The voice was quiet, with a faint foreign inflection. Each statement ended on an upswing that gave it the air of a question.

Torc nodded, and waving away the offer of water, got straight down to business. "I missed the boat back in Asurdun. A regrettable error but one for which I've surely paid."

The Athor regarded him impassively for a moment or two, then he spoke.

"It is not a matter of payment, prince." He smiled faintly. "You're simply too late. You've missed the initial stages of your sohurin. You couldn't hope to catch up."

Torc jumped to his feet, leaned down over the table. "I *can't* go home. So like it or not, I stay!" He smacked the table with his fist, setting the brass bowls, the pitcher singing musically on the wooden top.

The Athor kept his silence.

"It's a strange religion you teach, Athor," Torc complained. "You take the gifts and spurn the giver. Beware: golden rivers can run dry."

"It's no religion, prince, but a discipline for which you're poorly fitted, and fortunately so." The Athor's voice was smooth, even, perfectly controlled. "Were you to come to even the most basic appreciation of our teachings, your dynasty would perish."

He sighed to the distant roof.

"But never fear. Generation after generation of the Gnangars come and go unchanged, paying but lip service to the Quaur. I was frankly glad when the Gurnyac heir did not arrive."

Startled, Torc met the golden eyes.

The Athor spread his hands. "As for the gold, I know naught of that."

"Oh, come now, Athor." The gall of the man. "Why, one can see it from Asurdun! Your very walls groan under the weight of it!"

"Ah, yes. The golden roofs of Rm. The harnwood. The costly perfumes of Periaur. The green stones of Grell, the harsilk, the oils, and the wines."

The Athor once more turned his golden eyes upon Torc.

"Rather than refuse tributes from misguided folk who seek to purchase favor with the Quaur instead of earning it, we let the Rethi keep them. And why not? They prize such things, and they serve the Lothuri well."

"They keep all of it?"

"The Lothuri seek other wealth, princeling."

"Speak more plain." Torc longed to provoke this man, to goad those smooth features into some kind of expression other than a faint smile, to raise that even voice to some show of emotion.

"The Lothuri spurn appearance for reality. They travel light."

"You answer riddle with riddle. The Lothuri don't travel."

"Though we of the Inner Ring have not left Rm in one thousand generations, we've traveled farther than any other in the Known World. In spirit."

Still Torc couldn't understand him. So he changed the subject.

"These *Rethi*. I've never heard of them."

The Athor's eyes gleamed. "You met one in Asurdun. They are our worldly eyes and ears; our guards, our custodians and guides."

"Aha!" Torc understood him now. "Why, they're nothing but your melks dressed up in finery! You treat them too well, Athor, take a tip from me!"

The Athor didn't acknowledge him. "Their ministrations," he went on, as though Torc hadn't spoken, "free the Lothuri to live the inner life and serve the Pilgrims that come here. They are, if you like, the body and mind, the outer wealth of Rm, while the Lothuri are the soul, the inner wealth, buried where most men never see."

Torc regarded him doubtfully. In Gurnyac, a man's measure was nailed up in blood for all to know and fear.

"If the Rethi live out there under the golden domes, then where do the Lothuri live?"

"Here, under the K'haravim."

"*K'haravim*?"

"Our way of life. The very mountain itself."

The Athor's voice took on a final note. "I regret I can speak with you no longer. Your guide is by the door. Take heart, prince. There's always another time."

What, was he dismissed? Quickly, Torc drew his last weapon.

"I was told there'd be no sohurins for another half sunaround," he said, even as the guide came forward to escort him out. "And yet only this afternoon newly arrived pilgrims entered the gate."

The Athor nodded.

"And they wore blue, not white, if you remember, signifying that they come for their second sohurin at the eleventh level, having already survived their first at the twelfth."

"Blue? White? Return?"

The Athor appealed to the distant roof. "How great is the pride of the Gnangars that they nurture their ignorance with such care." He fixed Torc with such a look of infinite patience as made Torc's blood boil. "Prince, there are twelve steps on the Inner Path. Each step has its own disciplines and goals, and its own symbolic color. Those of the eleventh step wear blue."

Torc felt a stirring of hope. He knelt before the table, leaned forward eagerly.

"To take the eleventh level: is it a law that one must complete the twelfth first?"

The Athor, evidently catching his drift, smiled again his faint smile. "No. But what fool would embark on a second, more hazardous journey unless he has completed the first?"

Torc smacked his chest. "Why, this fool, Athor. I shall stay. On the eleventh level."

"Prince, each level is more difficult than the last." The smile was now tinged with pity. "Of those who come across the lake in white, full half of them don't stay the course. This newly arrived group, above thirty men and women—"

Women? Torc's eyes widened.

"—have paid their dues in full."

Torc leaned back. "Nevertheless, I shall stay."

The Athor looked at him most strangely.

"You are a determined young man—you who've not even learned to control your body, let alone your mind."

Torc stood up, looking down on the golden man from his full height. "I have the greatest control of any man alive, save Sharroc. With my bare hands alone I can fell a dozen."

"And yet you can't keep still for more than a few moments together."

So the chamber of mirrors had been a test after all. Torc's eyes darkened. Well, let the man think what he will. Gurnyac would prevail.

"I shall stay, then."

The Athor looked him up and down curiously. "Tell me, Torc, prince: in the chamber of mirrors—what did you see?"

Torc considered. "I saw myself multiplied to the power of infinity, stretching in all directions, line upon line of me, going forever."

At last a fleeting flash in the golden eyes. Of triumph? Or relief?

"What you attempt is impossible. Yet I'll not refuse you. You may stay long as you can, Torc-pilgrim. As long as you *can*."

A wave of the hand and the golden eyes closed.

The guide stepped forward and took Torc's arm.

The interview was over.

CHAPTER FOURTEEN

TORC, fresh-shaven, in new blue heisha and robe, filed through the cobbled streets with the rest of the conclaur toward a long, low stone building under the mountain wall.

One by one they passed under the lintel to sit cross-legged in neat rows on the cold flagstone, their heishas on their laps. From his place on the back row, Torc counted the heads. Nine rows, four to a row, two and two, with an aisle down the middle. Thirty-six neat shining scalps, counting himself. Hah! They should be grateful to him for rounding off the heads!

He scanned the skulls intently looking for the women, fidgeting against the chill floor striking up through his robe. *Skod,* what a depressing place. Even the rich colors of the Rethi guides flanking the hall were dulled within those man-thick, solid walls.

The little warmth and sunlight shafting through the doorway behind him was now blocked as a slow procession wafted past: four Lothuri in dark brown latik, their bright hair bound by knotted latik cord, set four braziers, unlit, before the front dais then stepped back to stand behind them, blocking them from the pilgrims' view. Women, they had to be, with that hair. Torc stared at them intently, willing one to turn around, by ever so little so that he could glimpse a breast, a face, but they remained still, looking to the dais. After them now walked twelve older Lothuri. Why "older," when he could see nothing but their backs? There were six men, and six women, tall, graceful, all dressed in the coarse unbleached latik robes that the Athor had worn.

These twelve climbed the platform to sit cross-legged save two. One was the Athor, the other, a woman. And what a woman! She was tall as the Athor, and as exquisitely made. Her hair was thick and long, two strands taken around the top of her head in fine braids. She was no fallowella, yet, like the Athor, she looked ageless. Torc's eyes moved down the length of her gown, trying to guess what might be beneath.

To his surprise, it was the woman who spoke, her chest rising and falling with each phrase. Her voice was soft, in the low register, yet it carried quite clearly to where he sat in the back row.

"Behold Hela, of the Inner Ring. Pilgrims of the Eleventh Step: welcome. You have come far. May your faith not prove vain . . ."

Torc watched her, disapproving. It was not seemly for a woman to stand up in public thus. In Gurnyac women kept to their place. Was she the Athor's woman? He tried to picture her naked, hair tumbled, straining under the Athor, grunting and sweating from climax to climax, and failed.

". . . your last opportunity before you take your final oath."

Oath? Torc snapped to.

". . . so if you have the slightest doubt, go now in peace, and without shame, bowing before the ancient law, for once you have sworn before the flame, you will pass under the K'haravim and from then on, whatever happens, though the outer world fail and whole dynasties pass—" She paused slightly, "—yet you must remain steadfastly under the

K'haravim, dead to all but the Inner path for fully two hundred and seventy days."

He leapt to his feet. Two hundred and seventy days! That was half as long again as the twelfth step sohurin! He couldn't stay that long! He was expected back in Asurdun in only one hundred and sixty-two days!

A sudden movement to the left of the hall and someone else stood up. This pilgrim bowed low to the dais, and replacing the heisha, walked quickly up the aisle past Torc and out the door. A moment later another followed, then another, and another.

Five in all walked out of there but still the woman waited.

For him? Was she waiting for him? She was clearly looking his way.

Realizing that he was still standing, he hastily sat down again.

They were not rid of him so easily. When he failed to show in Asurdun, Sharroc would send for him, and the Athor would have to let him go. There wasn't the man in the Known World who could defy the king of Gurnyac, not even this one.

As for this oath that the Hela spoke of: what was that but breath blowing in the wind?

Yes, he would stay.

At Hela's nod the doors shut out the sun with cold finality, and Torc sat blinded momentarily in the dim blaze of torches lining the walls.

The four women attendants leaned forward, and the braziers flared, then flickered with drafty flame.

The Hela raised her arms.

"Now is the holy fire lit. Now can there be no turning back. Now are you truly committed to taking the oath of Induction before your peers and Witnesses of the Inner Ring.

"Yet with the binding comes release from the fear of turning back. From this moment look freely only to the way that lies ahead."

She bowed her head and in one smooth, graceful, movement sat down.

Two of the Rethi guides, stepping forward, signaled the first row of pilgrims to rise and kneel, one to each of the lighted braziers.

The Athor stood now and raised his arms to the rafters. The pilgrims down below raised theirs.

"I swear," he began.

"I swear," they echoed, not quite in unison. A woman's voice in there somewhere, Torc noted with interest. A young one.

". . . by the sacred flame . . ."

". . . by the sacred flame . . ."

". . . to renounce henceforth for two hundred and seventy days all worldy thoughts, submitting myself wholly to the precepts of the eleventh step according to the will of the Quaur . . ."

Phrase by phrase they intoned the words, on their bare knees, their heads bobbing on the completion of each, and when at last they were done, they remained there in silence for an age doing the Dryac knew what.

Torc sighed.

Four heads down, twenty-seven to go.

How would he ever survive . . .

Torc shuffled toward the mountain gate, treading on the heels of the old gont in front whose legs seemed to be bound together at the knees.

Gate: the same dark cleft he'd gone through before.

Here, where light and dark comingled, one stood to greet them.

No Lothuri he, for sure. Torc looked him up and down. The features were blunt as the pitted Dryacs atop the Gurnyac keep. His scalp, furthermore, was shorn.

His robe was dark brown, whatever that meant.

"Behold D'huru Nor, your mentor. Look your last on the world out there, an you will."

There. By his broad flat accents, the "be-hawld," the

"yaw," the "last" as in "mass," the very gruff of his voice,
Torc had him. From the far north, he was, of barbaric
B'hadgazan. Now what was a man like that doing here? While
Torc stared down on him, wondering, heads had already
turned obediently for a last look out over the golden rooftops
glinting roundly under the late sun. By the time Torc turned his
head it was too late and the line was shuffling on again under
the darkness of the K'haravim.

Look your last . . . ?

Did that mean no more sun or stars?

Someone kicked his heel.

He swore, moved on again with the general mass, down
dark passageways, down and down, the air getting colder and
damper with each step until his breath came in clouds.

Finally, they reached a dead-end passageway lit by sconces
marking recessed doors down either wall. Through these doors
the pilgrims peeled off one by one until only Torc was left,
standing before the last.

Under the mentor's eye, Torc pushed it open and went
inside.

The cell was of rough-hewn stone, fresh whitewashed. The
door itself was of hard sugwood, black with age. In its center
at eye level was a carved round spyhole, the only source of
light in that place. Facing the door, a cot stood by the wall;
against the other two was a washstand, and a chair.

Torc crossed the floor—four short steps—and tested the cot.
Hard as the last one. He ran back out to find the mentor
waiting.

"When do we eat, *B'hadgazan?*"

The man's eyes flickered. "Yuh dawn't.

"What do you mean?"

"You 'eard the Athor. The first two weeks are for fastin' and
cleansin'. Now: go back in until I cum agen. And close the
daw."

The mentor turned away.

"Wait! I've eaten nothing since noon. My belly crawls."

The mentor waved him back. "Are you deaf, you young bruk? You're on a fast. There'll be no food today, nor tomorrow, nor for some days to come. Now go inside and shut your door."

Torc's anger flared.

He drew back a hand to push the mentor aside. But from there, his hand couldn't, wouldn't move. Startled, he looked down into the man's eyes and felt afraid as he never had before, not before Sharroc, not before Feric, or Brac, or anybody. There he stood, held in that look until, at a nod, he found himself turning about and reentering his cell.

The mentor closed it after him and snapped home an outside bolt.

Torc sat on the cot, staring at the door, at the spyhole through which one could look out—or in.

He was tired. He'd been mistaken. The man couldn't have stopped him like that, not without laying a finger on him. He couldn't have.

He lay down and stared up at the ceiling across which smoke-shadows fluttered from the sconces outside, and tried to think . . .

The mentor shook him awake. "Come."

The others were already waiting, of course.

D'huru Nor led them to a dim chamber whose floor and walls shone wet.

There, they were told to strip.

Reluctantly, Torc moved to obey.

The scrot next to him was potbellied and scrawny. He was also hairless, with flesh white and smooth as a woman's: scalp, chest, even his arms and legs.

Torc turned from him in disgust, only to find on the other side of him—his face stiffened with outrage—a female with dugs down to her middle and a rug of grizzled hair from navel to sex.

Pulling his robe back on, he strode to the door.

"Gurnyac warriors don't bathe with scrots and groles. I'll go elsewhere."

"This is not Gurnyac, and there are no warriors here. Neither are these folk scrots and groles, but pilgrims just like you—your soul-peers."

"You jest."

"Mayhap, for they're one step above you, 'avin' completed level twelve. But they'll not count it against you, I'm sure. Now—off with your clothes."

Torc wheeled about and striding back into the chamber, ripped off his robe, catching someone behind him a smart slap.

He spun about, braced for a fight.

This one was *not* old, but young, leggy as a new-dropped thar, with full breasts ripe as peculars and rich red nipples tight with cold. Her waist was lean above her belly, and her wide hips curved like dunes down to her thighs.

Slowly, inexorably, his krudt hardened and swelled, tilting like a lance at the charge. The grizzled one watched it with open interest until she caught his eye and turned away, but not before he'd glimpsed the laughter in her eyes.

He looked up.

They were all staring at him, every last one of them, as though he were some freak at a Gurnyac fairing—except for the girl, who'd turned her back.

None too soon, D'huru Nor turned a spigot, sending spikes of icy needles down onto them, deep mountain water piped in through latticed stone conduits overhead. Torc doubled over, gulping water and air.

"Nothing like water to douse a fire."

The accent was coarse, the voice, throaty. He glanced sharply to the girl, but she was looking the other way.

The water ceased abruptly.

At a signal from the mentor, the pilgrims followed him into the next chamber, dropped their discarded robes into a bin as they went.

There, they reached into great sacks for handfuls of dried crit needles to scrub themselves dry.

Torc edged around to the girl but she moved also, keeping herself an even distance from him. His anger growing, he moved on into a third place containing bins of clean dry clothing.

He reached out for a robe, just as she did likewise.

That was when he saw the Brandmark on her arm: an iron rose.

A melk—a runaway melk from the Brandings—here?

Catching the direction of his look, the girl went still, her arms upraised in the act of pulling her robe over her head. Then deliberately, she turned from him and let it fall. Still with her back to him, she reached for her sash and moved away.

Torc's mouth tightened.

He started after her, his gown forgotten in his hands. All around him the rest were shaking out, smoothing down, tying belts. He got her by the far wall, pressed her up against the rock, forcing back her head in order to see her face.

The strength of it shocked him momentarily: the broad cheekbones, the short, straight nose, the mouth, wide now and startled. She was tall, taller than Tanna by half a head. Taller than most of the other pilgrims in that place.

He pressed her harder against the jagged wall with the length of his naked body, and lowered his mouth to hers.

The next minute, he was flat on his back across the flagstones, his mouth twisted with pain. The she-frat! The melk! How had she done that! He scrambled up to find the girl gone and in her place, the mentor.

"Put on thy robe and get thee to the door!"

"Get thyself there, thou half-baked scrot. I'll see the Athor now!"

Without word or sign from the mentor, the pilgrims, all dressed and looking on, went to the door, and as they went, D'huru Nor repeated his words, picking up Torc's robe and handing it to him.

Calm brown eye met angry blue one. Torc saw that look again, and was afraid.

He slipped on the rough blue stuff, pulled it with great difficulty over his cold, wet skin. Then, shivering, he slipped on his sandals, and joined the line.

He stood behind his door until the mentor had passed. The rage and the shame had gouged their way through him, leaving him sullen. He lifted the catch and pulled. The door was locked. Rage caught at him again, a wave of angry frustration. He drew in a quick breath to shout, to send through the grille a string of loud and vulgar imprecations, but he let it out again.

Hadn't he provided enough entertainment for one day?

He took two strides to his cot and threw himself down, winced in pain. That mentor. Thick short fellow. Had he stopped Torc out there with but a look? Why, that was sorcery. Surely the Lothuri didn't practice the evil eye! Skod, but he was so starved his head was spinning. Perhaps that was it. Hunger played strange tricks on one.

His gut growled agreement.

He turned onto his back and watched the shadows twisting up the walls.

How was he going to get through one more day, let alone another two hundred and sixty-nine?

There'd been a hardness about the girl's body that he'd felt on no other fallowella. But then of course, she wasn't one, was she? She was a melk, a runaway melk! Absconded property of Gurnyac, and the Athor was harboring her.

He'd answer for that.

And so would she, the moment they set foot in Asurdun.

An iron handbell woke him. Groaning, he turned to face the wall.

Soft footsteps padded along the stone outside.

Someone coughed.

Silence.

Then his door opened, and someone stood inside.

"At the bell you get up and wash."

Torc addressed the wall. "And if I don't?"

"In future, I'll rouse you before the bell to give you more time. Now come, washed or no. Put on your heisha against the cold."

Torc heaved himself up and out to form the tag end of the line.

The pilgrims filed down long passages, then up steps that wound around a stone column in neverending coils.

How did everybody move so fast first thing in the morning?

Torc stopped as pain stabbed his ribs, and leaned against the wall, thinking resentfully of Tanna still lying abed, and of a warm stove; of vapor rising from fresh-baked shnihar, and pungent cups of hlath.

He realized that he was now alone on the deserted stair.

Where had the scrots gone?

Not to eat, certainly. Well, what went up came down. All he had to do was sit and wait.

Onward, prince. Onward, thou stout warrior of Gurnyac. Let not these lowly scrots and groles shame you.

Torc leapt up, peering in pitch darkness around the empty stair. D'huru Nor's voice, or he was the son of a pizac. But— *whispering in his right ear?*

I will, if you like, send back the last man to give you a push . . .

Bewildered, Torc turned about and about on the step.

It was the mentor all right. But where was he?

Up here and waiting. Hurry, or I'll come to fetch you myself.

Torc's skin prickled. The mentor had *answered* him. His unspoken words, his thoughts! He remembered the day before, when the mentor had robbed him of his will to move. Now had the man entered his innermost heart. What dark caznry was this!

Not caznry, prince, but mindspeech, that every pilgrim practices from level six.

Mindspeech. In Gurnyac they'd call it caznry, for sure, and that would cost the man his head.

Mindspeech. A strange word, yet apt, for D'huru Nor had both heard his thoughts, and responded to them—at a considerable distance.

Torc felt his way slowly, and a little fearfully, up the dark stair.

It occurred to him then to wonder: what might a king do with this mindspeech! Could he perhaps master it? Level six, the mentor had said. No. The price was too high.

He toiled slowly up through the darkness, every step a pain until he felt a sharp wind cut his cheek. Not a draft heavy with the stink of rock and mildew and damp latik, but cold fresh air, smelling of outside.

He emerged on a tiny plateau, under the stars.

Stars! Then it was not yet dawn!

In the near dark he could just make them all out, squatting, looking like so many gray boulders about the stony ground. What were they doing?

Meditating, prince. Meditating.

Meditating? Those scrots? On what?

That depends. If you were to sit down there and put your mind to it, what would you think about?

That's easy enough. The day I leave here, for one thing, and for another, shnihar and hot hlath.

There was no reply.

Torc looked around. Which was the mentor? And which, the melk?

He squatted. Might as well. Rest his legs. Skod, but it was freezing out there. His thick latik robe seemed no thicker than harsilk.

Silence.

His gut rumbled.

If they're as hungry as I, B'hadgazan, they're all thinking of food.

Still no reply.

He looked up, fixed his eyes on a star brighter than all the others: Forthyr, heaven's anchor, the wanderer's Eye. Even as he watched, it paled, and dull gold flecked low gray cloud streaking across the distant horizon. He stood stiffly, rubbed his legs, and wandered to the edge of the plateau to peer down into a mass of boiling mist coming up at him like steam from a cazn's pot. This must be the far side of the holy mountain that men never saw. A private, secret place. A tiny valley hemmed in on all sides by high peaks.

He stood, willing the mist to clear so that he could glimpse what lay beneath it, but just as it shifted and thinned, D'huru Nor had them all up and climbing back down the steps.

Where now, B'hadgazan? Back to our cells?

You're in great good luck, prince. You go to take sustenance.

Sustenance! Torc's spirits rose.

For all the fancy talk of fasting, they got to eat after all.

He hastened down the stairs, treading on everybody's heels.

The mess hall was a long, low cavern set with rush floor pads and low wooden benches on which were set pitchers, one to a bench, and tiny earthenware cups.

A faint sweet smell hung on the air. Torc sniffed appreciatively. Fresh-baked shnihar and honey.

His belly rumbled in response.

He sat where he was bid with alacrity while one of the pilgrims, an old gont with a mumbly mouth, took up the pitcher, measured out amber liquid with such slow concentration that one would think he handled the king's own wine cellar. Two, three short tips of the jug to each cup, and he passed it along.

While the man still poured for the rest, Torc seized up his cup, and tossed its contents to the back of his throat.

He immediately was taken with a fit of coughing. The liquid was fiercely hot with a strange sweet aftertaste that he wasn't sure he liked. Perhaps, he decided, it would grow on him.

He held out his cup for a refill but the man, ignoring him, sat down.

Torc leaned over, seized up the pitcher, and tipped it. Empty.

He looked to the others. Picking up the cups, sipping, rolling the stuff on their tongues, tilting their chins to let it trickle down their gullets. Torc's mouth came open in sympathy, his head tilted back with theirs. He caught himself and turned from them impatiently. Like his father's taster, they looked. He stifled an urge to laugh out loud, suddenly minded of Arcn, who in mid-swallow had flung up his arms and gone down writhing onto the floor, taking such a long time to die and Sharroc with a hall-full of guests.

He stopped smiling abruptly. Somehow, with him sitting there in that place, it didn't seem funny anymore.

The pilgrims were still sipping. Why, they were making a *meal* of it.

Heads came up. He must have said it out loud.

Quite right, prince, yet it will prove enough.

Enough for what, B'hadgazan? His thought was bitter. *For starving a man to death? On this—this piss of a forhar!*

No beast's staling is this, prince, but a decoction of hitaku, by the grace of the Quaur.

"*Hitaku?*" *What in Dryac's name is that?* Torc demanded, but D'huru Nor's attention had clearly gone elsewhere.

A faint warmth spread through Torc, pricking his skin, pressing back the chill. In spite of himself, he felt a surge of cheer the like of which came only at evening board after a second horn of red Gort wine.

When at last he stood with the others, he had to admit that he felt a new man, recharged and ready for anything.

Almost.

The mentor took from his robe a scroll, dividing the assembly into four sub-conclaurs. The first was to clean out the mess hall; the second, to clean out the cells. The third was to wash dirty linen, while the fourth . . .

Torc looked around. That was his group, to which, Torc noticed, the melk also belonged.

. . . the fourth was to empty the night slops and transport them to vats for processing into manure.

Torc sat down.

I'll not go! I'll not do this thing!

The Gurnyac stock is too delicate, it seems, to tread the path of enlightenment.

Torc folded his arms across his chest. *And just what has shoveling shlen to do with enlightenment? I'm sure my father never did it. One wouldn't have set him to it—and lived.*

True. But then he was on level twelve.

What if I refuse?

D'huru Nor considered him solemnly.

Let me put it this way: a pilgrim refusing the laundry chore stays in the same clothing until he comes to. One refusing to clean the mess hall keeps the same unwashed plate. Should he refuse to clean the cells, he sits in his own muck until he complies, similarly—

All right, all right. How long?

One week.

A week! Torc sighed.

Very well. He stood up again, looking down at the bare tables. *At least it can't put me off my food.*

The four sub-conclaurs filed out in silence, each to their appointed tasks, each led by a different mentor, D'huru Nor going off on business of his own.

Torc followed along from the back, as usual, eyeing the brown robe and heisha ahead sourly. He thrust out a thought.

I had understood we were to learn great truths, not to provide cheap labor for the Lothuri.

The answer came prompt. *Not for the Lothuri. For your conclaur. And already the learning has begun.*

A woman, not young, arguing like a man.

How? In scrubbing floors and tossing piss pots? You jest!

Indeed I don't. When you've done these duties a few times, you'll know what it is to be a scrot. And mayhap back home you'll remember. A ruler who knows not his subjects can't love them.

Love! Gurnyac ruled by love! He laughed out loud, causing heads to turn.

I don't know Gurnyac. But I say to you that a king who commands fealty through love is mightier than one who rules by force of arms. To be greater, you must learn to be lesser.

Starting with piss pots.

Quite so.

Torc regarded the brown heisha sullenly. Sanctimonious brat of a half-brained forhar. What did these people know of the outside world? Of the harshness of reality out there. Turn them out and set them down in the middle of Gurnyac and how long would they survive? It occurred to him that she might even then be listening in on his thoughts. Well, let her. And the Athor, too. All of them. They might learn something.

The sub-conclaur halted before the bins housing the pulp wagons. The mentor swung open the doors, wafting with them a faint scent of orat mingled with the damp rock smell. There were four wagons, one to a pair, of scrubbed wood lined with earthenware. They were heavy and cumbersome and seemed to have a mind of their own, as Torc found as he hauled on the front handles while his partner, man or woman he couldn't be sure, pushed from the back.

Two hours later, having emptied, scrubbed, and rinsed out the pots not only of their conclaur but of several others, they wheeled their contents deep under the mountain.

There, they decanted the stuff into a raw vat, and raked it in. In spite of the fresh orat branches lining the floor, and the bunches of it hanging from the roof, and the airy tunnels wafting out the fumes, Torc's gut began to churn.

He was so tired, and so glad to get into the bathhouse, that he forgot to watch for the girl until after he was dried and dressed.

No matter, he told himself. Next time. Next time.

D'huru Nor appeared to return them to their cells for noon meditation.

Noon!

How would they know it? Torc lay on his cot staring up at a damp patch on the wall, very like Rerry, the dairy queen, if he twisted his head about, so. The fitful torchlight coming in through the tiny hole in his door barely lit his cell. So dark. So dark. He'd never before been deprived of daylight. Had never thought what it might be like to live without it.

The only time he'd been in the dark like this during the daytime was when he went with his father to inspect the Foundings. The vast halls black with soot in the white-hot glare of the furnaces. The melks so thickcovered with fine black powder that one could see but the whites of their eyes.

It was not fitting that he, Torc, of Gurnyac, should be subjected to such treatment.

. . . *you'll know what it is to be a scrot* . . .

Hah! He pushed the images, the words, from him angrily. The sun, he craved the sun. Two hundred and sixty-nine days! Under the mountain cap a man must lose count of time. The use of his eyes—even of his mind . . .

Two hundred and sixty-nine days.

It had sounded so simple. A nuisance, but simple. Even had his father prepared him for some of it, which he hadn't, for the crown prince must prove himself blind, it wouldn't have helped him. There seemed such a wealth of difference between level twelve and level eleven. How was he ever going to get through?

He rubbed his belly.

Food, he wanted food. And daylight!

He smacked the wall with the flat of his hand and winced with pain.

How he hated the place. The stupid pilgrims, the holy-poly mentors.

He not only hated the place, but he also feared it. The

mentor still hadn't convinced him that he didn't practice the cazn's craft, stopping Torc in mid-stride, plucking his thoughts from his very mind. What, he brooded, might not that sort of thing work on a man, given time?

He turned onto his side and closed his eyes.

CHAPTER FIFTEEN

AGAIN the bell woke him.

He came up, rubbing his head. Not morning again already?

Not a hope, prince. Two hours have passed, merely. Come.

Torc rolled off the cot, stretched, and went out to join the conclaur, which was, as ever, already lined up.

I'm too hungry to move, B'hadgazan.

On. You're in for a treat.

Food?

Of a kind. On.

More tunnels, another flight of stairs, then Torc squeezed his eyes shut as suddenly he stumbled out into blinding sunlight.

He stood before a grassy courtyard walled in by white rush screens. In the center of the grass was a raised blue mat marked off by a thick latik cord. In the center of the mat sat a small golden man dressed only in a loincloth. His skin, his bald skull shone gold and shiny as a pinu nut. He sat quite still, legs crossed in an impossible position, eyes closed, apparently unmindful of the pilgrims being led to sit around the mat's edge, outside the cordon.

Behold the Harash D'ho, prince. Grand Master of the D'hogana.

In front of Torc was a neatly folded blue cloth.

Strip, prince, and put that on.

Torc looked around at the rest already well into the routine. At his left, the old grole with the rag rug was binding her sagging breasts with a second strip, while to his right, the hairless one was already sitting down.

He looked around for the girl.

There she was directly opposite him, in line with the Harash D'ho. He stared. For fallowellas in Gurnyac, undressing was an art, a fine and necessary art, calculated to show off the body with each loosened lace, each opened bodice, each dropped layer of petticoat, to bring men near to climax even before they lay down. He closed his eyes, for one moment seeing Tanna smiling on that last night, the second time, standing over him by the bed, her hands moving slowly, so slowly, rousing him once more as she knew best. And here was this—melk— stripping off her robe like that in broad daylight and yet his krudt was already beginning to respond . . .

Might I ask, Gurnyac, why you haven't as yet removed your clothing? You're not suddenly overcome by modesty, I hope?

Torc looked around.

The rest, changed, were sitting down again, some like the old man with their feet almost around their ears, some in the fashion of the Gurnyac gutter riff-raff. He was the only one left to undress.

So he was to entertain again, was he?

You have only yourself to blame. Now come, hurry, the Harash D'ho waits.

Torc obeyed, defying anyone to watch him, but all eyes were closed. He sat, staring straight past the old man to the girl. Like a goddess of Demiel, he found himself thinking. A statue, cast in palest bronze. From the Foundings, of course, complete with trademark.

The sun pricked Torc's skin. He tilted his head and closed his eyes, enjoying the pleasant trickle of sweat down the middle of his chest. Ah, this was better.

When the old man clapped his hands three times he came to with a start.

One of the novices rose and stepped up through a gap in the cordon onto the mat, where he advanced to stand face to face with the Harash D'ho.

The Harash D'ho bowed, the novice bowed. Then the novice dropped into a strange, sideways crouch, his hands before his chest and face, swaying like a langaur at the leap. Too quickly for Torc to see how, the Harash D'ho reached out, seized the novice's left wrist, and hurled him to the floor.

Torc leaned forward with interest. Now here was language he could understand. He waited for the novice to return the compliment, but instead of retaliating, the novice merely stood up, clasped his hands to his chest, then walked back to his place.

Torc couldn't believe it! To thank someone for besting you?

Three more loud claps and the next novice stepped up, then the next. Torc grew increasingly puzzled. It had to be a game.

He watched the girl go up, remembering how she'd thrown him in the bathhouse. A moment later, he watched the magnificent body arc through the air to land on its back. The sight angered him. Stupid melk to let herself be thrown like that. And the rest of them. Brainless scrots and groles.

They were going around the circle. Soon it would be his turn.

Dryac take him if he'd let the old gont throw him. Now was his chance to show them all a thing or two. His impatience grew as one by one the others fell, and did their obeisance.

The hairless one got up, took his punishment, came and sat down again.

Now it was him.

Torc was up on the first clap.

Sit down, prince. You watch only this time.

He turned in dismay. *Why?*

The conclaur revise their past skills before going on. You must watch and learn before you try.

Skill? You call that nonsense skilled? I would go up there.

Let him. The old man's voice was dry, thin, with the Athor's rising inflection.

D'huru Nor bowed his head, gestured Torc to step up.

The old man inclined his head, and after a slight pause, Torc did likewise. Then casually, he assumed the stance he'd seen the others take.

That is good. But move your feet, so.

The old man bent down, adjusted Torc's foot.

Why? It doesn't feel right. Torc kicked the old man's hand away, resumed his former position.

Mayhap not now, but it will later on.

That's for you to think, but I—

Prince! The mentor's thought came sharp. *Obey the Harash D'ho!*

How! You speak to me as I were a wayward child!

Quite so. Now move.

Torc, his mouth a tight, hard line, complied. At the old man's bidding he placed his arms, thus; head, legs, feet, so. He flexed his knees, checked his stance, and, at a warning, braced for the attack.

The next moment, he was lying on his back, staring up into the sun.

Thank you. Please sit down.

But I—

Sit down! The mentor sounded angry.

Fighting the urge to pick up the old man and hurl him from the ring, Torc obeyed, carefully avoiding the mentor's eyes.

He sat, his jaw tight-clenched.

He couldn't understand it. He'd never been so humiliated. And in public, too. Not even Feric had treated him thus. He felt the heat of shame and resentment wash over him, surpassing the warmth from the sun. He closed his eyes, shutting out the whole scene, wishing it away.

He felt a light touch on his arm, started. The old hairless one was patting him, and nodding his head the while. What! Did that old gont think he needed sympathy? He shook the hand off roughly, edged back.

How he hated them! He'd have no more to do with them, he resolved, and hear that if you will, B'hadgazan! And so he sat for some while, stony, staring down at the ground, disassociating himself from the thuds coming from the mat, but bit by bit his curiosity won out and he was looking on again until again it was his turn. This time, this time, he'd show them. The girl, the mentor, the old gont on the mat. He was prince of Gurnyac. No one, no one out there in the world could best him, hadn't Feric and his father always told him so?

This hold I take on your arm is called "griklok." Mark its feel well.

What's the point, if it enables you to throw me just the same? Drop all this stuff, let's go man to man, and then we'll see who comes off best.

The mentor cut in.

Hold your words, or you'll find yourself back in your cell. You won't defeat the Harash D'ho. He's the Master. The day he's bested will see a new Harash D'ho. As for you, you'll find that griklok works quite well against your peers.

His peers? He glanced around at the solemn faces looking on. His peers, again! Well, he'd show them. He'd show them the griklok all right! And—a new Harash D'ho!

Again, he went down, winded.

He struggled up, rubbing his shoulder, glaring around the ring. Of course, they made no sound, just as in the bathhouse, but they were all laughing at him, he knew it. How dare they! In a blind rage, he lunged without warning at the Master, reaching for his throat.

Once again, he arced through the air and landed on his face.

The old voice came gently into his mind.

You grow too excited, young man. It is not wise. Calm down and try again.

Torc got up slowly, and as he did so, he glanced at the girl. She was leaning forward, her lips parted, the sun glancing off the smooth wetness inside her mouth. His eyes narrowed. Was there a trace of mockery there?

By the Dryac, a little cunning this time and he'd succeed.

He suffered himself to be placed this way and that, to set his feet there, to raise his elbow just so. He bided his moment, then suddenly, just before the old man gave the ritual command, Torc struck, bowling him over with his sheer bulk. The Harash D'ho let go his hold on Torc and rolled, to rebound onto his feet.

Torc raised his arms in triumph, turning about and about, presenting himself on all four sides. For the first time ever, an outsider without any training had thrown the incumbent champion. He let his gaze linger on the girl.

Behold, the new Harash D'ho!

Out, Gurnyac!

The mentor stood by the cordon gate.

Torc stood defiantly. *But I bested him!*

Fool. He could have broken your back. Now do your obeisance and come with me.

Torc followed the mentor a short way along shaded paths into a sunken garden, a bright round space encircled by ancient dark green foliage. At the center of the garden, like a round dark eye, was a small pool, and at its edge, a stone seat.

"Come, sit."

The mentor walked to the bench, starting bright shapes in the water.

After a moment's hesitation, Torc went, sat.

"There are so many differences, prince, between you and your fellows, as is to be expected, but you'll have to overcome the greatest if you would stay."

If you would stay? There was question of it again? "And what is that?"

The mentor considered him narrowly.

"What would you say it was?"

"I am Gurnyac's son."

D'huru Nor shook his head.

"That is the most *obvious* difference. Not the *greatest*."

"Name it, then."

"The others are here because they *want* to be. You've no idea of the effort and hardship it took just for them to get here."

Torc thought of the Brandmark on the girl's arm. Of chains and guards and locks and bars; of walls and barricades.

Of a vast dark hall of soot and fire where daylight never came . . .

"Those people have come from all over the Known World. Have used their small hoards of piltshengs, have left their homes, their families simply to be here on level eleven. Whereas you—you're here under constraint.

"You don't respect the teachings. Your will, your desire is elsewhere. I tell you, you'll not last the course." The mentor sighed. "They say the young are saplings that bend in the wind. But to my mind there's naught so brittle as a stubborn youth."

Torc's chin went up. "You don't like me, do you, B'hadgazan? Or my being here."

The mentor raised his thick black brows.

"Like and *dislike* are beside the point. I have a conclaur to mind. I've told you what a privilege it is to be here, and I'd *like* to see you make the most of it."

"By emptying chamber pots?" Torc jumped up. "You who know so much—what do you know about me, or what's going on out there? All this scrottery is well for scrots. But I'm supposed to be becoming a king.

"And a king is supposed to wield his mind and body in defense of his kingdom, not spend his time shoveling nightfilth and dancing stately paradees with a decrepit old gont!

"At this moment Gurnyac may be going to the Gradhlzacs. Trouble was stirring when I left and my father's not the man he was. I tell you, this is no place for me to be, and yet, and yet I must, because custom would have it so. Oh, it's too much to bear!"

A bird started from the thicket behind him, took up Torc's loud complaint, and flew with it high up into the air.

To bear, to bear . . . Even the birds here mocked him.
He turned from the mentor to stare down into the water.

"Sit down, prince." D'Huru sighed again. "Such a mixture
you are of man and child. Your thoughts run random as the
lake kuzn skirring the currents without shell."

Torc remained standing.

The mentor sighed. "I believe, young bruk, that there's
nothing you couldn't do if you but set your mind to it. Your
father sent you here. You missed your sohurin, yet still you
came. The Athor would turn you away, and yet you stay.

"But now you withhold yourself. That is a conflict, prince,
that must be resolved if you are to prevail. Have you forgotten
that at the very least you swore to leave worldly matters at the
gate?"

"Words are cheap."

"You think? Prince, you have much to learn of the
K'haravim."

"Try," Torc sneered. "Try to teach me anything."

He sat himself down.

"I'd take you up on that, young bruk, but we have more
pressing business. Before we go back to the D'hogana, you
must know its rules."

Torc's nostrils flared.

Oh, his chest would burst that this scrot should be talking to
him, Gurnyac, of rules. The Gnangars were above rules,
didn't he know? The Gnangars made rules for the rest of the
world to follow. He caught his rage just in time, said merely,
"I see no sense in all that childish mummery."

D'huru Nor folded his arms.

"Its purposes are manifold. D'hogana teaches self-con-
trol—of which you're sorely in need. It directs one's energy
into positive use. And the ritual harmlessly channels our
violent tendencies. But most importantly, D'hogana serves to
prevent, not stir up, strife."

"You surely jest."

"Not at all." The mentor looked out over the pool. "The
other night, a certain young bruk came into the city uninvited

and unannounced, but instead of having the sense to use civil diplomacy, he would have stormed the gates, spilling blood had not two trained guards prevented it. And had blood been spilled, that young man would have been sent from Rm never to return."

Torc looked at the mentor slyly. "The art of D'hogana works wonders on the battlefield, mentor. The Gnangar kings are invincible. And when I know the secret, I'll go home more skilled than ever my father was, and win ever more campaigns."

"I'm sure. You think we don't know the way the Gnangars abuse the sacred art? Just by coming here, even if you learned nothing, your kings are thought to be invested with divine powers. By using our most basic skills against the common man—flouting your solemn vow of nonaggression—your kings command the battlefield. But D'hogana isn't a bag of martial tricks. It's a state of mind."

"Speaking of tricks—I did throw the old man. Doesn't that count for anything?"

"It counts you for a fool. I say again: you'd have stayed a broken back if the Harash D'ho hadn't let go your hand. You deserved it."

Torc leapt up. "The Dryac you say! No one speaks to me that way!"

"More's the pity. I tell you, I wonder how long you'll stay."

"The answer's simple," Torc retorted. "Until the end."

"Mayhap. But only by pitting yourself against us all. If there were no one to fight you'd never make it. Oh, well. These are early days. Who knows how much you might change?"

Torc laughed, sitting down again. "You do. And you judge right. As you judged my fathers."

"Oh? Well, mayhap the siopenar will alter that, prince."

"The *siopenar*? Who's he?"

"Not 'who,' but 'what.' It is the oath of total silence that the pilgrims take next week at the end of the fast, remaining in effect until the last day of the sohurin."

The Dryac! So that was why the silence. Obviously everybody was practicing for it.

"You mean—no one speaks? At all? My father never told me of this."

"Why should he? It's not—"

"I know, I know. '—required on level twelve.'" He regarded the mentor sourly. "What a stupid waste, B'hadgazan. After all this labor and sacrifice, they'll all end up like you!"

The mentor laughed. "A child I called you, and a child you are: a man-child, a warrior hurling childish insults. You think to goad this son of B'hadgazan to combat with such talk? I passed beyond all that many moons ago, my friend." He leaned forward, propping his elbows on his knees, and firmly clasped his hands together under his chin.

"I admit, I come from where you say. And I hadn't notched up many sunarounds before I left in a hurry—a little matter of careless fingers in a wakeful pocket. I fled to Kond, through Xangarat, down through Gurnyac to Asurdun and on to Rm, becoming a pilgrim in hopes of sacred gold.

"But I reckoned without the Athor. On my first day here he spoke with me, promising me all the gold I could carry at the end of my sohurin. I stayed and took my vows. That stay still lasts and will last until I draw my final breath, by the grace of the Quaur."

Torc stretched out his legs to the sun.

A fish leapt in the quiet.

"Who knows what I might have been had I not come into this place. A brigand, perhaps; a pirate, a petty thief of the marketplace, swinging in due course from the boundary gibbet, or hobbling minus a foot on the word of some spadebeard magistrate."

Torc laughed shortly.

"While here you are, virtue incarnate on the topmost rung."

"Alas, no." D'huru Nor tapped the brown stuff of his robe. "I'm but of level four. Third, soon, I hope. Past that it's not permitted to go."

"Ha! And why not?"

"It's not permitted to know that either. You don't question the Lothuri. To question them is to question the Quaur."

Demiel's fire flared on the pool's surface. Torc stared at it, transfixed. Presently, he looked away, shading his eyes.

"How many of those—pilgrims—will end up like you, poking and prying into people's minds?"

"Who can say? One or two, mayhap none. Few, if any, reach level six. And even then, there are some that stay on that level for the rest of their lives, the mindspeech the stumbling block. There are those who can only listen into other minds, those who can reach in but to speak, but success requires both."

"Does it take long to learn?"

"Oh, yes. And the learning requires great discipline in all the rigors of the sohurin except—"

"Except what?"

The mentor looked up, shading his eyes against the glare. "Some have that gift—and others—at birth, by the grace of the Quaur. But they're rare." He stood up. "Come. You've missed enough."

Torc followed him back the way they'd come. What had been the point of it all? Nothing was changed. Was it?

At least his rage was gone, and somehow he felt at peace.

The disciples, paired off now, were working on the grass around the mat—save the melk who, he saw with a quickening of interest, was sitting alone to one side.

You will work with the young female. She is your match, her superior skill balancing your superior height and bulk.

Superior skill. Torc smiled coldly. Had she been privy to that judgment?

Whether or no, the Harash D'ho obviously ordered her to join him. He wondered how she felt about that. The girl stood, made obeisance then walked to an open space and waited while Torc joined her.

Silently, she demonstrated the pattern of steps and movements she'd learned while he'd been gone, then stepped back, waiting for Torc to take up his stance.

Prince, and melk. Oh, how she must hate him. Almost as much as he hated her. He must not let her best him again. He must strike, for the pride of Gurnyac.

He glanced around. There the mentor was, not a dozen paces from them, squatting under the shade of a wide tree.

Torc took a deep breath, then, at her nod, lunged as she'd shown him. A moment later, he lay flat on his back.

Calm and peace were gone in a heartbeat. Rage swelled once again within him, rage and the urge to snap her neck.

Don't even try it, prince. You'll be sorry, else. Match her move for move. That's your only chance.

He got up slowly, his face set. He couldn't believe it. What would his father say, what would Feric say, or anybody, to see him now?

She nodded for him to try again.

The very movement of her head infuriated him. Calm, he must keep calm. Be wily, Feric would say. Put craft to strength if you would be invincible.

This time he was quicker. She staggered, almost fell. He also affected to stumble, rolling in toward her, hoping to bear down on her with all his weight, but at the critical moment she wasn't there.

His shoulder hit the hard grass floor with full force.

"You did well," she said.

Her surprise angered him more.

Aware of the mentor's eye, he went down again and again and again, until Demiel's rays dazzled the tops of the screens and they filed back under the K'haravim.

That night in bed he turned and turned again, felt her hands like iron graphooks on his slippery flesh, saw the broad sunlit planes of her face, her eyes dark, expressionless, the full round breasts straining their band as she braced to move, the sweat-sheen on her thighs.

For all her swell of breast and thigh, her body was hard and lean as a man's.

His skin tingled from the hot sun, his head felt light. His muscles ached and trembled at the same time, and the hole in his gut consumed him.

Oh, but how he hated that place and everyone in it. But most especially the melk.

He dreamed he chased her up and up the winding mountain stair, where he caught her at last, and took her, thrusting himself into her again and again then, wondrously spent, with one last mighty effort, he carried her to the edge of the plateau and hurled her out in a high wide arc.

CHAPTER SIXTEEN

11.27 Hours 12 October 2047
Estralita

THE space in the middle of the lab went dark, the shadowy figure of the prince faded.

"Lights," Ord called, getting up off the stool and stretching, but Shira knew that it wasn't yet over. Grandfather's mind was still locked into the beacon.

"Sir," Prosser said, and pointed to the psimeter, which was still going strong.

"Christ!" Ord looked at the chronister. "It's gone eleven! What's happening to him!"

Shira ignored him. A faint murmur was coming from the back of her mind. She closed her eyes, tried to go deeper. She'd been squatting by the wall now without moving since the visions began, not needing Ord's hologram, seeing the whole thing unfold within just as Grandfather was doing, hearing just as much as they via the synergizer—and feeling it as they never could.

Ord mumbled something about being hungry.

Suk went into the observation booth, brought out soycaf and cookies. Shira felt her nudge, waved her away without even opening her eyes. She mustn't lose concentration. She was tiring some, for she'd never stayed in continuous contact with anybody this long. Grandfather was tiring, too, she could sense it, but his energy level was still high, higher than it had ever been before.

The murmuring grew more distinct, voices, then just Grandfather's, in her head. And now out through the synergizer into the lab.

She pressed her fists against her forehead to squeeze her surroundings out.

. . . the first few days after her return from Pruth Tanna trod close by the wall, even though Gar had stayed behind.

Nothing seemed changed. Bells rang, folk went to board. There were the usual late-night carousals, and brawls and gossip. Intrigue there was a-plenty, but it concerned only who was sleeping with whom and who had won the latest jousting match. In the banquet hall Brac still sat at Sharroc's right hand; Feric his left.

The general looked just the same, and as ever occasionally his great loud laugh hit the rafters. Sometimes, perhaps feeling her eye upon him, he'd look up and along the tables in her direction but if he ever noticed her he gave no sign. It was as if they'd never met that night at all.

But not everything was the same.

Life was bleak without Torc. She felt lonely, bereft. Contrary to what she'd told Feric, no one bothered her. And that was strange. Torc must have made her position really clear about the citadel.

On the seventh night after her return, she was so unbearably lonely that she crept down to the scroll room . . .

A noise from Ord. Shira opened her eyes briefly, saw the TS shimmering. Saw Ord, soycaf in hand, staring toward the empty space as it filled now with dim lamplight in a low, wide chamber.

She closed her eyes again and there was the girl, looking not much older than Shira herself, sitting at what looked like a

Victorian writing desk, stroking it as though it were very precious to her.

She sighed a deeper sigh. And here the girl's thoughts came through Grandfather's mind; thought tinged with all the subtlety of her feeling. There was fear there, tension: the fear of being caught. But also a longing, a homesickness every bit as intense as Shira's own, but sadder, much sadder: it was for time that would never come again.

Tanna closed her eyes, savoring the special smell of the scribal chamber; a musky smell of parchment and ink and wax and old dry wood. Durac's chamber had been high and narrow, yet well lit with clerestory and skylights. Often she'd sat up in the storage gallery looking down on her father's bent head.

This chamber was low and wide with no windows at all. Only lamps, in wall and ceiling; one standing tall by the scribe's scrip-board.

She well recalled her father's desk: a plainer piece than this, having none of the heavy gilt and flying panels. There'd been birds on Florian's desk: fessbirds sucking on ripe peculars, well out of reach of leaping langaurs beneath. The lines had felt so smooth in the mellow wood, not harshly chiseled as the cronets and crests and crowns on this royal stand.

She rested her hand on the sloping scrip-board, remembering Durac's hands moving over his scrolls. Graceful hands, economical and compact as he himself had been.

Tanna got up from the tall stool. So long, since she'd sat on her father's, pretending to be scribe in his place. Sitting there brought back such happy memories. But she mustn't linger, mustn't be seen in there.

She crossed to the scrip-chest where, with the aid of a small knife from her pocket, she prised it open and stole two parchment rolls, and filled her empty perfume flask with precious ink.

Then she pulled down the chest lid and reclosed the lock. If the royal scribe found anything missing, or noticed the faint scratches around the padlock he'd never suspect her.

She went back to her chamber and bolted the door.

There she prepared to begin what was to be a nightly journal, which, she promised herself, she'd keep until Torc came back. Into it, in her fine neat script, she'd pour her loneliness, her thoughts, her feelings, filling the time she'd have spent in his bed until she could sleep.

From under her own narrow cot she pulled a small dower chest, and, lifting out the choice laces and semiprecious stones and rings that Florian had given her, she pressed a catch, raising the bottom. In the tiny secret space beneath lay a flat black box fastened with a gold clasp.

This she took up and sitting back on her bed she set it on her knee, and raised the lid.

Inside, on a cushion of gold harpile, lay her precious writing tools. First, the gleter: set of ink blades cut into different shapes and thicknesses; then the rille: bundle of quills—the quill being handle and ink-reservoir for the gleter; the shahn: hair-fine wire to ream a blade's ink groove while in the quill; a phoull: rod of pale hard green stone for sharpening the gleter; a morthe: pot of red chalk for canceling errors, and the grosch: small granular sack, blotter bag splotched with old ink.

She ran her fingers over the blades, lightly touching each one, mouthing their names silently, remembering how she'd learned to fit them to the quill, remembering the nights and nights she'd spent by the hearth learning their uses. How each one was shaped exactly to the scribe's needs: himele, curved like a young moon for short, blunt lettering; needle-sharp licene for lines no thicker than a spider's thread—her favorite. Indeed, for so long she played with that one, honing it to such a fine point and tracing wiggly lines all over the parchment, that Durac would search her box for the pet spider he said she kept to do her work.

Her face softened. For five sunarounds these tools had lain hidden.

Five sunarounds.

Durac was but bone by now, although she could never

picture him that way. Whenever she spoke with him in her mind, he was always as she remembered him in his gray harsilk robe, the color of his scant gray beard and the shrewd gray eyes under the hang of his gray brows.

She reached in and took up licene, sharpened it against the phoul. Now, Durac, she whispered, let's just see how well I've kept your mystery.

For three more nights she sat in the closeness of her tiny cell scratching away, drying the ink with the grosch, rolling the parchment up tightly and stowing it back under her dower silks.

Thirty-two days of loneliness, she wrote on the fourth night. *And this day dull as ever. I shall go mad. My body swells for love—but from only one lover.*

She paused. What a fool she was, pretending to a love that didn't exist nor could ever. She was living a fantasy. She was, and only ever could be for Torc, no more than a body to be used.

She pouted stubbornly. Not a fantasy. It had been done before. Hadn't Queen Teriane been born of a third equerry? Her blade had saved the then crown prince one night, when he would have fallen by his uncle's sword. Then there was Shour, born a slave, who won King Morhok's heart. He'd offered her freedom, then the bed of first concubine, but she'd refused, risking death in her pride. Instead of having her put down, Morhok made her queen.

As those women had succeeded, so might she.

She dipped licene, tapped off the excess ink.

Whatever happens, as I gave Torc my word, so shall I keep it.

She leaned back, admiring the perfection of her lettering, the straightness of the lines. She would have liked to embellish them with flowers and birds and curlicues, but she had to make the parchment last.

Promises.

She'd promised to stay faithful. An easy enough promise to keep, with Gar still in Pruth. But what when he came back?

She pushed that thought away uneasily.

She'd also promised to be Torc's eyes and ears.

Since her return she'd heard nothing, seen nothing.

And how could she expect to, going to ground straight after evening board? If anything were to be seen, it was in the dark hours—even now. Who knows what might be happening out there? Or who might be moving from stable to citadel—or barracks—and back again? What a coward she was. All she'd heard were rumors of riots and pillaging near the Weald.

Not rumors. It was the truth.

She began to write again. *Those troubles didn't start in the Weald, but from within this very citadel. Torc thought so, and I know so. And I know who might be behind them.*

She paused, then scratched out *know*. She didn't, not really.

She thought again of the night Feric had so suddenly crossed her path. Because of him the man had gotten clear away. But suspicions weren't enough. She had to be sure.

If only I had proof, she wrote. *I would be able to send word to Rm.* She halted, absently scribing the R with tiny, rolling waves.

How would she send word?

And what if it weren't Feric at all? What if he'd been keeping a weather eye around the place, and in turn, had seen and suspected her? Then was she in jeopardy indeed, for Feric did have the ear of the king.

She wiped the blade clean. If only she could talk to someone, anyone. But she couldn't. No one would listen to her. Not Sharroc. Certainly not Meltha. Not Brac—and *not* Gar!

She saw again Feric's eyes glittering in the starlight, the glint of steel as it pressed into her chest.

Who, then? Who, if not any of them?

She cleared her writing things away.

Then, wrapping her mantle close about her, she slipped out through the servants' door and down the back stairs.

The moment Tanna reached the shadow of the stables she doubted her impulse. Why had she come there? That first night had been but a coincidence. A dead man had been hidden, retrieved. If she suspected Feric, better she take a walk by the barracks, and not for just one night.

She was turning to leave when there came a sudden shout from the stable front, and the sound of thars coming, fast. She had no sooner made the shadow of the first rank of stalls when a rider burst into the stable yard, his gonfalon trailing in his wake. One glimpse of the Gnangar colors and brilliant yellow streamers inferior sent her fleeing back to the dim stalls where the dead man had lain.

Gar was back from Pruth.

She must take the side door, now, and get back to her room, fast. And if he sent for her this night, she'd say she had the flux. A lie, for she'd had it during the last week in Pruth, but he was not to know that.

She padded along by the stalls, and opened the side door a slit, just as she'd done that other night. Now, as then, the sky was clear. Overhead, and close enough to reach up and pluck, Ao hung like a ripe pecular, while far beyond her, tiny, remote, Forthyr glistened, still bright pin in the wheeling firmament.

She stepped out, drew back again, not breathing.

A man had rounded the stable front and was hurrying by the path leading to the barracks.

After a second, she slipped out and followed him, her heart beating faster and faster, and not just an account of the sudden exertion. What if she were seen again?

What if—she relaxed a little—what if the man were on some perfectly innocent errand?

Ahead were the bright lights of the compound. He'd have to turn aside soon or be challenged by the barracks sentries.

Suddenly, into the moonlight, stepped Feric, barring the

man's way. She waited, her blood leaping, for Feric to challenge the man, as he'd challenged her that night by the towers. But he didn't. Instead, at a word from Feric, they both turned from the bright path into the dark bushes dividing barracks from citadel.

She must go while she could. Run back to her chamber and into the safety of her bed. But her feet took her the other way until the two men stopped in a small moonlit clearing.

She moved closer, tree by tree, the murmur of voices growing louder, yet still not quite distinct. What could they be talking about, Gar's man and the king's general? What could they possibly—

Quite clearly she saw the man's hand come up, holding something out. Feric took it, turned it, and held it up to the light. Then, nodding, he slipped it inside his cloak.

She'd seen something like it before, in Aravac's hand: a small wooden stick, with teeth down one side of it. Torc hadn't told her what it was at first, not until after he'd taken her back to bed. A shuktek, he'd called it: call-stick to a cabal.

There was treason in the citadel, he'd told her, and that was the proof. Whoever had issued it was after Sharroc's crown.

Now there was Feric at that very moment standing but a few paces from her accepting a like thing from this man of Gar's. How? What could it mean? Was Gar a traitor also?

The men turned suddenly and came toward her.

Quickly, she slid around the broad trunk of the tree, and pressed against it, under the shelter of her cloak.

They reached her, and walked past.

". . . shall be there, and then we have Gar. After, I myself shall to the king. I'll pay you well for this, Ebral."

Saluting, Ebral took his leave, making for the stables, while Feric set off along the path leading back to the barracks gate.

When Tanna moved at last, her knees were so weak that she almost fell down.

*   *   *

She climbed the turret stair to her room, bolted the door, threw off her clothes, and burrowed under her covers.

But she couldn't sleep.

Gar's man, Ebral—she'd often seen him about the citadel—promoted from barracks sergeant into Gar's service as a minor aide—and Feric—doing what? She saw the shuktek in Feric's hand, heard his plain satisfaction:

. . . shall be there, and then we have Gar. After, I myself shall to the king. I'll pay you well for this, Ebral . . .

Feric! More Torc's father than Sharroc, they said.

She had been right! He was the one—and to think, Torc had gone to him on the night of his departure! Lucky for him that Brac had also been there, or perhaps Torc might not have lived to go to Rm.

Could she go to the king now? Or to Brac? She huddled under the sheets. If they wouldn't listen to Torc, and he with shuktek in hand, what chance had she to make them listen to empty words against the king's own man?

But Gar . . .

However much she despised him, was he not still the king's son? Could she stand by and watch him die by Feric's hand? After him, the king would follow, so Feric had said. *Then what of Torc thereafter?*

She sat up in the dark.

What a pretty pass things had come to. Not only was she Torc's eyes and ears, but arm, too. Whatever the cost, there was only one thing to do.

She slipped her feet to the floor and reached for her dress.

Gar received her in a small anteroom off his front hall. He was reclining on a narrow daybed, the sort much in use about the Citadel for dispatching quick and urgent favors. The insult wasn't lost on her. But, she reminded herself, she mustn't lose her head. On the way there she'd decided exactly what to say and do to escape intact from that place.

His teeth gleamed white in his beard. "How pleasant, lady, to see you. But I've not sent for you as yet."

"It's not that. I must speak with you, urgently."

Gar swung his feet to the floor. "Don't be coy. Everyone, including my brother, knows that you'll end up in my bed sooner or later."

He stood up, moved toward her.

"Highness," Tanna spoke quickly. "One of your household is working you grave harm."

Gar frowned. "Harm?"

"Before I say more—" She hesitated, but when he didn't interrupt her, she went on. "I would have your word that I'll leave here this night for the queen's tower as freely as I came."

She took a deep breath but all Gar said was, "Speak on."

Tanna told him everything, realizing as she did so what she was giving away: how she felt about him, how she'd hidden from him, and where, indirectly revealing her precious refuge. She told him of the night that Torc left, of following the man along the path behind the barracks. And of this last night, of seeing Feric with Gar's adaide, the shuktek that had changed hands.

"The last thing I heard was that Feric was first going to deal with you and then His Majesty, the king. I had the feeling that it was going to be very soon."

"And my man's name, lady?"

She hesitated. This was the hardest part, for in pronouncing his name she was condemning him to certain death.

"Ebral."

"Ebral!" Gar's mouth set in a thin, tight slit, like Torc's when he was angry. "You will remain here," he said, then went out.

She ran to the door, put her ear to it, heard only feet swiftly cross and recross the hall.

She went to the window, parted the harpile drapes, her arms opened wide, seeking Ao's comfort; saw instead red Hawcasyr, huge balestar that men called Death's Beacon. She snapped the curtains shut again, closing out the dread omen and her pale and startled reflection subtending it.

The edge of Gar's daybed sagged under her sudden weight.

She leaned forward, put her head between her knees, and there she stayed until she heard Gar's voice at the door.

"Here, lady. Now shall you call out the man face to face."

Ebral stood to attention in the center of the chamber, still the soldier for all his fancy harpile livery.

She met his eye briefly, looked down.

"Well?"

She bit her lip. "It was Ebral whom I saw. And his name that I heard."

"You're sure, lady?"

"Certain." Her voice trembled.

The flamelight from the sconces caught the man's eye. A baleful light. Like Hawcasyr's.

"You will wait," Gar said to her.

"But you said—"

He strode to the door, threw it open.

"The Lady Tanna will make herself comfortable in my bedchamber," he called. "She is to have anything for her comfort. Out," he added softly. "Unless you'd rather stay and see this one present his account."

She left, beside herself with fear and rage and remorse. From the doorway, she looked back. Ebral stood rigid, unmoving, betraying nothing of his state of mind.

He was dead already, she thought, going out. And by the Quaur, because of her.

Gar's chief adaide walked her into Gar's bedchamber and shut her in.

She waited a moment or two, lifted the latch, and opened the door a crack. The two men standing to either side presented arms. Gar's adaide appeared from nowhere.

"You wished for something, lady?"

"No." She shut the door in his face and crossed to the far wall to lean against it, eyes closed.

Presently, she began to move restlessly about the room, staring at the trophied walls, looking anywhere but at Gar's great bed.

Suddenly there came a sound that stopped her very breath. Not loud enough to prick curious minds, but full of agony.

Another sound followed and another, until they became one long continuous moan.

She leaned forward and pressed her hands to her ears.

Through the hissing in her head came a scream; short, sharp and high, too high, surely for a man.

Then silence.

She lowered her hands and slowly straightened up.

Gar was smiling when he came through the door.

"I shall now thank you, lady, for your services."

She backed against the wall.

"I asked leave to go," she whispered.

"So you did. And so you shall—after."

His smiled vanished.

"You'll not speak of this night to anyone, do you hear, or your life won't be worth a rak."

"Aren't you going to the king?"

"What, and repeat my brother's mistake? *Sairah*, I'll reveal Feric's treachery in my own way. And in my own time," he finished, moving toward her.

The attack was swift and fierce, and without preamble.

How, oh how, she said to herself over and over, could anything so short take so long? Torc's fierceness had been of passion with no ill intent—indeed, often it had only roused her to like response. But this savage and brutal . . . man had no idea . . . *O Torc, Torc,* she cried silently, *I never missed you as much as I do at this moment . . .*

At last, she lay panting on the coverlet.

Gar subsided onto her, squashing her very breath from her body.

"I see why my brother kept you so long. You only feed the appetite."

Laughing, he rolled off her and pulled her on top of him. She twisted in his arms, tried to sit up.

But the night had been too much for her. The stables, the shock of seeing Feric's treachery. The horrible moaning from next door. And now this, that she'd tried so hard to avoid.

With awful suddenness, hot caustic fluid welled from her gut, spilling out and down as though it would never, ever stop.

CHAPTER SEVENTEEN

14.12 Hours 12 October 2047
Estralita

SHIRA stirred, aware of movement around her.

The holoverter was off—how long? Ord, squashed between her and Grandfather, was leaning over to take off the headband.

She felt queasy; the sight and sound of Tanna's retching was still strongly with her.

"You feeling okay, hon?" Suk was peering at her from the other side of the couch.

Shira got up stiffly. "Thanks."

She watched Ord hand over the headset to Suk, who stowed it away. She turned from them in sudden distaste, stepping back to make room for the gurney that would take her grandfather back upstairs. Voyeurs, the lot of them. This whole synergizer thing had grown obscene, with those people sitting there, pulling out a man's private thoughts and spinning them out again, like a show on the public compuscreen.

She stopped with a blush. Hadn't she done worse?

Shira flipped back her hair in self-disgust, a mistake.

"Hey—careful."

MacAllister caught her, steadied her.

215

Suk and Prosser slid her grandfather onto the gurney, maneuvered him out into the passageway toward the elevator. She turned to follow, swayed, and fell back against the wall.

Again MacAllister caught her and held on this time.

"You don't look so great."

She could well imagine. She felt exhausted. Drained. God, was that how Grandfather felt after these sessions?

Of course not. He had the sense to sleep them off.

"May I borrow your arm?" Shira looked up into the sleepy eyes.

MacAllister's grip tightened. "Sure."

He walked her down the passageway, squashed them into the elevator beside the gurney. Shira saw Suk staring at MacAllister's hand on her arm. Oh, Lord, her legs were trembling so. Shira closed her eyes and, the devil take Suk, leaned her head against MacAllister's chest.

The girl, Tanna. She'd been raped, hadn't she? The barbaric prince Torc had as good as raped the innkeeper's daughter on the way to Asurdun, although Shira hadn't actually witnessed that. Even so, somehow that hadn't distressed Shira half so much as the conscious evil desire to hurt that she'd just seen. The white face haunted her. Its pain, its horror, its utter hopelessness. She made a small sound in her throat.

MacAllister leaned down. "You say something?"

She shook her head, her eyes closed. "No."

The elevator jolted to a stop.

Clang. Rumble.

MacAllister steered her out after the gurney.

As Suk and Prosser wheeled her grandfather through into the little apartment, MacAllister turned her around to face him.

"Can I do something for you?"

"I—no." She wanted to get into bed for a year. Dream the evil away.

"You haven't eaten since breakfast, you know. Tell you what: I'll get us both something on a tray, and after that you sleep. Okay?"

Suk, pushing past, looked back with pointed curiosity.

"Okay," Shira said.

She closed the door on them all, crossed into her grand-father's room. He'd gone deep. Actually, she thought, gazing down on him, he looked better. More rested than she'd ever seen him, even though she knew he'd reached his limit psionically.

However would she face him when he awoke? She dared not let him know that she'd eavesdropped upon his thoughts, even though most of them had ended up on display anyway.

She went out, closed the door quietly behind her.

The wonder was that he'd even let her stay, in view of the goings on on that planet. He wouldn't send her home now, would he? It was too late, she'd tell him, if he tried.

A light tap on the outer door, and MacAllister brought in a loaded tray.

Shira ate most of her share, drank four cups of soycaf.

She didn't speak.

MacAllister sat opposite her, eating with great concentra-tion, making no attempt at conversation either.

Presently, she began to feel a little better.

MacAllister loaded the tray to take it out again, inclined his head.

"You're looking human again. You'll look even better for a nap."

She stood up, promptly sat down.

"Here, let me."

MacAllister set down the tray, and walked her into her room and onto her bed. He took up her folded cover from the bottom rail, and spread it over her with a flourish, tucking in the edges.

"There. You want anything else?"

She looked up at him gratefully from over the edge of the cover.

"No."

He turned to go.

"MacAllister—"

He turned back, his eyebrows raised.

"Thanks."

He grinned. "That's okay, partner," he said, and walked to the door.

"Wait!"

He stopped again, came back to the bed.

"MacAllister—what do you think it all means?"

MacAllister perched. "Well, now." He crossed his legs. "We sent a probe out there once. A kind of space greeting card. It wasn't a whole lot of stuff: couple of diagrams, few formulas, in binary code. And yet it told a whole lot about who we were—where we were.

"This could be something similar, only in a different form, I guess."

"You think that?"

"No." He grinned at her. "I don't think anything."

She came up on one elbow. "MacAllister—trake that! It's me you're talking to!" She sat up, folded her arms about her knees. "If it's as you say, what's the point? They aren't there anymore, Grandfather says."

MacAllister shot her a quick look. "He hasn't told you why, eh? Perhaps he doesn't know after all," he muttered, as though to himself.

"What I don't get," Shira said, "is why this part of their history. I mean, it didn't start right there, did it?"

"Like dragon's teeth, you mean? I thought about that. I tried to decide what bits of Earth's past I'd pick to show the odd alien, and I couldn't. I thought ah! the Greeks, at one time. Then the Romans. But there was a lot before that. China. Mesopotamia. Africa, South America. The Levant. God knows what was crucial to where we are today.

"But they seem to know what they're doing. All this has some significance, some relevance to them. Maybe to us, as well."

He looked at her.

"Do you realize how astonishing that alien beacon is? It did its programmed job, undid the damage it caused, then selected an alternative procedure compatible with your Grandfather's capabilities—which are considerable, by the way."

"It sure makes you wonder." Shira stared down thoughtfully at her knees.

MacAllister stood up.

"Do you know where Phrynis is?" she asked quickly. She didn't want him to leave now.

"You think Ellisen would tell me?" He made her lie down, then he tucked her in again. "Young lady—sleep!"

"Are you going away this afternoon?"

He laughed. "Are you the mind reader!"

"Actually, it doesn't take much to guess. You daren't relay that much stuff to Ellisen, because of Hengst, so you're going to have to hop it to him. Will you be gone long?"

"I'll be back before you know it. Susann Ellisen was disappointed you couldn't come, by the way, when I gave her your regrets."

"Oh." Shira's face grew warm. She'd quite forgotten the woman. That morning seemed an eternity away now.

"I suppose we'll never get asked again."

"She sent you a rain check. Now: eyes closed!"

"Aye-aye, sir."

She heard him shut her door, heard the outer one click. She sighed, and settled down under the cover.

The moment she closed her eyes, there was Tanna's stricken face.

Shira snapped her head this way and that trying to shake the horrible playback from her mind. She imagined Gar's hands on her, imagined him lying on top of her, forcing her.

She groaned, and turned over onto her back.

Her thoughts quieted.

Tanna was beautiful. *Voluptuous*. What was it like, she wondered, to have a body like that? She herself was straight up and down, like a pole.

She traced her own small breasts, almost nonexistent when she lay flat. No man had ever touched them, not even Kirrin, but then one couldn't, not in the Bourg. Life was so different there from the outside world, as she'd seen on her travels with her grandfather. Not that folk didn't have their urges. Her friends did, she knew. In fact, sometimes she wondered if they ever thought of anything else.

But think and talk was all they ever did. Public morals were strictly guarded in the Hesikastor's community.

Out here, people joined up any old time, before marriage, after, or regardless altogether.

She'd tried many times to picture how it would be, making love. She had an idea that Aunt Marita had talked about it with her elder sisters. But she was still considered too young even to think of such things, even though she'd just promised to wed Kirrin.

And Kirrin himself was only a boy, she supposed. Certainly compared to those Gurnyac princes, although he must be about their age.

Seeing Torc and Tanna in bed together had stirred her strangely, made her wonder how Kirrin and she . . . but Tanna and Gar—oh, God!

She got up off the bed, walked into the sitting room.

MacAllister.

Now he was a man.

He'd never behave like that. She could see his blue eyes now, looking at her, his mouth in that cockeyed grin. If she and he were together, how would it be?

Her face grew hot. For shame. What was happening to her? No wonder the public compuscreen in the Bourg was run by the community elders.

She curled into the corner of the couch.

What would they say if they knew what she'd seen!

The next time the beacon contacted Grandfather, would they learn more about Tanna? About that horrible Gar? Grandfather wouldn't like it, but she wished that one dead.

And Prince Torc, too? He certainly was brutal, and yet . . .

He was different somehow. How? Was it because she'd gotten inside his head, had sensed not so much cruelty as ignorance? No. It was more than that. If she got inside that Gar's head she'd find a sadistic brute. Evil, malicious, and totally without redemption.

Torc needed a bump or two.

And was probably getting it under the mountain. *The K'haravim.* If he found that place uncomfortable, he should try the Bourg!

She sighed. Now they had to stay and wait for the beacon to make contact again. Two weeks since the first time. Would it be that long again? Two more weeks before something more happened to break the awful monotony of that place?

To Shira's surprise, her question was answered the very next day.

Her grandfather was in the middle of routine visualization exercises—via the 'verter, of course.

Ord's new toy.

One minute, Grandfather was sculpting color patterns, and in the next, the rainbow vortices in the middle of the lab floor were blown away by a sudden rushy darkness.

The TS flashed silver, went dark.

The beacon?

Dare she go in again?

Grandfather need never know. He hadn't seemed to suspect anything when he awoke that morning, and facing him hadn't been half as bad as she'd feared.

He'd only asked her if she'd been upset by what she'd seen. Yes, she'd said, but she wasn't going home, and he needn't try to make her. He hadn't said anything, only gotten on with his breakfast.

That in itself bothered her. He'd been distant from her, she'd almost think he'd forgotten she was there. And it wasn't the kind of distant he was when he was having visions. It felt different. . . .

. . . As though he were far away, even while he was sitting opposite her, sipping his soycaf.

She ought to be glad that he'd been too preoccupied to sense her unease. However, she shouldn't push her luck, but go back to watching the 'verter.

She looked to the empty space where the images would come at any moment.

Watching out there would seem so tame now. The difference, between seeing those people move, hearing them speak, and sharing their thoughts was extraordinary. If it were Torc or Tanna again, she couldn't bear to watch them from the outside. Not now.

She had to risk it again. She wasn't doing any harm, and she'd never eavesdrop any other time than this.

She cupped her hands around her face, so the others in the lab wouldn't notice, closed her eyes, and went inside.

All around her was darkness, and deep cold.

Her inner sight adjusting, she recognized the little plateau out on the holy mountainside, and very vaguely discerned the pilgrims sitting huddled in their robes.

How long had passed since the last time? she wondered. Was Torc there? Yes, Grandfather was slipping into his mind right . . . now.

Oh.

It felt different. There was a sense of . . . surrender? Certainly not. Resignation? Closer. He was very very tired, in mind and in spirit. And hungry. Maybe that was why the edge of his hostility was dulled . . .

You do well, Gurnyac.

It took Torc some moments for the words to penetrate.

Spare the eulogies, B'hadgazan.

Strange to think what bearable life came down to: a small degree of warmth above the freezing point, shelter from wind, a bite to fuel the blood, and sleep.

But you do. You're finer; tighter. Fitter.

A month's starvation would do as much for any other man.

You don't look starved.

I'd trade my cronet for a haunch of harmeat and a jug of hlath.

Mayhap. Yet you must admit to some improvement. Aren't you even now meditating?

Mentor: the stillness of my mind is born of torpor out of fatigue. This is the hour at which I'd end, not begin, my day.

Torc slid back into limbo, into a gray space through which at intervals floated gray-black images, grainy fragments slow-drifting aimlessly across his inner vision.

Not of Gurnyac. That seemed so far right now. Here was what mattered. The mountain. The mentor, who had so much power over them all. Or so it seemed. Over when they ate. When they slept. And rested. Over everything they did—and did not do.

Three times in one week he'd sent Torc back to his cell with but a jug of water to last him, and for comparatively trivial matters, it seemed to Torc.

He thought of Tanna much less these days. She, too, had lost solidity in his mind.

His mind dwelled these days on the precious hours of sunshine, the visits to the mess chamber, and his times alone on his cot.

And the melk . . .

. . . graceful body, glimpsed only now and then in the dim bathhouse, now that he kept from her lest he once again made spectacle of himself before the others . . .

. . . startled face the day before in the D'hogana at his first and hardly won success, and the fleeting smile with which she acknowledged it . . .

. . . cool eyes, firm mouth, controlled movements . . . total inaccessibility.

Still as mountain stone he sat, huddled in his robe while below the plateau the mists writhed and churned. He never would have believed he'd ever sit thus, but day after day of it did take its toll on one.

That morning, after a thimbleful of hitaku and a small skalu cake drenched in loile honey, the subconclaurs were reassigned to fresh tasks.

Torc braced himself. According to his reckoning, it was time for the pulp wagons again, but instead, his group was directed down to a level deeper than he'd yet been.

As he trudged through cavern after cavern, he began to feel a strange unease. Had something perhaps been not right with his cake and honey?

The conclaur came onto a long wide cavern filled with rows of oblong vats set up on blocks. The smell now was so thick he began to feel quite definitely ill.

The spore caves, prince, where our food comes from.

Torc peered into one of the vats.

It was half filled with a fine humus that gave off a strange blue radiance. From the surface of this humus was sprung clusters of globular golden fungi.

D'huru Nor handed Torc a rake. The others, obviously knowing the routine, were already reaching over and carefully gathering the fungi, one pilgrim to each vat.

This is yours, prince. Watch the others, and do likewise.

Torc took the rake, but no sooner had he made one or two halfhearted swipes across the humus, than he dropped the rake with a clatter and doubled over, heaving.

Come.

D'huru Nor led him by the elbow through the blue gloom into the cold flamelit passage outside where the air by comparison was sweet.

Bend over, that's it. Now breathe deep.

Torc bent over, his hands braced on his knees and did as the mentor said. It was worse than the sickest feeling after a winegorging.

He wanted to die.

Better?

Torc straightened up, his nostrils pinched against the stench.

No. I'll never be better. I can't go back in.

He put his hands to his nose. His very pores exuded the stink of the fungus. He smelled his sleeve. The stuff of his robe was impregnated with it. He closed his eyes again, his head swimming.

You must. You'll get used to it. Everyone does, in time. That—mold—in there: that's our food?

Don't look so disgusted, lad. Yes, that's what we eat, and drink, too. That's what the skalu cakes are made of, and from its fermentation comes the blessed hitaku. It's the greatest form of sustenance in the Known World—and the littlest known, for it grows nowhere but here. It's the humus. We get it from the deepest passages. We don't know what causes the glow, but that's the host for the holy fungus, by the grace of the Quaur. It's forbidden to take it from the mountain.

No danger of that, B'hadgazan. Torc, feeling marginally better, reopened his eyes, moved off the wall. *Why can't the Lothuri eat like normal people?*

The mentor grinned faintly. *It's forbidden to take life. And animal flesh coarsens the body and the spirit. Hitaku is better for both.*

Then the Lothuri are hypocrites, for isn't hitaku itself alive? To be true to their word, the Lothuri should not eat at all, but live on air.

To Torc's surprise, the mentor looked pleased. *Your skill in the Dialectic grows, prince. But argument aside, you speak true. One of these days, they'll do exactly that. However, until then we tend those vats. So come on, gird up your loins. We have yet a morning's work to do.*

The picture faded with the mentor's voice, but Shira couldn't move. She was vaguely aware of movement around her, somebody brushing past her, asking her something.

She must stir herself, not let them see her with her eyes closed like that, must not let anybody suspect.

But she just stayed there, keeping her eyes shaded from them all. She couldn't stir, any more than Grandfather could. She sensed him, lying on the couch, still as death.

Voices, the distant voices again. Lots of them, as in a large gathering, and Grandfather's mingled with them. What were they saying to one another—and to him? Whatever it was, he wasn't sharing it with Ord and Ellisen.

Or her.

She felt left out.

Grandfather's voice came alone now.

Out it came, the gentle syllables, through the synergizer, echoing through the silent lab. Strange, to hear it outside and inside the darkness of her head at the same time . . .

That night, between bathhouse and bed, the mentor led the conclaur to a new high rock-chamber . . .

Torc stood aghast on the threshold, staring around at the whitewashed walls lined with shelves, shelves stacked with scrolls such as were confined by royal decree to the royal Gurnyac castles and ducal palaces.

He moved forward and taking one up, unfurled it.

A chart of the northern heavens.

He took down another, found a listing of the ports of the Known World.

The Annals of the Five Kingdoms. Rules of weights and measures. Laws of numbers. The telling of letters. The Schemes of the Dialectic itself.

You will please replace them tidily, prince. You're allowed only one at a time.

Torc looked around.

Along the walls were set reading tables where already some of the conclaur were working. He looked to the mentor perplexed. These scrots could read?

Not only read, Gurnyac. Write also. See.

Along the back wall were scribal desks equipped with writing materials.

Torc eyed them angrily. *These things are for use only by royal license. These scrots are not members of the scribal guild. It is against the law for them to know the mysteries.*

This is not Gurnyac, prince. If the sight offends you, stay in your cell.

Even as the mentor's thought came, several pilgrims sat at the desks and with well-practiced hands took out pale writing sheets and flat boxes of the gleter, the rille, and the phoull.

Torc went forward, snatched up a sheet from the nearest pilgrim, rubbed it between finger and thumb, then sniffed it. It was not parchment. Not the skin of forhar.

Behold wephar, prince. Made by the Lothuri themselves from ligwood bark beaten to a pulp.

Torc threw it down again, and turning back to the center of the chamber noticed the line of tables down its length set with wooden chukar boards and matching pieces.

He sought the mentor's attention, outraged.

What now, Gurnyac? Cannot thee find something to occupy thyself?

They play chukar? The game of kings?

That's what you in Gurnyac call it. But the game is older than the Gnangars, prince, neither did they devise it. It is long played in many countries around the Known World. A fitting game for silent players, its two words "chak" and "chukar" being so easily signaled by hand.

I'd like to see them play. Only those trained to high battle strategy can do such.

I do believe I hear a touch of scorn in that thought, prince. Perhaps I should find you a partner to challenge.

Torc advanced to the first table, picked up the dark king, weighed it in his hand. *I think I'd not waste my time.*

Are you afraid, Gurnyac? I can't blame you, after all you've been through in the D'hogana.

Torc's anger flared. *You think I fear these ignorant scrots? There's not the one here who can better me.*

He scanned the chamber angrily, caught the melk looking his way, and such was the glance she gave him one would have thought he'd shouted the words out loud.

Then you have nothing to fear. Prince, sit down.

Torc sat.

D'huru Nor walked down the room, past the pilgrims who were even now applying themselves to various tasks about the place, and brought back with him the hairless one, or Old Glabrous, as Torc had taken to calling him.

The man, smiling broadly, sat opposite Torc, took up the two kings, enclosed them in his fists, and held them out.

D'huru Nor patted Torc on the back. *Now's your chance to shine, prince. I'll wish you luck. You'll need it, as you'll see.*

Torc clamped his jaw tight and tapped Old Glabrous's left fist. In it was the dark king. Bah! He'd given Old Glabrous the advantage.

Don't look so put out, Gurnyac. You can well afford to, as you said.

Smiling wryly, the mentor moved away.

The old man set down the kings in their places, and the game began.

Torc moved quickly, snapping the pieces about the board almost before Old Glabrous could finish his moves, impatient to be rid of the old gont . . . which looked to be easy, for the man responded just as promptly.

Torc could scarce keep the smile off his face. Why, the fool was moving all his pieces up the flanks, a weak and foolish strategy. He seemed not to recognize Torc's advancing spearhead.

On the tenth move Old Glabrous signaled chak.

Torc stared at the board uncomprehending.

Chak?

Old Glabrous traced his mottled finger about the board from citadel to priest to thar.

Torc sat stunned. His monarch was hemmed about on all sides. He studied the board through slitted eyes. Maybe if he—no. Or if he—not that either. The Dryac! Three moves and Torc was finished!

Fool's luck, they called it at home.

No matter.

He looked about quickly, so see if anyone was watching. No one seemed to be. He would play another, wipe this old man.

Torc snatched up the two kings, enclosed them in his fists, and held them out.

He lost the next game, and the next, and the next.

By this time, spectators crowded around the board.

The moment Old Glabrous signaled chukar, Torc upended the board in a rage. The board clattered to the floor, the pieces scattered.

So did the spectators.

A moment's silence, and the old man rose with a nod and wandered off to challenge someone else.

Torc got up too, strode to the scroll shelves, took down a chart of the northern heavens, and sat with it on one of the desks facing the wall.

There he stayed, elbows on the slope of the scripboard, chin in his hands, brooding over the parchment. All the advantages he'd enjoyed, that he'd been told belonged to him alone, by virtue of his rank and birth—these nobodies had here. Every skill he'd acquired according to royal privilege, these lowly scrots were learning now also.

And doing better than he.

It wasn't right. It was downright dangerous.

And he couldn't stand it. He was the best, wasn't he, at everything. He had to be, by virtue of his birth and breeding. That is what he'd always understood.

He started as someone placed a wephar sheet on the table before him. On it was Torc's likeness worked in charcoal, bent over the chukar board, frowning, jaws clenched, waiting Old Glabrous's next move.

He looked up into the face of a weedy, pale-faced scrot with bad teeth, then down to the tabletop.

What wickedness was this!

Enraged, Torc seized the wephar sheet, shredded it, and attempted to do the same with the scrot.

Really, prince. D'huru Nor forced them apart. *I'll admit that though it doesn't exactly flatter you, your vanity becomes you less.*

Torc scowled. *I'm in no mood for jests. That scrot shall not bind my spirit with his evil caznry.*

The mentor looked puzzled.

Do you not know? Torc smacked the desktop with the flat of his hand, making the portrait artist wince. *It is forbidden in*

*Gurnyac to make the image of any living man lest his spirit fall
into the power of the image-maker.*

*So that is why your throning room looks like a chamber of
the dead.*

Torc drew himself up at this slighting reference to the
chamber where the Gurnyac kings crowned themselves, whose
path to the throne was lined with pale columns topped with
busts, molded from the death mask of each fresh royal corpse.
How dare you—

*I repeat, lad: you aren't in Gurnyac now. Now are you
going to sit down quietly and not cause any more trouble, or
do I take you back to your cell again?*

*Not until you agree to keep that scrot from making any more
likenesses of me.*

That's easy done, for they're lining up to sit for him. The
mentor shook his head. *And you call these people ignorant!
Even if your nonsense is true, that you can hex a man from a
likeness of him—he wasn't keeping it but giving it up to you—a
friendly gesture wasted on you.*

*And you just hear this: that young man is no scrot but a
promising draftsman, and will be given every encouragement
at his mystery while he's here. Gurnyac may be the most
powerful country in the Known World, but it isn't yet the only
one. Now—find yourself something useful to do and keep out
of trouble.*

The rest of that evening, Torc watched Bad Teeth moving
about the room, drawing others, and presenting them with the
finished work, noting how pleased his subjects were with their
likenesses. Stupid, ignorant scrots and groles that they were,
putting themselves at such risk . . .

The next night, D'huru Nor bade Torc play the old man
again.

I shall not, Torc retorted. *I wish to work a scroll.*

They'll think, D'huru Nor's thought came sly, *that you're
afraid to.*

Torc scraped back a chair and sat. *I'm ready any time.*

Old Glabrous took the challenge with a nod and a smile.

Which he'd soon part company with, Torc resolved grimly, taking up the kings.

Torc lost the first four games straight.

At the last defeat, Torc ground his teeth to keep from crying out in anger and humiliation. He clenched his fists against springing up there and then and smashing the old gont against the wall. To think that such a lowly scrot not only understood the game's intricacies, but that he could win against the king's son! All those long years Torc had played the royal game he'd understood that only those of high rank could ever master it. It was not possible that the Hairless One should best him. It was not—

He looked up suddenly. The mentor. Was he helping Old Glabrous? Telling him the moves? To teach him, Torc, some kind of lesson?

Not a hope, prince. You face the champion of the conclaur. Think yourself lucky to have such a good opponent.

Halfway through the next game, Old Glabrous replaced a move of Torc's, and demonstrated what Torc himself could clearly see was a much better one.

Torc smashed his fist down onto the table making the whole room jump, then slammed the pieces back the way they'd been. The old man gently inclined his head and took up the play as before.

You young bruk. D'huru Nor stood at Torc's shoulder. *You could learn so much.*

Torc picked up another piece and banged it down, unable to stop himself. *Nonsense. I have him this time, can't you see?* he protested, but the mentor had moved on.

He stared moodily at the board, regretting his obstinacy, but it was too late to take it back. He played on, hoping for another chance.

It came a few nights later, when again Old Glabrous undid a move that Torc had made. This time Torc let it stay, studying it from all angles until he saw that in three moves more he'd have the edge and possibly the game.

Torc signaled the man to make his next move, then went on to win.

Old Glabrous grinned broadly—not *at* him, Torc was watching him most closely. Not at him, for he waved his palms at Torc as at a champion. It was, Torc realized with surprise, with pleasure at his win.

The young draftsman continued to make likenesses as before. Torc looked to him often, as the youth moved about the chamber. No one else seemed to feel threatened by him. Neither had anyone taken ill from it.

He began to wish he'd taken a more careful look at his own likeness before he'd torn it up. If he remembered right, the scrot had caught the set of his jaw and his narrowed eyes in a most remarkable way.

Torc got up, made as if to pass by the place where the scrot was working, covering the wephar sheet in sweeping lines with the burnt stick, shading in areas to create what looked strangely like shadows. Torc paused in his passing, looking over the youth's shoulder, not long enough to give rise to any idea that he was interested in the work in progress, or that he approved of it, but long enough to see that the mentor was right about the scrot's cleverness with charcoal.

He watched the likeness fill, take on uncanny solidity. He watched him hand over the likeness to its smiling subject, and move on, this time to the girl.

Torc turned away. He wished he could watch that likeness forming, but he pulled back, not wishing to show too much interest in either girl or artist.

When, a week or so later, while Torc was locked in combat with Old Glabrous, D'huru Nor handed Torc a second likeness. Torc took it gingerly, aware that some were watching for his reaction.

Compliments of Sheshu. He says if you don't want it, just tear it up. He won't bother you again.

Torc unrolled the wephar and studied it. Then he rolled it up again and set it aside.

It is well enough, he told D'huru Nor. *I accept it.*

He looked up to meet Sheshu's eyes, nodded curtly. The youth bowed his head and turned away to draw someone else.

During the evening Torc covertly unrolled the scroll. The likeness remained unchanged, and so did he. He began to relax, to look around at the others Sheshu was drawing. More likenesses, more scrolls given away, and still no one the worse for it.

Then, oh then a win, his first real victory over Old Glabrous. Keeping his face calm he looked around to see who'd witnessed it, noticed Sheshu over by the far wall, drawing the girl again, she bent over the writing table, her face soft and glowing in the light of the lamp.

In the joy of his triumph Torc got up and went over to see. Remarkable.

She glanced up to Torc, looked away.

Torc walked back to the chukar table, to challenge Old Glabrous to another game.

If the scrot would make a likeness of the melk for him, and maybe give her some hair, that indeed would be a gift. But the mentor would never agree to ask Sheshu for the kind of likeness of her that Torc would want.

But if he ever did, then, oh, then would Torc test out the Gurnyac lore!

CHAPTER EIGHTEEN

DAY followed day in ordered fashion. Summer swelled and burgeoned until it seemed that it must surely collapse and fall in upon itself.

Torc fell into a stupor from the endless changeless routine of plateau, chores, D'hogana, scroll room and bed.

Until the day just into the fourth month, when the conclaur went from the scroll room to a new chamber under the mountain peak.

It was high, higher than the level of the plateau. The air got so thin that Torc's breath began to labor in an unaccustomed way, and his head began to turn, just as it had when first he'd gone under the K'haravim.

On his arrival at the new chamber, Torc halted on the threshold, his hand on the lintel, wary, and heedless of the others moving past him.

For in the torchlight it looked like another chamber under the Gurnyac keep where sometimes maimed and tortured bodies surrendered their secrets to the crown.

Torc looked keenly around the space. What was he thinking of? This was Rm, the holy place. Here in this rectangular pit

was no stench of sweat and scorched flesh, nor air hazy from
the branding flame; nor was the pit floor slick with spilled
blood and human excrement. The stark whitewashed walls
rose clean and clear to unknown heights, the cold pit floor was
padded with soft clean rushes.

One by one the pilgrims stepped down to squat making a
rectangle as in the D'hogana, only facing outward to the four
walls.

Torc looked up.

High on each of those high white walls was painted a
striking device: two human profiles of unmistakable origin
joined at the jawline, one looking right, the other, left. In the
center of the device a third, great eye, worked in red and gold
and black caught Torc's gaze, held it. By the left profile the
word *Lothu* was beautifully inscribed in gold upon the white
wall, and to the right, *Huri*—in common characters for all to
read.

Common characters. But comprising words that Torc had
never seen.

Lothu. Huri. *Lothuri.*

The mentor came up beside him, to usher him down into the
pit.

What is this place, mentor? Why are we here?

*This is the meditation chamber, by the grace of the Quaur.
You are about to meditate.*

About to! We've been at it for four months!

*You think? You've only been practicing, prince. Practicing.
Now you'll have a taste of what it really is. When you're
ready . . .*

Torc felt easier taking a place facing the door, but by the
time he was seated, the door was closed and invisible, and
only the steps told him he faced the right way.

He crossed his legs, settled himself with a great stir of
rushes, put his hands on his knees, and tipped back his head.
Above that invisible door the painted eye caught him, held him
whether he willed it or no. The room was so still that Torc
grew first uncomfortable, then apprehensive.

What now, mentor?

At that moment the mentor's thought came, not in the usual dry way, but in a strange chant, and not, Torc suspected to him alone, but to all the others as well, and all at once.

Behold the Third Eye, which none but the Lothuri possesses, by the will of the Quaur.

The Lothu are They, who see back: Preceptors, Founts of wisdom, looking back to the birth of Time.

The Huri are They, who see forth: Leaders, Seers, looking to that which will be.

Lothu: Huri. Two in One are They, by the singular gift of the Third Eye.

To Their First estate none other might attain, yet by Their help might one raise oneself to greater heights under the K'haravim.

Empty the mind now of all thought, and see the Eye.

Through that Eye forward and back are the same, forward and back are the same, forward and back are the same, forward and back are the same . . .

Torc stared transfixed at the great eye while on and on went the mentor's chant without beginning or end, through Torc's head until softly other voices stole in, raw admixture from other minds. The others were taking up the silent incantation and the mentor was somehow combining their separate contributions into a chorus and projecting it out to each and every one of them as even now Torc's own voice joined in . . .

Black flecks danced in the air before him, multiplying, swarming, blocking out sight of the great eye, until those flecks turned white then flared, blanking his outer vision.

There came a shrilling in his head as of a thousand summer skeeches but he could not raise his hands to block it.

His eyes closed, yet all still was whiteness and in that whiteness stars flashed and wheeled until he spun to nothing under that vast firmament and in an instant all went still and he knew hadn't he always known the simple truth that time was a lie a delusion and that tomorrow was yesterday in disguise and that though he could not see them all his future deeds were done and his whole life was in the palm of his hand . . .

He settled himself down in the bitter darkness of the plateau, his hands up his sleeves against the cold.

Are you there, B'hadgazan? What went on last night? And how in Dryac did I get back to my cell?

You walked back with the rest, prince.

The corner of Torc's mouth twitched slightly. He'd been given only half an answer. If he asked for the other, likely he'd wait half the morning for it. He held his peace, wrapping his mantle more tightly about himself. Even this far into summer the air was raw before sunup.

And as to what went on: I told you that last night.

The Dryac you did. I suppose we'll be at it again?

Every night from now on. If you wish attune your mind to a level beyond that of ordinary men—

I am not an ordinary man!

Only through the Canticum can the Quaur reach you, by the grace of the Lothuri.

That stuff about forward and back being the same: that was the Canticum?

Had the mentor cut him off? Oh, well. He went on:

The Athor had no third eye that I could see. Nor had any of the others.

Neither have they two faces—that you can see. The device is symbolic only, representing a faculty far subtler than any gross physical manifestation—

The mentor's mindspeech ceased abruptly. In vain Torc waited for the conversation to resume. He stared morosely at the others huddled around him. Which of them had snatched the mentor's mind away? If he still wanted answers he'd have to bide his time.

He closed his eyes and composed himself to sit out the period.

When next he opened his eyes the sky had lightened. As

usual, he stood, the only one, and stretched, then he wandered to the edge of the plateau and looked down. The mists had thinned, revealing for the first time part of the crater below.

Under the lee of the plateau wall was a tiny blue rectangle, a single skystone tile set amid the rich dark pearlcrust of shrubbery and cabochon treestands touched to fire agate by the aging year. The D'hogana. How tiny it looked. Torc had not dreamed they were so high.

Oh? Judging by the heavy weather you still make of the stair, I thought you under the impression that we were twice the altitude.

Torc peered out. Way beyond, another boiling gap revealed a green-gray mass covered with tiny white dots inside a wooden palisade.

Houses? In the crater valley?

Mentor. Mentor!

The childrens compound, prince.

Children? Lothuri children? He stared down intently. The idea of the Lothuri in bed together defied his powers of imagination. *These—children—they're conceived and born in the usual way?*

Why not? You didn't think them to spring fully formed from the hitaku vats, did you?

Why are they kept out there, from the K'haravim?

There was a slight, but distinct pause.

They need the daylight for their growing years.

Then who cares for them, if their parents are under the mountain?

Why, their nurses, of course.

Nurses? Torc's eyes narrowed. That was nice. The women got the sunshine, while the men stayed indoors.

Wrong, prince. Both men and women care for the children equally.

Men—caring for children?

The Lothuri make no distinction between male and female save for the basic biological functions of begetting and gestation.

None?

None. In each Lothuri are the male and female properties blended equally. You are surprised.

Surprised? Repelled! A man was a man, a rider of woman and beast alike and a warrior on the battlefield. Anything less . . . he shuddered.

D'huru Nor stood up then, the rest as one following suit, and went down the stair for breakfast.

But all the way down, and for long afterward, Torc wondered about those children—and about the mentor's hesitancy when asked why they were kept out of sight. The mentor was keeping something from him. For that reason alone, Torc promised himself, he'd watch his chance and find out what it was.

The slow days deepened, turning with them, as the minute hand its gnomon, the slower seasonal pointer through fall.

A strange time came upon that high place then, of icy mornings and close afternoons broken by not one waft of air, as though the mountain were holding its breath. Leaves ripened, withered, hung brittle and dry, then spiraled down to lie still beneath their bare branches. The tinny shrilling of summer skeeches thinned to a fitful chirp and the mournful honk of the troon was heard no more. The slanting sun nudged the langaur's coat from sable to white, and lanced its balding lays; the tiny redcapped stone pipers gathered in jeweled flocks to flutter down to the warmth of the salt fens and sly old Pessar slithered under slab and shelf to coil in deathlock until the urgent drumsong of the late spring rains.

Only Ostryc, snow lord, screaming, wheeling aloft in the high still air disdained the warning signs, for wasn't he supreme ruler of the tall peaks? What need had he of camouflage, he already white as the coming snows and fearing none?

In the holy city, the granary was filled, and the apple lofts, and cellars with barrels of rich ripe peculars. Shutters were secured, eaves shored up, and lampshields bolted into the walls.

Under the K'haravim, a few last rites were administered to the dying year.

To one of these rites Torc's subconclaur was assigned, namely, to the herb garden, to cull the last of the summer harvest and clear the beds ready for the spring.

Torc looked about him curiously. He'd never had much truck with the royal gardens back in Gurnyac, but he was sure there was nothing like this place there. It was sunken and rectangular, like the meditation pit, and just as hushed within those secluded, evergreen walls. Torc took a deep breath of the close humid air, feeling more shut in there under that small square of sky than ever he did in his cell.

No, not like the meditation pit at all, but a charnel house, he amended, taking in the neat piles of cut and woody stems stacked on the paths like yellowed bones new dug from the earth, the piles of roots and bulbs like so many ancient skulls gaping blindly up at the light.

From the only gate (solid door in high stone wall, and shielded from the interior by a stand of aged orat), steps led down to the right, and to the left, an earthen ramp.

Already pilgrims were kneeling and plucking with care the dying leaves off espaliered vines and laying them in flat wide baskets to dry.

Torc got down also next to Old Glabrous and tried to follow suit.

He didn't get far.

Cease your labors, prince. The carnage you inflict on those poor leaves will render their potency useless. Come, I'll direct your energy elsewhere.

Torc stood up, scattering folia all over the path, and followed the mentor to the far end of the garden where tidy carts lined the wall.

Take up the refuse from the paths and wheel it to the compost pile outside. That you can't harm, no matter hard you try.

D'huru Nor watched over his first two trips then left to supervise the bunching, braiding, and layering inside. Which suited Torc well, gave him a welcome chance to work by himself. And it took him out of that oppressive place, if but for a brief spell.

He strode up the ramp, pushed the cart smartly through the gate, then, setting it down outside, leaned against the wall and wiped his face on the hem of his robe. It was so airless in that highwalled garth, a lung halted in midbreath, saturated with moist wasted air.

He shut his eyes and breathed out slowly, feeling fresh sweat start on his face. When would the weather change? Time seemed stopped, and the sohurin to go on and on.

Soon, the mentor said, winds would come to sweep the leaves down into the valleys.

Then the snows would arrive.

He recalled working through one wild afternoon in the D'hogana under the fury of a thunderstorm. Lightning flashing over wet bodies, bodies slippery with driving rain. What the fookar, he'd protested, gulping for breath. His skin had mottled in the cold, his lashes spiked with blinding wet.

On, Gurnyac, the mentor had goaded him. *Steel yourself for when the real weather comes.*

You mean the snow? We'll be out here then?

Until your sweat freezes on your skin, and your breath in your lungs. You'll see, Gurnyac, you'll see.

Right then, Torc would have welcomed storm of hail or sleet or even snow to cool his flesh and clear his head. Anything.

He pushed himself off the wall and dumped his load. He was just raking it in when, looking up, he saw two Lothuri, one male, one female, moving toward him along a shaded path leading from the D'hogana.

Seeing him, they halted, and waited while he wheeled his cart back through the gate into the garden, and shut the gate behind him.

Torc parked the cart at the top of the ramp, and peeped out through a low crack in the weathered gate.

The two Lothuri had already gone past, but hard on their heels trod a line of children, ranging in height from about waist level to near full grown, followed by two more adults in the rear.

Torc held still as they went by, blanking his mind as best he could lest they sensed him standing there. And when they'd gone he still stared after them.

He'd wanted to see Lothuri children, and now he had.

What had he expected to see? Something different, from the hesitancy of the mentor's response to his questions up on the plateau. Yet they looked miniature versions of their elders— except for strange peakless bonnets, curiously fashioned from cloth, encasing their heads, masking their brows completely.

He straightened slowly, wondering at children suffering such uncomfortable-looking headgear with such submissive conformity. Headgear that no one else wore under the K'haravim. Here was something, or he didn't know the mentor.

Hup—mentor!

He came to, seized the cart handles, and hurried down the ramp. Fool, letting his thoughts wander like that. He rounded the orat screen, glanced toward D'huru Nor, but the man seemed engrossed in the rest at the far end of the garden, and had his back to the gate.

Torc shoveled more refuse into the cart, hauled it up the ramp, through the gate, and tipped it onto the compost heap. Was D'huru Nor as all-powerful as he would have Torc believe? Was it really impossible for a son of Gurnyac to best him?

As Torc labored, the thought came on him that he'd certainly like to put it to the test, a desire he struggled to keep inchoate lest the mentor detect it. He wanted to see more of those children, learn why the odd headgear that no one else affected under the K'haravim. And he wanted to do it without the mentor's even knowing.

They'd come from the direction of the D'hogana. So for the next few days he'd keep watch to see if they came that way again, and at that time. If they did— He checked his thought, and bent his back to the compost pile.

For the next couple of nights before he went to sleep, Torc tried to practice emptying his mind and keeping it fixed and steady for a minute or two: an impossible task to perform cold without the benefit of Canticum.

Giving that up, he worked during the day on fixing his mind on his present task around the herb garden: struggling with an oversized cartload of compost, raking the growing pile over, and shoring up the sides with fresh planks. Any of these routines would serve to mask the time he left the garden to find the children. The mind-blanking exercise he left for emergencies.

For three days, he kept watch on the path outside the garden, and sure enough, the children filed past as before. Torc was convinced now that they were coming each time from the D'hogana.

On the fourth day, he decided to act.

Early on, while the mentor was busy with the others, Torc took out an extra large load of refuse, set it down by the compost pile, and sped away along the path toward the K'haravim, thinking all the while of tipping out leaves and hauling them up atop the main heap, just as though he were really there and doing it.

He slowed. If he was correct, the little pool would come up on his left, and just beyond that, the entrance to the D'hogana.

The path was there all right. But by the pool sat three Lothuri deep in meditation. He pulled back, and sidled around the fringes of the clearing, under cover of the bushes, blanking out the compost, blanking out everything—only for ten heartbeats, but maybe that was all he needed to get him past.

Leaving the pool and the Lothuri behind, he went on, imaging scraping the cart clean and setting it to rights again, tidying up the edges of the pile. His breath was getting loud and labored. The way from pool to D'hogana was longer than he remembered. Surely the mentor missed him now. Should he go back?

He checked, half turned, then carried on. Might as well, he thought, all thought of compost gone now.

He came up suddenly against the familiar screens surrounding the Harash D'ho's arena. He sidled around, searching for a vantage point, trying not to think, to send out anything that might alert those within the D'hogana to the presence of an intruder.

There was only the one approach, on the west side, the one the sohurin always took, leading from D'hogana to K'haravim.

He crouched among the shrubbery and peered through. To have gotten this far! It had been well worth the risk!

There were the children, their lean lithe bodies naked save for tiny loincloths, all going through their routines as well as any member of the conclaur. But he wasn't really aware of that. His eyes were fixed on their heads, encased by monstrous turbans that gleamed white under the hot sun.

Even as he watched, two of them, having finished their bout, made obeisance to each other and stepped out of the cordon, and taking off their turbans they shook out their golden hair and bared their foreheads to the sun.

Torc's eyes went dark with shock.

At the center of each brow was a livid cicatrice, a gnarled bossy mass standing out like a diseased growth on the creamy skin—or a Brandmark gone bad.

Stay, Gurnyac!

Torc whipped around at the mentor's command, but before he could move farther, two of the Lothuri rose from beside the D'hogan mat and came toward him.

He straightened up, looking out for the mentor, weighing his options. He could dash for it, but where, and what would be the point?

He turned to them and waited.

They led him, as he thought, back toward the herb garden, but to his surprise they halted at the seat, now vacant, by the little pool where they gestured him to sit, they remaining standing beside him.

Again and again he turned his head, expecting D'huru Nor any minute to come striding out from the bushes, spitting barbs.

Minutes passed.

Why am I here? What's going on?

Silence.

Torc stared at the two profiles on either side of him, each facing out away over the trees. Lothu. Huri.

Beautiful. Remote.

Useless.

He fought the urge to jump up and stride about and make demands.

It wouldn't get him anywhere.

Better to hold his peace, to show how well the barbarian prince could match them stillness for stillness, calm for calm.

His back erect, he folded his arms in his sleeves, closed his eyes, and, the warm sun on his lids, began the canticum of the meditation chamber:

Behold the Third Eye, which none but the Lothuri possesses, by the Will of the Quaur.

The Lothu are They, who see back: Preceptors, Founts of Wisdom, looking to the birth of Time.

The Huri are They, who see forth: Leaders, Seers, looking to that which will be . . .

You surprise me, prince. I'd looked to see you long since gone.

Torc opened his eyes.

Before him stood the Athor, his golden skin glowing against the roughness of his mantle.

The two other Lothuri were gone.

If that's true, then the Canticum is but a sham.

Well said. The Athor sat.

Torc slid away from him, to the other end of the bench.

Why are you here? Am I to be punished?

The Athor turned his head.

For what?

Oh, by the Dryac— Torc checked his impatience. *For what I just did.*

Why? Do you think you should be? Then how? How should I punish you, do you think?

Torc stared toward the sun flashing off the surface of the little pool, considering. Double his chores? Confine him to his cell? Send him—he pushed the thought away—from the K'haravim?

You'll suffer none of those things, prince. What you did was entirely according to the Will of the Quaur.

Torc looked at him in surprise.

If you left your labor to seek out the children, then that is exactly what you were supposed to do.

Torc's eyebrows rose further. *Meaning?*

My son, nothing in this world happens by chance. The Quaur directed you to do this thing. Therefore why should we punish you—or any man for what he does?

Torc grinned widely. *Don't tell my father that or Gurnyac's streets will choke with human trash. Athor, men move of their own free will, and therefore they must stand or fall by their deeds.*

The Athor smiled now. *Yes—and no.*

Yes and no? What sort of answer was that? The Athor made no attempt to reply but continued to regard him impassively. *If I've done no wrong, why wasn't I just sent back to the conclaur?*

Why this visitation from the great Athor, whom no one had had sight of since going under the K'haravim? Ha! Of course! Not for his disobedience but because of what he'd just seen: the vile disfigurement on the children's faces. No wonder they were kept out of sight. No wonder the mentor had hedged about them.

And here was Torc, an outsider, having witnessed the abomination of their faces in full daylight. The Athor was here to silence him. But how, if not by torture, or injury?

By bribery, perhaps? Or threats? Surely not, for they wouldn't last beyond the mountain gate.

Young man—don't waste your thought. I could remove all trace of what you saw at one glance. But yet I do not, according to the Will of the Quaur.

Then why? Why are you here?

The Athor sighed. *I obey, just as you, the Universal Will.*

He stood, his mantle rustling in the quiet, and went to stand by the pool.

Torc wiped his brow. There was no breath in that place. Nothing stirred save the grass blades at the Athor's passing. The golden fish hung just below the water's surface, gasping for air.

The Athor turned to face him.

The cicatrice is no disfigurement, prince. Come: close your eyes.

Torc obeyed, and leaning back against the bench, raised his face to the sun.

One minute Torc was staring at the blood-haze behind his lids, and the next he seemed to be standing in the D'hogana— *seemed* because at the same time he was very much aware of himself still sitting on the bench, arms draped along its back.

The Athor left Torc standing back by the bushes, and advanced toward the edge of the D'hogan mat. On seeing him the children, smiling, made deep obeisance, then crowded him, vying for his touch.

The Athor laid a hand on a golden head.

I'm sorry you find our children so repulsive, prince.

His long fine fingers delicately caressed the bossy growth on the child's brow. *For it's neither a disease nor, as you were pleased to think for an instant, a ritual Brandmark, but rather the badge of our inheritance.*

Badge? The child, the D'hogana disappeared instantly, and Torc found himself standing in the doorway of the meditation chamber staring straight up at the strange device on the wall: the two faces looking outward, the Third Eye in between.

The Third Eye! But . . .

The mentor said that it was not a gross physical eye, Athor.
The Athor nodded. *Even so.*

Then what is it?

The Athor turned, beckoned, and at once without surprise now Torc found himself back within the K'haravim sitting by the children who were lying on the grass oblivious of them, their heads bare to Demiel's rays.

How beautiful they were. Flawless. Save for the hideous cicatrice.

When the Athor's next thought came, Torc jumped. *Every man, as you know, has by birthright a brain by which he walks and talks and eats, builds his house, and counts the stars. Everyone, everywhere—save here.*

Torc looked up, shading his eyes at the dark form of the Athor standing over him.

The Lothuri, prince, have not one brain, but two, the second brain stemming from the main one, at the base of the skull. We call it the pyryx, that gives us our special powers.

Torc glanced to the knobs on the children's brows, perplexed.

The Athor went on. *At birth, the pyryx is but a bud. It grows with the child, matures with the child at puberty.*

The Athor spread his arms out to the sun.

Both need light to grow—but how to reach the pyryx within the skull?

The Athor squatted beside him.

From the pyryx four blood cords fine as harsilk arch forward under the skull to a point in the center of the brow. From there they pass through a hole, a natural lacuna in the brow plate where they flower into the cicatrix you saw. This cluster of knobs, or ganglia, that we call the opryx, takes in light, sends it back to feed the pyryx. The nature of the opryx being to crave light, it never knows when it has had enough. Hence the bonnets you saw yesterday prevent sickness of the sun. It is also delicate, easily damaged, hence the turbans to protect the children in rough play.

He tapped his own smooth brow.

At puberty, the pyryx being mature, needs no more light.
The blood-lines wither, the opryx fades, and the lacuna closes
at last. Then the pyryx stirs, moving the young Lothuri to
higher activities. You would know more?
You keep them from the K'haravim.
The Athor smiled.
Indeed we do, prince. See.

Another giddy minute and Torc stood inside the compound
he'd seen from the plateau. The doors of each small white
dwelling were open wide, and from them came sounds of
laughter and singing, mixed with the tinkling of the ghial and
the twang of the zonthar. All around Torc on the grass
helmeted children ran about, tossing balls to one another,
rolling huge wooden hoops while some were racing to and fro
on tall sticks with incredible ease.

They're healthy animals who need freedom to rush around
and make great noise—scarce fit company for pilgrims on a
siopenar, you agree?

This time when the Athor drew him away, Torc resisted
slightly.

The beautiful people.

Healthy animals . . .

Did the Athor also think of him as one? If so, it was as one
of a lower kind. One who, unlike the children, would never
grow up. How he suddenly envied those bright young things,
he, prince, Gurnyac warrior and second to none.

The mentor had said that only the Lothuri could attain to the
highest levels under the K'haravim.

If B'hadgazan could read a man's thoughts, and direct his
body against his will, what then could this man not do? He'd
already shifted him about the K'haravim at will even while he
could swear they hadn't left the little pool. And what had the
man said earlier?

. . . I could remove all trace of what you saw at one glance
if I wanted to . . .

Could the Athor really do that? Could he also see past and
future as the Canticum claimed? Was there truly a Quaur, and
were the Lothuri man's link with it?

The Canticum speaks true, my son. Through the pyryx the Lothuri see through the tangle of time, tracing each man's raveled clue from beginning to end.

End? Torc looked askance. *How can you see what's not yet done? I don't know what I'm going to be doing from one moment to the next.*

The Athor's mouth twitched. *Not even under the K'haravim's routine, prince? Seriously, I say to you, that from the moment of birth our actions are complete; every breath counted, every action weighed—yes, even to our meeting here.*

Torc shook his head. *If this is as you say, then ambition is dead, and we should all give up and become as stones on the high plateau.*

Indeed not. Rather we should turn our attention to our attitude. This we can learn to change, and this each disciple eventually strives for under the K'haravim.

Again Torc shook his head.

Be that as it may, prince, only remember what you've seen this day, not telling it to any man.

Why?

The Athor spread his graceful hands. *I may not say, by the will of the Quaur.*

Why not, Athor? And why all the secrecy about the second brain?

As long as men feel they can strive to gain our powers they accept them. Were it known that some must lie ever beyond reach, then cries of "monster" would echo throughout the Known World. When shall they know the truth? Maybe never.

I know it, Athor.

Aye, by the will of the Quaur.

The Athor left the pool to sit once more beside him.

Torc felt even more uneasy now, and not a little hostile. This man's abilities far exceeded the mentor's—and any that a prince might attain. He was superior to the Gnangars in ways that could never be surpassed—or even understood. And he, Torc, would remain inferior to him despite anything he did.

Rest easy, prince. The Lothuri look not to the lighted parade out there. The realms we would conquer lie under the K'haravim.

So you said. What was it? "We of the Inner Ring have not left this mountain in one thousand generations, yet we have traveled farther than any other men in the Known World."

Well said, prince. You have a remarkable memory.

Those are remarkable words.

Torc's envy yet grew. Those gifts could make a prince a god. Why, this man could read at will his own future down in Gurnyac, watch his life unfold as one watched the lowest pilpit toil with its grain of sand out of its slow hole.

Look at me.

Torc raised his eyes to meet the Athors' then could not turn away. His head, his whole body began to feel light, and the little clearing, the pool, the grass, and the trees, ceased to exist. He began to feel that sense of well-being, of elation, almost, that he felt after drinking hitaku, only better, much better. The tightness was gone, and with it, the bitter envy.

For a long moment the Athor held him thus, then closed his eyes, releasing Torc, and at once the prince felt a great, tight knot dissolve in his gut leaving a peaceful aftermath.

Torc closed his eyes also, and sat for long unthinking, not tired, he realized with surprise. Only relaxed.

He leaned back, gratefully savoring the peace. It was a while before the next question came.

What does the future hold for me?

A pause, then, *I may not say, by the will of the Quaur.*

There was trouble in Gurnyac when I left it. I would know if it is done, and that I will be king.

The Athor did not answer.

Torc sat up, swiveled to face him.

The golden eyes were on him fast.

What I know, prince, what I see I cannot put to words.

Then tell me only one thing, if you can: shall I be king hereafter?

The Athor regarded him long and solemnly, then slowly he nodded.

Yes, he answered. *You shall wear the crown.*

The Athor stood, and in that moment, a shiver of cold air passed through the arbor, stippling the surface of the pool, scattering the fish, and sending a faint frisson through the brittle bushes, showering dead and dying leaves onto the grass, chilling Torc's sweat-damp clothes.

A movement to the left and the mentor emerged along the path leading back to the herb garden.

Torc stood also even as the Athor began to walk away.

Athor! Torc called after his retreating back. *You never said: why did we meet here.*

But if the golden man heard him, he made no sign. Reaching the far corner of the path he went out of sight, leaving Torc and the mentor alone.

CHAPTER NINETEEN

TANNA paused under the lamp before the gatehouse. Courage. All would be well. She'd get through.

"The Lady Tanna." The gatehouse keeper hoisted up his belly and leaned over the barrier. "And where might you be going at this time of night without pass, or escort?"

Tanna moistened her lips, forced a coquettish smile.

"Come, Hock, you know how it is . . ."

And beneath her smile cursed her face for being so well known all over the citadel. Gar's property now, she was, and sneaking out the moment his back was turned.

Hock shook his head. "I can't let you out on the town whilst his Highness is away fighting for king and country, lady. His Highness'll have my head on a pole."

Tanna pouted prettily. "Who'll tell him? Come on, Hock. Here."

She took from under her mantle a tiny blue harpile bag, and loosening the drawstring, shook out a silver buckle set with bright white stones onto the counter. "It's yours, Hock, if you let me through."

The gatekeeper looked at her from out of the heavy folds of his face.

255

"My lady! What lucky man out there is worth this!"

He took up the buckle, held it to his vast middle, then at arm's length admiring the knot: Gremla, the knot around a man's soul protecting it from the Dryac's grim hand. It was old, very old, and worth five hundred shengs if a rak. Folian had given it to her for dowry; for her husband one day. But if she didn't use it now, she'd not have one—at least not the one she wanted.

Shaking his head, Hock shoved the buckle back toward her.

"Sorry, Lady Tanna, but much as I'm tempted, it's more than my life's worth than to let you out. Now you go back to your quarters. The town's not safe for a fallowella. And anyone who bids you go from here alone is not worth the effort."

"But Hock—"

Hock turned to the inner door where messengers sat idling the time away. "I'll have you an escort back to the queen's tower, lady."

"No—I'll make my own way back."

Tanna took up the buckle and put it away. Then pulling her hood about her face she turned from the lighted gatehouse. This gate was her last chance. She'd not give in if it took her all night, and the next. She must do what she had to do before he came back, and under cover of dark, for what reason could she give for wanting to go down into that place—other than the real one, and she was not about to reveal that.

Under the cover of her outer mantle she stroked her belly.

She'd hoped to steal through the servants' gate.

A whole hour she'd spent watching that postern, the scrots going back and forth from the town taverns, or to their hovels to sleep. All searched, all with passes. Times had become uncertain indeed.

She'd gone then to the barracks' gate, standing for long watching the sentries, the endless patrols going to and from the city.

Soldiers' gate, servants' gate, trade gate—what was the use of any of them without a pass?

Besides, no matter how she dressed, she'd never get out unnoticed, not with her face, her famous—infamous face. That face flamed as she thought of the gossip she'd overheard at board. Of how was Torc doing and what certain people were up to behind his back and what he wouldn't do to them when he came home. Tongues were certainly bold—in Gar's absence.

She'd sat miserably, unable to eat or drink.

She hovered, pulling her mantle tight against the cold wind. She had to get out somehow without being seen. Reentry would be easy, for that fool Hock couldn't afford to sign her in—one way!

Two people came through, up the steep drawbridge ramp, past the sentries and under the portcullis: the king's third equerry and squire, looking tired after a hard ride from the Weald, and, with a blast of horns and a loud clatter, a returning all-day hunting party delayed, they said, by storms beyond the hills.

No one came from the Citadel.

Her feet grew numb.

Maybe no one would pass through this night. Maybe she should try again tomorrow night. She hopped from one foot to the other, unable to decide. She hated to give in.

She was on the point of stepping out onto the return path when a pack of young squires rode up on thar-back, singing and laughing loudly, all of them brimming with Gort wine, all set to carve up the town; seven of them, to be exact, on six thars.

"Ho, Hocky-hock!"

The one riding behind his friend half slid, half fell to the ground, staggered out of sight around the corner into the gatehouse waving his sword dangerously in the air. "A thar, fetch us another thar, quick, before we pop your wind-bladder!"

Loud laughter. Hock's voice raised in reply: "Fetch it yourselves, sirs. That's not my job, you well know, nor my messengers' job, neither."

"You'll be sorry, Hocky-Hock!"

"Get away with you. I told you before: None but them from the king's own tower commands me. And you'd be wise to keep clear of those streets down there, lest His Majesty's patrols take you for spies and punctures your *wine*-bladders!"

"What, Hocky!" The squire's voice slurred slightly. "The Dryac take him for his impudence! Hoist him, fellows!"

More laughter, good-humored enough, then sounds of scuffling.

Tanna edged forward and peered around the door.

The lot of them had dismounted and were hauling Hock's vast bulk up over the top of the counter.

Hock called out loudly, and through the back door burst four sleepy messenger lads who grabbed Hock's feet and began pulling the other way.

"Put me down, you fools," Hock shouted. "And grab a-hold of them instead!"

Within seconds the gatehouse was a jumble of fists and feet, then steel as the two sentries came running in from their posts beside the open gate, pikes raised.

Seeing her chance, Tanna slipped across the lighted space and under the empty portcullis arch as one of the squires drew his sword and with a joyous whoop engaged the nearest royal sentry.

She ran headlong down the dizzy ramp, skirts about her knees, expecting at any moment a challenge, a shouted summons, down at last to the darkness at the bottom, her heart beating rapidly, her throat blood-raw.

Only there did she stop to gain breath. She leaned against the wall, fighting the weakness in her knees, the rising nausea.

What was she doing, anyway, playing double jeopardy at this time of night on half-heard kitchen gossip? If cutthroats and thieves didn't get her, the king's patrols were everywhere and she'd likely be hauled before Sharroc as a spy!

She moved off close by the wall, keeping to the main road. There were few people about. Most folk were indoors by their fires digesting their suppers, and the taverns hadn't yet disgorged their hordes.

Once she stiffened against the wall at the sound of booted feet approaching, all marching in step, but they passed and died away somewhere over to her left without coming into view.

It was some while before she went on.

Carefully she counted the alleys on either side until at a certain point she turned sharp right, following a narrow way all steps and cobbles to twist a body's ankles until she came to a low arch. Under the arch was a door, shoulder high. No more than a hole in the wall, really.

She ran her hands carefully over the door. It was thick, rough. Solid. No knocker. No bell.

She made a tight fist and rapped with her knuckles.

Then called softly, "Mother Rachy?"

There came a rustle, then silence.

She knocked again.

"Who's there?"

"Gordna Miry, of Tarith. Please—let me in."

Another silence, then a laugh which almost set Tanna running off down the alley and back to the street.

The door opened and in the darkness a claw shot out and pulled her through, shutting the door behind them.

"Come in, come in, Gordna Miry, and stop your row!"

Another laugh, dry, derisive, and bony fingers, still tightly clamped about Tanna's wrist, pulled her along an uneven tiled passage into a windowless room lit only by red embers in a rough earth hearth.

The low walls were crammed from floor to ceiling with shelves all awry; shelves filled with jumbled bottles and pots and bags. The smoky, greasy rafters were also hung with dusty dried sticks and bunched vines that had long given up their last fragrant essences. Most of the floor space was filled with a wooden table littered with the remnants of several meals, and surrounded by rickety chairs and a stool.

In a far corner was a sagging bed, unmade and strewn with rags. In its center a piebald she-frat whined and gnawed its own haunch.

The air was foul: a mixture of stale bodies long since gone; of bad breath and unemptied chamber pots and rotten food.

Tanna put her free hand to her mouth.

"Here, here, *Gordna Miry of Tarith*." The claw shook her. "Don't you go messing up my parlor here. State your business."

"I—" Tanna swallowed. "I heard you were a scorder—"

The laugh became a screech.

"Is that what they said, now! They wants their tongues a-pulled, for saying such a thing out loud about a body. You knows what they does to scorders?" Without waiting for a reply, the woman left her, went to rake the embers. She was very small, not even reaching Tanna's shoulders. And thin. Wiry under layers of heavy tattered skirts, all dark gray, and brown, and black. Wisps of gray hair straggled from under her doyshan, shadowing her grimy face, making empty sockets of her eyes.

On second thought, the old woman reached down and threw a small wizened log onto the embers, and at once the hearth filled with choking black smoke.

"The fookar take you!" she cried, and kicked it with her boot, starting a single sullen flame.

Tanna collapsed, unbidden, onto the stool and laid her head on the table.

She heard a chair scrape the floor next to her, and a claw patted her shoulder.

"There, girl. You look in sore need of old Mother Rachy. Let me guess—it's not a love potion that you're wanting!" Another sharp cackle.

Tanna raised her head.

"You guess right, old woman," she said. "I am with child. They say you have something to—to—"

"It depends. How much have you got?"

"No money. Only this."

She reached into her bodice, drew out the buckle.

"It's a man's buckle, I know," she said, "but it's worth a good few raks."

The old woman snatched it, placed it in her palm, turned it this way and that, and finally putting it between her teeth, bit it.

"Mmmn. Bohomon silver. Good, good—but not enough."

Tanna stood in dismay. "But they said—I heard—"

The old woman leaned over her and put her face close, wafting out a cloud of fetid breath. "Well, you heard wrong, missy. Tarith, indeed. In them clothes. You'll have to get up earlier in the day to fool me. From the citadel you are. Garahundts, the lot of you, in and out of this house of mine like fleas. Go home and find me something else. I'll hold this for you meanwhile."

"But—" Tanna held onto the table. If she didn't get out of there soon she'd make the woman a contribution of quite another kind.

"You're all alike, you fine fallowellas. Well, know this, *Gordna Miry of Tarith*—Mother Rachy's a woman of her word. If you don't go now, I'll send you packing and you'll never find this door open no more!"

Tanna subsided again. She might have known. She reached into her bodice and drew out a second, black bag.

"Here," she said. "That's it. I have nothing else. Nothing with which to buy my way back into the Citadel."

Opening the bag, she shook out onto the table a deep red stone. Garimony, they called it, or Gortstone, after that wine's color.

Her spirits sank. How she wished she'd not given the buckle. Now she'd lose both treasures after all. Oh, the pain of it. It were as though she'd given Florian herself into those filthy hands.

Mother Rachy grabbed up the stone, exclaimed as it caught the fitful flame of the fire. Red patches of light like bright blood whirled round the grimy walls, splashed the old woman's face and hands.

And Tanna's own.

She slid her hands under the table.

The scorder put the stone back into its pouch and slipped it into a pocket somewhere in her skirt. She patted Tanna's shoulder.

"There, there, my pretty Gordna Miry of Tarith. You just sit and take your rest. Mother Rachy will see you right."

From one of the shelves she took down several bottles, these not dusty at all, and a cracked bowl and brought them over to the table. Tanna watched in spite of herself as the old woman shook and measured and pinched the powders into the bowl and ground them all up together into a mixture which she then emptied into a glass phial and set down on the table. Then she went to the cot, smacked it with her hand sending the frat leaping from the room.

"There, now," she said. "You just come and lie down while I draw you a cup of water to take it in."

Tanna looked to the sagging cot in horror.

"No, no," she said. "I must take it at home. My— mother—will miss me if I stay out too long."

The old woman laughed harshly.

"An you wish, fine lady, but don't blame me if ought goes awry. Come to think," she muttered, and emptied some of the powder back out onto the table before stoppering the phial and handing it over.

"Take it in a cupful of hot water," she said. "Or, better, a handle of the strongest wine you can lay hand to. And take it in bed."

She leaned her head down again, took Tanna's chin in her claw, and tilted her face. "But as I said—if anything goes wrong, don't tell me." She straightened and walked to the door. "Of course, if all goes well, and you need me again, just knock on my door." She patted her skirt pocket. "And now for goodwill, I'll send Dagomal with you to see you on your way. *Dagomal!*" She tipped her head up and screeched into the rafters. *"Dagomal!"*

Heavy steps clumped slowly down an overhead stair, then the door opened.

Dagomal was as tall as Mother Rachy was tiny, and hairy as Djunu. He grinned at Tanna with huge brown rotten teeth.

"Dagomal—see this pretty on her way," Mother Rachy shouted. "Dagomal can be stubborn," she explained to Tanna in her normal voice. "But he's a proper boy for all that." She pushed them toward the door, down the passage, and out into the alley.

Outside it had grown colder and a stale mist rose from the cobbles.

Tanna set off back up the narrow way, conscious of Dagomal treading heavily on her heels. She picked up her pace nervously. It was so quiet and dark, she could hear his breathing.

Beyond the alley, the night was alive now with noise, the taverns having spilled out their drunken contents onto the streets.

Tanna had become so uneasy about Dagomal by this time that she almost welcomed the noisy brawling crowds singing and tottering from side to side of the road, arms linked to hold one another up.

But just as she was about to leave the dark of the alley for the light of the road, Dagomal seized her arm and pulled her back.

She struggled, tried to free herself from his grip, but he held her only more tightly, dragging her further back up the alley.

She opened her mouth to shout, but, with a curious grunt, he put a great fist over it, pressing her into the wall.

She drew back her foot to kick, and as she did so, there was a sudden shout and boots tramped past the alley entrance.

They froze, Dagomal with his hand over her mouth, she with her foot poised in the air.

There was a second shout, a stifled scream, the sound of running feet.

Then, in the sudden silence, the thud of boots died away.

Dagomal removed his hairy hand and nodded her on.

Shaking, she walked slowly back and into the street.

In the center of the deserted way a body lay unmoving. Dagomal turned it over with his foot.

Tanna took in a sharp breath.

The face was gone.

She looked around wildly, saw blood everywhere.

Dagomal straightened up, flapped his great hands at her, waving her away. Such a huge man, this rough ungainly son of an ugly scorder.

How she'd misjudged him, thinking rape even as he'd saved her life. Impulsively, she reached up and lightly kissed his wire-haired cheek.

"Thank you, Dagomal, and good-bye," she whispered, and turned away.

She'd not gone far when Dagomal reappeared beside her and stayed there until she'd safely reached the bridge.

By Dryac's luck, the drawbridge was down.

If the sentries were surprised to see her they gave no sign. But one of them did escort her into the gatehouse to confront Hock.

Hock was sitting behind the counter on a broad stool talking with a large gray woman whose doyshan was pushed back off her face.

At Tanna's entrance he stopped in mid-sentence, got up puffing and wheezing, and eyed her sternly from under his heavy brow.

He should denounce her, she knew; order her detained and taken to the king for judgment in the morning.

"The Lady Tanna says she's lost her pass, Keeper," the sentry said.

Hock's jowls waggled.

"That's so, Lady Tanna?"

Tanna nodded.

Hock nodded the sentry back outside.

"I'll take care of it." When the sentry was gone, he leaned

over the counter. "So you had your way after all, missy. Well, and now you'll at least tell me a-where-of you've been."

How generous of him. Tanna hoped he wouldn't ask for the buckle. But she couldn't tell him. They'd have to drag it out of her.

"Here, Hock." The old woman stood up. "The fallowella looks in need of a seat, not a scolding. Here, my dear. Do you come around here and sit you down a bit until you have your breath."

Tanna stared, surprised by the authority in the woman's voice, a deep voice, gruff as Hock's own, yet gentle and not at all coarse.

The woman met her halfway around the counter, took her arm, and firmly sat her on the chair she'd vacated. "Hock—hlath."

To Tanna's amazement, Hock fetched it himself from the back room.

"He's a kind man, my Lady Tanna—when he uses his noggin," the woman said softly. "Now—put your head down on your lap, that's it."

Tanna did so, and at once felt a firm square hand rubbing firm circles on her back.

Hock's heavy tread and he was back with the hlath.

The woman spoke in her ear. "Now, I know you don't feel like this hlath at this moment, but drink it down. You'll feel better for it."

Tanna raised her head, took with both hands the scalding cup that Hock had wrapped in a blue and white kerchief. Her gut heaved at the first two or three sips, but as the hot fluid scored its way down her throat and chest, its flutterings slowed, then stopped.

No one spoke until she'd drained it all.

The old woman took the cup, handed it to Hock, and stood up.

"Hock—I'll see the Lady Tanna back to her quarters for you. As for me—I'll come again tomorrow."

She gave Tanna a hand up and put an arm about her shoulders, steadying her.

Out in the darkness of the path leading to the main pile, she paused.

"Here. Stop a minute and take in a deep breath or two, if you can stand the cold." The old woman herself had on no outer mantle, only her doyshan which lifted in the chill wind.

"You're very kind," Tanna said. "I don't know you."

"No more you should," the old woman said. "For I keep to myself much these days. I'm Harbeli, that raised up that young bruk of a Torc and the rest of Sharroc's brood. For my pains I got a pension and a hole in the wall and since I've no one out there after all these years, I'm pleased enough to bide beneath the king's hand."

Tanna glanced to her face sharply at a note in her voice, but the old face seemed genuine enough.

"You're trembling," Harbeli said. "Let's move on."

They went on in silence until they reached the outer ring of buildings adjoining the great arch which led to the inner courtyard and the royal towers. The old woman stopped and pointed to a squat stone building three stories high to the left, partway along the wall.

"There's my dwelling place," she said. "Two flights up and then a half one to the little turret you see on top. The widow's peak, as they call it, a fit place for me for longer than I recall."

They walked on. At the foot of the queen's tower, she stopped again. "Lady Tanna, I'll leave you here. Take your time up the stairs." Tanna was aware of the eyes scrutinizing her face. "If you go ahead and do what you mean to do," Harbeli went on in a low voice, "—have a care. You'd have best had it done out there while you could. Her Glorious Elevation won't like it, you know, and you'll have no help from her. If you need me—" She nodded back toward the great arch. "—you know where to find me. If you can't make it—send for me. I'll come."

Before Tanna could speak a word, Harbeli was walking rapidly back toward the outer arch.

She leaned against the doorway.

You'd have best had it done out there while you could . . .

Harbeli knew. How? Did it show so plainly?

She set her feet to the stair, shaking away the idea. No. Nobody had yet guessed, or they would have said. What a remarkable old woman she was. Tanna smiled. She'd have to be, if she was Torc's old nurse.

She climbed on.

As silently as she could, she stripped her bed, lined it with sheets she'd hidden away those past two weeks. Then, putting on her oldest gown, she filled her bedside goblet with water and shook the precious powder in.

She sat for long on the side of the bed, the goblet in her hand, staring down at the dark contents.

The floor was silent.

Boards creaked.

Someone—probably Magla—snored softly a few doors down.

When it started, she told herself, she'd have to keep silent, whatever she felt. She took a kerchief from her mantle pocket to bite on. What of the little life within her body? Would it, too, feel the pain? Would it, too, cry silently in the darkness of her womb? Her hand tightened on the goblet. Enough. She'd been around all that too many times. She'd made her choice. It had no right to be there. Her first child must be Torc's, or she'd have none. She swung her feet up on the bed, raised the goblet, and tipped the contents down her throat.

The taste was bitter, metallic.

With a faint after sting.

She lay back, waiting.

A cry awoke her. She sat up in the dark.

And realized then that the cry had come from her. Her belly was burning. A rolling pain ripped through her body, wrenching from her another moan, which she quickly bit off. Through the next wave she held herself rigid. Had anyone heard? She sat there, in the chilly dark, listening. Another wave of pain, swelling, then tightening to a point.

She curled up, her fist to her mouth.

Her breathing quickened. She fought to slow it, even with the next wave. She was going to be sick. Loudly sick. But she couldn't be, not there.

She swung her feet to the floor, groped for her mantle, then pushing through her door, made for the stairs.

Halfway across the deserted compound, a sentry stopped, saluted.

She took two paces past him, staggered, went down.

The sentry hovered somewhere above her.

"Lady Tanna?"

She looked up at his tall shape against the starlit sky.

"Harbeli!"

"Harbeli, lady?"

"You know her?" Tanna ground the words out.

Out of the dark the old woman's voice came. "I'm here. Pick her up, young man, gently, if you value your splendid outfit, and follow me."

"Harbeli!" Tanna was vaguely aware of being lifted, of the old woman's face hovering somewhere upside-down against the wheeling stars then in a flash of pain the face and the stars winked out.

CHAPTER TWENTY

THE early morning sun woke her.

She opened her eyes onto a warm room bright with stitched panels and cushions. In one corner hlath steamed on a broad, black stove. The stone floor was polished and littered with rough rag rugs.

She sighed, her breath a feeble vapor cloud against the sun's rays.

She moved slightly, winced. Her whole body, even her scalp was sore.

When she tried to raise her head, she fell back against the pillow.

"Good morrow to you, lady."

"Harbeli?"

Harbeli bent stiffly over her. "Here, sit you up." The old woman slipped an arm under her, raised her, and piled up pillows behind her. "I put your bed to rights over there. As far as anyone knows you're on an early morning walk. In those." She pointed to a set of day clothes lying over a chair. "You can go back this afternoon, I'll help you. You'll be ill—a slight chill-fever. Send for the apothecary, buy yourself a day or two in bed. He'll never know the difference. Here."

She crossed to the stove, ladled hot hlath.

At the smell of it, Tanna turned her head away.

"You must try," Harbeli said. "Slowly, a sip at a time. The sickness will go away sooner."

Tanna took the cup, watched the surface of the hot brown liquid tremble in her hands. She looked up.

"Did I—did it—"

The old woman shook her loose wiry locks. "No, it did not, though you yourself nearly died with the force of it. The child lives, the Dryac knows how. Your breath failed three times during the last hour of the night watch, yet that babe has not issued forth, nor will it, now. Perhaps—" she paused. "Perhaps it's not meant to, lady."

The bed sagged as she perched on its edge.

"Is it Gar's?" Her voice was low.

Tanna's eyes went wide.

"No. Oh, no."

"Torc's?"

Tanna nodded miserably. Harbeli held her gaze long, until at last she looked away and folded her arms. "Drink," she said.

Tanna drank, staring broodily around the old nurse's chamber. How spacious it was. Why, it was large and airy as the queen's own sitting room, and brighter, for all that it was only three and a bit stories high. That was because—she looked toward the dormers through which she glimpsed the cluster of royal high towers—there was space all around it. She thought of her own windowless box off the back passage leading from the queen's bedchamber. "Lady" sounded so grand, carried with it so many privileges. Yet she'd have traded some for a place like this. One day, maybe, when she and Torc—

She remembered Gar and the incubus clinging to the walls of her womb.

Oh, that she had died. It wouldn't have mattered, would it? She'd not have known the difference.

But she hadn't.

And here she was with no more poison, unless she went down again into that awful place with the last of her precious stones.

"Why would you want to be rid of the heir's child?" Harbeli's eyes were hard upon her.

Avoiding them, Tanna stared into the cup. "He'll not take me back like this."

Harbeli made a scornful noise. "What makes you think he'll take you back at all—from his brother's bed? Lady, that child is your only salvation! Bear it—and pray! Now down to sleep with you!"

Harbeli took the cold cup from her hands, and pushed her gently into the clothes.

"I say again—have the child. Take your chance."

Take your chance! Tanna lay back and squeezed her eyes shut. She dared not. The idea was too apalling. That thing was going to go on growing inside her into another Gar. And what was she going to say when it didn't come out at the right time? She had to do something, something, some . . . *thing* . . .

The days, the weeks—the months passed, and fall passed into early winter, with threat of deep snows.

Tanna's body grew rounder, heavier; her breasts fuller. It was remarkable, Harbeli said, how little her body showed her pregnancy, being as Tanna had told her, over five months gone.

But it wasn't over five months, Tanna knew, but under— well under. Still Gar made demands on her, clearly meaning to keep her at least until Torc arrived, and that idea terrified her.

The only relief came from his increasing absences.

He'd kept close to Feric these months, Tanna had to admit, going about with him wherever the king sent him to quell the spreading troubles.

And not just to the Foundings. Unrest was spreading wider even as far as Gortland and the Eastern Seas. Even Kond, toothless merchant city to the northwest had had wind of it, and spies were in and out of Gurnyac like starving felmars sniffing for offal.

People looked increasingly to the skies for relief, to the heavy snows that would bind peoples to the earth for the duration, giving the king's armies rest and respite before taking up hostilities again in the spring.

Everyone, that is, save Tanna.

If the snows came early, she prayed, then let them come between Gurnyac and Gar.

But the weeks passed and still the weather did not break.

One night, little more than a month to Torc's return, Gar arrived unexpectedly after only five days with Feric in the Weald. For more troops, so he said. Unrest was spreading north even to the kingdom of Kyrion, where that king was getting bold enough to send quick raiding parties into the borders of Gurnyac for women and booty.

Naturally, he sent for Tanna.

As she walked across the bedchamber to greet him, his eyes narrowed.

"You grow heavy, lady. Look to your victuals."

There came a tap on the door, soft and short.

"Stay," he said, as though she were a she-frat. "I'll be back."

As soon as the door closed behind him, she ran across the room and put her ear to the lock.

A murmur of voices, the sound of another door closing. To the anteroom.

She straightened up, walked slowly about the chamber. So many men these days, secretly coming and going. Spies, watching Feric and his allies, Gar said. Watching, and waiting. She paused by the tall chest, where Gar had laid his sword in its richly carved scabbard.

In all that time, Gar had really done nothing but work his way into the counsel of those who had the king's ear—the better, he said, to topple Feric when the chance arose.

Why, why, she'd urged Gar. Why do you let him go on so long? Go you to the king before he topples you all and Gurnyac crumbles under his sword.

Gar had slapped her for her pains. Leave men's work to men, he'd warned her. And hold your tongue if you would keep it.

She bit her lip. Gar was a fool and a coward. How fortunate that he was the second son. With him on the throne, Gurnyac wouldn't last five minutes. Oh, that Torc were there. He'd have long since gone to the king.

She drew the sword from its sheath with a faint scraping sound, and lightly ran her fingers along its edge.

What was Torc doing up on that holy mountain all this while? She couldn't imagine. But of one thing she was sure: he couldn't dream how bad things were or he'd have been back by now.

Courage, she told herself. One more month. One more month, and—

Still holding the sword, she folded her arms across her belly.

The light sparked the blade drawing her eyes. She looked from its point to the soft mound below her waist. She placed the tip against that roundness denting her dress, just as Feric had done that night. What would the point feel like inside her? Would it hurt so very much? Time and again she had resolved to beg the royal chirurgeon cut the monster from her womb, but what woman had ever walked away from his bloody couch? She returned the blade to its sheath, put it down.

Coward.

But the coward's was the hard way out.

The door opened.

Gar came back in carrying a bundle of parchment which he stacked carelessly on top of his desk in full view of her—and why not, she being but a fallowella and supposedly unable to tell a character from a cipher? They belonged in his secret drawer and he wouldn't open that while she was in the room.

If you only realized, she thought, as he went toward her. I know about your secret drawer. Every desk has one. My father taught me so, and how to find them.

"And now—" Gar shucked off his buffer gown. "—for you."

*   *   *

Tanna slipped from the covers, stood still watching Gar's chest heaving in and out. He was lying on his back, one leg bent, the other outflung under the covers. A deep sleeper was Gar, particularly after lovemaking.

She padded across the floor, lifted the edge of one of the scrolls.

Accounts of some kind. Tanna was surprised, although she had not known what to expect.

One quick backward glance, and she took up the scroll and unwound it.

Down the left-hand side was a column of names—unfamiliar names. Next to them a figure denoting—her eyes went to the head of the column—hundreds of shengs.

She laid that scroll aside and took up a second one.

More names. Some with dots beside them, others with dots and lines through them, besides.

Gar stirred.

She dropped the scroll and moved back to the bed.

As she eased herself between the sheets, Gar opened his eyes, murmured something, and began to move against her.

As his movements grew more purposeful, she thought again of the chirurgeon's knife.

Coward, she thought, in time with his thrusts; *coward, coward, coward.*

Gar left at dawn.

Tanna stood by the barracks gate in the bitter light: a chattel, a public slur on the Gurnyac heir; there by Gar's command to watch him from the outer ramparts ride out with three hundred of the King's Reserves.

She turned as soon as she could toward the inner citadel.

Remembered with a start of fear another departure five months earlier.

She walked faster.

Soon the king would send the escort to await Torc's return to Asurdun. And then, and then . . .

She reached the archway at the foot of the queen's tower and stopped. She should go and lie down for an hour or two before morning hlath. But the prospect of that bleak little box was too much. She turned away and walked, almost ran, across the damp grass toward the Great Arch, and through to the squat building on the right.

Harbeli's building.

Tanna tapped on the old woman's door and without waiting for answer, lifted the latch and went in.

Harbeli was sitting in a rocker by her stove, hands folded in her lap, eyes closed. Her sleeping cap was awry and her wispy gray locks lay untidily down either side of her face.

"Tanna?" The old woman opened her eyes. "Lady—how good to see you. Come sit." She stood, took Tanna's outstretched hands to draw her to the fire. "Oh my dear. Why are you always so cold?"

Harbeli chafed Tanna's hands vigorously between her own rough dry ones, tutting all the while. Then, still tutting, the old woman sat her down in her own rocker, and set fresh hlath on the stove.

"I see His Highness is back."

Tanna nodded. "But he's gone again, the Dryac be praised."

Harbeli pulled up another chair to the fire and sat.

"Was it so bad, child?"

Tanna moved from the chair, knelt at Harbeli's feet, and laid her head in the old woman's lap.

"There, there." Tanna felt the old hands on her hair.

"Oh, Harbeli—stand by me or I'm lost."

"Nonsense. You did well enough before I came along, and you'll do better when I'm gone. But it's good you came."

Presently, Tanna sat up, and leaning against the old woman's skirts, picked up her hlath and stared into the flames of the stove.

"What's on your mind, lady?"

Tanna didn't answer her.

"It's not that babe, or even bully Gar, I'll wager."

Tanna kept her head toward the fire. How she wanted to speak. To tell the old woman everything. About that last night before Torc's departure. Of Aravac and the shuktek; of her meeting with Feric, and her going to warn Gar. Of Gar's ineptitude, his dalliance, in putting his own small interests above that of king and state.

But she couldn't, even though here, of all people in Gurnyac, was the one to find for her feet strong and swift enough to reach Torc before the king's men.

She sighed.

Too long. She'd walked alone too long to change now.

Oh, she badly wanted Torc home. For her sake, as well as the people's. And yet—she would lose him, she knew. Maybe even her life. Yet maybe not, if she did him service enough. If she came through for him, why, who knows she might not still be queen, and deservedly so.

She looked up, her eyes brightening some.

"Tell me, Harbeli, something of His Highness, Prince Torc as a child."

"As a child?" Harbeli's brows went up. "As a *child!* Well, now."

She leaned back again, closed her eyes.

"He was wild as he ever is now, you know. All the Gnangars are. And Torc hated having anyone so close to him, breathing down his neck, you might say, while Gar never forgave Torc for getting himself born first.

"Do you know—the nursery was like a battlefield, with them fighting one way or another from morn to night." The old woman looked Tanna squarely in the eye. "I suppose you might say you're only the latest trophy in the war, the latest in a very, very long line. But I recall the first big one.

"I don't know if you're aware, that when a gentle-born lad reaches double figures, he fights his first tournament—with others of the same age. Not with metal swords, mind you, but wooden ones, broad, and blunt, like paddles, which they wield like clubs.

"The winner of the Wooden Tournament gets a sword of gold, called the Brandelac; a purse from the king, and a seat at high board for a day.

"It's a grand occasion. The boys line up before His Majesty, all in their new guards and hauberks. They kneel down, hold their sword hilts to their right cheeks and the blades up in the air, and swear to do their best to the honor of kith and king, or may those blades shatter at their words, then they bring them down across their knees with a great slap. 'Tis most heartening to see."

Tanna nodded. She could just imagine Torc kneeling before Sharroc, standing out from the rest, of course, and his high harsh voice outsounding theirs.

"It's the first big occasion of a boy's life. He who wins the Brandelac can boast of it for the rest of his days."

"It must have been discouraging for the rest," Tanna said, "to know they were going against the king's son without hope of besting him."

"And so it was, especially for the young lord Aravac who next to His Highness was most like to have won it."

Tanna nodded again. The poor Lord Aravac had been so far superior to the rest, save Torc. " 'Tis a pity they didn't give two Brandelacs that year," she said.

"It wouldn't have made much difference," Harbeli said, "for His Royal Highness wouldn't have won either."

"No?"

Harbeli grinned, her color rising. "His was the first bout, against the Lord Aravac. A fair match, a close one, yet His Highness should have had the edge.

"But—I can still see it now: he swung that sword of his as though his arm were of lead—and so it was! For someone—" Harbeli looked slyly, "—*someone* had made an exact copy of His Highness's blade and filled it with pellets to make it so heavy that I doubt General Feric himself could have hefted it."

"But," Tanna said, "surely whoever gave it to him on the field must have realized—"

Harbeli laughed harshly.

"He did, indeed. For that was the one who'd made it. I remember it now as though it were yesterday. For ages that Gar pestered his brother to let him be his squire. To look good before the people, he said. And please the king. Of course His Highness let Gar carry his sword at that. Oh, you should have seen Torc's face when Gar dropped the blade onto his hands. 'Tis a wonder the lad didn't keel over under the weight of it.

"Feric beat him for losing, and his father had him whipped. But except to me, he said nothing. Not a word, not even to Gar himself. But the next year—" The old lady chuckled, "was Gar's turn to compete for the Brandelac.

"He lined up with the rest before the king, swore his oath to do his sincere best for kith and king or may his sword shatter at his words, and brought his blade down across his knees." She leaned forward. "It splintered into a thousand bits. For one whole minute you could have heard a pilpit sneeze, then folks starting laughing and laughing—not loud at first, mind, but soft and embarrassed. But by and by it got louder and louder until Gar ran from the field. Torc was standing by the arena gate to watch him go by. I feared there'd be blood spilled, but Gar simply looked at him and said, quietly like so's nobody heard but Torc—and me: "One day," he says, serious as a full-grown man, "the sword'll be real and blood shall flow between us, and it'll be yours, brother." It still gives me goosebumps to think on it. With that, Gar pushes past and on to the citadel. I went after him but he'd have none of me. Now you've done it, I says to Torc. Gar never forgets. I'd as soon have taken old Shufar by the tail. Rubbish, Torc says. I've only evened up the score. Oh no you have not, Your Highness, said I. Nor will you ever. And I was right."

The old woman's smile faded. "And even now His Royal Highness, Prince Torc, underestimates that one. As for me—I take good care that Gar's shadow doesn't fall across my path. He grows more cunning and dangerous the older he gets. Don't you agree, lady?"

Tanna shrugged. Her smile had left her face also, and the

warmth, leaving it bleak. The tale was over, and here she was, a trophy in a war.

"Now," Harbeli said briskly. "Maybe you'll tell me what's on your mind. And mayhap you'll feel better thereafter."

What was on her mind? So many things. Which was the safest? She must tell something, for this old lady would not let her be until she'd done so.

She sighed. "I'm worried," she said, "about the troubles. I've heard things. From the Weald."

Harbeli's face went grim.

"Aye, and with good cause," she said. "Not that I'll raise my voice against king or country. But it's true there's a current a-blowing out there that chills my flesh." Harbeli took up her hlath, sipping, then set it down again. "My father was a merchant, middling to fair. My mother liked to play the midwife. Many was the trip I took along of her out on a dark night through the back alleys. As far back as I recall, I learned about the other Gurnyac, the one the fine ladies and lords never see. Folks's so poor you wouldn't believe—but then you must have seen some of that the other night, lady. How you had the courage to go out there, the Quaur only knows.

"But if that was bad enough, my mother said it was much worse out in the countryside. Take the crofts. There's big ones, and little ones. For every big crofter, there are a dozen bonded melks from the Weald. Poor miserable creatures stamped with a cruel mark, bought by the crofter to do the dirty jobs around the place. They live like animals in sheds, made to breed to give the crofter more folk to do his work.

"Of course, not all crofters are like that. There's a lot as do their own dirty work, and stay just as big as they can handle. But then they stay poor as slaves themselves.

"There's a lot of folk as would like to see things a bit more even around the place. And I heard—" She stopped.

"Heard what, Harbeli? Come on, you made me speak."

Harbeli smiled. "That's true." Her face went grave again. "I heard that many of those folk all across the king's very own country are getting ready to rise up and join the melks in the Weald."

Tanna's heart jumped. What would happen if all those people out there did get together? Could the king and his generals handle them all?

She felt faintly excited, faintly frightened.

Could Gurnyac fall?

If so, what would happen to Torc?

If he were no longer prince, then he might know at last what life was for folks like her.

Ah, no. She dismissed the idea. The Gnangars were too strong, had ruled too long to let that happen. They were secure.

Harbeli was watching her.

"You're not looking much happier," the old woman said. "I should have minded my words, I seeking to comfort you."

Tanna smiled. "Oh, no. I live a too-sheltered life. Especially since I got here. When I lived with Folian I saw much more of the world. Why, we even went to market in Kond on high and holy days. You never saw so many people as there are there then."

"Kond." Harbeli's eyes gleamed. "Now that's a place I'd like to visit one day. They say all the richest merchants of the Known World live there in great houses winding up a high hillside."

"Oh, yes," Tanna said. "And the richer the merchant, the higher is his house. My father told me he worked atop that hill before he was taken by Florian. But that was before my time."

"Your father was a good man," Harbeli said. "And a farsighted one, teaching his little fallowella to read and write like that, while folk have not yet even dreamed of such a thing."

Tanna smiled now, a sad, fond smile.

"Aye. He used to tell me so often just what you said, how things should be more evenhanded. And not just among the rich and the poor, but between men and women, too."

"Well, I'd like to see that," Harbeli said. "But knowing men, if there's a change, that'll come the very last." Harbeli hoisted herself up with a creak and a groan and hobbled to a chest of drawers by the back wall. "Anyhow." She bent down, and pulling out a roll of cloth, brought it back to the fire. "See what these old knobbly fingers have been working for you these past few days. For His Highness, Prince Torc's favorite fallowella. Why, 'tis fit even for a *concubine!*"

So saying, she slowly unrolled the cloth and out flowed a white silken gown with embroidered front panels and lace about the sleeves.

A birthing gown, and, on the top of it, a birthing cap seeded with shiny white seapits and silver petals—one not quite finished with the needle still in it.

Tanna put her arms about the old woman and hugged her close.

The following day four men were brought before Sharroc for high treason.

So Tanna learned that night at board. The whole hall buzzed with the news, and talk of the death's heads staring out eyeless over Gurnyac from the poles by the outer Gates. Weald men they'd been, brought in by Gar.

"They say," Leylin looked toward the High Table, then leaned toward Tanna, "that General Feric had hard words with Gar for going over his head in rooting out their tongues too soon. They say that His Highness is growing altogether too tight for his own cuirass!"

"That Bundraic—the way he rushed at the king! Right to the throne steps he got!" Magla's eyes shone across the table. "Did you see it, Tanna?"

Tanna shook her head.

"She doesn't have the stomach for that sort of thing, as you well know, Magla," Leylin said. "Me, I watched until their blood congealed, and their lips turned black. I hope to see many more, too. May the king find every last one of his enemies!"

"Shut up, Leylin," Magla said. "No one's listening—no one to do you any good, anyway." She lowered her voice. "Now that Baldod had such a body on him. Pity." She stabbed up a piece of harmeat with her knife, examined it carefully, then popped it in her mouth. "He was," she went on, "head of the main work gang, and second only to the Hall Master himself. They say he was behind the last riot in the House of the Iron Rose. Kudry told me we lost two hundred good men putting it down."

There was a general shifting of feet as the assembly rose. Sharroc was leaving the hall.

Tanna stood with relief. Now he was gone so might she be. How she hated those two. Ghouls, they were. But as the queen's women they all had to sit together, unless Gar were home and had Tanna by him at board.

She nodded to Harbeli as she went out. The old nurse was sitting alone at one of the lowest tables near the door. Tanna looked at the empty seat beside her. How much nicer dinnertime would have been spent there.

She slept badly.

Dreamed of bright swords arcing down from a great height to sever mutilated heads.

She opened her eyes. She was lying on her side curled up tightly as a womb-bound child. A bare second later she scarce remembered what had woken her, scarce recalled her nightmares. Yet the feelings remained. Of fear, and revulsion, and pity. But mostly fear.

The Dryac take the dinner talk. How she hated it, she, the eyes and ears of Torc. Her mouth twisted in self-disgust.

And as for Magla and Leylin—carrion birds, they were, their beaks foul with shredded gossip.

She tried to go back to sleep, but their voices went through and through her mind.

Baldod. Bundraic. Two hundred dead men. The House of the Iron Rose.

She'd never seen the Brandings.

And never wanted to. Such hateful places, the Smeltings and the Foundings where humans were bred like forhars to keep the Brandhouses filled.

As they deserved to be, so the saying went.

But did they? Her father had whispered differently to her; of how no man should be the chattel of another. Of how everyone, from slaves in the Foundings, to little fallowellas, yes, and even to scribes—his eyes would twinkle slightly—should be free to shape their own destinies.

She could quite well imagine what the death's heads had looked like, and how the jeering crowds would have been that afternoon, hurling stones to knock them from their posts, in traditional sport. And now those ghastly heads were all alone out there, stiffening in the night air. Tomorrow they would begin to rot and then the watchful shar-birds would spiral ever lower waiting their chance to shred flesh from bone.

Four men with no tongue to plead either guilt or innocence.

One called Bundraic. Another, Baldod.

Baldod.

She came wide awake. She knew that name.

Had seen it only the night before in clear, bold script—on the parchment scroll on top of Gar's desk.

She paused at the end of the passage, listening.

What would she say if anyone saw her? What possible reason could she have for being in Gar's wing?

She moved on. No one would see her. Why should they? The pikes had passed through but minutes before and wouldn't be back for another hour.

The apartment was another matter.

She stopped before the door, looked back down the empty gallery.

When Gar was here, the door was locked and guarded day and night.

What now that he was away, and with his most trusted equerries?

She lifted the latch and pushed.

Locked. It was locked.

She glanced up and down the passageway.

Farther on was the menials' door.

That opened so easily and noiselessly that she all but fell inward.

Someone had slipped. And if Gar ever came to hear about it, that someone's head would roll.

The tiny side hall was deserted; the wall sconce almost out.

Off the hall the four narrow doors to the servants' cubicles were shut. Someone coughed, rolled over.

She moved swiftly through the far door into the servants' hall.

Empty also.

From there she must swing open the door leading into Gar's public quarters.

She pressed her hand against it and pushed by slow degrees.

The entry hall was brightly lit—and deserted. And why not? Why should anyone in his right mind stand to attention all night behind a stout locked door with no one to see?

She crossed the hall, paused an instant before Gar's chamber door. What if someone had taken to the secret comfort of his master's bed?

Courage. She turned the latch and went in.

She groped her way across the floor to where she remembered the lamp and tinder to be. Bumped into Gar's washstand rattling the bowls.

She stood still, listening.

Nothing.

She moved on, slowly.

But not too slowly, for soon it would be the end of the night watch. And when the dawn bell sounded, then the citadel would come alive with menials, including the ones in these very chambers.

Were the drapes closed?

She stumbled across to the window. Yes.

She moved out again, over the room until her hands found the high chest, slid open the front drawer, closed on the cold tinder box.

One strike and the night light caught. She turned it low, to a faint blue glow, then set one of the bed rugs across the bottom of the door.

The desk was over by the far wall, beside the window.

She'd looked it over many times, wondering where the inner compartment was. There had to be one.

She ran her hands over the carving, as her father had taught her.

Tapped lightly with her knuckles for a certain echo. Many of the cavities were lined with metal, for extra safety. She traced leaves, animals, birds, curlicues. Nothing. She pressed knobs, bosses, depressions in the polished gobyrwood. She tried various combinations of them all. Nothing.

She got down onto her hands and knees and tried the bottom. Still nothing.

Then she remembered what her father had told her about the work of Gitu, master carpenter from Hirand, and reaching under gave each of the back legs a quarter turn, one out, one in. Then raised the desk lid.

There was a slight scraping sound and a panel slid out at the side.

She dipped in her hands and pulled out the scrolls from a thick steel-lined well; four in all.

One by one she spread them out on the desktop under the lamp's dim glow, sliding her finger down the left-hand side.

There, halfway down the third one.

Baldod.

And just below his, that of Bundraic.

There was a dot beside the names, and a line through them. And on the right of each was written in strong clear figures, five thousand shengs. A considerable sum.

She bit her lip. What did the scrolls mean? And what was Gar doing with them? She must study them, find answers, and before Gar came back.

She closed the desk, slipped the scrolls inside her robe, replaced the lamp, doused it, and crept out the way she had come.

* * *

It wanted but minutes to the dawn bell when she reached her room.

She knelt by her bed and pulled out her dower chest.

Too late now to read them. She raised the lid, took out her treasures, then slipped the scrolls down beside her scribal tools. She was just replacing her bridal clothes when without warning her door opened and Magla looked in.

"I thought I heard you. You *are* up early."

Tanna continued to fold with deliberate care.

"So are you."

Behind her, Magla moved forward, bent down, peering over her shoulder.

Tanna lifted a length of blue harsilk, snapped it open in front of Magla's face, starting her back, set it on the bed. Then lowering the lid, she slid the chest away.

Tanna took up the blue harsilk and stroked it. "I am thinking to have myself a new dress, Magla. This blue is a lovely color, don't you think?" She threw the silk about her shoulders, let it settle. " 'Tis a waste to leave our treasures under our beds for others to enjoy when we're gone, isn't it?" she said, keeping her eyes on the folds falling about her.

Magla made a short, angry sound, and ran out.

Tanna rose, shut the door behind her, and stood with her back against it. Such an evil thing to say, and everyone knowing how Magla and Leylin practically *lived* in their old dower chests, counting and fondling the things they'd never use, but she had to be rid of the woman fast and that, she knew from experience, was the only way.

She moved to her bed, sank heavily onto it.

If she'd had any notion of studying the scrolls there, it was gone.

Then where?

There was only one place, and that was Torc's apartment.

It would be stale, and thick in dust, remaining so until they broke the seal on the front door on his return. She would have to be careful to leave no trace of her going there.

Dare she? She must, and that very night by the back

passage, at the end of the third watch. She knew exactly when the pikes passed by.

The trembling gave way to faint excitement.

What if—what if Gar came home again before she returned the scrolls? What if she couldn't get back into his bedchamber? Or someone saw her leaving the queen's tower and followed her there? She rocked back and forward slightly, considering. So many ifs. What *was* she doing!

The excitement faded. But after another minute, so did the fear. If they caught her, so be it. At least she'd have tried.

CHAPTER TWENTY-ONE

TANNA, stooping, stepped through into the silent bed-chamber and straightened up, her throat pricking with dust. She stood quite still, looking around the room at the shrouded furniture: the bulky chests, the tall bureau, the empty armor stand holding the center of the floor like an agonized shrookt.

The place looked haunted as a Gradhlzac's Hollow, so haunted that she all but started back the way she'd come.

There, on that very spot where she now stood, Aravac had died in a pool of blood.

She closed the glory hole panel behind her, tiptoed to the great bed, set the scrolls down, and, kneeling, laid her head on the soft furs, stroking Torc's place, remembering . . .

Enough. She had much to do, and little time in which to do it.

She moved to the window, glanced across and up to the darkened casements of the queen's tower then edged the drapes shut, lit a lamp, set it on the bedside table, and curling her legs under her, leaned back on the cushions and opened the first scroll.

One after another she read down the names, all written in the same strong, bold script. This was a roster of sorts, that Gar had somehow come by, and somehow without Feric's yet suspecting. But a roster of what? And by whose hand? Feric's? It had to be.

Name after name had dots beside them, with many crossed out as well.

When she came to Baldod's, and Bundraic's, she paused.

Why the dots? And why the lines? What did they mean?

She glanced over the last page. Names only on that one. No sums of shengs yet. Nor dots. Nor lines. Names of treachers like *Baldod,* and *Bundraic.* All ready, like the others before them, to be bought by the promise of great wealth.

Where could even Feric have come by such sums?

She looked down the columns again, at the dots, and the lines through the names. Of course.

Those sums had never been delivered, for the poor wetches had been neatly disposed of when they'd done their stint, those dots marking their proscription, she'd stake her life on it.

And the lines? She thought of the heads rotting out by the gate. When they were done, Feric simply crossed them off his list. Those ciphers were worth no more than the parchment they were written on.

Clever.

But not clever enough. Gar had these scrolls now, surely evidence enough to take to the king. So why had he not yet done so? Maybe—maybe he was on the brink of more, out there beyond the Weald.

So much for her boldness, meddling in affairs over her head. What should she do now? Why, return those scrolls at once before she found herself in real trouble.

She slipped from the bed, took up the scrolls, and carrying the lamp with her, left the chamber the way she'd come.

She entered Gar's apartment just as before, slid the scrolls into the secret cavity, back down beside a stack of other, flat sheets.

One of these she crumpled so badly that she took it out to smooth the creases with her fist.

As she lifted it, the bold clear script caught her eye. More of Feric's work? Correspondence this time. Correspondence about—Pruth? She looked to the signature over the page, then, dumbfounded, she reached for one of the scrolls.

The writing was identical.

And the hand not Feric's but Gar's!

How she got through that next day she never knew. The scrolls she'd taken out with her again, resolved to go to the king. That resolve had lasted but to the foot of his tower. Once she stepped out into the open, there'd be no turning back. She needed time to think.

She placed the scrolls once more in her dower chest and lay down to catch an hour of sleep before the dawn bell.

She turned this way and that in the darkness.

Gar.

All this time he'd been working not *against* Feric, but *with* him.

And all this time she'd lain with him, even now bore his abomination inside her, on the brink of stirring to life.

Oh, why didn't she go to Sharroc?

Because . . . she turned over . . . a rash act in this place could prove one's last. Oh, what to do? Giving up all idea of sleep, she lay on her back and tried to think.

That afternoon, even the queen remarked on her pallor, and sent her to lie down.

She lay facing the door, listening to the faint sounds of chatter and laughter coming from the queen's sitting room.

She thought of afternoons spent with her father; sunny afternoons in the scribal chamber, watching him bent over his high desk, watching and dreaming of a lady's life of love and harsilk and wine.

Her head ached. How many hours since she'd slept? She'd

lost count. But she couldn't afford to now, not until she'd resolved the problem one way or the other . . .

When she awoke, her transom was dark.

She lit her lamp, wiped her face, dressed quickly, and looked out.

It was warmer. The wind had dropped, and snow was on the way.

The tower was silent, deserted. Everybody was at evening board.

Well, that was good, for now she knew what to do.

She pulled out the scrolls and all her secret treasures from her dower chest, bundled them up, put on her cloak, and went out.

As she hurried through the darkness toward the Great Arch, the first flake fell.

The bundle she stashed behind the dresser. Then she stoked up the stove and pulled up a footstool to watch flecks of soot flare into life, and fly foolishly up and out into the night.

Presently, she heard the sound of feet laboring up the stair.

Harbeli showed no surprise at seeing her there, but only took off her doyshan, shook off melted snow.

" 'Tis slippery out there already. You just take care when you go out." Her eyes went from Tanna's face to her belly. "You look ill, lady. It's not the child, I hope."

She pulled up her rocker, sat, put her hands to the fire.

"Harbeli—I need your help."

Tanna fetched the scrolls from behind the dresser and spread them out on the hearthrug between them, pinning them flat with small bowls from the dresser shelves, for the first time catching the old woman surprised. She read out some names, tracing each with her finger, read off the sums beside them.

Then she spoke of their meaning and Gar's treachery.

Harbeli rocked back and forth. "I knew it, I knew it," she said at last. "Haven't I always called him a very Shufar, with cunning and venomous tooth? No one, *no one* saw it, not even his closest brother. I ask you, lady: where—*where*—will it end?"

"I thought to take the scrolls to the king."

Harbeli shook her head.

"You'd never live to reach him."

"Then what?"

"First: get those things back where they belong."

"Agreed. But first, since they're the only proof against those two—" She jumped up again and brought out her writing tools on the table.

Harbeli asked no questions. Instead, she helped Tanna transfer the scrolls to the table, spread them out, and anchor them with the bowls, then pulled up a chair to watch while Tanna copied each one.

"Now I'll take these back," Tanna said. "I just have time. But after that—then what, Harbeli?"

"We must send word to His Highness, Prince Torc, that's what," Harbeli said, helping Tanna on with her cloak. "I know the very men. My sister's son and his boy. They work the morning shift in the kitchens scrubbing pots. They'll not be missed."

"Then," Tanna turned back to the table. "I'll write a note."

"No. No note. Nor mention of your name. Only a message—a greeting by word of mouth from an old nurse to her former charge—the full meaning of which only Torc will understand. Such secret language did he and I have in the old days—never Gar. He'll have remembered it, I'm sure. As for those things—" She nodded to the table, "they'll stay here for safety. Now let us be off. I shall stand by while you take those things back, then see you safely to bed."

The old lady went to the door and reached down her doyshan.

"But, Harbeli—I can't let you." Tanna bundled the things up to take them to the door.

"Nonsense. You had the sense to come to me in the first place, didn't you? Anyway, 'tis not you I'm thinking of, but His Highness's child. So put those things back where they belong and come."

After a moment's hesitation, Tanna obeyed. Harbeli, nodding, threw her doyshan over her shoulders, and tied it firmly under her chin.

"You know," she said as Tanna walked to the door, "The way you wielded that pen. . . . Your father must have been proud."

The snows came and went, came and went again, and for some days Demiel shone brilliantly down from a cold clear sky.

Gar also came and went.

For a few days after his return, Tanna walked in fear that he'd notice something, the creased parchment sheet, something. But he didn't.

Only Tanna's changing shape.

And not only Gar.

The queen in the bath one morning looked hard and long at her.

"I see you're with child, girl. Gar's, I suppose."

"Oh, no, so please you, ma'am."

"No?" The queen looked askance. "Then whose?"

"His Highness, Prince Torc's, ma'am."

"Indeed? Prince Gar will not be at all pleased."

The queen stepped out of the bath, the rest following, looking at Tanna with interest. The queen's toilette finished, Tanna went to her own room to attend to her own. Magla poked her head in.

"By Her Majesty's desire," she said, "you are excused from royal attendance until further notice. She is confident that you'll have no trouble in finding other quarters as soon as possible. She also ordered me to inform you that in accordance with her promise to the Lady Folian you have permission to remain within the protection of the citadel for as long as you wish."

Protection!

Tanna raised her hairbrush to throw it after Magla, then

subsided onto the bed. She, and Magla and everyone else knew what that meant: that she was henceforth out of favor, but must stand by in case son Gar had any further use for her.

She got up, put on her cloak to go to Harbeli, sat down again. Hadn't she resolved to keep clear of her until Torc was safely home?

She slid her bed from the wall, traced her fingers along the scratches she'd made, ten to a bunch. Only one bunch left.

Ten days and then they'd all see.

Maybe Harbeli had been right after all.

When he came home and saw the scrolls, learned of the risks she'd taken for him, when she told him that she bore his child: his first—to be recognized, anyway—he'd be bound to take her back, wouldn't he? And that being the case, the queen's crown might still be hers. If not—what were her chances in life? Out of favor with the Royal Dowager, the royal bastard coming to naught if unrecognized by its sire—where would that leave her? Finished, as far as Gurnyac was concerned.

Enough!

She slid the bed back. She must lie low. Only ten days to go until Torc came back. Surely she could hold on till then.

The days passed. Nine. Eight. Seven.

On the next day, so Magla told Tanna, the king sent the escort to Asurdun—a large escort, well armed, for the heir's protection—though, as everyone was saying, what need would he have of that, coming back as he was, from Rm?

The day after that a weak damp southerly blew in to unlock ice-bound ditch and eave; the citadel moats, and the gray moraines along the sides of the roads. Stagnant wastes long festering under the ice seal oozed, mixed, and evaporated into the humid air; foul gray fog pressed down over the citadel, spread eastward, smothering traffic on the Weald road.

Tanna kept to her room, brushing her hair, oiling her skin, soaking at dawn in the baths' ghostly steam. She avoided going to board. Pleading indisposition, she had food brought to her room.

If her spirits were low, she cheered herself by looking on the brighter side of things. At least Gar was still away. And what a relief it was not to dance at the whim of that willful, spoiled old woman.

But her isolation brought hardship and growing anxiety.

How she missed Harbeli.

Time and again she almost went to see her. But Harbeli was safer left alone.

Four days before Torc's expected return, Magla and Leylin tapped on her door.

"You look peaked, Tanna," Magla said. "Come for a drive with us. The queen's given us leave to see the decorations down in the city. Every building flies banners and victory wreaths, and there's to be a great fair. Isn't it exciting? Once in a lifetime it happens, and here we are. So up and out with you. It'll do you good."

A fair! Memories of the Kondish fairs and Durac filling her hands with sticky sweetmeats. Of jugglers, and dancing dogs, and men walking across ropes strung up on high poles. The thought only saddened her.

"Thank you, but no," Tanna said. Anyway, she couldn't risk meeting the queen, or being out on public display.

"Suit yourself," Magla said over her shoulder. "We thought you'd be glad—considering the show you put on when His Highness went away!"

On the day of Torc's arrival Tanna awoke with a headache.

But even so, she forced herself down to bathe, to put on her best gown—loose-laced—and dress her hair elaborately atop her head.

She took stock of herself in her glass.

Her face was pale, her eyes dark-circled and puffy underneath. Face it—she'd lost her looks, not to mention her figure. How could Torc want her now?

She turned this way and that, eyeing herself, curling her

mouth up at one corner. She put the glass down, covered her face. It didn't work. Not even the smile, anymore.

Noise came from the passage outside; the queen's laugh, the deep-throated one that she kept for Torc and Gar. Then high-pitched thar whinnies. The queen's daughters. Her Majesty was in a rare good mood. Finally, there was quiet.

Everyone had gone to morning board.

No menial came to see how she was.

She dozed.

Awoke to the dimness of early afternoon.

The Dryac! Had Torc returned already and she there in bed!

She opened her door a slit to find the hallway deserted. She slipped out and peered through the hall windows toward Torc's wing. No. Not yet. His standard still lay furled at the foot of his mast.

Dare she cover herself and creep out, melt into the crowds?

She could resist it no longer.

She pulled her mantle over her, threw a doyshan about her face, and went down the back stairs.

Halfway she paused, breathless, dizzy. How many days since she'd gone out? Since she'd eaten a decent meal?

The courtyard was empty.

Everyone stood by the main moat watching for the outrider. A faint cheer came from far across the city, rolled over the distant masses like a wave toward the Citadel. Torc? Did they see Torc? She reached on tiptoe, trying to see.

Presently, a high black thar rapped over the king's draw-bridge and under the Great Arch. He's gone, someone said behind Tanna, to present the prince's greetings to Sharroc. A signal for the king to come down to the Citadel door, and by that time, the prince should be in sight.

Tanna put a hand to her chest. She breathed deep, but fear and excitement had taken hold. She could feel the heat in her cheeks, the quickening in her blood.

Minutes passed. No further cheers came from down below. Neither did the king appear. The crowd shifted restlessly. Streamers, released prematurely, drifted sadly down over the outer wall.

Tanna leaned against a post.

The air about her grew dim, there came a rushing in her ears. She heard a cry, "Give place, give place," then, "Here, make way," from a familiar voice somewhere overhead.

Tanna looked up. She was lying on the cobbles amid a circle of faces—one of them Harbeli's.

"Here," Harbeli pointed. "You—bring the fallowella this way."

Strong arms lifted Tanna and bore her out of the press. A guard with a gate insignia on his collar—one of Hock's men— was carrying her over to Harbeli's apartment, Harbeli walking alongside.

Tanna struggled to get down.

"No!" she cried. "I am all right. Let me go!"

"That he'll not!" Harbeli said. "Lady—you are in no fit state to be standing out like this."

Tanna deliberately ignoring her spoke directly to the guard.

"Put me down. I'll stand out here until His Highness is safely in the citadel."

"Then you'll stand alone, lady," Harbeli said. "For he'll not come home this day. Didn't you see the rider bore no gonfalon? Come, before the crowd breaks up."

She took Tanna's wrist, gave it a quick shake. "Go, lie down, lady," she muttered in Tanna's ear. " 'Tis likely His Highness is delayed by the fog. I'll send to you when he arrives."

The dear old, lovely old thing. Didn't she realize what a risk she was taking, speaking to her? Ignoring her, Tanna looked up into the guard's face. "Take me to the queen's tower." Only when the guard moved away did she acknowledge Harbeli's existence.

"I thank you for your kindness, Mother," she called over his shoulder, "and bid you good-day."

At Tanna's command, the guard set her down at the foot of the deserted tower stairs, saluted, and marched quickly back the way they'd come. One step at a time, Tanna climbed back to her room.

What did it mean, that Torc had not yet arrived? The light was fading, way past the hour for men to be within city gates in these uncertain times, especially the precious Gurnyac heir. She thought of the scrolls, the names bought for gold. To do what? To bring down the name of Gurnyac? No. Rather to create chaos and in that chaos who knows but what Sharroc might not fall—and his heir—and who would then be king? She went to the door, wrenched it open, and ran out. What better chance would treason have to dispatch the Gnangar heir than on his journey home from Rm?

But yet—hadn't Harbeli sent him timely warning? Torc was more than a match for any motley, misbegotton scrots that Gar could send against him.

No. The fog had simply hindered him, as Harbeli had said. And she was but giving in to womanish fears. She went back into her room, and closed the door behind her. She held her shaking hands before her face.

Hungry. She had eaten nothing all day. And would not for a while yet, with everyone still outside.

She lay down on her bed, despite the loose combs in her hair, the gown creasing under her, and closed her eyes, listening for sounds of returning feet.

When she awoke it was dark.

How long had she slept?

She raised her head.

The tower was silent, still.

It couldn't be night, could it?

She sat up, her head spinning with the sudden movement.

Then she realized what had woken her. Smoke. She smelled smoke. She ran to the door.

She took a deep breath to shout, choked. The passage was full of it. She ran back into her room, took up her washcloth, soaked it in water, put it over her face, and opened her mouth to shout again, just as a strange light erupted through the passage windows, and a loud wild bell sounded tocsin over her voice.

The king's tower was afire.

She ran, hammered on the first door she came to, and the next and the next, and in moments the space was crammed with shrieking women all pushing and fighting to reach the tower stairs.

But the stairs were already alight. They turned away, stampeded back toward the aerial walkway leading to the king's tower, bearing Tanna along with them.

"No!" Tanna struggled against the tide. "The king's tower is alight!"

No one heeded her.

Instead they trampled past her, to the Royal sitting room, burst through the doors.

Tanna backed away, watched figures, among them Magla, flying into the burning chamber, saw the queen, her hair in papers, start from her bed, saw her run with the others through the far door onto the aerial walkway just as it gave way with a roar and cracking of timbers leaving ragged darkness shot with sparks and falling brands.

Tanna labored for breath. Her eyes streamed, her throat, her chest were raw.

She retreated along the back passage to her room, resoaked the napkin, then seizing up her mantle, she emptied the rest of the water over it, threw it over her shoulders and pulled the hood over her head. Bent low, she ran through the billowing smoke toward the burning stairs.

She started down, crying out at the river of heat, fixing her mind on the next step and the next, and the next all but tripping over a body lying face down athwart her path, its clothes alight. Oh, the Dryac—the smell! She steadied herself, moved on headlong down. How much farther? All those times she'd used the stairs and never counted them. Surely she was through by now.

There came more cracking, loud and long, then a rumble and all about her was falling blazing wood. Something hit the side of her face and she went down.

CHAPTER TWENTY-TWO

S HIRA came to in the dark, her mind filled with the images of fire. She was lying curled up on her side. Her face was wet, as though she'd been crying.

She had been crying.

And futhermore she was lying on her bed, fully dressed, her covers over her. She rubbed her eyes, reached out and touched the bed-light behind her head up to dim. A glance to the chronister. Lord, it was almost midnight! How long had she been there? How had she gotten there?

Unsteadily, she threw aside her covers, slipped her feet to the floor, and hurried across to her grandfather's room.

Someone had left his bed-light on "glow."

He was asleep. Deeply so.

She crept out to the galley for a drink of water.

The galley light was full on, brilliant, blinding her.

Suk was in there, leaning against the sink, hot soycaf in hand. Ignoring her, Shira went to the cupboard, took out a cup, and splashed water into it, and headed out again.

"You feeling okay now, hon?"

Shira turned to face her.

"Don't call me 'hon!' " Regretting her outburst, she added, "I'm not quite awake. What happened?"

"You fell asleep, hon—Shira. We couldn't wake you, no matter what." Suk balanced the hot cup on the palm of her hand. "And no wonder. You've hardly slept or eaten since you've been down here. You know—you ought to loosen up a bit. Your grandfather's okay, really he is."

The look in Suk's eyes irritated Shira. A mixture of condescension and pity. Totally misplaced.

"Who brought me down here?"

A smile flickered across Suk's face. "We did, I'm afraid."

"And what's that supposed to mean?"

"Prosser and I. MacAllister's not back yet."

Shira's face flamed. She spun on her heel and headed back to her room, would have slammed the door had not Grandfather been sleeping.

She set the cup on her bedstand, undressed, and climbed back into bed.

There, she leaned against the pillows, dipped her mind down to alpha.

Poor, poor Tanna. After all her trouble. Oh, God.

She put her face in her hands.

Why, why was that beacon showing those terrible things?

It occurred to her then that it hadn't exactly received a bouquet of roses from Earth. Earth's entire human history was almost all a bloody struggle for territory, power, religion, and wealth.

Thomas Hobbes had been right. Man's life was nasty, brutish, and short. A baby even now on the evolutionary scale, he was going the way of the mastodon unless—unless somebody turned him around, now.

Strange, how things turned out. Grandfather had come to see Ellisen and here they were, in this deep place talking with the stars.

Well, one star, anyway.

Demiel.

Well, not so much the star, as its planet, a place so like Earth.

How beautiful Phrynis had looked that first day, without the people to spoil it. Earth must have been like that once. A veritable Eden.

She sighed, closed her eyes. It would be so wonderful to walk topside, breathe in the air, smell fresh new growing things. Recycled air came out stale and chemical whatever they did to it, and the stink of hydroponics was sickening.

What had it been like to walk about under the sun, to hear other living things around one, telling the seasons of the year? She'd never heard the sound of real live blue jays and cardinals, the mockingbird telling the spring, the noise of summer bees gathering honey, and the honk of geese gathering in the fall. And now she never would, for her only knowledge of those long extinct creatures was via the nature files shown over and over on the public compuscreen.

It had been so good, sitting out on Torc's plateau, with that wind on her face, working in that garden, against the buzzing and chirping of insects, even if only through the mind of the prince.

She yawned drowsily.

Tomorrow, if the beacon signaled, would she see that holy place again, and the prince? Would he know by then of what had happened at home? Of Tanna's passing? Would he care, being so full now of the melk?

Would anyone shed a tear for Tanna?

Harbeli would.

Wiping her eyes, Shira took up the cup, drained it, turned out the light, and lay down to sleep.

She was alone at breakfast in the little mess room when her grandfather came in. She got up, hugged him, kissed his cheek.

He squeezed her absently, obviously preoccupied.

He took a dish of soynuts and kaolait and sat down.

"Shira, you're going home as soon as Chairman Ellisen can send you."

"No!"

He looked up at her from under his brows. "Shira, my child. Look at you. This is no place for you to be."

There was an awful finality in his words that she knew well. Yet she didn't give in without a fight.

"But you said we had to stick together. You need me. Nothing's changed."

The door opened, Ord came in.

Grandfather—leave to speak inside.

Granted, Shira.

If you send me home now, I'll—I'll—there's no telling what I might do!

To her surprise, and to Ord's manifest astonishment, her grandfather laughed aloud.

I've told you before, but do you really know how like your mother you are? A stubborn young woman—brat, even.

He took up his spoon, got on with his soynuts.

"Aha," Ord said, rubbing his fat little hands together as though he were trying to light a fire with two sticks, "you're in good spirits, I see, and all set for another session. I spoke with Chairman Ellisen last night."

Her grandfather said nothing, only kept eating.

"MacAllister's coming back this morning. Reason he's taken so long is Hengst shipped us down some spare transducer plates. Lord knows where he dug them up. Ellisen had them checked out security-wise." He smiled slyly. "Doesn't trust Hengst. Trojan horses, and all that, hm? I must say, we shouldn't look gift horses in the mouth." He laughed loudly. "We've been damned lucky we haven't broken down before now. You know the trouble we had in the beginning. Old equipment deteriorates even when you don't use it. And we were down to our last spare, right, Prosser?"

Prosser, who'd just come in on Suk's heels, poured himself a cup of soycaf, grunted.

"What we need," Suk chipped in, "is the personnel reinforcements they promised us. I for one need spelling."

Shira eyed Suk with distaste. As if Grandfather needed that

one. Or any of them. Why didn't they all just go to bed and sleep. If that stupid machine broke down it won't make any difference to Grandfather—or to her . . .

Oh, how she wished that the two of them could go home together right then.

She sighed heavily, bringing up her grandfather's head sharply.

Nervous now, she got up, fetched them both a cup of soycaf.

"Still feeling tired, Shira?" Ord said. "Pity you fell asleep last evening. You missed quite a lot."

"That's all right." She looked at him from over her steaming cup. "I can see the strips later, can't I?" She glanced deliberately to Suk. "Maybe when MacAllister gets back, we can see them together."

"Doubt it," Ord said. "He'll have to turn right around and take yesterday's strips first."

A quick short laugh from Suk.

Shira, catching her grandfather's sharp look, took a firm grip on her thoughts. There were at least two fronts on which she didn't want to invite Grandfather's attention: Phrynis, and MacAllister.

Although her grandfather would not presume to read her, he'd certainly pick up on her mood. That being the case, she concentrated her thought on Aunt Marita, her two sisters; on Kirrin, keeping her mind busy on anything and anyone not connected with those two subjects. And what an effort that was all through the rest of breakfast, all the way down to the lab.

Not until Grandfather was down once again on the synergizer couch did she relax her thought, not until she actually heard the murmur of his voice in her head, out through the speakers; not until the TS flickered, and the figure of Prince Torc sprang from the slits in the 'verter did she sit back and dare to let her mind go free . . .

Days drifting past on the high mountain: fall idling into winter; bitter winds gouging the mountain face, scouring the inner valley.

Torc, in the D'hogana, flesh raw red with cold, impervious now to the whirling snows, striving, still striving to pluck the Iron Rose . . .

Torc, sitting out on the dark plateau, frozen body, frozen mind, oblivious to who he was, what he was, to everything but the warm spot of his existence in the wide endless cold.

Torc, over the nightly chukar board, horns locked with Old Glabrous, determined to win this night, and on his own, for once.

Still the days drifted past, slowing, slowing, until it seemed to Torc that time itself was caught in winter's entropy.

Torc lying in his cot thinking, thinking of the melk. Who would have thought one such could move so well. The memory of her cold flesh was still on his hands, the chill of her touch. Oh, there was no love lost between them, he knew it. So why was she always in his thoughts? Time and again he put her from his mind, only to find her back, before sleep, on waking, and, if he didn't watch out, up on the high plateau. Only in the meditation chamber did he find release, taking refuge in the Canticum . . .

Dead. The whole world was dead, locked in ice.

And yet, imperceptibly, there came change.

He took to studying his fellows covertly. Old Glabrous, who had taught him so many tricks of the chukar board—where would he go from Rm? Who would give him a game out there, where only kings were kings and beggars rode no more? And the hairy old grole, Artil, who night after night pored over the stars—out there her charts would be only the very skies. And Sheshu—how would he draw those remarkable images without being either imprisoned for scribing illegally, or sent to the stake for a cazn?

And the Iron Rose—what of her? His mouth briefly tightened in the old way. He pictured her breasts straining against the chest band, her round chint braced against his hip. Cold, her eyes were. Insolent. Well, he'd cure that. To the Foundings she'd go, when they got to Asurdun. The moment she left the ship he'd have her seized . . .

And the mentor? What of the wily one who'd seen so many
come and go under the K'haravim? How soon would he forget
a future king?

The darkest day came and went.

Then, Torc could not exactly pinpoint it, time began again.
Then wanton Asticalys, harlot wind, blew hot and cold upon
aging winter; sculpting seas of shining ice, turning trees to
glass.

Torc caught her restlessness. Soon the twelfth step sohurin
would end. But when, exactly? The marks begun on his cell
wall were long neglected. How could he ever have let himself
lose count of the date?

Say—B'hadgazan—what time of the year is it?

That is not a proper question for one under the K'haravim.
Consider only the moment, and how you should be using it.

Cut the blather, mentor, and answer straight. I've been in
this place too long.

Whether or no is not for you to say, nor when you'll take
your leave. As for the date—you vowed to leave that behind
outside. If the Athor wants you to learn of it, he'll let you know
in his way.

And that was that until one morning, as Torc's group was
leaving the mess hall, D'huru Nor halted them to let other
pilgrims pass—the first Torc had ever seen outside his own
conclaur. Strange: they were in white. *White!* Signifying
pilgrims of the twelfth, or lowest step.

Mentor—is that my conclaur? The one I missed?

No reply.

Torc stared after them. What were they doing there at that
hour, where everything ran in grooves? Why hadn't he seen
them before?

It was not until he was back in his cell that he had time to
wonder. They were either coming—or going.

Going. It *was* his original conclaur, and they were on their
way out.

Correct, prince, but don't fret yourself. It's no concern of yours.

Torc kept his eyes closed, his legs crossed, his hands on his knees.

How long to Asurdun, B'hadgazan? And how will they travel?

Five days by ice-ship, prince. Or four, with favorable winds. You've never seen the silver sails, have you? Nor will you, for the thaw will be ancient history by the time you leave. So be easy, forget what day this is, and bend your mind to its proper work.

Proper work?

Torc uncrossed his legs and set his feet to the floor, elbows on knees, and chin on hands and set to brooding on thoughts of home, and of the king; of Tanna, of a city streaming with banners and loud with bells. He thought of the banquet in the Great Hall, the toasts, the heavy gold chain Sharroc must place about his neck, token of his success in the sohurin, official seal of the heir to the throne.

He stood, paced the cell. That tiny space, his blue robe, the daily rites suddenly lost their relevance.

You shall wear the crown . . .

Not for the first time he thought of escape. But that medal was contingent on even exchange: a token from the Athor that the heir had served out his term. No token: no medal. No medal—no heir.

Five days to Asurdun. He smashed his fist into his palm.

Five days hence the white robes would arrive at Riverside. What would his escort say to find he'd stayed behind? How long would it take them to come for him, the holy ship taking none but pilgrims aboard? With guides and fast sled teams, one week at least—maybe two.

By then it would be almost time to leave anyway.

He sighed, recrossed his legs, and closed his eyes.

From that day on, however, Torc kept count, mentally following the pilgrims' descent, from the upper level over the falls, down the river to the marshes, around the meanders closer and closer to the sea.

The day he was to have arrived in Asurdun the mentor read the duty roster later than usual.

The third phase of your sohurin draws near, he told them. *And the Hour of Augmentation when you shall receive the hmlic.*

All went totally still.

Torc looked around, then to the mentor. *That's good. What is it?*

The mentor sighed. *On the day of Augmentation you shall go not to the meditation chamber but to the Hall of Visions to take the hmlic, that is, a decoction of hitaku, triple distilled. You should find it to your liking: 'tis a mite stronger than your Gortwine. But unlike your Gortwine which addles the mind, the hmlic expands it.*

How?

Who can say? It depends on him who receives it. There are those who have soared to regions beyond great Forthyr himself, while others have simply snored the night away.

And when is this fateful day, mentor? Or shouldn't I ask?

The mentor shook out his chore lists; peered at Torc over the top of them. *You may—and I'll answer you, for what it's worth. In three days time you take it, with the rising of Ao.*

Three days.

As he filed out with the rest, it came to him suddenly that on that day he was to have arrived home.

The long drafty hall was fragrant with censers, darkly lit by guttering flames.

Torc followed the rest past lines of bare cots, lowered himself onto the one assigned to him.

Mentors moved about the hall with flasks.

Here, Gurnyac. Lift your head.

Torc obeyed, feeling cold metal against his lips, cool fluid burning his throat. Like hitaku, he thought, lying back, a mite disappointed, until the full force of it hit.

His eyes streamed. He coughed, cried out for water but the sound stuck in his throat. Someone wiped his mouth. Who? He tried to open his eyes but could not.

He began to feel afraid. This was no ordinary drunkenness, for even as his body became as a dead man's his wits grew quick and keen.

B'hadgazan! B'hadgazan, I say!

He saw D'huru Nor in the distance, bent over a prostrate form. Or was it the mentor? The lines of both figures blurred, shone faintly golden.

He looked about him. The walls of the cavern were gone, and the fitful flames, while over each body hovered a pale light, slightly different for each one.

Even as he saw this he was lifted high into the air by a great wind.

He shouted, heard nothing but the wild slipstream bearing him away. He reached out for something, anything to cling to but all around him was only empty air.

B'hadgazan—B'hadgazan!

At once he felt something solid under him, opened his eyes to find himself lying on his cot, as all the others were on theirs. The mentor, recognizably, was standing looking toward him from halfway down the hall. He relaxed, took a deep breath. He hadn't really been anywhere.

Hadn't D'huru Nor said something about one's mind soaring beyond great Forthyr himself? He thought of old Glabrous, and Sheshu, and the Iron Rose, all lying alongside. Scrots, groles, gonts, and melks, the lot of them, all doing the same thing. Well, was he not a warrior? Wherever they went he'd go, nay—further.

When the force drew him up and out the second time, he was ready.

In fact this time he looked down, saw the lines of bodies on the cots, watched the lights wavering over them, fast receding. Why, there he was, he was sure. The vague outlines of his body seemed taller, and thin—scholarly. A body quite unfitting for a warfaring prince.

He let himself be carried out under the cold stars, on and on until the stars faded and all at once he was sinking through a chill mist that clung to his robe.

Below him, Gurynac's citadel reared silent under ominous snow-cloud. From every turret flags and banners flew, save his own, still furled at the foot of its mast, against his non-arrival. It was early morning, as near as he could judge, well into the fourth watch.

He looked toward his father's tower, wondered what Sharroc had made of it. Had they canceled the feast? They certainly weren't dancing in the streets.

The scrots wouldn't have liked it either, losing an excuse to be idle.

Suddenly, a light flickered through his father's casement window.

Dark shadows in armor surrounded the king's bed, one bent low over Sharroc's sleeping form.

Torc saw his father start up, and hands thrusting him back down again.

Father! he shouted. Father!

A moment later, there followed a roar of rage and shock. Abruptly it ceased, and blood starting from the king's chest ran in spouts over the coverlet and splashed to the floor.

Fire sprang, crawled up the king's tower right to his banner atop the spire. It caught, flared—and was gone, and in that moment Torc knew his father was no more.

The air filled with the clamor of the tocsin.

The king was dead.

Long live the king!

He cried out in anguish. Sharroc! Sharroc! What hand had dared do this thing? Dared—and done? He tried to claw his way down through the windy air toward the leaping flames, but firm currents pulled him up and away until the Citadel was but a speck of distant fire.

Raging, grieving, he let himself be carried over the dark lands, upward over the shining lake to the fastness of Rm, where for a time he lay, his mind a blank.

He came to, not on his cot as he'd expected, but standing upright, closed in on all sides by—he reached out in the blackness and touched walls smooth as glass.

He drew back his lips, shouted into the darkness.

Light! Bring light, I say!

No one answered him.

His head began to spin.

Images passed before him: of the whole of Gurnyac afire, of great masses running amok. He saw the Brand houses ranked banner to banner, fighting for ascendancy; the Smeltings, the Foundings, idle and dark, while beyond the Weald, farm and orchard and croft stood ravaged and bare.

Everywhere, from city to city was ruin, chaos, and waste.

His inheritance! His nostrils flared in anger. This was his kingdom that he was to inherit!

His fury swelled, surpassing even his grief for Sharroc. He looked about him in the darkness, demanded angrily, *Who has done this thing? Show him, that I may know mine enemy!*

Light came up from hidden recesses above his head.

He revolved slowly, realizing at last where he was.

On every side a face looked in upon him, a death's head, stark shaven skull with hollow, sunken eyes. A ravaged face, pale and sick with shock.

In the chamber of mirrors he stood, the place where he'd stood on the eve of his sohurin: and the face that stared in on him was his own.

Mentor.
Prince?
Did you see?
Rest now. You're not done.

For a space he lay, conscious of those all around him, of the mentors moving silently up and down the aisles, bending over this pilgrim and that.

All at once he saw the runaway melk moving purposefully toward him. He looked around for the mentor, expecting him at any moment to come striding across the hall to send her back, but the hall was gone, leaving only darkness around them . . .

She halted beside him.

Come, she said. *I have something to show you.* The voice was just as he'd remembered it from the bathhouse: throaty, and coarse.

All this time he'd dreamed of speaking with her. Now all he could cry out was, *Out, melk! Back to your own dreamspace!*

Like it or no, you shall go with me.

Never! He pushed her away. *Get off, melk, or I'll have your head on a pole!*

The girl's image wavered, dissolved.

At once Torc rose in the air a third time, to his great satisfaction leaving her behind.

Where to now? And what to see?

He came to an abrupt stop, on his feet. There was a smell of summer blossom, sweet hay, and the warm stink of fresh thardung. Faintly through the darkness came the sound of singing; a woman's voice.

There came a sudden glare of noon sun on whitewashed stone. Before him stood a crofter's cottage, and on a seat beside the door a young woman dandled a girl-child on her lap.

The woman's face was familiar.

The Iron Rose, her glossy black hair just how he'd pictured it, tumbling in waves down her back.

Resisting lullaby, the child struggled up, put her arms about the woman's neck, and kissed her face. Then, twisting about, she jumped down and ran off to play. The woman smiled, turned to a man who'd appeared in the doorway. A gentle man, Torc saw, with an odd pang of jealousy; older than the Rose by some years, yet strong and sturdy enough.

The Rose's father?

The man pulled her close and kissed her.

Not her father, but her husband.

Torc shrugged off a faint pang of jealousy. Had the melk had her way after all? He began to struggle against his presence there, but a mind as strong as his own—and more adept—held him fast as the body had done in the D'hogana all those past months.

Even as he sensed her presence, the girl suddenly appeared beside him.

Be still and watch. The woman is my mother. The man, my father. I am the little girl.

So? What is that to me? His thought was haughty now, and harsh.

Wait and see, prince, wait and see. Was she mocking him? Did she know how often he'd had that from B'hadgazan?

The sky darkened. The man picked up the child and went with the woman into the house.

Armored riders came over the hill, their captains' helmets bearing the Gnangar crest. They dismounted at the little gate. Torc caught his breath. Wasn't that Feric? The Feric of his boyhood. His hero, his second father, his champion. A younger, leaner giant, with lusty beard and hair about his iron shoulders. Back from some campaign, by the look of it, stopping by the croft to demand food and ale as was his right.

Feric strode to the door, and without knocking, went inside.

He soon emerged with the crofter, who carried food. As the crofter served it, Feric called for the wife to bring ale, which she did, with bobs and anxious smiles, the girl-child clinging to her skirts.

Having passed the jug, she made to go back inside, but Feric caught her arm, pulled her close, forced his mouth on hers. Bewildered, the child began to cry, but yet stayed by her mother's hand. Beside himself, the crofter watched until he could bear it no longer, and, running forward, tried to prise her loose, but hands caught him, felled him, shackled his feet.

Feric, smiling, shucked off his armor, seized the woman, dragged her to the ground, and had her, fierce and fast while the child stood by.

The woman cried out as Feric climaxed, and the child, whimpering, ran from her at last but the men caught her also, tied her small ankles and brought her to where her father was.

The mother, grimy and bloodsmeared, tried to crawl away. Feric let her go so far, then gave the nod to the second in line.

And so it went, until every last man had had his way.

In the twilight they loaded the crofter onto a spare thar, the sobbing child behind him. But when they hauled the woman to her feet, she fell back.

Shrugging, Feric seized a spear, ran her through, pinning her to the ground. She writhed a little, like a ruptured pupa, then lay still.

They fired the house, then girding themselves up once more, they moved off, under the high stars, leaving the woman's body for carrion.

I never knew my father, Gurnyac. Only that he was born a free and honest man. But that day we were taken without witness as slaves by our own king's men.

As for my father—if he's still in the Brandhouses, I've never found him out. And I—

She bared her arm, displayed the iron rose. *Feric did well for the Founding Masters that day, didn't he? See? From that time on I labored in the forges day and night until puberty, when the Masters found other work for me to do.*

We're much of an age, you and I, prince. I wonder what you were doing when your general rode by?

He looked at her, strange feelings stirring in him. Oh, the pity of it. He wanted to protest his innocence, Feric's. Tell her that there must have been some mistake.

She must have read his thought, for she started back as from some threat of gross contagion.

He drew himself up, hiding his confusion. So much enmity there was in her face, it wouldn't become him to grovel. And so he answered her in terms that much belied his turmoil:

How should I know? Or care? I wasn't responsible for what they did. His thought hardened. *Nor was my father. It's against his law.*

Oh? Her eyes flashed. *But didn't you wish that very thing on me that first night in the bathhouse?*

That, he answered harshly, *was only after I saw—*

—the Brandmark on my arm. That one small mark that transforms free human beings into things. The Houses are crammed with hundreds such!

No!

Yes! Or where do you suppose your slaves to have come from?

From the spoils of war!

Fool! If you don't know the truth, your father must! But the people have had enough! One day they'll rise up and the Gnangar flag shall burn!

Torc whirled on her, seized her arm.

What do you mean? Answer me!

Could she have had anything to do with what he'd just seen at home? He let her go. No. Her struggle was not with the iron of the sword, but with the iron in her soul.

Gurnyac: know that I hate you, and shall hate you until the day I die. You, and all your kind.

She looked up at him, loathing in her eyes, such as she'd never revealed in all the months they'd spent working together in the D'hogana. *I've heard your thought many times: in the D'hogana, out on the plateau, sometimes in the middle of the night. I've heard you thinking on all of us, looking down on us as though we were a herd of filthy forhars. Well, you're the filth. You don't deserve to be here.*

In the D'hogana? In his cell? His anger stirred. She'd intruded upon his innermost thought? He recalled the mentor's saying once how some had powers naturally. Is that what this melk meant? That she had powers like that? And did D'huru Nor know about them? Had the mentor known that she'd pried into his mind?

If so, the hypocrisy of it, chastising him for merely infringing upon her body even as she had been trespassing with impunity upon his deepmost being.

Why, she must have read his thoughts on her, time and time again.

He didn't know, Gurnyac. He didn't guess. I was very discreet.

Discreet? She had that power, that he, Torc had so long desired, to deceive the mentor and come off undetected and unscathed?

D'huru Nor certainly could not have guessed her powers. Even now, she had crossed into Torc's dreamspace. Her gifts must have been strengthened by the hmlic.

He watched her warily. He felt violated. Filthy melk—no— not a melk but a freewoman, a crofter's child.

There you go again! Her voice was bitter. *Can't you see even now? There's no real difference between "freewoman" and "melk." Only a Brandmark on the arm—and in the mind. As for me—born free or no, I've lived the melk's life. I've suffered the melk's miseries and injustices, endured the Brandmasters' tyranny.* She waved him away. *I give you warning: we're at war, you and I, and war gives one leave to set rules of nicety aside. Now go—unless you've stomach for more. Unless you'd like to see more infamy.*

Almost at once, he found himself looking down on Gurnyac from a great height, on banners and bunting flying from every tower for a coronation day. There was cheering, and shouting; bells rang, bugles sounded, the harness jingled on thar and tasseled ambaree until, in the very midst of it all the tumult died and slowly, slowly the banners faded like smoke and shredded bunting fluttered down to the dirt.

She, turning away, walked into the distance, climbed a far slope which Torc saw to be not the hill leading up to the citadel, but the path to the holy city's gate. She reached up to toll the bell but even as she took the rope in hand, the gate swung, groaning, of its own accord.

Inside, bodies littered bloodied streets, the white walls lay in ruins, and the golden roofs were gone.

Torc watched, incredulous, unable to move or speak a word.

As the girl made to pass inside, D'huru Nor appeared, leaning on the gate.

Back, child, for the way is closed.

She made obeisance, then still tried to pass.

The mentor spread his arms before her, and as he did so,

deep gashes opened in his flesh, letting blood in dark shining rivulets until at last he crumpled, to lie with all the rest.

The Iron Rose turned, looked blindly out into the darkness where Torc still stood.

Look what you've done! she screeched at him, her face twisted. *You hated thing—now are you satisfied?*

CHAPTER TWENTY-THREE

HE came to lying in his cell.

The all-too-familiar bell had awoken him, to call him out and up onto the predawn plateau.

He turned his face to the wall.

He would not go out that day. Would not face anyone.

There came the sound of shuffling feet from outside, then silence.

He drifted, dreamed bad dreams of fires, of falling from great heights, called out as his father uttered his death cry.

He sat up, his breath coming short, his heart pounding.

The cell was empty. On the floor by the door was a tray and on it sat his sip of hitaku and honied skalu cake.

He turned from it and lay, blindly facing the wall.

Look what you've done!

O Father, Father. He should have stayed at home. Should have insisted. Called his father's bluff.

If he hadn't missed that Dryac-crossed boat, he'd have been home by now and then—and then . . .

He sat up slowly.

And then he might also have been dead, taken in wine-drugged sleep. Because—because whoever had done that terrible thing to the father must have planned to include the son, or *why else pick the night of his expected return?*

He drew up his knees, and hugging them, rocked back and forth.

Oh, Sharroc! The things he'd said, the times he'd dismissed him for an old gont, the times he'd wished the king dead and he already in his place. He hadn't meant it. It was too soon for his father to die. Things hadn't yet been over between them.

He closed his eyes, gave himself up to grief.

The fires in the keep! The dark figures about the royal bed, his father's roar of rage, the blood everywhere.

He looked up suddenly.

Perhaps it hadn't really happened. His spirits rallied a little. Perhaps what he'd seen had been simply a nightmare conjured by strong liquor after too long a fast.

No.

What he'd seen was the truth, he was sure.

But how? His hands tightened into fists. Who had done it? The sweat broke again. The last time he'd asked that his own face had looked back at him from mirrored walls.

How? How could he have been responsible when he'd been there, in Rm?

He groaned, curled his arms about his head.

His thoughts had come full circle. He should have stayed at home.

Look what you've done! You hated thing—now are you satisfied?

What would he expect when he got home?

He saw again the coronation bunting fading, the crowds melting into mist.

The Athor had said that he'd wear the crown.

The Athor.

Torc's mouth compressed into a tight, thin line.

Had that one known?

He got up, walked to the door.

There, he bent down, took up the hitaku cup, tossed the

liquor back as he'd not done since his first day in that place. He felt it going down, heating the back of his throat. He breathed out, savoring its aftertaste.

He bent down a second time, took up the cake, and stopped, his hand halfway to his mouth.

Look what you've done! You hated thing—now are you satisfied?

The girl hadn't been speaking of Torc's own grief, but of hers, as they'd stood before the ruins of Rm.

He lifted the cake again, nibbled on it miserably.

Had the Athor known of that vision also?

He threw himself down on the bed, turned back to the wall.

All of this was too much for him. They had been fevered wine-visions only. Even so—it was strange that the mentor had let him alone in his cell that day . . .

He drifted, in and out of sleep. Sometimes grief was so strong and keen upon him that he couldn't bear it. Sometimes he dismissed what he'd seen as unreal, impossible.

A dream.

But his grief was real enough.

Yet—had he not times past had nightmares that left him with very real feelings of fear and sadness, feelings that lay upon him well into the waking state?

He shook his head.

This was different, and he knew it.

Three times more he slept and awoke, and each time his tray was replenished with food and water and another cup of hitaku. But no sign did he have of the mentor that day.

The next morning, awkwardly, Torc took up life again. In the D'hogana, he braced himself to meet the girl's eyes. But all during that day, and throughout all the days and weeks following, she remained just as before, never betraying by so much as a look what had passed between them. Her manner was cool and correct as ever as became a pilgrim on the eleventh step.

Had they really shared that dreamspace, Torc wondered,

more than once. Perhaps they had and the melk had forgotten it. Or had it all been but his own private nightmare after all?

Whatever the answer, he never felt the same again, not about her, not about the rest of the sohurin. More and more he took to studying them, watching them go about their business, trying to know them more as persons than scrots and groles.

But he never really succeeded, however he wanted to.

And yet he took to wondering more and more, though, what Gurnyac would have to be like if his fellow pilgrims would live out there as they did under the K'haravim. Someone, certainly, would have to make changes such as hadn't been seen since the first Gnangar king ascended the throne and crowned himself.

Time passed, the pain, the immediacy of the visions faded, until the end of the sohurin drew near. Life about them quickened, spent forces reemerged from decay to rise again and build another year.

The last day of the sohurin was almost springlike.

Having bathed and put on fresh pilgrim's clothes a last time within Rm's walls, Torc filed from under the K'haravim, back into the Induction Hall where he'd taken his oath full two hundred and seventy long days before.

From his place at the back Torc brooded, his mind on Asurdun; on danger, and survival as must the langaur in a felmar's vale, for the force of his visions was back upon him.

Being there in that place brought to mind long forgotten words, spoken by the Hela at the beginning of the sohurin.

. . . though the outer world fail, and whole dynasties pass . . .

She might well have been thinking of him.

Who had killed Sharroc? And did that one even now sit upon a stolen throne?

Unthinkable.

Feric and Brac would surely have brought the assassin to account. But if so, why hadn't they come to Rm for him?

Perhaps they had. And perhaps they'd been turned away as the Athor had promised.

If so, who was minding the throne until his return? Gar was second in line, but not tall enough. The throne lay empty, for sure. The generals would rule through the king's Council until Torc's coming.

The Council.

He ran yet again through the noble names, found not one with courage and cunning enough to do what had manifestly been done. He thought of his father's old friends, comrades, the equerries who'd escorted Torc to Asurdun. Loyal, every one of them. But—loyalties could change—as Sharroc had discovered to his cost.

After his long isolation, Torc had no way of knowing whom to trust, whom to watch out for.

He'd trust no one: would not disembark at Riverside.

So what to do instead?

Only now did he notice the morning brightness flooding in through the open doorway, warming the back of his scalp. It was with a sense of unreality that he stared around at the familiar heads in that hall.

Strange, how they'd once all looked alike to him. There, halfway to the front was Bullneck, champion of the D'hogana; there, Artil, the hairy Starwife. To the right, further back, Torc saw almost with fondness, shone the smooth cheeks of Old Glabrous, while over there was Sheshu's long skinny nape and bony skull. And somewhere—his eyes raked the heads from side to side—up front, the Iron Rose.

The fondness leaving his eyes, he stared fixedly at the back of her neck, focusing upon her, willing her to acknowledge him.

Nothing.

A slight stir and the Inner Twelve filed onto the dais as before, followed this time by a bearer holding aloft an earthenware urn.

Torc sighed resignedly. More ceremony. For how long this time?

Don't wish your last hours away too fast, and don't dismiss that oil too lightly, either, if you would speak again.

Torc scowled at the mentor's broad back. Would he evermore grow used to the privacy of his thoughts?

The door closed behind him, shutting the sunlight out.

The Athor spoke.

Behold Athor, of the Inner Ring. With joy we greet you, and release you from your Induction oath. Go forth this day with lasting strength and heightened vision, your attainments on the Eleventh Step sustaining your feet ever on the upward Path.

The Athor paused.

Torc, looking up, met the man's eye, sensed a strange hesitancy.

Should you wish to return, the Tenth Step sohurin begins on the first day of summer.

The Athor summoned the bearer forward, took from him a cochlear of polished stone which he dipped into the urn as the mentor ushered the front line of pilgrims to the dais.

Torc closed his eyes. That odd awkwardness: so unlike the man. As though he were not certain of the new sohurin's date. He hugged himself against a sudden chill.

. . . though whole dynasties pass . . .

Could the Hela have meant the Lothuri themselves?

He thought of his vision. The dying mentor, the roofless walls, the bloodied streets.

Could this happen—and could the blame somehow be laid upon him?

He fixed his eyes on the Athor, willed him to answer.

Will my vision come to pass? Will it? Will it?

But the Athor continued to watch the pilgrims filing up for their swallow of throat-loosening oil without even looking up.

Torc turned his attention to the girl.

You! Melk! Speak to me! Could it happen, could it? Could it?

The girl rose, followed her fellows to take the oil, sat down again without once glancing his way.

Torc calmed himself with the Canticum.

The whole idea was preposterous, that was why no one answered him.

Soon they'd all part ways, go about their proper business. Sharroc would have his hide for staying this long, until he recognized what status the stay would give Torc with the people. A wave of homesickness came over him.

He wanted to be out of there, and on the boat, skimming the waters toward Asurdun.

It was already past the tenth hour, as he would judge. After this they'd all have a last audience with the Athor, asking of him one boon—and only one, the mentor had repeated, his eye on Torc.

The pilgrims stepped down one by one. Oh, what the fookar. First. Last. They were all going by the same boat in the end.

Side by side Torc and the mentor trod the passages, Torc swallowing, pushing his breath against his palate, savoring the lingering flavor of the oil the Athor had dropped onto his tongue.

"Well?" The mentor's voice sounded rusty, too. "How do you feel?"

Torc opened his mouth to reply, closed it again. Long ago, in the beginning, when he'd come into that place, he'd insisted on speaking aloud against the mentor's mindspeech. Now he was reluctant to use his vocal chords.

Eager to be gone from you, B'hadgazan—that is, if one ever can. What guarantee have I that you'll not follow me all the way home?

"Ha! Rest easy, Gurnyac. Once you're through that gate, we're done."

They walked on.

This boon, mentor—can it be anything?

"I've already told you: yes, except what *you* want." D'huru Nor shot Torc a sideways glance. "Again, prince: it's forbidden to speak of one's visions under the hmlic."

You'll be sorry, B'hadgazan.

"Maybe. Maybe not. But though the very mountain fall, you mustn't speak of them. As I 've said, it's no arbitrary rule, but a universal law of consequence. Just try to express your visions aloud, and you'll forget them before the words are off the tongue. That's the way of it."

But some of what I saw concerns the K'haravim.

The mentor stopped in his tracks. "Have you learned nothing after all? The future is already written. The only thing we can change is—"

—our attitude. I know, I know. But I don't believe that.

"That's your privilege. Meanwhile—" He nodded toward a small door behind him. "In there and wait."

But—

The mentor opened the door onto a room that Torc knew only too well.

Their eyes met.

The mentor knew.

"In, Gurnyac."

After a moment, Torc brushed past him into the light—and the door clicked shut behind him.

He stood in the middle of the room, eyes closed, a small boy hiding from the Gradhlzacs. How foolish. This was not the Hour of Augmentation. Not his vision. This was real, and he was leaving. He opened his eyes, threw off his heisha and lifted his arms, turning and turning about in deliberate parody of the first time in that place.

Behold Torc the now and future king of Gurnyac.

How thin this tyrant had become. Gaunt. He remembered the sight of himself from above during the Hour of Augmentation. *More like a scholar than a warfaring prince.*

He lowered his arms slowly, and all the other Torcs lowered theirs.

He tilted back his head and laughed aloud, a short brittle sound cracking the space around him: the first sound to come from his throat in all that time.

He revolved slowly to watch all those other Torcs laughing also. Yet for all those ranks upon ranks of laughing faces in that place, going back and back to infinity, there came but the sound of one man . . .

The Athor received him as before. But this time he handed Torc a cup and bade him drink. Torc took it, sniffed, sipped.

"Now try your voice."

Torc made a dry sound in his throat.

"Drink more. It is an effort after so long."

Indeed. It feels so—unnecessary, too.

He drained the cup.

"But yet it is not. Mindspeech is indeed rare beyond these gates."

Rare, but not entirely nonexistent, Torc told himself, minded of the girl. He looked quickly to the Athor. Had the man read that thought? Hard to tell. The golden face remained expressionless.

"And speech does have its uses, prince." A brief smile. "What king can afford to share his every thought? Even we observe strict restraints in our mindspeech practices."

Oh? No one told the mentor.

Another smile.

I think, Athor, that it wouldn't be such a bad thing for every man to know the measure of another's words. Truth is rare in Gurnyac.

The Athor's eyebrow went up. "You've changed indeed, prince."

As well you know.

"Indeed. What boon would you ask of me before you go?"

What I saw—

The Athor raised his hand.

"If it concerns the Hour of Augmentation, stop. Surely the mentor told you that to talk of it, even to me, would be to lose it. Then your experience will be rendered useless, to you and everyone else."

Torc pulled at his lower lip.

I thought you knew everything anyway.

"Perhaps, but not to speak of it, by the Will of the Quaur."

"In that case, only tell me," Torc hesitated, "whether what we see is real, or just a warning."

"Only time can answer that, prince."

"Then the Dryac take your hmlic!" Torc's voice broke in a fit of coughing. *It's a sick philosophy that holds a man can't shape his own future. And if it's true, then a man's life isn't worth a shilpit!*

The Athor refilled Torc's cup, held it out. Torc took the cup, drank.

"I don't make the rules, prince. Only bide by them, just as you and everyone else. Some things can change, by the grace of the Quaur, but I don't know which any more than you. I only wish I did." He sighed.

I've wasted my boon.

"No. Ask again."

Torc considered. *It's been long under the K'haravim. I've wished many times to be out of here. At the end of it the mentor says I've changed; you say I've changed—yet—I haven't, not in the way I'd want to.*

I've watched the others, and it's plain that they've gained more than I have somehow. And I think— He paused, then tried again. *I think the cause is in me. In the D'hogana all I wanted was to win. The mentor told me over and over that that wasn't the point, yet I couldn't change my goal. I've worked hard, learned all the rites and rituals, how to win and lose with equal grace, but it's only show. Inside I still seethe with rage and the urge to kill. I've never felt the true spirit of the D'hogana. Further—*

He stopped. Always his thoughts went back to the Hour of Augmentation.

"Wait." Again the Athor raised his hand. "I shall close my mind to yours so that you may be free to consider your next words."

Torc nodded thanks.

The king might well be dead. Thinking him to be initially, Torc had grieved for him, as much as any Gnangar could. But how paltry had been the measure of his sorrow beside the girl's.

Athor—I must mention the Hour of Augmentation, but not specifically.

The Athor nodded him on.

I saw great evil done, but yet—and this is my trouble—I could not feel it enough.

The Athor smiled. "This is in itself change, Torc-prince. A far cry from the one who first came in here. The change is begun. It is just a matter of time."

Athor—I haven't time. When I go home I shall be exposed to such pressures as you wouldn't believe. What I don't achieve now, I never will. I beg you—I want to feel more the wrong that I witnessed in my vision. Torc spread his hands on the table between them, leaned forward. *One of your mentors told me that a king must know his lowliest subject in order to become great. I want to be great. I want to feel the pain of my people. I would be feared—and also loved.*

The Athor closed his eyes, and at once Torc felt himself at a vast distance from him. Minutes passed, until Torc wondered if he'd not been dismissed. He looked around, but saw no one in the darkness beyond; no guide, no mentor. So he stayed, uncertain, until at last the Athor stirred and reopened his eyes.

"This is no small favor you ask, prince. This that you desire, this *empathy:* it is more powerful by far than mere sympathy. Be warned that it is a two-edged gift that only the strong should wield. And its application is universal. Once possessing it, you may not use it selectively, choosing what you will or will not feel at whim. Neither, having once received it, shall you ever be able to lay it aside."

"I can have it?"

"If the Quaur wills it—and you really want it."

"I do."

"Then close your eyes while I intercede for you."

Torc did so and waited, curious to know what the Athor would do.

With a slight shock, he felt cool, dry hands grasp his head

from behind, and the fingertips spreading fanwise over his brow. Such a light, soft touch, yet Torc's skin burned. He felt momentary elation. Was it happening already?

All at once he felt a surge of energy, a humming in his ears, and his body tingled as though fine wires were passing through the soles of his feet and out through the top of his head.

Was it pain that he felt? Or joy? Anguish? Or ecstasy? His whole being dissolved, flowed out at high speed through the Athor's hands, and out, into space.

"You may open your eyes."

The Athor was seated as before across the table, as though he hadn't moved.

Maybe he hadn't.

"You must go now." The Athor folded his hands before his face.

"But—"

"I have done. Only time will tell if your wish has been granted. And remember this: you have been granted only that which you already possessed by the grace of the Quaur."

Torc stood up slowly.

"Tell me one last thing," the Athor said. "In the chamber of mirrors this time—what did you see?"

Torc looked out into the darkness, frowning in concentration. "I saw myself multiplied as before by the thousand thousand, a vast army of Gnangars, I at their head. I smiled, they smiled. I raised my arms, so did they. And when I lowered them, they did likewise, even as before.

"But when I looked again, I saw that vast host was but an illusion, and at its center just one man, an average man, at that."

The golden eyes flickered, then closed.

"Farewell, prince. May the Quaur go with you. Remember: whatever happens, hold fast to the process, for that is all that matters in the end. That, and your attitude."

For a moment Torc stood gazing down on the golden face, unwilling, unable to move. Here was the real world where important things happened. Out there was all show and shadow play. For a moment he had a wild urge to beg to stay, to sit at the man's feet, to share in his serenity, to learn to reach for truths of whose existence he could not as yet conceive.

"Come, prince."

Torc turned to find D'huru Nor standing behind him.

"Don't be dashed," the mentor said, leading him out. "He has that effect on anyone when he so chooses. It's a mark of his favor, you know."

Torc's anger flashed, and as abruptly, died. For the first time he heard not condescension but a peculiar kind of fondness— and—pride?—in the mentor's voice. The mentor liked him, and Torc had never known it.

Warmth surged through him. The Quaur had granted his wish, and it was working. It was working, even now!

He moved on, pausing only for one last look at the solitary figure seated under the flame before following the mentor from under the K'haravim, then out through the gates of Rm at last.

The long boat skimmed the smooth, bright waters of the lake. Torc, shading his eyes, turned for a last look at the golden city. Too late. It was already gone over the horizon.

His face lightened. Already the mentor was gearing himself for the next lot of shorn innocents to be delivered up, sacrificial harlings under the knife-edge of his wit and tyranny.

"Farewell, B'hadgazan. May your next whetstone have no less grit than this one—who nevertheless is sorely abraded under your blade."

"Farewell, prince. And mark: wear your crown to bed, sleep with your back to the wall—and don't fall too quickly into your old ways."

Torc smiled at the memory of the mentor striding back up through the gates, until he was minded suddenly of his terrible vision; of D'huru Nor's bloody body slowly crumpling to lie in the dust.

Look what you've done!

The girl's words haunted him.

If ever he was to find out their meaning, now was the time.

Besides, he'd also been thinking of the dangers that might be lying in wait for him in Asurdun, and if he was right, if the girl really did have the power of mindspeech, he might very well have a use for her.

He stood up unsteadily, pushed past his fellow pilgrims, and lurched forward with the movement of the boat into the prow.

She was looking over the side, gazing down at the water patterns curling outward from the boat's side. He half fell, half slid onto the bench beside her, staring down the Rethi guide who sat facing them.

"I would speak with you."

The words were lost in the swish of wind and the slap of sail.

He leaned across her, pushing his face under her, tried again.

"I would speak with you!"

The girl did not even turn her head.

"I said, I would speak with you!" He seized her arm, shook it, ignoring the turning heads, the Rethi half risen in his seat.

"Get away."

"I must speak with you before Asurdun."

She turned to him at last. "Why?"

"I've been thinking. I would make amends. Find your father. Set you free."

"Why?"

"I'm sorry. Feric shall also pay."

She made a short, sharp sound, turned back to the water.

You're in trouble, Gurnyac. And you want to use me. Go away.

He studied the back of her head, her heisha riffling in the wind. She'd used mindspeech. He'd been right. Which meant—his gut tightened—which meant that his visions had had some kind of weird reality after all.

I am in trouble, I'll admit. But I still mean what I say about helping you.

She did not reply.

Anger should have come then. Words formed in his head. *Is this what you learned under the K'haravim? Where's the love they taught you to show your fellow-man?* But there was no heat in them. He'd seen her grief, and its cause, had watched her vent her pent-up hatred and bitterness, and understood.

Hadn't she suffered enough?

Oh, he felt so confused. Things were not so simple anymore. He wanted her, he needed her, and yet he wanted to let her go.

Very well. I leave you in peace. If you're still listening, I promise you—you're free. Go your way. I wish you good speed.

He waited a minute, then, when she still didn't move he slid to the edge of the seat, braced himself against the lift of the boat.

You'd be a fool to trust me. I told you: I want you dead.

He waited.

In the Foundings they called me Katanaia.

Katanaia! Iron's bitter aftertaste.

The name became her well. And yet—

When you were small—do you recall your name then?

She turned to face him.

Ramoni, my father named me.

Ramoni. Bridge of love.

Between my father and—and my mother, you see. Her eyes had filled with tears.

He slid back toward her, took her arm.

Ramoni—I need your help. Will you come with me?

She looked down at his hand, made no move to free herself.

You're a fool. I thought so, and now I know it. Go, while you're yet safe.

Fool you may think me, but when a man must choose between a raging fire and an uncertain ledge, surely the ledge is worth the risk, for at least it buys him time. Maybe I can change your mind about me between here and Asurdun. Say you'll at least consider it.

CHAPTER TWENTY-FOUR

13.00 Hours 14 October 2047
Estralita

S HIRA, hearing voices outside in the passage, went to the door, put her ear to it. There—MacAllister's clearly above the rest.

He was back.

Footsteps, his. A light tap on the door.

She darted back to her chair, sat.

"Who is it?"

"MacAllister."

"Come in."

He poked his head around the door, obviously spotted her lunch tray.

"Well, well. Eating alone." He stepped inside.

Shira made no attempt to welcome him.

"Have I done something wrong?"

"No." She stared down at her tray. "It's just wonderful around here."

He came forward, dropped into a seat opposite. "I had to wait for Ord's replacements."

"The Trojan horse?"

335

"Don't even think it." He looked toward her grandfather's closed door. "The Hesikastor okay?"

"Uhuh. Sleeping, as usual. That's all he ever does these days, when he's off the synergizer. But this whole thing seems to agree with him, so it's all right, I guess."

"And you—you okay?"

"I guess."

"Have I missed much?"

Shira, relenting, told him what had happened the last couple of days.

"Thanks," he said. "Though it's not the same as seeing it. By the way, Susann Ellisen's renewed her invitation."

"We can't go right now," Shira said hurriedly. "Grandfather's busy."

"She didn't say your grandfather, Shira. She thinks you need a break. I'm going back tonight with the latest batch of strips. She's asked me to bring you too."

Shira recoiled. "Oh, no."

"Well, I have to relay the message to your grandfather." He attempted to smile. "Do they still shoot messengers?" He leaned forward, took Shira's hands in his. "Listen, young lady, far be it from me to tell you what to do, but she has a point. You're looking like the Lady of Shalot." He tightened his grip, pulled her toward him. "There's a husky young bruk, as they say on Phrynis, just waiting to meet you. Wants to know whether you play slingball.

She pulled away, feeling her color rapidly come and go, leaving her paler than ever.

The Lady of Shalot. She knew about her. Elaine, the young girl who in King Arthur's time fell in love with the great knight Lancelot and died for love of him, he not even knowing. She glanced keenly at MacAllister's face. No. He hadn't meant any more by it than that she looked peaked.

"I shan't go, and that's that."

MacAllister got up. "That's okay, then." He moved to the door.

She got up also, went to open it.

Her hand on the knob, she paused. "Did you really mean what you said about our seeing the strips together?"

He looked surprised. "Sure. Be fun. I'll take me a rain check until I get back." He held out his hand, smiling.

Suddenly, impulsively, before she knew what she was doing, she reared up on tiptoe, aimed a quick kiss at him, missed his mouth, hit the corner of it and a bit of his cheek.

"Hey, hey." He took her elbows, held her at arm's length. "Steady."

He must have caught something in her eye for the laughter died in his.

"See you," he said, and went out.

She closed the door on him, stood with her back against it. There'd been something, she was sure of it. She'd seen it in his eyes.

She pushed off from the door, went to sit down, wrapped her arms around herself.

Fool. What did she know about these things? She'd made a spectacle of herself, worse than that Elaine had done. At least that girl hadn't literally thrown herself at the man's head!

She rocked back and forth in misery. What was happening to her?

Damn MacAllister.

She'd never marry Kirrin now.

Grandfather awoke around four, took his afternoon snack in the mess room with her.

Shira picked at her food, aware of MacAllister sitting with Suk and Prosser at a side table. She watched him closely, watched Suk making eyes at him.

MacAllister glanced up once, met her eye, and winked.

She looked away.

MacAllister caught her grandfather as he was leaving the mess room. At a nod from Grandfather, the two men took a table in the far corner. Shira went back to the little apartment, sat moodily, waiting for her grandfather to come in.

The moment he walked through the door, she knew what he would say, knew that this time he would brook no quarrel.

"Shira, my dear. You are going to take a break."

"No!"

He smiled at her gently. "You shall pack and be ready within the hour to go with MacAllister."

"You said we had to stay together. You need me."

"Shiralee. I have my reasons." He reached forward, took her hands in his. "Trust an old man. Everything will be all right here, I promise."

She bit back her chagrin. That wasn't the whole of it. She looked down. She couldn't tell him, couldn't—

"You think I didn't know?"

Startled, she looked up and caught the gleam in his eyes.

"I might well have done the same in the circumstances. At your age, anyway. Let us go within."

Keeping her eyes on him, she nodded.

Shira, I want you to continue. Listen: while you're away, I'll let you know the moment the beacon contacts me, and you shall share my experiences just as before. I'm sure you'll find a way.

This time, he actually smiled at her.

She jumped up, threw her arms about him.

"Hey, hey. Leave this body some breath."

"How long? How long will I have to stay?"

He sighed. "Let's wait and see, eh? Maybe you won't want to come back down here after a day or two of luxury. Okay, okay, now go and pack. MacAllister's waiting. And Shira—" He patted her shoulder. "Take care."

She turned from him, hurried into her room.

He knew. He knew about MacAllister, just as he always knew about everything.

She reached for her bag, began to throw her few belongings into it.

But—he hadn't forbidden her, hadn't said she was wrong.

Had only warned her to be careful.

She went back out into the sitting room, found MacAllister there. She set down her bag, embraced her grandfather.

"Take care of yourself, Grandfather." Her voice was wobbly.

What was she doing, leaving him there with those people who didn't give a dam?

It's all right, Shiralee. Nothing's going to happen to me, I promise you.

It wasn't until she was strapped in and under the slam of the hopper's acceleration that it occurred to her to wonder. He'd not only not punished her for eavesdropping on the beacon, but he'd given her permission to continue. No—he'd actually asked her to do so. She bit her lip, suddenly anxious. That wasn't like him, not at all. She fought the urge to tell MacAllister to turn back. It wouldn't be any good. Grandfather had told her to go to Bentnose Peak, and that was final.

Why?

Her anxiety grew. What did he know? She forced herself to calm down, let go. There was nothing she could do but as he said: trust him.

20.00 Hours 14 October 2047
Bentnose Peak

Dinner lasted forever.

And soy tasted like soy eaten off bone china with real silver as out of struzar cups with myplast.

There were six of them at the table: Ellisen, Susann Ellisen, their son, Sven. She herself.

MacAllister was there, but he might very well not have been for all he said. It was almost as though he didn't exist, she thought. And then, that's how he'd been at first in Estralita.

And Katz, silent, his eyes missing nothing.

Conversation was smoothly awkward.

Ellisen?

He was impatient to go and see the latest tridi strips,

obviously, but there he was, having to go through the ritual of the dinner for her.

The son didn't want to be there, either, Shira could see that quite clearly. He'd taken one look at her and clearly wasn't impressed.

The judgment was mutual. He had spoiled brat stamped all over him. The handsome face, so like his father's, was overwritten with a sulky resentment.

It occurred to her then that her face might be looking pretty much the same. She glanced toward MacAllister, and smiled.

She liked Susann Ellisen a lot. Found her to be every bit as nice as her writing had promised. She seemed so genuinely concerned about Shira that Shira quite forgave her from pulling her out of Estralita. She asked Shira many questions about her grandfather, and the Bourg, about the way of life there, the Spartan conditions. It was rough, Shira told her, "but no worse than many other places. We're lucky to be anywhere."

She looked around at the opulence of the dining room to find her hostility gone, she couldn't think why.

"You have a young man, or shouldn't I ask?" Susann Ellisen said. "It's so difficult to judge these days."

Shira's face flared. "We're considered too young to think about such things," she said, deliberately not mentioning Kirrin. She avoided MacAllister's eye.

Ellisen stood up.

The rest followed. With a mumbled apology, Sven ducked out and away.

Ellisen bent politely toward her.

"I'm going to run today's strips. Would you care to join us, Shira?"

Shira paused. She was desperately tired, after the morning's viewing. She looked toward MacAllister. He'd probably be gone again by the morning. "Thank you," she said. "I'd like that."

It wasn't the same, watching the holograms. How could anyone assess what was happening just by seeing and hearing from the outside? Even being privy to Torc and Tanna's thought as voiced through Grandfather's mind was nowhere near the same as being inside, actually feeling what they felt, physically and emotionally. Between watching and being part of it lay a world of difference. If ever genius found a way to make that kind experience viable—better yet, commercially viable—he or she would amass a fortune!

She and MacAllister sat on the couch on either side of Susann Ellisen. MacAllister said nothing, only watched the hologram through half-closed eyes.

Shira kept falling asleep, so much so that in the end they had to wake her to get her to bed. The hologram was off, MacAllister and Katz were gone.

"Don't worry, you can see the strips tomorrow. And if you want to sleep on in the morning," Susann Ellisen said at Shira's bedroom door, "please feel free. That's why you're here."

Shira thanked her, closed the heavy oak door behind her, and throwing off her clothes climbed into a high four-poster bed that smelled of French lavender.

But the business of getting herself upstairs and into bed had taken her clean over her sleep curve. She lay wide awake, thinking about her grandfather, worrying and wondering over his strange behavior and his repeated words, trust an old man.

He'd known—how long?—that she'd been sharing his visions first hand! And yet instead of packing her off home in disgrace as she'd have expected, he'd sent her here. Why? Not because she looked peaked. She always looked peaked. She was too impatient to waste time sitting around sunrooms.

She blew out a long slow breath of frustration. The very next time they spoke together, she resolved, she'd confront him with the question direct. She tossed about onto her other side, then struggled upright. It was no good. She just couldn't settle now.

She slipped out of bed, and paced about the room. The only thing that would take her back to sleep now would be a hot drink. Where would she get it? She hadn't seen any of the usual wall dispensers about. Like the silo, was this place too old to have any? Perhaps. Perhaps not. Perhaps she'd been too preoccupied to notice them.

There was only one way to find out. She dressed, and crept through into the hall.

It stretched right and left through a series of curtained arches, gloomy with real imitation gas lamps suggesting Victorian days. No hot drink dispensers. At the end of the hall to her right was a darkened window. Curious as to what lay beyond it, she padded along past rows of recessed doors on either side.

She was halfway there when she heard the sound of voices raised behind one of the doors.

She hurried past, not wishing to eavesdrop, but before she got out of earshot she clearly heard Susann Ellisen say "old man" and knew that meant Grandfather. And then she heard Ellisen say something like, "can handle Hengst okay."

She stopped still, frankly listening now outside the door.

". . . I say it's wrong, Pitar. Stop before you're in over your head."

Ellisen's reply began as a mumble, too low to hear, then rose almost to a shout. ". . . it's the only way, can't you see that? I don't like it any more than you, but look what appeasement got us last time. Look what a hellfire mess Chambertin got us into in spite of all that your father could do! Christ! Come on—you're General Cleary's daughter, aren't you?"

"Pitar, you're going around and around and saying nothing. Fazhakian said this was the end of everything unless you act— his way. Pitar, he's the one you must move with, not Hengst. *Disarm,* don't *escalate* the madness."

"I'm not for escalation. Only redistribution. Goddammit, Susann, you don't know what you're talking about. I wish I'd not told you anything!"

There was a pause, then Susann Ellisen's voice answered.

"You haven't told me anything, Pitar. Not anything that

matters. You think me a fool? You think I don't know what you're up to? You're going to sell that old man out, aren't you? *Aren't you!"* she demanded, then went quiet again. "We've come a long way, Pitar. Maybe as far as we can go."

Shira heard the sound of muffled feet rapidly crossing soft carpet, toward the door. The door!

She dove for the nearest arch, made the drapes just as Susann Ellisen came out.

Through a gap in the velvet Shira saw her leaning against the door, eyes closed. A moment later, the woman pulled away to walk past, down to the end of the hall and around the corner. There'd been tears on her face, Shira caught a flash of them in the glare of the phony gas lamp.

She went back to her room feeling sick.

Ellisen was planning to betray Grandfather to Hengst? Hadn't she tried over and over to tell Grandfather to beware? Maybe she should go inside to eavesdrop some more.

She recoiled quickly from that idea, though not necessarily from fineness of feeling. It would be more than her life was worth if Grandfather found out, even if she did it to save his.

She lay down, pulled the covers to her chin, frowning up into the dark. Tomorrow she must contact Grandfather, inside if necessary, whatever he said.

Contact him, and warn him . . . somehow. . . .

08.16 Hours 15 October 2047
Bentnose Peak

Shira opened her eyes.

It took her a moment or two to place the creamy flounces surrounding her, the whorled posts rising to the canopy overhead.

A slight chinking sound brought her upright against the pillows.

"Oh, good. You're awake."

Susann crossed the room bearing a gate-legged tray laden with breakfast, which she set on the bed before Shira.

"Stay where you are. You're looking better, but I still think you need to rest more. Try the fruit drink first. It's the latest orangeade."

The bed dipped slightly as Susann perched herself on the edge.

Shira surveyed the tray. There was even a plastic red rose in a glass.

She took up the cold yellow soy drink, sipped. It was cold and tangy. No better, no worse than any other brand claiming to be like the real stuff. Who remembered what the real stuff tasted like anyway? She shot Susann a look. Her hostess, in a light blue jumpsuit decorated with silver fake buttons looked bright and cheerful. Too bright and cheerful.

"Pitar's gone off to New Washington. MacAllister'll bring him back for tea though, with new strips." Susann smiled, held it. "I hope you like toasted muffin, Shira."

Toasted muffin! How could the woman sit talking inanities with Grandfather on the block! Shira took a quick angry breath, let it out again. That wouldn't get her anywhere with Susann Ellisen, except out.

"Susann—" she began, then stopped. No good blurting out that she'd been eavesdropping, either. So how to find out about Ellisen's intended treachery without making an unpardonable intrusion upon Susann's privacy, perhaps a humiliating one?

She looked up, saw that Susann was watching her, waiting politely for her to finish her sentence.

"I'm—I'm concerned for Grandfather, Susann. I'm worried that something bad might happen to him down in Estralita."

Susann's smile cut. "Bad? What do you mean, bad?" she asked quickly.

"It's Hengst." Shira picked her way through the minefield. "The man's a snake. There's no knowing what he mightn't put over us all. Even the Controller," she added quietly.

Susann looked down at the carpet, biting her lip.

Then she suddenly looked up again, meeting Shira squarely eye to eye.

"You're so young to be so sharp, Shira. Yes, I'm afraid too. I won't insult you by denying it."

There followed a silence. Susann didn't say any more, didn't offer to speak of her quarrel with her husband the night before. And yet it hung heavy in the air between them, even though Susann could have no idea that Shira shared her knowledge.

Speak, Susann, Shira willed her. Tell me. I'll not forgive you if you don't.

Susann stood up abruptly.

"Finish your breakfast, my dear," she said. "And if you feel like coming downstairs, I'll be in the kitchen."

She hurried to the door and went out without a further word.

Shira watched after her, her anger rising. The woman was suffering tremendously, she knew, and she must still feel such loyalty to Ellisen. But to Shira that didn't excuse the silence.

She swept the tray aside and prepared to swing her legs off the bed. She'd follow Susann downstairs, have things out with her after all. She had to. She must save Grandfather. Maybe there was something, some small thing more Susann could tell her about Ellisen's planned deal with Hengst.

Her resolve rising, Shira threw back the sheets.

And at that moment Grandfather's calm mild voice came through. *Shira: shall we begin?*

Shira caught her breath. *Grandfather? Oh, Grandfather, I've the most terrible news. Listen!*

To her dismay, there was no reply. Why not? Because . . . Because the beacon must be active again.

He'd blipped in only to alert her to join him! What else could she do but comply?

But she wasn't sure that she could, away from the synergizer.

She lay back, pulled up the covers and closed her eyes, trying to relax. No good. She was too rigid. Too worried. With a great effort, she set her mind adrift. Only then did she begin to hear faint background noise. Voices. Shouts. The cry of a bird.

A burst of exasperation surged through her. *Oh, Grand-father. What are we doing, lying about listening to all this when our world is tumbling about our ears!*

The sounds were gone.

She clenched her fists, unclenched them. Breathed deep. In. Out.

You can't do any good while Grandfather is under, she told herself. He's asked you to go under with him—and that's as good as an order!

She relaxed a second time, went deeper, deeper.

Images floated, disjointed. Sounds came and went. Not clear enough yet.

She imaged her grandfather lying on the synergizer couch, she squatting against the wall beside him. The others, moving around him, quietly, efficiently.

A gentle wave of sound echoed through her head.

The TS flickered.

At last she was inside . . .

Lots of people, chattering, milling around.

Where were they?

She heard lapping of water, the creak of timber, smelled tar and a fresh dank stink that she didn't recognize.

The crowded quayside was noisy as ever it had been, year in, year out, whenever one of the holy barges pulled in.

—salibas fish oil! Cures all! Insect bites, sores, ulcers, the running shales!

—what a pretty sail! What a lovely blue!

—blue for level ten! I've seen them once before, you know.

—pompous ignoramus! Blue's for the eleventh step. My grandfather, he went to level eight!

—don't get too close. There's no knowing what they teach up there!

—fresh parafish! Cooked to a turn! And live chouls in their shells!

The noise died as the boat bumped the dock and the Rethi guides leapt ashore to secure the moorings and set the neat

white gangplank in place. Broke out again—though quietly—
as the blue-robed figures moved off the dipping vessel one by
one onto the shimmering cobbles and the blue sail slid slowly
down to the foot of the mast.

Shira shifted in the bed. Where, she wondered, looking
about her, was the prince? She couldn't guess from his
thoughts yet.

He wasn't on the dock.

She turned over, curled up on her other side. Wherever he
was, he was uncomfortable, and . . . she pushed her covers
back . . . very hot.

For a few minutes, the blue-clad pilgrims stood about, as if
a little bewildered by the noisy crowd, then, talking among
themselves, they moved off across the quayside, through lines
of stalls laden with the fish of the estuary: smoked fish, fresh
fish, pickled fish, and fish steaming in kettles; jars of lamp oil,
skin oil, polished shells, bits of flotsam and jetsam for
souvenirs: past the inns and taverns and more respectable
trading posts lining the waterfront, and on up the Asurdun
road, the crowd giving way before them, closing in on them
behind.

Only one of the pilgrims—a woman?—it was hard to tell
under the coverings—showed any curiosity toward the onlook-
ers, scanning each face as though seeking someone she knew,
someone perhaps who'd promised to meet her there, but after a
minute or two, obviously disappointed, she moved off after the
rest.

A moment later, and Shira knew exactly who it was.

*There are three of them, prince, standing close by the
plank. Watching the Rethi unhitch the sail.*

Torc, in the closeness of the sail locker, thanked great
Forthyr for his decision to hide the night before.

What manner of men are they?

They're big fellows, dressed as fishermen.

Armed?

They've fish-knives at their belts.

Where are you, Ramoni?

Moving toward the Asurdun Road. I'll double back once I'm out of sight. Prince—the boat is in full view of the dockside. You'll not get out till dark.

The fookar he wouldn't! If it got any hotter in there, his blood would boil! The question was—what would the girl do now? Why was she helping him, considering how she hated him so much? Was she waiting her chance, to offer him up, a harling to the sacrifice?

All his talk of fires and ledges had locked him into a pretty trap.

He listened to the screech of sea-hags, the fishwives' shouts, a man's coarse laugh.

He ran his tongue around the inside of his mouth. The last of the hitaku from his wayfarer's pack was gone, and he was dying of thirst.

Time passed.

Gurnyac. Gurnyac!

Ramoni—where are you? So far so good.

Across the way. They're still here, watching the guides. If you ask me, they're waiting for them to leave the boat, but the guides look as though they're going to change the sail now— yes, they are.

Change it now? Change the sail with him in its storage place lying under the new one? And without the Rethi's knowledge? It had seemed such a good idea at the time.

One of them is talking to the chief guide. Can you hear anything?

Torc tensed, listening, heard a low murmur, muffled through the yellow canvas that weighed him down.

Suddenly, the boat rocked violently. Then he heard clearly enough:

"Thou wilt step back whence thou came, young fellow. Only pilgrims set foot on this holy bark!"

"Answer me, and I'll do as you say."

The accent was low Gurnyac, the voice of any or every footclar to tramp a campaign trail. Three 'clars dressed as fishermen, asking for him. It occurred to him that Feric might have sent them to help him on the quiet.

No, prince. These harbor no good feelings toward you. Quite the reverse.

"Prince Torc of Gurnyac sailed for Rm these nine months past. He didn't show up on the last boat. Nor on this. Where is he?"

Folded sail thumped against the locker side, rocking the boat, slapping water up against the dock.

"I can't answer that. You'll have to ask the others."

"Did he or didn't he come down on this boat?"

"If he did, I didn't pick him out. Only pilgrims travel this river and they're all alike to me."

More talk, then, "Say he was on this boat—could he have jumped overboard?"

"He could, but if he did and lives, he's following the river, for he'll never have survived the Fens. Now, leave. 'Tis dinnertime and I've a sail to change before I sup."

Torc held his breath, waiting for the boat's answering bob, but none came. The man was clearly staying put.

A second later, the head guide slid back the locker bolt and raised the lid. More footsteps approaching, and two pairs of hands gripped the yellow sail, heaved it out over the locker side, exposing Torc to the light of Demiel.

Squinting up, he saw two startled heads transfixed against the blue. An instant later, the Rethi hoisted the old sail up off the deck, dragged it over the locker's edge, and dropped it smartly over him, winding him. He must have cried out.

The locker lid came down again, the bolt slammed shut, and he heard the Rethi hauling the new sail over to the mast.

The 'clars hadn't found him, nor had Ramoni denounced him.

What was she waiting for?

He was just beginning to breathe again, when there came an angry shout. Had she gone to them, had she? His heart began to pound against his chest.

Gurnyac, can you hear me? It's not over yet. The 'clar must suspect something for he's seized the head guide. Everybody's coming back to watch.

Torc braced himself, heard only the sounds of scuffling near the mast.

Where are the other two?

Standing on the plank. I can't see very well through the crowd.

The boat suddenly tipped, sending wash up and over the quayside. Then there was a loud splash.

Don't take alarm, Gurnyac. The 'clar's overboard!

With her thought came a roar of laughter and an urgent cry.

The other two are pulling him out. They're coming my way. I must move on. Now—stay put. I'll bring you clothes, but not till dark.

Wait! Ramoni! The Rethi saw me! Will they help me, do you think?

There was no answer.

The Dryac take her! What if she never came back; left him trapped in that bolt hole at the mercy of any that cared to open it! What if she were waiting to bargain with the men at a safe distance. What if—

He made an impatient noise in his throat. He could almost hear the mentor saying it: calm yourself, prince. What will be, will be.

Fine comfort that was!

Sweat streamed from him. He put his mouth to a hole in the locker side. Air. He needed air.

He put his eye to the hole. Through the narrow sliver of gangway he glimpsed people staring. At the new sail going up, or in the hopes of more excitement? Torc cursed them under his breath. His throat was choking dry, and his tongue swelling like a ripe pinu nut . . .

"Prince?"

Torc snapped to.

The Rethi guide knelt by the air hole.

"Are you all right?"

"Just. Thanks for what you did. If only you—"

"Nay, don't tell me. Do you need anything?"

"Water. I need water. I've been in here since sunup."

"By the Gates! I'll see what I can do!"

Presently, the lid opened once more and the guide let down a flask and a pack of food while ostensibly putting away a coil of rope.

"We go to the inn opposite," he murmured. "There'll be a guard by the boat, a new pilgrim. We'll tell him of your presence, and none other. And we ourselves will keep an open eye from across the way. Until nightfall, prince. Good fortune—and farewell."

"Wait. I would have the hatch unbolted."

A silence, then, "An you wish."

The sound of the bolt sliding back, another little boat dance as the Rethi stepped ashore, then the rhythmic rise and fall of the river flow.

Torc relaxed a little and reached for the flask. He removed the bung, took a swallow. The water left a metallic tang in his throat. Where was the aftermath? The flush of bubbles to prick the skin?

His hand closed on the pecular, brought it to his face. Real food again at last.

Hungry as he was, he paused, his teeth against the wrinkled skin, remembering the sweetness of the fruit, the rich smell. Then he sank his teeth into its flesh, flooding his mouth with warm juice.

And wished for hitaku.

He closed his eyes. His left leg was totally numb. His right one throbbed. If only he could stretch. The early afternoon sun warmed the locker lid. Timbers creaked in the waterswirl. Sweat trickled slowly from his skin, soaking his blue robe.

When he got out of there, what then?

What of Feric? Why hadn't he come to Asurdun? What had happened at home that these low scrots should come for him? To do him ill, he had Ramoni's word on that.

So many questions, and none of them answered.

But his instincts had been right. And he was even more

resolved to get back to Gurnyac un-named and un-noticed until he saw which way the wind blew.

His father dead. His mother, too, no doubt. And Gar? Whoever had murdered Sharroc wouldn't have neglected him as next in line.

And Tanna.

Poor Tanna. It were well if she'd died in the fire. Such hopes the girl had had of him. How long was it since he'd thought of her?

His mind turned to Ramoni. Bridge of Love.

As if he were not heated enough already.

He squirmed a little, then relaxed his body joint by joint and in the closeness of that cramped space sought comfort in the Canticum.

CHAPTER TWENTY-FIVE

PITAR ELLISEN

11.48 Hours 15 October 2047
New Washington

ELLISEN had just reached his private office when Katz buzzed him.

"Yes?"

Katz ignored his snap. "Ord, sir."

"What about him?"

"They have trouble."

Ellisen swore. "Put him on."

One look at the man's face and Ellisen swore again.

"Sir: it's the synergizer."

"You losing strippage?"

"Yes, sir."

"How much?"

Ord's face shone with fine sweat. "We, er. Half an hour to date, sir."

"And the old man?"

"Er, going strong, as far as we can tell."

Ellisen blew out hard. "Get to it, Ord. And what you've lost—you debrief the man as soon as he comes to, you hear?"

"Yes, sir."

"Expect MacAllister about thirteen hundred hours."

"Yes sir."

Ellisen cut.

He sat back, feeling anger and relief at the same time. He'd been seeking some excuse to be rid of MacAllister. Now he could send the man off to Estralita with instructions to wait for strippage, and slip off with Katz unnoticed.

The door swished open to admit Katz.

"Sir, the shuttle's here. Cargo bay."

"Good." Cargo bay, where a spaceside shuttle wouldn't attract undue notice. "Let's see MacAllister."

Alone again, Ellisen got up and walked around his desk.

We've come a long way, Pitar. Maybe as far as we can go . . .

He smacked the desk with the flat of his hand. Why couldn't she understand? Things had never been simple. She should know more than most that it wasn't always nice or easy. She knew well enough what he'd had to do to survive, what sacrifices he'd had to make—of others.

A game, that was what it was. You learned the rules, how to break them, how to win clean and dirty.

He spun around in sudden self-disgust, and leaned against the desk facing the door. Susann was right. It wasn't a game, this time. The old man was for real. He was a man of truth. And yet— The Hesikastor was also very wise. He'd delivered himself bodily into Ellisen's hands. Deliberately. Intentionally. They both knew that. There was no doubt that the old man knew full well the risk he was taking. Why, he'd as good as offered himself as coin for world ransom . . .

Hadn't he?

Ellisen rubbed his brow. Right again, Susann. He was going around and around in circles. Getting where? *He had to stay on top.* God knew he hated Hengst. Despised him. And he knew that in going to see the man he was as a fly visiting with a spider in its web. The trick was not to get too close. Right now, Hengst called the shots. For now, Ellisen must do as he'd always done to come out on top: go with the flow and bide his time. He wasn't betraying the old man for all time, only using him for temporary bait. He'd bail the man out, at the right moment.

Encouraged, he straightened up and walked back to his chair.

All things being equal, he'd get Hengst in the end. After all, he'd promised.

. . . *take that Hengst apart. It's you or no one* . . .

And it was now or never, while Hengst was so sure of himself. First he'd offer the strips as bait, then the old man himself, *if* the hellfire syngerizer didn't fall apart.

Damn Ord and his machine. All the time Ellisen was spaceside he'd be worrying. No synergizer, no more strips. No strips, no deal. Well, he had enough clips already to keep Hengst interested—minus the one giving Demiel's co-ordinates.

Why worry? Ord had his replacements. Transducer plates shipped down post haste from spaceside: clean plates. Ellisen himself had had them checked three times by three separate Security outfits. Surely the man would have the thing working again soon, maybe he had already.

MacAllister walked in.

"Ha, MacAllister. There's been a slight hitch. I want you to go to Estralita right away. Wait for strippage. I'll send you further orders. Okay?"

"Okay," MacAllister said, but the cool blue eyes told differently. Ellisen looked down. The man suspected something was up, but he dared not say anything. A radio rat didn't challenge the Controller.

Ellisen clenched his hands. Why, dammit, couldn't he look up again?

Fires of hell, he was *ashamed!* Ashamed, at this stage of his career!

He got rid of the man, sat with his head in his hands, recognizing the old familiar ache. Those times he'd gone about picking up after Grandfather's dawn massacres in the marshes . . . He sat up. He had to get a hold on himself, or they'd all go to the wall! He pressed for Katz.

"Sir?"

"Are we ready?"

"Yes, sir."

"Okay, then. Let's go."

He paused at the door, looking back over his familiar office. The antique film likeness of Susann on his otherwise bare desktop. When he came back, he wondered soberly, would she still be there for him? For the first time in their whole lives, he wasn't so sure.

Whether or not, whatever happened, he thought, sighing heavily as the door shut behind him, nothing would be the same after that day.

11.48 Hours 15 October 2047
Bentnose Peak

Shira's bedroom door opened and closed slowly, but she didn't hear it. Neither was she aware of Susann Ellisen walking away to leave her young guest, as she thought, to get some more much-needed sleep.

Shira lay unmoving, curled up fetus-wise, in sheets damp with the dew of her sweat, deep-locked into Torc's processes . . .

Pain pounded Torc's skull with the force of a twelve-man battering ram. The air was suffocating. He blinked the sleep from his eyes, took up the flask, sluiced his mouth, and swallowed.

Ramoni?

So you're still alive. How do you feel?

Relief flooded through him. *Like a rockfish at the bottom of the pile*. He put his eye to the hole. Not dark yet?

The fog's rising. It's safe enough. I'm coming across.

He chafed his dead legs, remembering the long way back to Asurdun.

He strained his ears in the silence, heard quick footsteps across the cobbles, then the murmur of voices as she came aboard.

Good to know the guard had been there.

She raised the lid and with difficulty pulled up the corner of the sail.

By the Dryac this is heavy. How did you manage to breathe under it, Gurnyac? Here—squeeze out this way—steady. Lost your legs? She gave them a perfunctory scrub with her knuckles as Torc swung them over the locker side. *As soon as you can shift you've a thar waiting over there.*

Torc looked about him in the dark. The road had a bad feel to it. The thought came to him that she might be leading him into an ambush.

I feel exposed, Ramoni. Can't we go faster?

No. We're Riversiders. We don't travel eager. Trust me.

Trust her? That was rich, after all she'd said.

What news of Gurnyac?

Not good.

Out with it.

There's been trouble. They say the king's dead. And the queen.

He hung his head, blinking down at his hands on the reins. He'd known it, had lived with it, had been braced for it—so he'd thought. *Go on.*

So are you, some say, but not all. They say your General Brac died with the king. And that Feric keeps order until your death is proven.

She'd dropped the name as though it were a foul disease.

There's a deputation waiting for you in the Thar's Head. Soldiers. A man called Enkalt. He's the one that sent the 'clars to meet the ship.

Enkalt? But he was chief adaide to Brac. The Dryac! If it were not injury enough that he turn traitor, he'd sent but three common 'clars for him, likely not daring, in broad daylight, to be seen himself at what would be known as the Gurnyac heir's assassination.

His thar stumbled slightly. The road here was particularly

narrow and overgrown, folding back upon itself as though unwilling to go on.

That's the spot I told you about, that next bend. You should have seen us! They grabbed him you call Old Glabrous. Two held his arms, the other put a knife to his throat. "Where's the prince of Gurnyac?" the Knife said. "Speak up, afore I slit your gizzard!" The next thing you know all three are in the bushes flat on their backs with us staring down at them. They took off like flitbugs and that's the last we saw of them—on the road.

They're waiting outside the hostel now, you say.

Aye. Your guard of honor, Gurnyac.

Skod, if she wasn't laughing at him.

You're sure they didn't follow you here?

'Course I'm sure. Blue pilgrims went in the front door, and a fisherboy come out the back. Even if they saw me, they'd not have looked twice.

True. Torc remembered his first full sight of her on the quay with her woman's body gone inside such clothes as he now wore: rough jacket and breeches, striped hose, and a red tasseled cap pulled over one ear. At the very thought he reached around to scratch his back vigorously.

Stop that, Gurnyac. That's Kabun's best jacket that he keeps for high days. What did you expect? A harsilk tabard?

This Kabun—what did you tell him about me?

That you're a friend of mine. How's that for effort, Gurnyac? Don't worry, you're as safe under his roof as anywhere here.

He's a friend of yours?

Maybe.

They'd reached the outskirts of the town.

There, Torc drew rein.

What is it, Gurnyac?

He turned blindly to face her. *Why are you doing this?*

She shrugged. *I thought that was clear on the boat. We struck a bargain, remember? You said you'd find my father. And make Feric pay.*

So he had.

Anything else? The thought was tinged with irony.

It'll do for now. Come, we'd best move on or we'll be noticed.

She turned them aside down a lane to a low shack, where, signaling him to dismount, she led him across the front yard, through piles of nets and broken mollusc jars, around to the back where they left the thars tethered beneath a tree.

A tap on the shack door brought boots crunching over grit and a moment later they stood inside an ill-swept scullery stale with fish and turboil.

The man led them through into a kitchen lit by two reeking lamps and a banked fire.

"Well."

Kabun, a full two inches taller even than Torc, and twice as wide, looked him up and down.

"So this is your pilgrim."

Ramoni nodded.

"Here." Kabun took Torc into a lean-to off the kitchen and left him there to wash. The water was icy, the towel, sour and wet. And where was there blade to scrape his stubble?

He smiled at his foolishness. He had no need of razor now, being no longer pilgrim, but once more man of the world.

He dipped his hands into the water, swilled his face.

When he stepped back into the fug of the kitchen, there was an awkward silence.

"Ramoni tells me you don't want my rockfish chowder."

Torc looked to the pot of gray sludge on the table and shuddered.

But even had it been game meat stew from the king's own kitchens, he realized with surprise, he couldn't have touched it. The very thought of dead meat turned his appetite.

"Well? Say up, lad."

Torc looked to Ramoni. "No—thank you." It was a passable imitation of Ramoni's accent, he thought. And so did Kabun, apparently.

"You didn't tell me he was from the Weald, gal."

"No more should I. Shut up and give him some bread."

Torc took a bite. It was stale, and moldy around the edge.

Kabun took a noisy spoonful of chow, and pointed to Torc's arm. "Show us your mark."

Mark? His eyes flickered to Ramoni's sleeve. "I—flit before they branded me."

"Oh? Where were you before that, then?"

Ramoni raised her hand. "Here, Kabun. You know better than that."

"Gurnyac," Torc said.

Kabun spat. "And she took up with you?"

" 'S right. What you got agin Gurnyac?"

Kabun reached out and seized Ramoni's sleeve, pulling it up to show her scar. "That's what I got. Best thing she ever did was to get out of there. And now she says she's going back— with you."

Torc looked at her startled. Since when had she decided that? The bargain had been for her to get him off the boat.

Kabun spat again. "Ramoni's my friend. You think I like the idea of her back in that place? Specially now, with all the goings-on. What with the old man finally dead, praise the Quaur—"

"Kabun!"

"And his brood along of him. Except for the eldest, who got hisself lost halfway to Rm." Kabun began to laugh. "Likely chewed up by one of them langers. Did you hear about him missing the boat? A reg'lar pizac he was." He stopped laughing suddenly, and leaning forward, the huge, menacing man poked Torc in the chest. "I'm only sorry I didn't get to him first because you know why?"

"Kabun! That's enough!" Ramoni stood up.

But Kabun had pulled his fishing knife and was waving it slowly before Torc's face. "I'd like to have got him down this road on a dark night to carve some nifty patterns on his hide— like this!"

As Kabun lashed out, Torc leapt, scraping back his chair with a hard wooden sound but no sooner was he up than he felt a force smack him sideways. He twisted, would have recovered, but for the chair. As he went down, he distinctly heard Ramoni's horrified cry.

Gurnyac! I thought you were going to—

And Kabun's loud laugh, but afterward he never could recall how his head hit the table's edge and how he crashed to the floor, his legs entangled in the chair.

Torc felt something cold pressed to his head. He was resting against a rough jacket under which lay great softness and warmth.

"He's out for the night, 'moni. Just look at him. Why don't you go and leave him here with me. What are you doing with such scum?"

Ramoni's voice was cold. "I have my reasons."

A short laugh from Kabun. "You allus do. I'll give you that."

"Kabun, can I still take the thars?"

"Aye." The voice sounded sullen. "Though Dryac knows how I'll ever see them again."

"Don't worry. I'm buying them."

She took up the cloth, swilled it around briskly in some nearby bowl, and wringing it out, applied it again. "Just keep what you owe me. It should buy you three, even four new ones, if you know where to go, and one of those newfangled fish wagons you told me about."

"Don't be a harbrain, child." Kabun sounded hurt now. "I don't want a rak of your money. I'm worried about you, that's all."

"Save your energy. The Quaur'll take care of me."

"So you keep saying. But me—I'll see It first. When do you leave with him like that?"

"As soon as he comes round."

"Tonight!"

"Aye, and soon, I hope."

"You're not taking him by the Route?"

"Mayhap. Get his other clothes."

A pause, then Kabun crunched across the floor and out. Ramoni shook Torc urgently. ·

Gurnyac? Gurnyac, wake up. I'm that sorry for what I did, but when you got up like that I didn't know you were only moving out of reach.

Torc lay, painfully aware of the hardness in his krudt. It had been a long time. She shook him more vigorously, with greater urgency.

Prince—wake up!

He affected to stir, opened his eyes, and nuzzled against the jacket front. It was all he could do not to fall upon her. Ramoni, obviously catching his drift, dumped him smartly onto the floor and leapt up.

"Come on. It's time to go. Kabun's fetching you more clothes."

"More?"

"When did you see a fisherman in Gurnyac? On your feet."

"About Kabun—"

"He'll give you no more trouble, I promise."

"Well, that's good." He got up and faced her. "I don't mean to complain, but he's crazy. If, as you said, he's one I'd be safe with, I'd like to see one who wished me ill!"

Torc slowed up, uneasy. All night they'd traveled along no road that he could see. *Ramoni—where are you taking me?*

She didn't even look back. *Like I said—around.*

It's getting light.

She glanced back now.

There's a shelter over the hill. Hurry.

He held back. How did she know? Her words back in Kabun's kitchen, "You're not taking him by the Route?" What route was that? He nudged his thar to catch up with her. Whatever, he'd soon find out.

Over the next ridge low wooden sheds huddled in the dawn mist.

A typical grain croft.

There was no sign of life: no lamps lit, no smoke from the crofter's chimney, no smell of toasting grain or brewing hlath.

Reaching the yard, Ramoni dismounted and led Torc to a stable where they left the thars alongside two others and an aged daur, then, to his surprise, instead of going to the crofter's house, she steered him into one of the outer granaries, strewn with bales of winter feed.

She shut the door behind them, closing out the cold light. Then she drew him to the back wall where she knelt and fumbled in the straw.

What are you doing?

There came a faint creak, and the smell of cold and mildew rose into the comparative warmth of the shed.

Here: feel for the ladder. Careful. It's quite rough.

He swung a leg over the hole, felt the first rung with his foot, and started down.

The bumpy floor was just plain dirt.

She leapt off the ladder behind him and nudged him aside. A moment later in a shower of sparks a lamp flared, to Torc's surprise not the dull yellow glow of turboil but the costly flame of agria. In a lowly crofter's cellar?

She set the lamp on the floor.

The place was rough; the dirt walls shored up with wood and stone; but it was clean and spare, and lined on two sides with shelves. In one corner lay bedding enough, Torc noticed, for at least a dozen.

The shelves held boxes and sealed jars: food. Skod, but he was starved.

Ramoni set out grain cakes, flat-bread, butter and honey on a rough wooden box, and poured water from a large pitcher.

Sit. Help yourself.

Ramoni looked tired. Which was not surprising, since she'd not slept in—forty-eight hours—on his account.

What place is this?

She kept her eyes on her food.

A storm shelter.

The Dryac it is. Even I know that's under the crofthouse. Try again.

She closed her eyes.

Another time. Be thankful—and quiet.

They ate steadily and in silence.

When they had done, she stood up. *Pack up the things.*

He found himself obeying, while she took out two bedrolls and laid them out side by side.

Then she pointed wearily to a low doorway in the far corner. *Through there, prince.*

He strode over, opened the door onto a tiny closet and the nostalgic catch of orat. He turned, with a flourish, *After you—sairah.*

She nodded, passed through, and closed the door in his face.

The closet, he found, was scarce big enough to turn in. Yet it contained a table, a pitcher of water, a small cracked bowl, a covered chamber pot.

He relieved himself, stripped, and washed himself down, blowing out like a sea-thar in the cold. Reached for the damp napkin, remembered with nostalgia the bracing sting of dried crit needles. He draped the napkin over the empty water bowl and got dressed again. So many bits and pieces. He longed for the simplicity of a robe.

Why hadn't he stayed in Rm? He'd wanted to, then. Up there on that last day all this had seemed so unreal and— irrelevant. And now? The world was steadily pressing in upon him. Now he must go home to trial and tribulation and the Dryac knew to what outcome.

Torc put his hand to the latch. The girl: she seemed genuine enough. But how far could he really trust her? He didn't like traveling blind like this. She could be setting him up for a bigger fall.

He checked the thought. She could still be reading him. *Gurnyac: is all well?* She sounded faintly anxious.

He lifted the latch, went through.

Ramoni peered at him over the top of her pallet. *Good night, Gurnyac. Sleep well. We've a hard ride tomorrow.*

Good night . . . and thank you, Ramoni.

A second's hesitation, then, gruffly, *Cordially returned.*

He climbed into his bedroll, wriggled down.

Ramoni dimmed the lamp and shuttered it.

He relaxed, felt the aches and pains drain away, heard the sharp clicks of the lamp chimney cooling in the chill air, faint rustling as Ramoni removed some of her clothing within the warmth of her bedroll, and tried, as ever, to focus on home and the dangers ahead.

Inevitably, his thought went to the girl, already asleep by the sound of it. How many nights under the K'haravim he'd dreamed of lying with her. Roused, he remembered his urgent need in Kabun's house.

He turned abruptly, forcing his mind back to Gurnyac: to images of fire and blood; to treason and death and to Enkalt, Brac's man. Enkalt, waiting to take him. He had to be, and with stealth. Feric would never have sent just that man for him, neither would a loyal man dare send scrots for him without coming himself. For whom was Enkalt working?

It was no good. He reached out, touched the sleeping head beside him. Her skin was cold and damp. He felt the prickly stubble on her scalp. Black, it was, and growing thick and fast. He trailed his fingers lightly down her cheek, his desire for her awakening.

She was a woman: she must respond to him.

He pushed down his coverings, half climbed out, then stopped.

Apart from the fact that she could throw him clear across the floor without even touching him, there was another consideration: Ramoni was no fallowella, and no man's tool.

He sighed, climbed back into his roll. It had grown cold.

They rode well throughout the following night.

Although Ramoni refused to discuss their hideout, and how they'd left it, going off after sunset without setting eyes on a human soul, he'd had all night to think, so it was no surprise when they stopped at dawn on the second day at another croft, a dairy croft this time: tiny meager dwelling, dairy, loom-house, and forhar byres.

The hiding place was under the last byre, the entrance a loose flagstone.

They ate, washed, lay down against overhead sounds of clanking and scraping as the crofter milked his forhars and mucked them out.

Tell me, Ramoni—when I went down in Kabun's—I'd swear you never touched me.

A pause.

What difference does it make?

I want to know. Did you?

No.

I knew it! With your mind! You threw me—just as the mentor! He lay for a while, thinking about it, resentment rekindling within him at the memory. He'd been too grateful then to take issue with the fact that she'd once again gone into his mind, read him, manipulated him and with a speed that would have done credit to D'huru Nor.

Resentment flared into anger. He came up again. Even the Athor didn't do thus.

She came up now also, regarding him solemnly.

That is true. I did wrong, and for that I'm sorry. Yet I had my reasons. I shan't do it again, I promise.

You had your reasons, he sneered. *So you told Kabun. I demand to know what they are.*

I thought you knew. She sounded surprised. *We have a bargain, remember? That we settled on the boat and just before we went to Kabun's house.*

You keep changing it. Why are you still helping me?

You just said: I have my reasons.

I must know them.

Later. They're nothing that would bring you harm. I swear.

He lay down again, thinking over what she'd said.

When you use the mindspeech—how far can you hear? I

mean, you spoke with me on the quayside, but never from Asurdun.

I don't know how far I can hear. It doesn't always work, anyway. When I'm tired voices go in and out, and I can't always get through. I'm no D'huru Nor. That's why I go under the K'haravim. Until I am as good as— She stopped abruptly, and though she didn't say why, Torc was sure she was, like him, thinking of her vision under the hmlic. Of the ruined city, and bloody D'huru Nor. *I'm tired, Gurnyac. Sleep well.*

Wait: when we get home, will you use your powers of mindspeech for me? I would know what certain people think truly of me and my house.

So! You would have me use it when it suits you.

I'm at war, Ramoni. Fighting for my life. Those ends surely justify the means. Please—just to see me through.

A pause.

I'll think about it, Gurnyac. Now: good night!

She turned from him and fell asleep almost immediately.

Torc tossed and turned. The girl's easy breathing began to irritate him. So sure of herself. And of him. His breathing deepened with anger. Like a child she treated him, telling him only what she thought he should know. He struggled out of his bedroll, shook her awake.

This is a slave haven, isn't it? There's a whole chain of them, from the Weald to Asurdun. And Kabun is its end link. What halfwits you must think us Gnangars.

She didn't answer him; made no move in the dark.

"Hey—you!" His sudden shout whipcracked off the walls. "Answer me!"

Light flared and she was looking at him, her eyes cool as ever they'd been in the D'hogana.

He seized her to haul her to her feet. The next moment he lay on his back clutching his nose.

Here.

A wet rag, to stem the blood flow.

The anger came again, then, as suddenly, went.

Old habits die hard, Ramoni. And the new aren't set.

I know.

I want you.

I know.

You don't care?

Why should I? I neither give nor lend myself to any man. Not even a prince. Now—you try that again and it'll go hard with you.

In what way?

I'll go off and leave you.

That surprised him. He'd expected her to threaten to denounce him. Even so, he couldn't let the argument go at that.

Do that and you're finished—your houses too.

Rubbish. There's no malice in you. Now: behave yourself.

There! She was calling him to heel again. Almost he was tempted to try her but what would be the use?

He turned from her.

The lamp went out.

A moment later, her touch startled him.

I neither give nor lend myself to any man—but I'm not above a bit of bartering now and then. Move over, I'm freezing.

He lay awake long after she'd fallen asleep. The lovemaking hadn't been the best. He should have known she'd have her say in how things went, but she'd taken him by surprise and so he'd responded awkwardly, and yet—

What they needed was practice. Plenty of it.

He shifted in the cramped space, molding his body to hers. How soft she was, yet hard. Was there anyone like her anywhere?

I neither give nor lend myself to any man.

He'd see about that.

Having tasted her, he'd not let her go.

The third night was their last stop before Gurnyac. They made love deliberately and with great concentration then, satisfied, lay back to sleep.

Stay by me, Ramoni. After it's all over.

No. Hey, listen, I've gone from betraying you, to not betraying you, to going along with you, to helping you get back home. Don't be greedy. After I've seen you through that's my side of the bargain done. Oh, the beauty of bartering! It's good, clean trade with no strings attached. Anyway you're forgetting Tanna.

Tanna? What do you know of her?

Gurnyac: you made her promise to wait for you—have you forgotten?

Momentary anger, quickly controlled.

No. But she's likely dead. If not, I might make her a concubine, if she's kept to her own bed at nights, which I doubt. Even then, I still might, for I don't think she'd have had much say in the matter. But, Ramoni, a king has many concubines.

She rolled from him, laughing. *You're offering to make me one? You're truly generous, prince.*

She was laughing at him again.

Very well, he said, stung. *If not concubine—queen!*

She was sober now. *I'm impressed. I don't want to sound ungrateful, but I couldn't live in Gurnyac.*

You know about Broda, don't you? You don't think I can get out of wedding her, do you?

That's not it.

He looked to her sharply in the glimmer of the lamp.

You've seen something? A vision?

Aye, but nothing clear. Maybe tonight I'll be lucky—if I can get some sleep. Help me, Gurnyac. As you drift off, dwell on what you'd have me dream about.

I can dwell on only one thing at this hour, Ramoni.

Too bad. Now—drift away.

Within minutes she was asleep. Torc lay on his back, his mind hopping. Tomorrow they reached Gurnyac. Where would they go? To the Citadel? Not until they'd sniffed the air.

What then?

He twisted and turned. He didn't know.

* * *

He suddenly awoke to a well-known shout: from a Gurnyac drill captain falling out his men.

Prince!

I hear it.

They'll not find us.

Nevertheless, she sat up, and strained to listen with him to sounds from above.

Boots struck the flagstones overhead.

He heard muffled noise as men poked, stabbed the fodder bales and meal bins. The grate of heavy feet climbing to the loft. The shout that all was clear. Heard the captain's order to move on.

Silence settled in. Did the crofter even know they were there?

Of course, Gurnyac. By the thars.

The thars! But so would the soldiers!

No. The crofter will have put them out among the forhars. The soldiers wouldn't notice anything amiss. Rest easy, Torc.

Rest easy! Skulking like a low melk under a forhar shed!

What now, Ramoni? What do we—?

She put a hand on his arm. *Wait.*

He waited, listening.

The crofter was talking overhead to somebody about an all-out search across the countryside. For runaway slaves, the captain had said. The captain also carried an edict. No one went into Gurnyac from now on without a pass.

Torc frowned. An edict? Only the king signed those.

The search for him was widening, he was sure of it. Who was behind it? Who had signed that edict?

The crofter had been issued four trade passes for the morrow's market day: one for himself, one for his wife, and two for melks.

That's us, I suppose.

You suppose right, and count your great good luck. I'll speak with the crofter after nightfall. Meanwhile, there's the rest of this day and one more night to pass down here. Time enough to meditate.

That's a funny name for it, he said, reaching out in the darkness and pulling her close.

He ran through the city gates to find the streets lined with folk cheering and throwing their caps into the air but instead of hurrahs he heard only growling. Atop their human bodies sprouted felmar heads with wicked eyes, pointed snouts, and wide, murderous mouths.

He raced on, the crowd streaming after him, to the citadel.

He paced the length of the throne room to stand before a shadowed figure on the dais.

Who sits in my father's seat! he called, while behind him the beast snouts crowded in. Show yourself! He drew his sword and leapt the throne steps and seizing the usurper by the hair, dragged him to his feet.

The head went back, and Torc cried out to find it was his own.

His twin plucked the crown from out of the air and put it on. With an angry cry Torc struck out. Off came the crowned head and rolled while behind him the beast-men leapt and squealed.

Stooping, Torc took up the bloody crown and climbed in sudden silence to the empty throne.

There he turned and held the diadem high for all to see—the felmar faces, and human faces in between.

"Thou shalt not have this diadem!" he cried. "See! Upon this head it goes, who have the reason and the right!"

With shaking hands he brought it down upon his shaven head.

The instant it touched, there was wild laughter from the felmar faces, while the humans spouted flame.

What have I done? he shouted.

Only what you should, the mentor sighed before he too was engulfed in fire.

Torc started awake, sweating. Had he cried aloud? He reached for Ramoni.

She didn't move.

He said her name.

Still no response.

He groped for tinder, lit the lamp.

She looked dead. Was she having visions?

He turned the lamp low. He couldn't sleep now. He'd keep
watch. Wait for her to wake.

It was a somber vigil. His thoughts went again and again to
the old visions: of tattered flame and blood and masses
crowding the countryside; of his father's last cry, of the tocsin,
the screams of those dying in the fire. Of Ramoni toiling up the
hill and the mentor falling in his own blood.

Those hours were among the loneliest in his life.

CHAPTER TWENTY-SIX

H E was watching her when the signal came: three light taps on the flagstones. She was up in an instant.

They doused the lamp and climbed out into the predawn dark.

The crofter's wagon was large, built for the heavy brass urns and cakes of yellow cheese, with a high front bench for the driver and a tail board for bondsmen scarce wide enough to perch a pettiwik.

A 'Hiyah!' from the crofter and the wagon began to move.

"They didn't speak, Ramoni."

"No. It's the way."

"You cried out in your sleep."

"I'm not surprised."

He hardly dared ask it. "Did you dream?"

"Sort of. A revelation, more like."

The heavy wheels ground over the ruts, setting the urns clanking and rattling against one another. The stink of cheese was sickening.

"A *revelation*. About me?" His heart quickened.

"Yes." She turned from him, her body swaying and bouncing with the movement of the cart.

"Well what, then?"

"It was different from any I've had before. I saw colors and shapes, like clouds boiling in a high wind, and heard voices in my head."

"What did they say?"

She hesitated. "You'll not be happy."

"Why? What is it? Ramoni—tell me!"

"A time of great change is on us, prince."

"Change? What change? Woman—speak out!"

"I'm not sure. But Gurnyac is its birthing place."

Gurnyac! Then that change concerned him. That thought brought back the vision of the mentor's death. Of Ramoni calling out: "Look what you've done!"

"It's bad, isn't it? And you don't want to tell me! Ramoni— what we saw in Rm—"

"Hush. I'll not speak of it. And as for talk of bad and good—what is that? Did you learn nothing back there? Be proud to hear that one day your line will help save the people of the Known World."

His line? One day? What about him? Now? Was not his head already teeming with ideas for reform?

"Not you, prince. My vision was more far. I speak of a descendant."

A *descendant!* What kind of talk was that! "That's it?"

"Yes."

Torc bumped along sulkily. He'd hoped for visions of a new kingdom rising from the ashes of his father's pyre, but all he'd learned was that he'd live long enough to spawn an heir— small comfort for a Gurnyac prince who must wed on his coronation day.

"You're not happy—just as I warned you."

"You saw no more?"

Again the hesitation. "No."

Was she holding something back? How would he know? If there were more, she'd tell him in her own good time.

Maybe.

* * *

Near the city gate the line of wagons stretched back and back. Slowly they moved up, while all around them crofters gossiped and grumbled.

The new edicts, they said, were ruining trade. By the time they got to the market it was almost the hour to go home and their produce was spoiled. And the guards everywhere scared folk away.

Torc lay back among the urns.

Why the passes? And who had ordered them?

He looked up constantly, for a glimpse of the citadel, his father's blackened tower, but all he saw was wall. His impatience grew, and the urge to push to the front of the line.

Calm yourself, prince. Use your training. We'll get there exactly when we're supposed to, and not a moment before.

Torc regarded Ramoni sourly.

You sound just like the mentor, he said.

It was mid-morning when they finally reached the gate.

From the moment he sighted it, Troc braced himself, and each roll of the cartwheel tightened his wariness.

But one look at the passes and the guards prodded on the cart without so much as a glance at the ragged bondsmen clinging to the rear.

They were through.

So much, thought Torc, for edicts.

From every post and rooftop flew black banners, just as in his vision.

Torc looked at them, uneasy.

They rumbled on toward the mart. On every hand people hurried by, heads down, purposeful—and with good reason, as Torc soon saw.

Guards were everywhere. Footclars, in pairs, armed with pikes, stopping folk at whim.

One they stopped, a frightened youth, ragged, barefoot, just as the crofter urged the cart up a steep incline.

Torc, his eyes on the road slipping under his dangling feet, heard every word as he went past.

"Name?"

"Ferdin Gorl."

"Business?"

"N-none. I—I'm just going home from work."

"*From* work?" The guard backed the youth against the wall at pike-point. "What work brings you home at this hour?"

"I'm bonded to Jundar, the baker. We bake at night."

The cart rolled out of earshot.

Torc watched the youth fall under the pike, the guards kicking him where he lay. By the Dryac! The lad had done no harm! The fookar take him if he'd stand to see him treated thus!

He knelt up, poised to jump off the back of the bumping, swaying cart.

No, Gurnyac. There's nothing you can do.

He glared at Ramoni, subsided angrily. She was right. He looked back along the road. The youth lay on the pavement; the guards were gone.

Was he dead?

Torc stared at the youth's dwindling outline, his mouth set in a tight, grim line. Soon, soon the people of Gurnyac would learn what true justice was.

The cart crested the rise.

The mart was crowded, but quiet.

Once the cart was in, they slipped off without a backward glance at the crofter or his wife.

It was the way, Ramoni told him.

"What now, Gurnyac?"

"I'm not sure. Give me a minute." They stood in an alleyway, sheltering from the wind, two more "Ferdin Gorls" in thin, ragged clothes.

For a space, Torc felt lost.

The king is dead. Long live the king.

Sharroc standing above him, the snowy heisha raised for all to see. Torc remembered the coolness of the stuff descending on his new-shorn head, his father's words:

May the grace of the Lothuri cleanse your soul, prove your mind and spirit, and send you forth from Rm a future king!

Sharroc lay now in the Hall of Tombs. Sharroc the warrior, big as Feric, loud as Brac.

Oh, Father, Father!

He saw the great head thrown back in laughter at some jest of Brac's. His enraged face the day Torc failed to win the Brandelac. His proud smile after the victory of Gortland: *Soon, my boy, you'll ride by me and learn to be a king . . .*

"Gurnyac?"

"Pardon. Come."

"Where?" Ramoni strode along beside him.

"Home," he said.

"Well? How do we get in?"

It did look difficult, Torc had to admit, with every gate secured, every drawbridge up.

It looked somber, uninviting. Even forbidding. Is this how strangers saw it for the first time?

He turned away. "We wait till dark."

"Then what?"

"There's a conduit under the outer moat, leading to the inner one."

Ramoni stared down into the foulness.

"Under *that?*"

"It's the only way. You're game?"

She shrugged. "Aye, I suppose."

They walked on, dodging guards, keeping to the meaner streets, looking purposeful, and staying on the move.

Torc saw for the first time another Gurnyac: filthy, dangerous—alien.

Curfew notices were everywhere, scribed in symbols used for the illiterate: a crude image of a barred door beside a setting sun.

The afternoon crawled. So did Torc's gut. They'd not eaten since the early morning, and didn't look like to for some time to come.

The sun went down. Black banners merged with sky.

Curfew sounded over the rooftops. The taverns closed, and the crowds dispersed, vanished, and fog filled silent streets.

Torc led the way through dark wasteland to the moat's edge and into the still, icy water, then across carefully, so carefully, to the far side.

The conduit was under the lee of the servants' gate. Torc well remembered the year the moat was drained and cleared. The stench from it had hung about the citadel for days. Even so, it hadn't stopped him and Aravac and several other like-minded spirits after it was refilled from trying that way in without being caught—a way which had nearly gotten one of them drowned. Yet no one had ever found out.

Could he remember the way? He got his bearings, took a deep breath, and dived, Ramoni following after.

The water was shocking cold and totally black. A few seconds and already he began to feel confused.

Ramoni? Are you there?

I am, and if I come any closer, you'll kick me in the face.

Torc felt for the hole. It wasn't where he'd expected it to be. He moved sideways, kicking, feeling the slimy stones.

There!

The moment he found it, his breath gave out.

Ramoni! Up! Up! I need air!

They came up together, sputtering, spitting out water. They rested, clinging to the wall until their breathing slowed. Icy as the water was, Torc didn't feel the cold, not after all those months under the K'haravim.

Now, Ramoni. Let's try again.

He dropped, straighter, faster, found the hole and kicked his way inside, his fingers gouging slippery ooze on either side. Weed caught his legs, smothered his face. He calmed himself, fought the panic. It couldn't be that much farther. Only the thickness of the outer wall, after all. Two more kicks—

—and he was through.

He shot upward, Ramoni close behind him, gasping for air.

They waited a few minutes to get their strength back. Then Torc pushed off the bank.

Over here.

Torc swam across to the inner bank, climbed out onto the stretch of no-man's-land between the barracks and the stables.

He was home.

He led her into the stables through a rear door to a grooms stall with clean dry gear hung on pegs. They swilled themselves down from a thar pail then changed into breeches and smocks, thrusting their wet clothes into a pile of dung outside.

There came a sudden clash of bells.

The tenth hour, the changing of the watch.

Where to now? Torc looked toward the empty blackness where once the king's tower had stood. He wanted above all to see it, to stand in the ashes where his father had lain.

Later.

He must see Feric first.

The sentries paced the brightly lit front stoop of Feric's hutment.

Torc turned aside.

Down here.

Not a fitting entrance for a future king, but wise: through the flap and down the chute the way of fuel for the general's stove.

The main passage was deserted.

So was Feric's outer chamber.

The lamps were lit and the stove was banked ready for Feric's return from the changing of the guard. A pot of water steamed on the hotplate and the general's mug was warming in the hearth.

Through here.

Ramoni didn't move. He glanced to her face, saw it tight and set.

He drew her through the far door into the dark of Feric's bedchamber; a chill bare cell containing a single cot, a wooden soldier on which an officer hung his uniform at night, a washstand, and a commode.

Once in, she didn't move, but stared at the wooden soldier as in a trance.

He felt a moment's compunction. Here she was, in the very home of the one she hated, in his very sleeping chamber.

'moni—would you rather go now while you can?

She stirred herself. *I'll be all right. Give me a minute.*

She glanced quickly to the window beside the cot: their only means of escape.

No one will walk in on us. Not until Feric's ready for bed. And that is late.

From outside came the commands of drill sergeants and the sound of feet marching across the wide compound. The new watch on its way out. Strange to hear the familiar routine again.

A door opened and closed. Voices sounded through the chamber wall.

Feric was back.

Now what, Gurnyac?

His handle of hlath and the day's dispatches before he goes to evening board. Can you read him?

She shuddered slightly.

I'll try.

He watched her eyes close in the light from under the door, felt her withdraw from him. Felt the resentment returning; of her power, and at being shut out even as he pitied her for having to touch the mind that had destroyed her life.

He heard the stove being raked and refilled, the familiar tinkle of spoon on cup, the sounds of feet coming and going on the polished floor. Gibbal, probably. And the dispatch-bearers. He smelled smoke from new-kindled logs, the pungency of fresh-brewed hlath.

Skod, but he could taste it now.

A low voice, unknown, singsong, making report.

Feric's then, upraised. "Is that all you have to say? Where are the men I sent out two days ago? Why aren't they back?"

Torc remembered the voice as being strong and resonant. It

sounded harsh and strident now. Strange, but in spite of Rm and all that he'd done his old fear of the man was returning.

I'm finding it hard, Gurnyac. I'm tired. It's coming and going in waves. He's worried. Over you. He fears you've come to grief. That man has great love for you.

Love? His throat constricted. That word, coming from Ramoni.

He caught her, pulled her to him, held her tight. What must she be feeling! How could he have brought her here!

Peace. It's all right, praise be to the Quaur. She laid her head on his shoulder and clung to him.

The next room fell quiet.

Feric had dismissed his adaides and would be sitting at his desk in his black and silver general's uniform, his hlath at his elbow.

That brief interval was and had always been the most precious hour in Feric's day; an interval of peace and privacy invaded only ever by a small boy squatting beside that stove scarce breathing so's not to be sent out.

Ramoni raised her head.

The rising is officially over. The assassins' heads rot by the citadel gates. And yet—Feric is uneasy. He fears there's more to come.

He fears right. Ramoni—I'm going in.

She nodded, once.

He touched her shoulders, then slipping past her, went through into the next room.

Feric was on his feet, one hand on his sword hilt, the other on the bell.

"I shouldn't, Fer."

Torc went to the stove, stood with his back to it.

Feric's chair went over as he rounded the desk. How tired the general looked. Haggard. *Old.*

"Torc?" Feric gripped Torc's shoulders, and held him at arm's length.

Torc suffered the general's scrutiny. Haggard he may be, but he was a giant still. A very Djunu. Torc must look slight beside him. But he wasn't. *Oh, Feric, if you only knew my strength now.*

Feric let him go at last. Moved back a step. Torc braced himself. Here he was, back home after all this time, against all expectations, without a word or sign of warning and looking like the worst scrot. Would Feric scold him for a wayward child, or greet him as his king?

Feric clicked his heels and bowed. "Majesty."

"How did it happen, Fer?"

Feric sighed heavily, moved to the window, looked out into the dark.

"It was on the night of your homecoming. I don't know how much you've heard."

"Go on."

"I was still in the Weald. About one hour into the first watch, five men took the duty guard. The adaides. And Gense. They found him by the alarm bell. They say it was he who sounded the tocsin."

"The king didn't have a chance."

"Five men? *Five* men, you say? How did five men get into the king's chambers unseen?"

"We may never know. All five men were dead by the time help arrived. Brac, too, and fire raged through the Keep. We managed to put out the fire at last before the tower was gone completely, so we were able to bring out the king's body, thank the Quaur, to bury him in a fitting way."

"He lies in the hall of tombs?"

"Aye."

"And my mother—what of her?"

Feric looked surprised.

"The queen is dead, also, sire. The wind carried the flames across the walkway even before the tocsin sounded. We could not save her tower. Nobody survived."

"Nobody?"

Feric walked back to the stove, held his hands to the flames.

"The Lady Tanna has not been seen since the fire. One can

only assume that she died with the rest." He cleared his throat. "A number of bodies were pulled out too charred for recognition. Pity, sire. She was heavy with child. Yours, they said. Her position in the queen's household had become quite difficult."

His child!

Poor Tanna. Loile blossom. The idea of her engulfed in smoke and flame sickened him. Yet he merely shrugged, as Feric would expect him to.

"What," he asked Feric, "of the rest of us?"

"All dead, sire, save Gar. He had just arrived back from the Weald when it happened. In fact, he was the first to reach the tower. In your absence, he acts as king. By order of the Council, of course."

The Council! Of which Feric was a part.

"And you? What did you say? Is your hand on that?"

"Sire! You know that answer as well as I!" Feric hesitated. "Say it, Fer."

"They think you dead. Gar seeks the crown. It's been all I could do to hold him off. I still hoped you'd been somehow delayed."

"The fools! Is Gar the one behind the edicts?"

"Aye. There are those who think the trouble not yet over. Gar is one. He holds that there are still rebels out there waiting their chance to move against the crown again."

"It's not over, is it, Fer?"

"No."

"Twitch of the nose?"

"If you like." A ghost of a smile touched the general's face.

"Where is it? Out there? In the Weald? Or where?"

Feric didn't answer at once. "Let's say I'm looking closer to home, sire."

"There was a welcome party waiting for me in Asurdun, Fer."

"Welcome party?" Feric frowned. "It came back three weeks ago."

"An unofficial one, under Enkalt."

"Enkalt! But he's in the Weald!"

"Not anymore, he isn't, by someone's order. You have no idea whose, have you, Fer?"

"Sire!" Feric stood up.

He's sincere, Gurnyac. And utterly shocked.

Torc told Feric about the scene on the boat, the way the 'clars had followed the pilgrims all the way to their hostel. "They were not there for my welfare, Fer. Had they found me, I'd not be here now."

He told Feric then about his journey home, the search parties moving from Gurnyac to Asurdun.

"Looking for slaves, they said. I heard them tell a crofter. But I think they were looking for me. Under pretext of carrying edicts. Somebody doesn't want me home, Fer. Any idea who?"

Feric shook his shaggy head. "None. And it's not for want of trying. As I said, I don't think it's over, and I've eyes all over the citadel. But this is too much—" His face had gone a deep red. "Whoever it is has got to our very vitals! Sire, I'll have Enkalt brought back at once. He'll give us our man. Do you know exactly where he is?"

"I do. You say Gar is acting king. How does he survive?"

"He doesn't move without a bodyguard of twenty men. And three tasters at board. He's a frightened man, sire."

"But not too frightened to want the crown. Does he look to home for treason, too?"

"Who knows? He keeps his own counsel. But I'll tell you one thing: he's deeper than we ever thought him. He's won the Council over. He can do no wrong in their eyes. To hear them, you'd think he quelled the riots single-handed. Over half the Council would crown him right now. But that's all over, now you're back. He'll not be pleased to see you, sire."

"But he won't just yet. Nor will any one, until I've flushed our felmar from his lair. Think, Fer, how free I am to move about like this."

"And hard to protect. What do you plan to do?"

"Nothing, until I've eaten. But first—meet a friend of mine. A fellow pilgrim from Rm."

Torc glanced at the bedchamber door. *Ready, Ramoni?*

No reply. Was the thought of confronting this man now too much to bear? Was she still there?

Hiding his sudden anxiety, Torc waved toward the door. "I'd not be here now but for him. He saved me back in Asurdun."

He threw wide the bedchamber door and there Ramoni was, standing by the window, almost as though she'd been about to go through it. He took her arm and drew her out into the light. "General Feric: meet Ramon, of Rm."

Ramoni advanced slowly into the room.

She looked grubby and unkempt, in the ill-fitting grooms clothes. A scrot of the lowest kind. Like him.

The general clicked his heels.

Ramoni made no move of any kind to acknowledge him. The set of her head made Torc very nervous indeed.

"You are of Gurnyac?"

Ramoni's eyes flashed. "I move around."

Her voice was steady enough. Deep and husky for a woman, it was somewhat high for a man. He caught the flicker of Feric's eyes. Knew the general had judged her that instant as an "undescended man." Now nothing she did would ever gain her favor with him.

He can't help thinking as he does. The man is an animal in human clothes. But loyal as the most loyal of frats, Gurnyac.

Even as her thought came, Feric turned from her, dismissing her, ignoring her completely.

"Majesty: I am at your command. Say what you need."

"Food, Fer, while we talk. We've not eaten since sunup. Who's your man?"

"Gibbal."

Torc nodded. "Call him in."

Feric moved to the wall behind his desk, pulled the bell.

Gibbal was in at once.

"Sire!" Gibbal smiled delightedly. His eyes glanced off

Ramoni, then back to Torc. Then realizing his lapse of discipline, he went rigid, looking stiffly ahead.

"Gibbal: His Majesty requires food and hlath. And water for baths. Be fast, and quiet. No one must know of His Majesty's return."

"Sir." Gibbal clicked, saluted. As though trying to make up for his lapse he looked not once to Torc or Ramoni again, but addressed himself wholly to the general, wooden as a shrudkt.

"I think, Fer," Torc said, when Gibbal was gone, "I'll visit the king's tower while you're at evening board. What do you think?"

"I think it—risky."

"Not in guard gear, with special passes signed by you."

"Hm." Feric folded his arms across his chest. "Well, if you must, you must," he said gruffly, but Torc knew the man was really pleased.

Within the hour he'd be standing where the king had died. What would he find there?

Not long, then he'd know.

Gibbal led them to a small room three doors down where uniforms lay ready.

The moment the door was closed, Ramoni whirled on him, her face tight.

You expect me to wear—those?

She pointed to the black tunics, breeches, silver-trimmed, shiny black boots, leather cuirasse, black steel helmets winking in the lamplight.

Torc stood stricken. He'd never thought. Since he was a child that uniform had always meant comfort to him, and security. And as a young man it represented the might of Gurnyac. But to her— Oh, how could he not have realized. He went to her, tried to put his arms about her, but she pushed him off.

Ramoni—I'm so sorry. The words sounded lame. What a gulf lay between them, him and Ramoni. How could he possibly breach it? *But what could I say out there? Look—you stay here. I'll go alone.*

He began to undress.

After a long moment, she did the same.

Ramoni: don't.

It's not for you, prince. I have my reasons.

Ha, thought Torc, feeling a sudden kinship with Kabun. You always have those.

He watched as Ramoni went to the stand, pick up the breeches, and with set face, draw them on.

Ao was at her first great fullness: the spring tide moon in Asurdun, when homing fish sprang to the net; the sower's moon on the plains. The soldier's moon in Gurnyac, signal to shake off winterlock and hit the campaign trail. She was wasted that night over the citadel, obscured as she was by mist that clung about its ramparts like lingering smoke.

Ramoni stopped in the shadows of the central courtyard. Had she seen something? Torc fingered the passes in his tunic pocket.

What is it?

Feric. He wants me gone.

Torc relaxed. *Well, too bad for Feric, for you're staying.*

No, Gurnyac. When this is done, I go. You promised.

But that was then. Surely you've reconsidered.

Maybe, once or twice. But not for long. I can never belong here. You must see that.

He looked down at her, incongruous in her guard uniform.

I see nothing of the sort. Ramoni—I need you, and I'll need you more after I'm crowned.

She shook her helmeted head. *Sorry. Remember what I said about barter? It's good clean trade with no strings attached. I must feel free to go.*

He sighed and moved on, around the courtyard, through an archway, and across the cobbles to the king's keep.

He could see nothing.

He put his hand to Ramoni's shoulder, felt a shudder go through her.

Are you cold? She shouldn't be, under all that gear.

No, she answered, then he felt it too. Chill air, tinged with the stink of Sharroc's funeral pyre whose blackened ribs curved up above their heads, invisible in the midst.

She was trembling now, engulfed in that dead smell. Their thoughts touched, and at once Torc was overwhelmed by grief, her grief as she stood once more a child watching her own world explode in bright sparks and crash in ruins about her tethered feet.

He put his arms about her.

You shouldn't have come. Wait for me back there.

It's nothing. Continue.

They trod the outer stair carefully, keeping close to what was left of the wall, their boots crunching soft carbon and rain-flocked ash.

As they reached the king's chamber at last the mist partially cleared revealing the waxen moon; high, small, remote from that ruined roofless place: the charred hangings about the burned-out bed, the shapeless hunks of molten lead—remains of priceless chests that had contained the king's robes and furs. There, the boot-chair in which the king had received him that last night, and there, his writing desk. And everywhere under their feet, Torc could all but smell it, the blood: Sharroc's, Brac's, old Gense's, the guards' and the assassins' all mixed together in the brittle charcoal that had been the floor.

Torc's throat tightened.

He glanced up, remembering how he'd looked down upon the fire, heard the king's last cry, the tocsin bell.

He edged forward feeling around holes in the floor, through to the reception room beyond. A splendid chamber this had been, with its vaulted windows overlooking the three royal courtyards: east, to the queen's tower, west, to Gar's, and south, to his own.

It is exactly as I saw it.

Ramoni was standing close to the outer wall, staring out toward the ruin of the queen's tower.

Torc turned away to look east, toward the lighted windows

of the banquet hall where at that moment Feric dined beside Sharroc's empty seat.

He crunched around to the west side, to the line of dark casements that marked his own apartment—still sealed—and guarded, Feric had told him, as they had been since he'd left for Rm.

Aravac had died there. And Tanna had been sworn to him.

And Torc had walked from those chambers new-shorn to go to Rm.

How lightly he'd left then, secure in the knowledge that he'd be king one day, that one day it would be his turn to play the game, a game he'd thought better than chukar with real blood and rules to break at whim.

He'd also left behind him a father he'd not yet come to grips with, a mother he despised.

But all was changed; with Gurnyac, and with him.

Now there lay on him the sudden weight of that crown, with nothing solid under him. There lay on him also grief for Sharroc and the queen. How could he ever know his father now? And how could he ever make amends to the queen for all his slights and insults?

As for the future: the path to the throne was now a dangerous one, uncertain and bloody. Did he have the stomach for it anymore?

He turned away. They should go back to the barracks. He'd promised Feric he would before folk rose from evening board. Yet the sight of his windows beckoned him strongly.

Who lives down there? Ramoni stood beside him, looking down.

I do. Why?

He felt her shiver slightly. *It is so dark. And cold.*

Which is not surprising, considering the place has been sealed for three quarters of a sunaround against my return. Come, I've a mind to raise the dust down there.

Ramoni hung back. *Must you?*

Aye. Don't worry. There's a back way. No one will see us. He steered her toward the stair. *Watch your step, Ramoni.*

Nay, she answered him. *Do you watch yours.*

*   *   *

The rear gallery was deserted, as he'd known it would be.

Here, on that last night Tanna had scrubbed away Aravac's blood.

Poor Tanna. The smell of charcoal was still strong upon him.

He raised the faded tapestry, slid the panel aside, and gestured Ramoni through. *Mind your head.*

He stepped in after her, let the tapestry fall behind them, closed the door again.

He squeezed past Ramoni to lead the way. *Keep your head down; there's a low beam in front of you. Not much farther. Wait—there's a step—there.*

He reached for the inner door and slid it aside.

It was pitch-dark in there, of course, the curtains being drawn, but he knew how it looked, the shrouded furniture, knew where every piece was.

He stood quite still, sniffing. There, over the old familiar smells: the faint mustiness of the langaur skins, the bitterness of dry harn-wood, the tang of armor on the wall came another odor. The catch of smoke. He sniffed. Could it be from the burned towers?

No. It smelled fresh, and— He sniffed again. Above it came another scent, of fresh doused candlewax. Nay, more: over it all was yet one other, as from human flesh too long confined in dark and airless space.

Gurnyac!

Even as Ramoni's warning came, a slight sound came from the window.

He crossed the room, felt his way along the thick harpile, slipped round into the bay.

A figure stood opposite him, pressed up against the windowpanes. A shapeless figure, heavily swathed. With a cry, the figure ran, flinging the curtain in his face.

Quick, Gurnyac! Light!

Torc moved out, crossed to the bureau—uncovered—and taking up his tinder box from its customary place, struck flint against steel and at once he saw the figure lying by the glory-hole.

He moved across, bent, and pulled back the hood. The face was beautiful, death-pale. The eyes were closed.

It was Tanna's.

CHAPTER TWENTY-SEVEN

*S*HE *took us for guards.* Ramoni helped Torc lay her on the
bed, then stepped back. *She was very frightened, yet she
struck out at me before she fell.*

Tanna stirred, looked up, her eyes dark with fear, even
though he'd taken off his helmet so that she could see who he
was.

"Tanna."

He knelt, put his arm about her shoulders to comfort her.

For a moment, he would swear that she looked more afraid
than ever. Then her arms went around him, first limply, then
tight, clinging to him, pulling him down. And thus he stayed
for a while, aware of Ramoni's eyes on his back.

Presently, he pulled away.

"Better?"

Tanna nodded, her eyes still wary. "Torc—sire—" She
stopped, looking past him to Ramoni.

"It's all right," he said. "Ramon is a friend from Rm. He
saved my life in Asurdun."

"I want to speak with you—alone."

Torc patted her hand. "Ramon is *hrodm,* blood-friend.

Nothing's hidden between us. Tanna—it is good indeed to see you. They said you'd died in the fire."

Her eyes went wider, darker.

"I almost did. Oh, you can have no idea." She closed her eyes.

There was water on his washstand. Torc fetched some, made her drink, he himself holding the cup to her lips, for her hands were shaking so.

"The flames and the smoke. And the screaming. They all went mad. Rushed onto the walkway. It gave under their weight. I still hear them in my sleep. I went the other way, by the outer stairs. I can't remember exactly what happened but I must have been near the bottom when they gave way. I woke up in here."

"In here?" Torc frowned. "How?"

She hesitated. "Harbeli brought me."

Harbeli! His face cleared. He might have guessed! So. She must have known of his comings and goings all that time. Old Harbeli! A female D'huru Nor if ever there was one. Outgrown these many years, but never outdone!

"Were you hurt, Tanna?" His eyes went to the mound of her belly. She, following his look, pulled her mantle about herself.

"I was burned. On my legs and back. But Harbeli knew what to do. The scars have all but gone. But at the time it was mainly hard to keep quiet in here, I hurt so."

Torc bent down, put his arms about her again. "But why here, Tanna? Why did Harbeli bring you here? Why do you hide?"

Tanna struggled up against the pillows. "Because—" Again she stopped, her eye on Ramoni.

"Go on, Tanna."

"—it was the only safe place."

"Safe, Tanna?"

She hesitated, then whispered, "From Gar."

"By the Dryac—" He pointed to her belly. "That is Gar's doing?"

For one moment he thought her about to faint. "It's not that at all." She closed her eyes. "He seeks me for quite another reason." She struggled up away from him, and slid her feet to the floor. Torc, thinking her about to break loose, reached for her.

Leave her, Gurnyac. She knows what she's about.

Tanna moved to his desk and pressed the carvings in the side. Torc sprang up in surprise. His secret drawer! How?

She's a scribe's daughter, isn't she?

He held his tongue.

From his secret drawer she took a wad of fine parchment bearing the royal mark. Every sheet was covered in fine, neat script.

"Remember how I was to be your eyes and ears?" The old Tanna smiled up at him. "Well, soon after you'd gone I saw strange men coming and going from your brother's tower. I watched, and waited, and—" She was watching him closely. "—until once when he was away in the Weald I stole into his apartment and found these—well, not exactly these, for these are copies I made before he returned. You can ask Harbeli if you don't believe me, for I made them in her apartment."

Tanna looked again to Ramoni as though wishing her gone.

Torc took them, unrolled them, looked them quickly through, then stunned, let them snap up again and handed them to Ramoni, who was smiling faintly. "You can read— and write, Tanna?" *I know, I know—she's a scribe's daughter.* "Then you know what all this means."

Tanna nodded. "And Harbeli, too. I had to tell her about it. There was no one else to turn to. We—she sent after you some weeks ago. Two men, her kindred, to Rm, warning you. In special words. That you'd understand, she said. Did they not—"

Torc shook his head. "They've not returned?"

"No."

Torc spun on his heel, paced up and down beside the bed. Gar! He couldn't, wouldn't take it in.

Well, Ramoni?

She rolled the parchment up, and handed it back.

Looks like you have your man. You owe Tanna much.

That he did. In fact he owed her everything—unless—

"Tanna—you must have known all this before the fire."
Before the king's death.

"Yes." She looked up at him, a trace of fear returning.

"Why, *why* didn't you go to the king?"

"What, a fallowella like me? I'd never have gotten through
alive."

True. But there was Feric.

"Feric, then? You could have gone to Feric!"

"No! Not Feric!" She shook her head violently. "He's Gar's
man!"

Ramoni?

She speaks the truth—as she sees it, Gurnyac.

He leaned forward, took Tanna's hand. "Why do you say
that, Tanna?"

There came such an outpouring from her. Garbled tales of
meeting Feric by Gar's tower, of half-heard snatches of talk.
Of shukteks exchanged in the dark. Nothing concrete. Not like
the scrolls. He dismissed it all and stood up, his anger
sparking. But for her Sharroc might be alive today. But for her
Gar might have been long ago called to account. How could
she not have acted!

*Gurnyac—she did what she could! She risked her life to give
you the scrolls—don't do anything now that you'll regret!*

He turned back to Tanna, forced a smile. "You've done
well, Tanna. As well as warrior or scout. Did Gar find you
out? Is that why he wants you dead?"

Tanna sat down heavily. "Yes."

Torc knelt beside her, put the cup in her hands. "Drink," he
said. He watched her tilt the cup to her lips. Lips he had no
more stomach for. Ripe lips. Ripe breasts. Riper with the
burgeoning child.

To think she'd been able to read and write all this time, and
could have unlocked the secrets of his desk at any time and
he'd never have guessed it. She was braver and more
resourceful than he'd ever realized.

And yet—his anger flared again—and yet for all that the king had still died and so might he had it not been for Ramoni.

Prince—she did well. Think of her stealing those scrolls, copying them, and daring to put them back. Of Harbeli, sending out her own kinsmen to warn you. Both have done so much for your sake.

True. His anger subsided, and his resentment. Who was he to judge Tanna? He'd done no better armed with Aravac's shuktek and the gosheng piece, and he the king's own son. Tanna could never have hoped to see the king. Or to reach him and live. As for her view of Feric—what was the use dwelling on that now. What was done was done. He had the scrolls—and Gar. And he had survived.

"Tanna—you've saved my crown, and my life. And as I'm king, you'll be my first concubine." He placed his hand lightly on her belly. "I see I barely came back in time to give a certain fratling the seal of respectability."

The cup tipped in Tanna's hand, spilling water over the furs. He took it from her, set it aside, then pushed her down against the pillows. "Rest now. I'll be back. And keep this lamp lit. It's not good to lie in the dark."

He unbuckled his regulation sword, and throwing it aside, strode to the hearth and took down his own from the wall. He slid it from the scabbard, lightly ran his fingers along its edge.

Tanna sat up again, her eyes wide on the blade. "Where are you going?"

"To do what I have to. Now, Tanna. Don't look that way. All will be well, I promise you. When Harbeli brings your supper, keep her here—understand? Now—smile for me."

She smiled. A brief, pale smile. Why, why did she look so miserable and afraid? She had so much to be happy for. He was back. She was safe. And he'd just offered her the highest post in the kingdom next to queen.

He slipped the scrolls inside his cuirasse, turned to leave.

"Prince—"

"What is it?"

"Nothing—except—you're quite different." She smiled

suddenly, reached for him. He bent over her, suffered her to pull him down, then with a warmth that surprised him, he returned her embrace, Ramoni notwithstanding.

Very nice, Gurnyac, and only proper, if I might say.

A brotherly hug, no more. I owe her much.

Ha! So you see it at last!

He straightened up. "Stay close," he said. "Until I come back."

He saluted her and went out.

Halfway along the passage he stopped. *I can't believe it, Ramoni.*

He closed his fist over his sword hilt. *Gar!* In one quick glance he'd seen the cunning. The enormity of what his brother had done. And of his own ignorance—no—not only his own. Gar had fooled them all so well: Feric. Brac. The king himself.

Still he couldn't believe it: that puny Gar, not yet in his majority, starting the riots in the Weald, carefully controlling their spread, ridding himself of unwanted conspirators who'd outlived their usefulness. All this without one breath of suspicion. And now he was within one hair of the crown. No, he couldn't, wouldn't believe it.

But for the scrolls.

What now, Gurnyac?

Back to Feric.

But that was not what she meant, and he knew it.

That night he must have Gar's head.

With a single stroke he must shatter the threat to his life and crown, avenge the death of Sharroc as a true Gnangar son.

With one single stroke.

And with that single stroke shatter all that he'd become, all that he was in the process of becoming.

And widen the gulf between him and Ramoni.

Once and once only must I spill blood. Whatever the cost to me, I must have his head if I am to wear the crown.

Why tell me? It's not my concern.

He took her arm, shook her. *Must you be like this? The Dryac, woman! I want you to stay.*

How many more times must I tell you—no. Besides, the post of chief concubine in now filled.

Ramoni, this is no time to jest. I already told you, I would make you queen.

But I don't want to be queen. I don't belong here. Look, prince—don't make it hard for me. Our paths are separate, crossing but this once. I have kept my part of our bargain. Soon it will be time for you to keep yours. She gently disengaged herself.

So be it. He released her. For the time being. But she wouldn't leave him. She couldn't. He'd not let her. *Tell me— why was Tanna so unhappy?* No—more than unhappy. Afraid.

Ramoni sighed. *Why do I always have to be the bird of ill omen, the giver of bad news? I've been agonizing within myself whether or not to tell you. Well, I must, for your sake, and for Tanna's too. And maybe for the crown's. She carries a secret that weighs on her, and will weigh on her more and more, strong as she is, until it bears her down.*

She put her gauntleted hands on his shoulders.

Now I trust you'll do right by Tanna when you know the truth. She promised to be your eyes and ears, didn't she? She said that over and over to herself in there to keep her courage up. Well, so she was, and a terrible price she paid for it. Yet I tell you that she did it only for you. For your sake alone she's endured Gar these past months. For you only she's suffered herself to be used as only Gurnyac women can be used. And through her alone Gar stands exposed. You owe her every- thing.

In the darkness of the passage the silence was absolute.

So that was it. Now he understood her fear of him. The pallor. The shaking. The tears. He remembered his threats on leaving if she proved unfaithful to him. Almost he turned back to tell her that it was all right. That all was well.

But why couldn't she tell me? Even she said I'd changed. Am I still that terrible?

No, you're not. And it's not her sleeping with Gar that weighs on her now. There is something more, that she fears will make her abhorrent to you, even after all she's done for you. Gurnyac—her time is not anywhere as close as she'd have us think. She fears you because the child in her belly is not yours but Gar's.

It was one hour into the first watch when they took Gar—at Torc's specific direction as near to the time of Sharroc's death as they could guess.

The outer chamber they took with no trouble.

Torc himself opened the bedchamber door to find Gar asleep, and alone.

Feric's guards ringed the bed with torches, routing every last shadow from the far corners of the room.

" 'Tis almost a pity to wake him," Torc said.

Gar lay on his back, mouth open, a hand curled like a child's by his ear.

One day the sword shall be real, and blood shall flow between us and it shall be yours—brother!

Torc drew his blade, touched its tip to Gar's throat. A single drop of blood, welling up around the point, reached critical mass, split, then slowly trickled down either side of his neck, tracing a thin red line.

Gar twitched in his sleep, and with his fist tried to brush away the irritant. The saber's edge slashed the side of Gar's fist, and more blood flowed. Gar snapped awake, focusing upward at those about him.

Torc steadied himself. Not his blood, but Gar's. Gar must die, now, at his hand, before Feric and his men.

Gar lay very still, his eyes on Torc.

"Up."

Torc withdrew the saber point, waved Gar upright against his pillow.

Gar, glancing past him, saw Feric at Torc's elbow, the men standing around. "What is this?" He lifted his gashed hand. "The Dryac! There are those in Gurnyac who'll make you pay for this!"

"You think? Show me the man who'd defend the son that killed his father for the crown."

Gar's eyes narrowed. "Wild words don't win men's minds."

"Maybe not." Torc produced the scrolls. "But these will."

Gar's eyes went to his desk. "What are they?"

Torc unrolled them and began reading down the first page.

Gar leapt up. "Where—" he began, then realized. "The she-frat! The garahundt!" He struggled out onto the bed, snatched at the parchment in Torc's hand, but guards grabbed him, held him back.

"The originals, Gar. I want them."

Gar looked puzzled. Then, "Find them," he said.

Taking down a two-edged blade from the wall, Torc walked to the bureau and carefully prised each drawer open in turn. No scrolls. Not so nicely now he levered off the front and broke it up piece by piece. The cavity was in the side, a steel bin under the main body of the desk. How Tanna had found it he couldn't begin to guess. Reaching down, he lifted out the original scrolls and riffled through them.

Intact.

At Feric's command three of the guards seized Gar, lifted him struggling to the floor.

"Now, sire," Feric said in Torc's ear. "Do what you must. Get it over and done."

Torc nodded.

He was glad now that Ramoni hadn't come, that she'd elected to stay back in the barracks. *Sorry, Ramoni, Athor, D'huru Nor. But I must show this brand of strength this once.*

He met his brother's eyes. "Have you any last thing to say?"

Gar's eyes flashed. "That I have, you double-tongued Pessar. "Frat eat frat." Isn't that our motto? How can you fault me, then, for living by it? Our very foundations rise on the blood and bones of those that stand in our way. Father stood in my way. So did you. And now as I went to him, so do you come to me like a thief in the night. Where is the greatness in that?"

"Have you finished, brother?"

"I have. Now—do what you have to do to me without trial and behind closed doors, O brave king—and sorry am I not to see the aftermath!"

At Torc's signal, the guards shoved Gar down onto his knees and bowed his head. Gar's hair, parting at the nape, disclosed the dark necklet of dried blood from the throat wound.

Now. Torc raised his blade with both hands, preparing to bring it down with full force. He closed his eyes momentarily, swallowed against the sudden dryness in his throat.

Feric was waiting. The men were waiting. And Gar, he was waiting, too. He must show strength. Yet there was strength and strength. With strength went freedom. But where was the freedom here? A reign begun in blood would continue in blood, and end in it, no doubt, someday.

There must be no more blood.

He lowered his saber.

"So my brother would call me a coward," he said softly. "He dares me to call him out in broad daylight. Why then, General—so we shall." He looked up, including the guards now in his address. "Shall this rotten seed, this—*parricide* die so clean? I think not." He waved the scrolls before them. "Why should we spare him what these remaining miserables must now endure? I, Torc, heir apparent, warrior, pilgrim, not of the twelfth but of the eleventh step will make him eat his words. Stand him up."

The guards seized Gar's shoulders, pulled him to his feet. Torc looked straight into his brother's eyes.

"One cry of agony my father gave before mercifully he went to join the Quaur. That mercy I now deny you. Before long you'll cry for death continuously, and wish you'd kept your mouth shut.

"Now hear my judgment: Tomorrow from a felmar cage you'll see me take up the crown and from that cage bear witness to your judgment with all those who supported you. A thousand, thousand curses they'll heap on your head, and even then you'll not find relief for you'll then watch the woman you abused come into her own.

"All that is yours, both wealth and lands will pass to the

Lady Tanna, and my child that she bears in her womb will assume your titles as First Lord of Suther and of the Wades.

"And after, brother, you'll be stoned through the streets of Gurnyac with your fellows and, if still living then, you'll put your flesh straightway to the public Branding Iron, and your miserable body for slave in the Foundings for the rest of your days!"

Torc turned to look into Feric's stony face.

"Take him, General. Make him a guest under my father's keep."

For a moment, Torc thought Feric would refuse, but then the general, coming smartly to attention, rapped out the proper commands and followed by his entire squad, marched Gar from the room.

Left alone, Torc sheathed his saber, and sank onto the bed. He'd done well.

Gar was finished. And set to pay a higher price for what he'd done than the expected one.

But Gar's blood was not on his head . . .

Ramoni would be as pleased as he was, certainly.

Not Feric though. Not yet.

He stood up to go, looking idly round Gar's cluttered room; at its hanging weapons, its mounted scrolls, medals won in the lists, his bits of gold and silver, buckles, necklets, trophies of the battle, and felt a kind of pity for this second son, this unloved, loveless one.

With a sigh he picked up the scrolls and went out, through the hall, past the guards on the door, and pausing momentarily outside, looked down the passage in the direction of his chambers in the west tower.

The seals on his outer doors had been broken, Tanna removed to a royal suite and put to bed under Harbeli's care.

While Feric had paced impatiently outside, Torc had told Tanna he knew of the child's parentage, and his plans to recognize it as his own child for her sake.

He'd never forget her face, the fear giving place to disbelief. "But how did you know?"

"You'd be surprised what they teach in Rm," he'd answered her, in such a way that she couldn't be sure whether he meant it or no.

He'd kissed her, and made her smile at last, but she was still not happy, he knew. Tanna had changed. Something was gone.

He stood still, listening to the sleeping citadel.

Right now guards were out in numbers, seizing from their very beds all of those whose names were on the scrolls. Others were riding to the Weald to do likewise and by dawn all traitors should be behind bars.

How fast the news would spread in an hour or so of his return and of Gar's arrest. In hours Torc would come into his own by the grand stair that he'd left by.

His father's face in the morning light: it haunted him.

The king is dead: long live the king!

He moved off down a dark back stair, and out.

It pleased Torc to walk through the barracks a last time unmarked, and unchallenged by virtue of the insignia on his sleeve. He ran up the steps of Feric's hutment, along the passage, threw open the guest room door.

It was dark, and the stove, untended.

Sleeping—at a time like this?

Ramoni.

He moved into the room, saw by the light from the passage that both cots were untouched.

On one of them lay a sealed scroll.

He lit a lamp, closed the door, took up the parchment, and turned it over. It bore Feric's official mark, carried his official seal, but the inscription was not in Feric's hand.

Torc cracked the seal, unrolled the scrip, and read.

Gurnyac,

I promised you I'd see you through, and I have. By the time you read this you'll have done what you must and laid your ghosts to rest, I suppose. And tomorrow, you'll crown yourself king. What more could you want?

I know you asked me to stay, and may have thought to

persuade me to, but I really can't. Not that I consider myself unworthy. It's as I tried to tell you: my path lies another way.

I wish you well, Gurnyac, with your plans to change things. And I also caution you—go slow. Keep your own counsel for a while. Don't antagonize Feric for he's your best ally. And don't take him for granted. Mark, prince—he may be as a father to you, but with him the crown is larger than the man. See you fit it well!

I'm glad we touched, and at this time.

Tomorrow your new life will wrap itself around you and when and if we ever meet again it won't be the same.

May you ever walk with the Quaur!

Ramoni

What had she done?

He started to reread it until in a rage he tore it across, and seizing the poker, wrenched off the stove lid and threw the fragments in.

For a moment they lay, then slowly curled, flared, and were gone, leaving only sheets of brittle carbon lying on the coals.

What had she done!

He stabbed the coals viciously, pounding the carbon to ash.

Just let her wait! When Feric came back he'd have her picked up within the hour! He knew where she'd gone! She'd taken one of Feric's passes, too.

He banged down the stove lid, went to sit cross-legged on one of the cots, and took up the Canticum.

Not for long.

He eased his legs over the edge of the bed.

I trust you to let me go, she'd said.

Was this any way for him to behave?

Anger gave way to remorse.

How many women would refuse a royal diadem? Only Ramoni, who'd just as soon wear the cheapest trifle from the wharf at Riverside. How could she ever be anybody but herself?

What had he done? Destroyed the one token that remained of her.

He went back to the stove, looked into the coals as though hoping by a miracle the parchment would reappear.

What had she told him? To keep his own counsel. For a while, at any rate. And not to antagonize Feric. Well, too late for that.

The door opened and Feric strode in.

"Sire."

His face was stiff with rage.

"There's hot hlath next door. Where's the boy?"

"Gone."

Feric stood aside to let him pass.

Gibbal had placed the steaming mugs by the stove and retreated to his cubby across the hall.

Feric raised his. "To the king!" He drank.

It was hot. Too hot, Torc found. It must have burned Feric's mouth.

Feric set down his mug. "Why? *Why?* Why didn't you take his head? Are you mad?"

"On the contrary. I've never been saner. It's time Gurnyac saw what strength really is."

"That kind of strength, keep to yourself. It's not for a Gurnyac king. Tomorrow, take Gar. On the rooftops if you must. Only take him."

"If you say, Fer, but after he's been on show. The people will love it, you'll see."

"Maybe," Feric said gruffly, and drank.

"Fer—the king is dead. Tomorow begins a new reign. Time moves, and with time comes change."

Even as he said it he regretted it. Feric's eyes narrowed.

"And just what *change* have you in mind?"

Torc spread his hands. "Nothing—specific." He raised his cup and drank down the scalding liquid, holding his peace.

Feric may be your second father, but with him the crown is larger than the man . . .

There was trouble ahead. Ramoni was right. It was going to be harder to change things than he'd thought. He'd have to bide his time. But there was one matter that could not wait.

"Have the messengers gone to Cray?"

"They are to be sent momentarily, sire."

"Hold them. I shan't wed tomorrow."

Feric lowered his hlath ominously. "The king takes his queen at his crowning. Give me one good reason—sire—why you shouldn't."

"I can give you several, Fer. The sairah Broda is hardly prepared. Tomorrow's coronation is strictly business; a rattling of swords. And Gar in his cage will be hardly conducive to happy wedding bells.

"In addition, there's no queen's tower, so where will the queen live with her women, eh? In the apartment of a concubine? I've done, unless you can think of further insults to offer her. As it is there're enough there to start a war!"

Feric regarded him silently.

"I will, if you like, personally invite the sairah and her kin to honored seats, stressing the true nature of our purpose. But wed her I cannot, will not do at this time."

Without waiting for response, he raised his cup and took a long draught. *How's that for dialectic, mentor?*

Feric still didn't speak, but watched him narrowly, obviously not yet satisfied. Torc fought his irritation. Was he not king? Why should he have to justify himself so, as though he were still a little boy!

. . . with him the crown is larger than the man . . .

The Dryac take Feric and Ramoni both!

Torc drained his cup, wiped his mouth, tried another tack.

"Feric—do you recall that I never wanted to go to Rm in the first place? Maybe if I'd stayed at home all this would never have happened. But I was ordered to go, and I went as a dutiful son should. Now who in all this kingdom rooted out Gar? No one. No one suspected him—and for that Brac and my father paid in blood. But within hours of my return I had him smoked out and spiked." He let the old notes of petulance and willfulness into his voice. "Is that not the mark of a strong Gurnyac king? I am strong, Fer, and shall be stronger. I'll wed my bride when I see fit, and Gar shall keep his head till I've had my sport.''

Feric relaxed slightly.

"Well said, sire. I'll allow postponing the bridal bed to be of secondary consequence—provided a date is set before too long. But as to the other matter—think on this: the crown is not affixed to the king's brow by some cazn's cement. Two things keep it from slipping awry and they are blood and fear. The direct Gnangar line has just weathered the most dangerous challenge since recorded time, and that from within. Gar is an ever-present danger while he lives. For that reason he must die before the sun sets on your crowning—and there'll be edicts tomorrow for you to sign to that effect. If not, I'll not, nor would any man within the whole Known World vouchsafe your future as king.''

CHAPTER TWENTY-EIGHT

16.30 Hours 15 October 2047
Bentnose Peak

S HIRA walked unsteadily down the stairs.
Four-thirty!

She desperately wanted to sleep, but Susann would surely suspect something was wrong if she went right through until tomorrow. Besides, she must talk to Susann, to find out news of Grandfather. The only question was, how? She wasn't up to head-to-head confrontation just yet.

She stood for a minute at the bottom of the stairs, holding onto the newel post until the dizziness went away.

"There you are." Susann Ellisen emerged through a small green baize door behind the staircase. She studied Shira's face critically. "Hm. You look better, but still a bit peaky."

Shira drummed up a smile. "I always look like this."

"Even so." Susann looked worried momentarily. "Pitar won't be back tonight. He sent word that he's in over his head with conferences." She took Shira's arm and drew her toward the green baize door. "We shall console ourselves with a cup of tea." She led Shira through into a large airy place, the kind the history files called "Colonial Country Kitchen": wide stone floor, pots hanging from beams; brick fireplace with inglenook, mantelshelf, and real fire; wooden butcher's block in the middle of the room, and a dining booth made from what looked like old church pews.

Through the fake windows over the sink, smoky hills dipped back into haze.

Susann waved her to a stool by the fire and took down a caddy from the high mantelshelf, shook dark leaves into a teapot warming by the hearth, then poured boiling water onto them from a kettle hanging on a hook over the fire.

The tea tray had three cups on it. Shira eyed the third cup dubiously. Not Sven's, she hoped. Susann poured the tea into two of them, handed one to her. She took it, sniffed. The dark brown liquid had a strong, pungent aroma, definitely different from soycaf. *Hlath,* she thought, making a face.

"You'd like a little kaolait, Shira?"

"No thanks, it's fine." Shira put down her cup with a clatter. How could they sit there, going through this charade with all that unspoken stuff between them.

"Susann," Shira began.

MacAllister walked in.

"Alistair!" Susann almost ran to meet him. Then she stopped, looking back to Shira.

Alistair!

MacAllister held out a small package. "I got instructions to bring these over and wait. We're allowed to see them."

"Any word when he'll be back?" Susann was trying not to look anxious.

MacAllister shrugged. "Nope. Hey—is that real tea?"

Susann made an effort. "It is, and it's just made. And there's your cup, all ready. Drink up. Tell you what: if you're hungry enough, we'll make this high tea and then go to the study."

Shira put her feet up at Susann's insistence. She didn't want to see the strips. She'd not long since seen them in the making and now all she wanted was to get MacAllister alone. *Alistair.* She glanced sourly at Susann. Was there something between those two? Surely not. Jealousy was certainly warping her view.

Even while MacAllister set up the 'verter, Shira's head began to droop. The next thing, she opened her eyes to see Gar kneeling before Torc, his neck exposed to the prince's blade. She'd slept that long? She glanced sideways at the others. Had they noticed her sleeping? Maybe not. They seemed wholly absorbed in the hologram.

She stretched surreptitiously. How long before she could talk to MacAllister? Despite her impatience, Torc's anger and misery at losing Ramoni drew her in. But it wasn't the same. Watching, listening, she thought again, wasn't as good as being inside.

At last it was finished. MacAllister closed up the 'verter, and Susann went for soycaf.

Shira sat up. Now was the time.

MacAllister came to sit beside her. "That poor guy. He's sure going through it."

She nodded. "No more than Tanna. When he walked through that door, I thought she'd die. MacAllister, I want to know—"

"Wait." MacAllister put up a hand. "Say that again."

"Say what?" He was looking at her most oddly.

"About Torc and Tanna."

"Why?" Something was wrong.

"Do me a favor, Shira. Don't ask questions. Just say."

She eyed him suspiciously. What was he up to? "I said, when Torc went back into his chambers through the glory-hole, I thought Tanna would die of shock." She waited for his response, but he just stared back at her, that left eyebrow of his raised in that maddening way. "Well," she snapped, "didn't you?" Something was definitely wrong. Something in what she'd said.

"Well? What is it?" she demanded, angry now, and for some reason, a little frightened.

He took her hands in his.

"Shira—there was nothing of the kind on those strips."

"Not on the—" She felt the blood draining from her face.

"But they were the strips from this morning. I don't understand."

"For over two hours this morning the synergizer wasn't working. By the time Ord had it going again, Torc was on his way to get Gar. There's no strippage of any meeting between Torc and Tanna in his apartment. So if it occurred, no one knows of it yet, except for your grandfather. And you."

Silence.

"I suspected it," MacAllister said. "When you found that tracer. It takes one to know one. I myself," he ducked his head in mock modesty, "have a touch of the Sight from my maternal grandmother. I must say," he added, "the old man's a sly dog, not letting on he had a backup system."

Shira flushed deeper. "Grandfather didn't know—" She stopped. It was not true.

"Oh, come on, Shira."

Her eyes flashed. She tried to head him off. "You're calling me a liar? I'm not allowed to go in without permission."

MacAllister's grin widened. "But you did."

Her chin went up. "It was an emergency."

"And so you decided that the ends justified the means. Like Ramoni."

"Why, yes." She tightened her grip on his hands. "MacAllister, you won't tell, will you?" Now, now she'd speak about Grandfather, what Ellisen was planning to do.

"My lips are sealed." MacAllister pulled her closer to him. He wasn't smiling now. "Listen, Shira, would you read someone for me?"

He knew. "Ellisen?"

MacAllister nodded. "I overheard something this morning."

The word stuck in her throat. "What?"

"He's gone off with Katz."

"Where?" Her voice shook with panic. "MacAllister— *where?*"

MacAllister pointed upward. "I think."

Shira sprang up. She'd been right!

"Here." MacAllister pulled her down again, so sharply that she fell onto his chest. "Shira, I won't mess about. I have a bad, bad feeling. Quick, patch into Ellisen, right now. Can you?"

She regarded him doubtfully. "I—I'll try."

"Like Ramoni, Shira," MacAllister said softly, setting her upright again.

She leaned back, closed her eyes, took a good, deep breath, and let her mind settle down. She ignored MacAllister, tuned him out; focused instead on Ellisen. She imaged him standing by the hearth. Tried to remember his voice.

"Oh." She covered her ears. Terrible noise. Shrill whining.

Ellisen was sitting, no, lying back, strapped into a kind of harness. His face was contorted, flattened, blurred. He was moving fast, so fast it looked slow. Around him were controls of some kind, everywhere, crowding the cockpit.

Cockpit.

"He's under stress," she murmured. "Great stress. He's going up, and accelerating."

MacAllister's voice sounded softly in her ear.

"Good girl. I was right. Ellisen's really going spaceside."

Shira's eyes flew open. "That's how he's selling Grandfather out! I heard Susann say he was last night!"

"Oh? And what else did you hear, Shira, my dear?"

She whipped around.

In the doorway stood Susann, a tray in her hands. The woman's face was ashen and hollow as a death mask. Shira was struck dumb by the sudden change in her.

In the silence, the woman came forward, set the tray down and straightened up to face them, tight-lipped. She hadn't been crying, but her eye sockets were deep purple shaded, making her look quite ill.

Stricken, Shira spoke out. "I overheard—by accident. I never meant to." Before she knew it, the anger, the resentment burst out again, swamping any feeling of sympathy. "But what does that matter beside the fact that you knew? Last night you knew Grandfather was going to be betrayed. And this morning, *you knew* the Controller wasn't coming back tonight—"

"That's not true!" Susann cried, more in grief than anger. "I was hoping, *praying*. I couldn't believe—oh God!" She sat down.

"—and you never told me!" Shira continued, over Susann's protest, heard her voice rising shrilly, but couldn't stop it.

"Listen, both of you," MacAllister said.

Susann spoke through her hands. "We all have our loyalties." She looked up wearily. "Even the wives of politicians."

"Susann." MacAllister sat beside her.

Shira glared down at them both. "What," she demanded, "is he going to do to Grandfather?"

"Do?" Susann's eyes were large and dark with distress. "You know as much as I. My guess is that he'll trade your grandfather for what he wants. Which is armaments."

"Armaments? He'd trade the Hesikastor for—for—" Shira clenched her fists. "You mean he's going to hand Grandfather over like a sack of—"

"Yes. Yes. And yes! And don't look at me like that. For there's nothing you or I or anyone can do to stop him!" Susann leapt from the couch and ran from the room.

Shira went to follow, but MacAllister took her by the shoulders. "Let her go."

She tried to break free, but MacAllister, holding on, shook her. "Listen, Shira. Listen to me. You think your grandfather didn't know that all this was going to happen? Come on. He's the Hesikastor. Why do you suppose he sent you here, eh?"

She stopped struggling. And saw with a shock compassion in the blue eyes. "Oh. Oh, *God!*"

"Shira." MacAllister stroked her hair. "Courage. Remember what I said? We're at war. If we're going to come through, we'll need cool heads, and the strength to do as we're told!"

04.28 Hours 16 October
Bentnose Peak

Shira was awakened suddenly by her grandfather's voice sounding close by her ear. *Shira?*

She came upright in the dark. *Grandfather?* Where was he calling her from? Horrible images flashed through her inner vision. Of him bound in chains, being delivered into bondage high above the Earth. *Grandfather!* The call was almost a scream.

Stop your fretting child. You are letting nightmares scatter your thought. The beacon signals us. We must answer it.

"The beacon?" She sobbed the words out loud.

. . . *You think your grandfather didn't know?* . . . *if we're going to come through, we'll need the strength to do as we're told* . . .

She lay back again, tried to relax, to suppress her hysteria, the many questions she wanted to ask.

Oh Grandfather! No answer, of course. He was already gone ahead of her. It was up to her to join him. Slide, slide, focus.

She began to drift at last, to hear the silence in the space around her. Whose space? Hers? Grandfather's? Or Torc's? It was difficult to tell . . .

The rasp of curtains woke him. Light streamed through the bay that Tanna had crouched in the night before. Above him through those windows loomed the blackened ruins of his father's tower.

"Majesty?"

He rolled away to face the wall. "Go away."

"Majesty."

It was no use fighting it—the day had begun. He turned his head. Arad stood there, hlath in hand, looking anxious.

"Majesty—General Feric reminds you respectfully that it is already three hours past sunrise. The whole of Gurnyac waits to greet you, he says, and did you not hear the bells?"

Torc sat up, stretched his naked arms, took the scalding cup from Arad's hands. Skod, how quickly he was taking to hlath again.

"Arad—my clothes."

"Majesty."

To Torc's surprise Arad brought in not only his morning suiting but a length of rough blue latik—no—*two* lengths: a pilgrim's robe of the eleventh step and a heisha. "I thought—when I heard the news—you might instead like to wear this, sire."

Torc looked at Arad with renewed interest. A good man, Arad. Maybe he'd misjudged his father's choice of adaide. "I would indeed. In fact, I think I'll shave my scalp as well." It seemed fitting then, to come as he'd gone.

Torc had scarce begun his bath when Feric arrived. The place, he said, was crammed with well-wishers. There was congestion and confusion everywhere and preparations for the coronation were being hampered, and would he hurry down to breakfast.

It took a full hour to reach the dining hall through the press. Yet that hour was a necessary one; men falling before him, pledging their loyalty, congratulating him on his victory over Gar; and he binding their pledges with a nod or a look or a squeeze of the golden palm.

When at last he reached the dining hall, it was crowded; every table, every bench, and people were four deep all around the walls.

All stood in silence at his entrance. No one moved until he reached his father's chair. For a moment he stood, head bowed before it, then sat, not in the king's seat, but in his old one beside it. In response to this gesture there came a spontaneous roar: "Long live the king!"

"Good move." Feric eyed him opposite. "Feeling for you runs high. And the crowds already await Gar's head."

Torc nodded, looking down. The stink of meat was sickening.

Sitting there felt strange after so long. He was aware of the noise, and of them all staring at his blue robe and heisha, at his new-shorn head and chin, and at his plate on which sat a lone pecular. Dish after dish of spiced meats he turned away, conscious of the murmurs.

Feric's eyebrows, too, went up, but he said nothing, addressing himself only to his own heaped plate.

Torc gazed out over the milling chamber, searching for but one face.

Ramoni!

She'd be miles away by now.

Had she gone because he'd been set to kill Gar? No. He let out a sigh. Now he knew why she'd made herself wear the black and silver of a royal guard.

I have my reasons.

She'd been planning this all the time he'd talked of making her queen. His face went bleak. If not her, no one. He looked out across the hall, thinking of the night under the byre, the lovemaking, the fights.

Ramoni.

By now she'd have reached the Weald, in her guard's uniform, and, he'd bet on it, with an order under Feric's seal to search the Brandings for a certain slave . . . His lips twisted into a faint smile. And she'd get away with it, too. Should he send after her?

No. Let her be.

Maybe when she'd found her father she might not be averse to reconsidering the throne.

Throne. There was but one in Gurnyac: the king's. Queens since time immemorial had stood behind their consort's seat on the rare occasions they appeared there. He could just see Ramoni settling for that! His face brightened. He'd commission a queen's throne just as soon as he'd—somehow—disposed of sairah Broda.

Feric leaned across the table. "It's good to see you smile. It makes the people feel secure. Shall it please you to go now, sire?"

"I had these drawn up last night, Majesty. They need only your signature and seal." Feric set three parchments down on the table before him.

"What is this?" Torc took up the first scroll and unfurled it, saw the annual requisition order commanding every family with a son of age to deliver either him for a five-year stint in the military or a ransom of five hundred shengs—a sum past the reach of any in Gurnyac below the rank of second noble.

"A formality only, sire, as you no doubt know, but an urgent one. We are one month behind already with our spring campaign. We've an urgent score to settle with Brugad of Kyrn. It should go out today."

Torc put it down. He didn't like it, he didn't like it at all. How many Sheshus would get themselves spiked this sun-around because they hadn't the money to buy themselves off? Ill trained and ill fed, the footclars merely served as buffers in the field. Dare he refuse to sign? No. Not this time.

He must not antagonize Feric.

He took up his quill and signed it, then picked up the second sheet.

A formal declaration dispossessing all traitors' families of wealth and lands and an order for their immediate exile.

Feric stepped up to him, read over his shoulder. "Is there something wrong?"

"The words are strong."

"Indeed, sire. And they're yours."

Torc hesitated. Stripping the traitors of land and title had sounded all very well. But now it occurred to him: what had those families done, for the most part innocent women and children, that they should be put from Gurnyac's gates without a rak to their ruined names?

"Sire?"

"I'll think on this awhile."

"But you cannot. Already noise of it has gone out and a declaration is expected within the hour."

"Let them wait."

"Sire—the people watch for you to show a strong arm."

"But, Fer—"

"Since Sharroc's death, our borders have been breached, our name for power eroded—even the fat Kondishmen are looking askance at Gurnyac. I warned you last night and I say now to you that the whole of the Known World will closely look to what you do this day."

Torc picked up the quill, held it, suspended over the sheet.

This went sore against the grain. In his mind now it was tantamount to treachery against all he felt and thought. But it was plain that he had no choice at that time. He signed, and, still bent over the table, took up the final scroll, knowing even as he did so what it was: a proclamation, inviting all the citizens of Gurnyac to watch Gar's execution straight after his branding that afternoon.

Now was Feric truly calling him out, and Torc himself could see the right of his purpose. Had he not gone to Rm but a bruk as green as an unripe pinu nut? The man sought only to guide him, this seasoned general of a thousand campaigns, being rightly concerned for the throne. But he was mistaken in that concern. For the boy who'd ridden away was now a man.

Torc dropped the scroll.

The glove was now thrown down between them, the challenge to each to show the measure of his strength. Feric sought to force him, to bend him to his will, the way he'd always done as Torc's mentor and second father. But whatever his intention, was not Feric in effect setting himself *above* the king? Is that how he saw himself? As one who pulled the strings to make the new king dance? A dangerous precedent indeed. Where would it end?

"I won't sign this. I said that Gar wouldn't die until I decided. You've gone against my word."

Feric's face darkened. *"Word?* A king doesn't *speak.* He *does.* And you know nothing yet of what a king does and doesn't do. I warned you last night that this must be finished today. This is but the seal upon it."

"Well, again, I say, no."

"You will please," Feric said, his voice going very quiet, "tell me why you go against the military and the Council in this matter."

So many times in the past had Torc cringed inwardly at the threat in that voice! Even now he felt its force. Yet he pressed on.

"Did military or Council smoke Gar out? No. I did. He's mine, and as I'm king I'll have my day." He deliberately turned and walked toward his bedchamber.

"A king's not crowned with gold on a high throne," Feric called after him. "But in blood, on the battleground. That's where he shows his mettle. You've proven nothing yet, save that you're as willful as ever and no wiser—*stay!"*

Torc halted before his bedchamber door, the old dread rising in spite of himself.

Feric still stood before the table on which the scrolls lay.

"One thing your father knew, young bruk, is that a king's might is in his arms. If they're lost, he's lost entire." He jabbed a finger at the proclamation. "I ask you once more—sign."

Torc swallowed. "No, Fer. Not now."

He turned from Feric and went through the door.

He collapsed onto his boot-chair and put his head in his hands. *Don't antagonize Feric!* He might as well have challenged the man to a full-scale tournament! But what else could he have done? The question was—what would Feric do now?

There he sat, staring at the floor, until at last Arad came in. It was time to dress for the ceremony.

One hour later, anointed and dressed in his coronation robes, he set off down the Grand Stair for the last time in his life as prince, unattended save for Arad as was the custom.

Step by step he descended past the packed galleries amid slow thigh slapping. Behind him trod Arad holding high a plain wooden rod bearing the Gnangar colors. Torc's hands were empty and would remain thus until they raised his own crown.

The king's mantle was of heavy harpile; its train dragged the stairs behind him. His shaven head must surely look small atop it, he thought.

Beneath the mantle, his doublet was of heavy harpile also, the same gold; his breeches of thick white harsilk embroidered with gold filament. Gold weighed heavy on his chest, the buckles of his shoes.

The last time he'd trodden that stair he'd worn but a simple pilgrim's robe. To think he'd considered that heavy! And Sharroc had been waiting down by the Great Door with his heisha.

May the grace of the great Lothuri cleanse your soul, prove your mind and spirit, and send you forth from Rm a future king!

Hah!

He looked around. No sign of Feric, but then he should be already waiting in the throne room.

What if the general weren't there?

He thrust the thought away. They'd had their bouts before, hadn't they? It always came out right in the end.

He reached the bottom step, treading the golden carpet not used since Sharroc was made king, around through the central hall.

Young bruk, Feric had called him. On that last coronation day, both Feric and Sharroc had been but young bruks—and Feric only a captain. How had his father felt walking this route? Surely not as badly as Torc felt now.

Through the gathered lords and nobles he was to walk, through the high archway and down the long aisle that led past the pillared busts of past kings to the foot of the throne.

Which is why your throning-room looks like a chamber of the dead . . .

His father's bust was in there now. Not taken from a death mask, for he'd been too badly burnt. But as near to a likeness as the royal masons could judge. There it was, just by the doors. He paused before it, head bowed, paying respects for the last time as prince to monarch.

Then amid an appreciative silence, he went on.

There were nosegays and wreaths everywhere, and bunting, and ribands in the Gnangar colors. The people must have worked like slaves to have it ready so fast. *Like slaves.*

He nodded to the kneeling figures on either side.

The hall dazzled in the sunbeams lancing down through high clerestories. Torc smiled faintly, remembering the gloomy chill of the Hall of Induction.

Way down the front, near the foot of the throne, Tanna waited in the concubine's gallery, attended by Harbeli. She looked pale, he saw as he approached her, but he wasn't surprised, not with Gar in his felmar's cage facing her across the aisle. At the very front, sat the sairah, Broda, conspicuously veiled.

To think—he was just about to be the first bachelor king in the history of Gurnyac. Comforting thought, for hadn't Ramoni guaranteed he'd stay alive long enough to spawn an heir?

He drew level with Tanna, smiled as he went past but her head was bowed. Behind her, Harbeli went down stiffly, looking most solemn.

He gave Gar one quick glance, then looked away. They'd bound him, and muzzled him, leaving him unwashed and unkempt, and still in his bloodied nightshirt, and lashed him upright to the bars of the cage.

A cluster of figures stood at the base of the throne steps, the Council, for the most part.

He nodded their way, looking for the general, saw him nowhere.

Feric wasn't there.

Fear started in him. What to do? What could he do, but go on.

He reached the foot of the steps, began to climb. He was halfway up when he paused, his legs trembling.

A king's might is in his arms. If they're lost, he's lost entire.

On again, ten, eleven, twelve . . .

What if Feric was still not there when Torc reached the top?

He fought the overwhelming urge to turn around and look.

A fine sweat broke out on his forehead. He was going to suffocate.

He looked up to the empty throne, shining under the dark mote-laden air high above the hall.

. . . nineteen, twenty. He reached it, breathing deep and fast. He stood before it, his back to the brilliant company, his arms raised.

When he turned at last, what would he find at the foot of the steps?

He forced himself at last to face about, his skin pricking.

Feric was there, stiff-faced, with the crown.

Torc nodded him up.

Feric obeyed, but as the general climbed, Torc's sense of dread only increased.

At the top, Feric, breathing hard, knelt and held up the cushion on which sat the crown.

Torc looked down searching Feric's face for the slightest sign of relenting, but the general's eyes were fixed on the crown.

And so at last Torc bent, closed his hands on the gem-encrusted band, and raised it high, looking to the cage, remembering his dream.

He looked toward Gar and cried out. "Thou shalt not have this diadem! See! Upon this head it goes, who have the reason and the right!"

He lowered the crown onto his head then sat and all at once the air filled with shouting:

"Long live the king! Long live the king!"

Torc looked around the crowded chamber.

There were no felmars, no flames of his vision, but only

solemn patrician faces upturned, opening and closing dry mouths on ritual as old as their very names.

Torc dipped his head, feeling the unaccustomed weight of the crown, and as he did so, it slipped slightly on his bare scalp so that he had to snatch at it and push it back into place.

Feric, still beside him, his back to the crowd, bowed.

"I think, sire," he murmured, "that the crown sits insecure upon a shaven head."

Torc looked sharply to him, even as the man backed down the steps. Feric was still angry. No matter. It was over. He lifted his chin and gazed over the hall, looking truly a king. But that feeling of dread persisted, and a sense of irreversible wrong.

Look what you've done, you hated thing. Look what you've done!

Done what? Only taken up a crown that was rightly his. And with it he intended to become the greatest king ever in the Known World.

CHAPTER TWENTY-NINE

TANNA sat on the bath's tiled ledge, the steam curling about her ears, the water up to her chin. Only there did she find relief from that alien body that had once been hers. She stared down at the swell of her belly, at her bloated breasts floating like drowned dead things under the water.

Her body was ruined. And not only her body.

Her eyes pricked at the thought of the years ahead.

Such high hopes she'd had. And only a short while ago. Of wearing the queen's crown and of bearing the Gurnyac heir. And what had all her struggling and suffering brought her? The hateful parasite, that *dahorg* growing inside her, barring her forever from the throne.

But worst of all she'd lost Torc. Oh, he told her every time he visited her that he'd lie with her after the birth of the child. But she doubted it, and even if he did it wouldn't be the same. For he'd lost his desire for her and all the kindness in the world couldn't make that right.

She leaned back, pressed her hands to her eyes.

The best she could hope for now was to stay his confidante.

She lifted her feet, waved them gently up and down in the water.

She should be glad that of all the people in the Citadel he talked only to her of his plans for Gurnyac. Such strange and exciting plans as they were—incredible, coming from Torc's head. Unheard-of plans for freeing slaves, providing hostels for the poor, training centers where scrots and scroles alike could learn to read and write openly. She shook her head fondly. Such talk as she'd only ever heard from Durac. Could it all come to pass? Harbeli doubted it. She, too, was worried for Torc. The Council, she said, the nobles would never stand for it. Tanna wanted the plans to work. But knowing that they couldn't she'd be relieved for Torc's own sake when his Rmish ideas faded and he got back to reality.

She sat up, pressed her hands to her eyes. Where would that leave her?

She should be proud, Harbeli told her. She, a scribe's daughter, in the place of First Concubine. But Harbeli couldn't guess, and Tanna could never tell her, what it had been like that day to watch Torc ascend the throne and she confined to the concubine's stall.

What would become of her? What when the child was born, if it grew to be another Gar? What would Torc do with it, with her?

"Lady?" Tanna sat up. Harbeli was bending over her with the towel.

"It's time already?"

"Aye, it is. And not good to lie too long as near to your time as this. Come on now—here, you take my hand. That's it." Harbeli, grunting, hauled her up and out.

A while later, Tanna lay on her favorite couch in her sitting room overlooking a little rear courtyard. She felt warm from the bath and knew she must have a color. A pity that Torc was not there to see it, he saying all the time how pale she'd grown.

It was seven days since she'd last seen him, on the morning that he set off for the Weald himself with Gar.

Ugly, evil, mutilated Gar. She never told anybody, but she'd heard the cries of the branding that day from her bed.

Gar, they said, had lain under the Keep for seven days raving like a madman but still Torc hadn't taken his head.

At the time, the choice had sat well with the people, and Feric, clearly out with Torc over it, had lost face. But Harbeli said now folk were changing their minds, saying now that there should have been a blood-let and that there'd have been one had not Torc's mind been turned in Rm. Torc should never have taken the eleventh step, they said, for it had softened him. That—dare she even think it?—that he had gotten more of the Quaur than was good for a king.

Oh, why hadn't Torc taken Gar's head?

When she'd tried to tell him of the talk, he'd dismissed it with a wave of his hand.

"Don't worry," he'd told her. "Gar is no more a threat to anyone. He's been broken, and disgraced. There's not a man alive who'd speak with him now."

He'd kissed her, and left straightway with Feric for the Weald. The very thought of that man made her uneasy. There was something about him that she'd never trust.

She brushed her hand across her lips. She still could feel Torc's mouth on hers. A cruel mouth always, until his return from Rm.

She lay back among the cushions, sighing.

"A rak for your thoughts, lady."

Harbeli, sewing in hand, came to sit beside her. A gown it was, a tiny, lovely thing, for the baby. Harbeli knew it was Gar's baby, Tanna was sure, although they'd never discussed it, and Harbeli kept up the pretense that it was Torc's. Maybe Torc had told her, but she doubted it. She wouldn't be a bit surprised if Harbeli hadn't known it all along, even when they'd first met.

"I was thinking of His Majesty."

"Tell me something new!" Harbeli's needle moved in and out.

"Harbeli—"

"Yes, lady?"

"The things you told me: I tried to tell Torc, but he wouldn't listen."

"And wasn't that always the way?" Harbeli said soberly.

"I think," Tanna said, meaning to say, "I must try again," but just then came a loud fanfare and the clatter of a drawbridge.

Torc was home.

It was several hours before he came to see her.

He sat beside her as soon as they were alone, on the couch.

She thought he looked tired and strained, and would have said so but he spoke first.

"Tanna—you're still looking peaked. I've had a word with the apothecary. Tomorrow you're for Pruth."

"No!"

He pretended to look stern. "And why not?"

"I would remain with you. I'm all right, really I am. Please don't send me there."

"You're going, lady, and no more argument. You've been cooped up too long in closed rooms without light and air. The apothecary himself is attending you. And Harbeli is already packing your things. I shall miss you, Tanna. Hurry up and have that child. You and I have some catching up to do." He smiled down at her, but not with his eyes.

He was dismissing her. Getting rid of her. So soon.

"But what about our afternoons? Who shall you tell about—" She dropped her voice. "About the changes?"

"I'll keep a journal instead," he said. "It's time these things were properly set down. I'll not go to work though until after the child is born. I promise you'll not miss anything."

"Journal?" Had she heard him right? "You mean you're actually going to write out the things you've told me?"

"Not *going to,* Tanna. I already have: charts, lists, laws and all. It must all be worked out most carefully before I present it."

She couldn't believe it. She placed her hands over her belly and closed her eyes.

He half stood, leaning over her. "Are you all right. Tanna? Shall I call Harbeli?"

She shook her head. "You are not keeping those scrolls in your desk? You see what happened to Gar."

"Tanna: this is no insurrection I'm planning; or a parricide. I'm a king bringing timely change to my own people, in my own realm. You look unhappy still."

"I am. Torc—what you say makes me afraid."

"But why? Did you not yourself say that these changes will make me the greatest king in the history of Gurnyac?"

"Aye. I did. But we were only talking then." Oh—what had she said! She watched the displeasure spring to his mouth. "Sire—"

He sat down again, heavily. "On with it, Tanna. You might as well."

"I've been hearing things."

"*More* things? What about, this time?"

"Feeling is rising worse over Gar, and your quarrel with Feric. Torc—I still don't trust him." Had she gone too far?

"Tanna—there's no quarrel with Feric. Always people exaggerate. Is there any more?"

"They also say a lot of the nobles grow tired of waiting for largesse. The properties you confiscated—they expected them long since."

Torc frowned. "I've bound all those to me that I want with gold—and generously. But I promised those lands to none. The greed of those men! There's no noble in all of Gurnyac who lacks estate to fit his rank. The Dryac take them. Hah! Avarice and disaffection are common enough coinage in a king's realm. So don't be anxious on that account."

"But what are those nobles going to do when you use those properties the way you mean to? I tell you again, Torc—you're likely to make many enemies."

"And I tell you again that all kings do that, Tanna. Especially the king of Gurnyac."

She didn't return his smile.

How could she? He wouldn't listen to her—not that he ever had. And her day was over. He was packing her off, and this was the last time she'd see him before she left for Pruth.

Maybe ever.
Come to Pruth. Come to Pruth and die.

Shira stirred slightly on the bed. Almost as though she
wanted to break concentration, to pull away. She needed to rest
away from the energy flowing through her, so she told herself.

But she couldn't.

Her own deeper desires held her fast, her mind locked on
the new currents of energy flowing from her grandfather's
mind. She gave up the struggle, allowed herself to drift back
into the reality that was Gurnyac.

Torc stood at his window looking up at the king's keep: at
the new timbers rising already from the ruins; beams, shoring,
scaffolds, spars, strong and black against the great white
fullness of Ao.

He slipped his hands into the sleeves of the blue pilgrim's
robe that he now affected to wear, satisfied. From the ashes of
the old was rising the new. He lifted the window catch, pushed
open the casement.

Over the warm air came distant sounds of laughter and
singing from the city below. It was the night of the Quendaree,
Carnival of Fools, marking the first official spring day.

As this very hour one year before he'd gone down into
Gurnyac with Aravac and the rest looking for sport on the
night where more men were parted from their gold and
fallowellas from their virginity than on all the other nights of
the year put together.

Tonight Aravac was dead and the others had been sent down
without him.

He walked back to his desk, took up the scroll he'd been
writing on.

"From this day on," he read, "the Brandings are under my
direct jurisdiction, I solely having power to appoint or dismiss
Masters, and to constitute the laws by which the Houses run."

He took up his quill and wrote on.

"Be it known that the slave system in its present form is
abolished. All civilians formerly taken as spoils of war shall be

freed, together with free men disenfranchised for bounty. These shall be replaced by criminals and military prisoners, whose choice at judgment will be branding or death.

"Those slaves who wish to remain in the Brandings shall as free men be given decent dwellings and a gratuity to train and oversee new slaves.

"If any Brandmaster complain he shall resign and be replaced by one of the aforementioned former slaves.

"As to the slaves that elect to take their freedom and leave the Weald: royal hostels shall provide free shelter and training for them from the king's own coffers, said hostels comprising lands confiscated from those who sought to overthrow the Gnangar line."

He paused, reread what he'd just written, then set down his pen.

His hlath was cold.

He got up, poured himself some fresh from the stove, and stood before it, cup in hand, staring into the flames, seeing there as he saw in all unguarded moments the image of Gar being wheeled into the open market place, hunched on the cage floor while the royal crier read out his list of crimes before the silenced masses crowding that space and spilling back in all directions to the very city gates, it seemed.

The list being read, they dragged Gar, the first of the conspirators to the branding irons.

Never would Torc forget it.

Four times they seared his battered flesh; each arm, his back, and brow with the mark of the hammer.

Not one sound did he make until the last.

They left him to lie moaning in the filth of his cage while one after another they branded the others, squad after squad of them until the air above Gurnyac filled with screaming and wailing and Torc sickened to his very soul but he'd had to stay through to the end.

How he envied the Athor and D'huru Nor among the clouds.

How easy was the life up there.

Already he was at odds with the Council for settling on the

traitors' families annuities, modest enough, Dryac knew, to keep them off the streets, and those out of his own coffers, too. Feric, also, had come out particularly strongly against the measure, and had said so, to Torc's own great displeasure.

Feric.

Something must be done, and soon, to breach the widening gap between them. The general had obviously not forgiven Torc for Gar, and would not, save over Gar's spilt blood.

Hah! He had a single blinding image of the solitary throne shining high upon the dais. No one had told him how lonely it was to be a king.

How could they know?

He wandered back to his desk, to the piles of edicts and drafts and proclamations and lists.

How could he hope to change these people?

They were worse than animals, and there was he trapped among them for the rest of his days.

He swept his arm across the desk, scattering parchment over the floor and not feeling any the better for it.

But not all the news was bad.

He bent to retrieve two scrolls from the pile at his feet.

One was from Tanna. She was feeling better, she said. Her time was drawing near. She didn't say so, but she was begging him to go and see her. Well, maybe next week, when Feric got back from the Weald.

He dropped that scroll onto the desk, turned to the second.

He'd found it tucked under his saddle one day the week before when he'd gone riding at sunup. Whoever had put it there had done it somehow in the instant between stall and stable yard. The moment he'd seen the seal—a crude sign representing a bridge—he'd pushed it further under his saddle without a word.

A note from Ramoni.

Gurnyac, know that my father's safe with me. In the Smeltings, he was, under the sign of the double axe. I won't distress us both by describing him, but only say he has the black lung and not long to go.

As for you and me—I said our paths lay separately. Well, something has happened to change that—somewhat.

Gurnyac, I am with child.

I intend to keep it, this living seal of our friendship. But it shall never come to Gurnyac, or know its sire.

But as you are the father, so you shall see it one day and so after it is born we shall meet on some common ground—say, by some crofter's house?—and you shall witness this wonderful creature we have made.

Don't resent me, Gurnyac. You above all men shall not lack progeny, whose queen shall shortly give you your heir. Be glad for me and rejoice that something remains of a strange and wonderful time in our lives.

I think of you every day—and how could I not, with your name in every mouth from here to the Far Seas—and not all of it bad, either.

You move through dangerous times. Remember—lose your Iron General and you lose all. I know it went against the grain, but maybe you should have taken Gar's head after all.

I pray for you and your success. Take care, Gurnyac, until we meet again.

Ramoni

I am with child!

His child!

He dropped the letter on his desk.

Hadn't Ramoni said that from him would come a descendant who'd one day change the destiny of the Known World?

In that moment such a surge of pride and gladness took him that he leapt, clicking his heels in the air. If only he could fly, soar out above the ribs of the rising tower and look down as he had that night only now with elation in his heart.

Failing that—he took up his empty hlath cup—he'd toast his son with his last hlath of the day.

He rang the bell for Arad, and in the brief wait, took up Ramoni's letter again, rolled it, and slipped it inside his robe. Arad's eyes were everywhere.

He rang again, a little longer this time. The Dryac take the man. Where was he?

He crossed the room, put his head through the door to shout.

The hall was half dark, the lanterns turned low. Arad sat sprawled in his chair, asleep.

"Arad—Arad, I say!"

Arad didn't move.

He went forward, took Arad's arm, dropped it, his hand slick with blood.

He stooped to turn up the lamp.

"Leave it, brother."

Torc wheeled about. Across the hall in the shadow of Arad's own doorway stood Gar in guards' gear, save for the cap pulled over his brow.

From behind him came guards to line the hall.

And—"Feric!" No time, no time for more.

He glanced past Gar, measuring the distance to the outer door.

"Don't bother." Gar laughed. "There are guards outside. There's no one alive in this wing to help you now. Take him!"

Torc ran, back into his chamber, locking and barring the door even as the ramming began. A dozen strides to the glory-hole and he was clear.

How had this come to pass? Oh, what a fool he'd been, and how badly he'd underestimated Gar.

Reaching the end of the passage he opened the outer door a crack, moved aside the arras. The gallery was alive with guards.

His chamber window—maybe he could jump from there.

He sped back up the passage, ran to the window, only to find the courtyard below brilliant with torchlight.

There came a sound of splintering. In another moment they'd be inside. There flashed into his mind then the thought that Feric had deliberately let him through, had given him this time in which to take the only way out.

But he hadn't taken it.

He suddenly remembered Ramoni's letter.

Quick—he must burn it.

At that moment the door burst open and men spilled into the room.

Before he could take up the poker to raise the stove lid, hands seized him, pinning back his arms, and Gar stood before him.

"Well, brother. Now I take you just as you took me. The Brandelac reversed—except that this time the last laugh is mine."

He went over to the desk where Feric was already turning over the scrolls, picked up a sheet and read aloud.

"As to the slaves that elect to take their freedom and leave the Weald: royal hostels shall provide free shelter and training for them from the king's own coffers, said hostels comprising lands confiscated from those who sought to overthrow the Gnangar line."

He looked up and laughed.

"You were indeed right, Feric." Gar eyed Torc up and down. "I see, General, that you were also correct in saying how Rm has addled our brother's mind. See—he still thinks himself a pilgrim dreaming under golden roofs!"

"Your Highness," Feric still avoided Torc's eyes, "move— fast, before folk come back from the Quendaree."

"Yes." Gar went to the wall, took down Torc's own sword. "I said once, if you recall, brother, that one day there'd be a real sword between us and blood would flow and that that blood would be yours." He laughed again. "It seems I'm a greater prophet than you for all your fancy pilgrimage. Down."

Torc braced himself.

Here, in his last moment, would he need the best of all he'd learned. They must never know of Ramoni, of the child. He must burn that letter—*now!*

Twisting suddenly, he freed himself and lunged for the stove.

Gar ran at him, only to spin away an instant later, snarling in pain, across the floor, fetching up against the desk with a smack.

Torc seized up the poker, and with deliberate haste engaged its hook into the niche in the stove lid and hefted it.

Gar screamed for the men to take him.

Feric himself came sword drawn, crouched.

A moment later he, too, was over on his back, down the far end of the room, and in that instant Torc slipped his hand inside his robe and pulled out Ramoni's scroll.

I am with child . . .

Gar scrambled up, and came on again, waving Torc's sword before him, but Torc turned the poker, still with stove lid dangling, to ward off Gar and at the same time dropped the letter in the flames. Gar, too late to check the momentum of his rush, took the poker, the lid full in his groin.

He cried out, doubled up, and probably would have fainted but for the fact, Torc realized in that interval, that infinitely small interval when clocks stand still and one has all the time in the world to wish and hope and regret, that Gar's very hate was bearing him up. Poor Gar. One child he had unknowing and would never have another. But from his own loins was sprung one of prophecy, and it was his own line that would one day change the face of the Known World.

Many hands held him now; his arms, his head, squaring his chest to his own blade. His chest? Oh, yes. Gar would want him to see. Time enough to hack off his head and post it on the Citadel gates afterward.

He called to Feric somewhere behind.

"Fer—how can you crown the very head you wanted stricken off! Is this what you want? A king without an heir? Think—it's not too late to change your mind. At least I have one."

"Oh, no you have not!" Gar lowered the blade, the sweat pouring from him in his agony. "No progeny for you either, for I sent within this past hour to Pruth to have the child ripped from the she-frat's womb!" And so saying, Gar raised the blade and rammed it through Torc's chest with all his remaining strength, spilling blood out onto the blue harsilk.

It hurt, oh, how it hurt, just as Torc had always imagined it would. But he steadied his mind, sought for breath.

There must be no more blood!

He mustn't let Tanna die. His mouth twisted. How she'd wanted to be queen! And how ironic: now she'd get her wish, but at what price, for she and Gar would have to wed to make the child his heir.

"Pity," he made himself say, with a ghost of his old smile. "You—lose—after all—child in Tanna's belly—not mine—but yours!"

The room began to spin, and as the spots swirled thicker, faster, flocking out the light, he heard Gar screaming for riders to overtake the first.

Torc looked to Gar's bloodied groin and tried to laugh but something bubbled up and choked it off.

Gar snarling, fell in toward him but he never got there.

"Yours," Torc said, and let his head fall at last.

Ord, gazing at the blood flowing from the young king's chest, closed his eyes in relief as the images faded.

It was over.

The old man had lapsed into sleep.

Wearily, Ord reached to help Suk unhitch the Hesikastor to wheel him back upstairs. He felt totally drained, and not wholly on account of the long day's stint. The brutality. The treachery. The overriding irony. Had that poor young bugger gone the way he was supposed to, he'd have made it through. Christ! Earth, Phrynis. It was all the same . . .

Well. At least this last batch of strips should restore him to Ellisen's good favor. Ord wiped his brow, feeling better on that thought. He'd clear up, steal a quick nip from his secret store, then take a well-earned rest—on the qui vive, of course, for a summons from his bleeding nibs.

At a quiet exclamation from Prosser, Ord whipped about to find men crowding the doorway.

He stared blankly. Not psi team reinforcements, surely. Not in those gray and black plasti-leather getups. Or those black, shiny helmets.

One of the men stepped forward, raised an arm in salute.

Ord drew in a sharp breath. On that arm was a black armband bearing a silver insignia on a blood red ground, subtending the letters S.T.I.

"Stand quite still, and you'll not be harmed," the soldier commanded, nodding to the weapons his men had trained upon them. "Director Manfred Hengst has instructed me to inform you that this station is now under his command."

Vowels are short unless otherwise indicated. e.g. c*a*t; m*e*t,
p*i*n; c*o*t. n.b: short *u* usually as in p*u*t.
ch as in lo*ch*, *ch*utzpah, indicated by **k*.
Initial *h's* sounded as *ch* above also indicated by **k*.
th's are rare, and soft, as in *forth*.

achan *(a'kan)*: fragrant herb with soothing properties.

adahi *(a-dah'hi)*: fierce dog-like creatures used for guarding
and tracking.

adaide *(ad'aid)*: equerry; confidential attendant.

agria *(a'gri-ah)*: costly refined lamp oil(mineral) of odorless
blue flame.

ambaree *(am'ba-ree)*: traveling platform or cabin atop a daur,
like Earth howdah.

bruk: brash young man full of hubris or chutzpah.

cazn: healer; one skilled in herbal lore; witch. Northern var:
cathn.

charnu *(chah'noo)*: hot whole grain cereal.

chint; ass; buttocks.

'clar: abbr. for *footclar*.

conclaur *(con'claw-uh)*: class; study group; work detail.

crit tree: mountain evergreen akin to Earth's pine.

daur *(daw'uh)*: huge domestic beast, between elephant and
dinosaur.

d'hogan *(duh-hoe'gun)* mat: area on which the D'hogana is
practiced.

doyshan *(doy'shan)*: shawl, used like eastern chadar.

fallowella *(fallow-ell'uh)*: virgin, originally; later used to
denote anything but.

felmar *(fel'mah)*: large rodent; hunts in packs usually; vicious
cunning creature, preying on injured, smaller animals;
though has been known to attack new-born langaur while
dam away.

fookar *(foo'kah)*: either home of evil spirits or spirits themselves.

footclar: common soldier; infantryman; conscript.

forhar *(faw' hah)*: domestic ruminant beast, like Earth's bison. Source of milk, cheese and meat; thick curly coat chief source of cloth throughout Known World.

frat: dog-like animal, domestic.

garabol *(ga' ra-bol)*: bastard.

garahundt *(ga' ra-hunt)*: whore.

ghial *(guy' ull)*: musical instrument comprising hollow glass columns of varying lengths and thicknesses, suspended within vertical brass frame and struck with fine silver tapers (lins).

gobyr *(go' beer)* wood: extremely hard wood found only north of Gortland; trees very small & slow-growing, yielding whorled and knotted wood of warm golden hue; highly prized for carving.

gont: dotard (m).

gort-red: rich blood red, color of gort wine.

gort wine: strong choice wine from the vineyards of Gortland.

gosheng *(goh' sheng)*: equals one thousand shengs.

griklok *(grik' lok)*: arm/shoulder grip used in the D'hogana.

grole: dotard (f).

harling: forhar yearling.

harmeat: meat of the forhar.

harnwood: choice hardwood used for paneling; like Earth's cedar.

harpile: any pile cloth, from finest velvet to coarse carpeting.

harsilk: fine yarn or cloth made from the coat of the harling.

haryarn: coarse yarn made from coats of mature forhar.

heisha *(hay' shuh)*: headpiece like Arab kaffiyeh and agal.

helak *(hell' ak)*: approx. 6 Earth kilometers.

himlic *(*kim' lic)*: potent fomentation of hitaku : having strong psychedelic properties.

hitaku *(hi-tah' koo)*: edible fungus found only under Rm. Staple nutrient of the Lothuri.

hlath *(*klahth)*: herbal brew, thick fomented syrup, laced with liquor.

hrodm *(*kro' dum)*: blood brother.

krudt *(kroot)*: penis.

kuzn *(koo'zun)*: freshwater protoplasm; a small blue medusa found in Lake Asn.

langaur *lang'gaw-uh)*: beast of prey like Earth's somewhere between a lion and a lynx.

ligwood: tree having many forms, each prized for different reasons. Silver ligwoods for papery bark; spindly twisted black ligwoods as delicate (& costly) ornamentals.

loile *(loh'eel)*: wild nectar flower, source of choicest honey in Known World.

melk: slave.

opryx *(op'rix)*: bossy growth on brow of Lothuri child; cluster of light-conducting ganglia serving immature *pyryx*. Disappears at puberty.

orat *(aw'rat)*: ancient evergreen herb; vine with dark shiny leaves; disinfectant, deodorant, and cleansing properties.

paradee *(pa'ra-dee)*: stately court dance punctuated with sudden leaps; performed in pairs and entirely on the spot.

pecular *(peck'yew-lah)*: soft-fleshed fruit, size of peach with grape-like pellucidity; remains in prime ripened state for months; good winter food.

pettiwik *(pett'i-wik)*: tiny bird of plains; gleaner of the grain crofts.

pilpit: like Earth's ant lion.

pinu *(pee'noo)*: hardwood tree, yielding choice edible sweet nut, size of plum.

pizac *(pie'zac)*: idiot.

pyryx *(pi'rix)*: secondary brain of the Lothuri, set at base of main brain. Believed to be source of their extraordinary powers.

rak: small coin, exact value unknown. Used for emphasis, like Earth's mite, or farthing today.

sairah *(say'rah)*: "Mistress," in Southern dialect; term of respect to woman.

scrot: churl, layabout, bum.

sea-kuzn: salt-water form of lake *kuzn*.

shnihar *(shnee'hah)*: coarse grain cake, like rock-cake.

shrudkt *(shrookt)*: scarecrow.

shuktek *(shuk'tek)*: small flat stick, notched down one side; coded summons to secret meeting or cabal.

siopenar *(sigh'oh-pen'ah)*: oath of silence taken by pilgrims under the K'haravim.

skalu *(skah'loo)* cake: puff pastry made from powdered hitaku.

sohurin *(soh-hoo'rin)*: sojourn under the K'haravim.

thar: horse-like creature; with sleek brown fur and cloven hoof; red eyes and a stiff fringe of striped black and silver hair under belly from shoulder to haunch, and along underside of long whip-tail.

tharling: young thar up to one year.

troon: sloth-like creature, size of seal, in marshes between Rm and Asurdun.

turboil *(turb'oil)*: unrefined lamp oil crudely rendered from forhar fat; gives off acrid fumes and poor, sickly yellow light; only source of fuel in rural areas.

wember: common wild vine; used as twine and rope in rural areas.

wephar *(wep'hah)*: writing paper devised by the Lothuri from silver ligwood bark.

zonthar *(zon'thar)*: multi-stringed instrument, stroked, not plucked, with *deba (dee'buh)*, resembling Spanish shell comb.

The Atheling

Glossary of Proper Names

Asur *(a'zuh)*: river flowing from Lake Asn (q.v.) west to the Wide Sea.

Asr-Rm *(a-zuh-rum')*: the holy mountain, home of the Lothuri.

Asurdun *(a-suh-dun')*: large fishing port on the estuary of River Asur.

Athor *(ah'thaw)*: male leader, with the Hela (q.v.) of Lothuri (q.v.).

Adiga *(a'dig'guh)*: cazn (q.v.) of legend, said to have irrigated eastern plains with limitless water.

Ao *(ai'yoh)*: the moon of Phrynis.

Asticalys *(ast-i-cah'lis)*: wind of vernal equinox.

B'hadgazan *(buh-had'gaz-an')*: wild barbarian region far to north of Gurnyac, unconquered in Torc's time.

Brac *(brahk)*: one of Sharroc's two chief generals.

Brandings, or Brand-houses: Halls in the Weald where slaves are housed, each having its own Master and brandmark; serving Foundings, Minings and Smeltings.

Demiel *(dem'i-ell)*: the sun of Phrynis.

D'hogana *(duh-huh-gah'nuh)*: i. the art of self-preservation, like kung-fu; ii. the area in which it is practiced; iii. a certain code, or way of life.

D'huru Nor *(duh-hoo-roo naw')*: name of Torc's mentor in Rm.

D'junu *(duh-joo'noo)*: giant bear-like, legendary ceature.

Dryac: *(dry'ack)*: ancient god of wrath and anger.

Feric *(fe'rik)*: one of Sharroc's two chief generals; Torc's first mentor.

Forthyr *(forth'ear)*: the north star; fixed star, chief of the mariner's quadrangle, comprising Forthyr (N), Racacta (W), Syrcyr (S), and Thyrle (E); shines with clear blue light. Named for ancient Phrynis hero, legendary enemy of balestar Hawcasyr's namesake.

Foundings: forges where weapons and utensils for Gurnyac are made.

Gnangar *(guh-nang'gah)*: dominant royal line of Known World.

Gradhlzac *(graddle'zak)*: demon, gremlin, bogey-man.

Gurnyac *(gern'yac)*: name both of country and city at center of Known World.

Harash D'ho *(ha-rash duh-ho')*: Master of the D'hogana.

Hawcasyr *(haw-cuh-seer')*: fifth planet of Demiel, shining red in the spectrum. Balestar.

Hela *(hay'luh)*: female leader, with the Athor (male leader), of Lothuri.

Katanaia *(kat-an-eye'uh)*: Ramoni's nickname in the Brandings. Bitter taste left in mouth after handling iron.

K'haravim *(kuh-ha'ruh-vim)*: literally, area under the mountain peak; deeper connotation, the sphere of spiritual brotherhood.

Lothuri *(low-thoo'ry)*: spiritual super-race of Rm.

Pessar *(pess'ah)*: mountain serpent, size of a boa constrictor.

Quaur *(kwah)*: the Universal Mind; Universal Will; thought by the Lothuri in *The Atheling* to be the source of creation.

Ramoni *(ram'on-i)*: runaway slave, pilgrim of Rm.

Rethi *(rath'ee)*: caretakers of Rm; the body of the mountain, as the Lothuri are its mind and soul.

Riverside: a small fishing village outside Asurdun, on the estuary of the River Asur.

Rm *(Rum)*: holy mountain; seat of the Lothuri; comprising both outer "Golden City" and inner K'haravim.

Sharroc *(sha'rock)*: king of Gurnyac; father to crown prince Torc.

Shufar *(shoo'fah)*: serpent of Fens; revered as symbol of worldly wisdom; a good totem; the antithesis of Pessar, mountain serpent, symbol of cunning and deceit.

Smeltings: smelting houses east of the Foundings where metals are extracted from ores mined in the Weald.

Surdun *(sir-dun')*: country west of Gurnyac; capital, Asurdun.

Tanna *(tann'uh)*: Torc's mistress.

Torc *(tawk)*: crown prince of Gurnyac, pilgrim to Rm; the atheling (Anglo-Saxon for "prince." "heir-apparent.")

Weald *(wield)*: line of barrier hills east of Gurnyac; source of all significant mineral ore in Known World; ruled by Gnangars.